Also by Ernest Francis Schanilec

BLUE DARKNESS

To my parents, Herman and Emma:
Their hard work made it possible for
me to earn a college education.

THE TOWERS

By Ernest Francis Schanilec

THE TOWERS

Author - Ernest Francis Schanilec
Publisher - McCleery & Sons Publishing

International Standard Book Number: 1-931916-23-3

Printed in the United States of America

ACKNOWLEDGEMENTS

THE FOLLOWING PEOPLE are on my thank-you list for assisting me in writing *The Towers*: My brother Vern and his wife Faye, my daughter-in-law Paula, my daughter Kris and my son, Clayton.

PROLOGUE

Tom HASTINGS HAD MOVED TO MINNEAPOLIS and rented an apartment on the 20th floor of a high-rise. The apartment had a breathtaking view and was located near numerous lakes in the suburbs. There was a network of bike-trails, which appealed to the semi-retired computer consultant.

His motivation for moving had been to escape the traumatic incidents he'd experienced living at his lake home in central Minnesota. A fanatic had murdered one of his neighbors. Tom's life was threatened and he barely escaped the same fate as his neighbor.

At his new location, in Minneapolis, he'd met new people and established some friendships. Life was good and he was happy until one of the tenants was found dead next to a bike-trail.

The adventures that Tom Hastings underwent after the murder made him wish he had never moved.

1

T OM HASTINGS WAS SITTING ON A BARSTOOL and enjoying dinner at O'Leary's bar & grill. His attention was drawn to a man who had arrived about fifteen minutes earlier. The dark navy blue sport coat seemed out of place, since almost everyone there was dressed casually. Even more out of place was his fidgety manner. The man's head was constantly turning toward the door, looking for someone. Tom habitually studied people at the bar. Humans are similar to trees, he thought, never two alike.

The man took a stool, one of the two empties next to the server station. Tom was sitting on the middle stool of five at the closed end of the horseshoe-shaped bar. The sport-coat man had thick dark hair combed straight back. One of the overhead bar lights enhanced his smooth cheeks. A roman-like nose complemented his prominent chin and dark Italian-like eyes.

The man lit a cigarette and waves of smoke clouds drifted upward, partially blocking the view of the television that Tom and others were watching. A hairless basketball guard was shooting his second free throw when a billow of smoke blocked Tom's path of vision.

He looked over at the smoker and watched him take a deep drag, tilt his head back and blow out the smoke. It reminded Tom of pictures he'd seen of ocean whales that emitted huge sprays of water above their heads.

The play in the basketball game resumed after a timeout. Tom and some of the other patrons were relieved when the sport-coat man ground the remains of his cigarette in an ashtray. Their relief was short-lived—the smoker lit another. Tom's eyes left the screen and meandered over to the smoker.

Could be the ninth or tenth by now, thought Tom. Besides smoking, the man was gulping drinks that looked like scotch or bourbon. The basketball game resumed after a lengthy commercial. Loud laughter broke out on the side of the bar opposite the sport-coat man as two ladies responded to a joke. A man next to Hastings, second stool to his right, was shuffling through a stack of papers, uninterrupted by the basketball game and the laughter.

The man in the sport coat got some company, a tall blonde lady. She stood next to him in front of an empty stool. He laid his cigarette in the ashtray and rose from his stool, giving up an inch or two in height. The blonde lady was dressed in a red blazer, easily outclassing the other females sitting at the bar. Like a gentleman, he assisted her up onto the empty barstool. Returning to his seat, he took out two more cigarettes. She accepted one and within minutes was contributing to the density and size of the smoke clouds lingering over the bar area.

The lady wore thin-framed glasses perched on her narrow nose. Her bright, prominent red lips offset her pale complexion, which matched the blonde hair that partly covered her cheeks and extended down to her shoulders. As Tom continued to observe the two, he noticed she was doing most of the talking. Scanning the other patrons sitting at the bar, he noticed the blonde lady was also attracting their attention.

Tom took another sip of wine, and his thoughts drifted to a series of traumatic experiences that had occurred just over two years ago. He had been living in the quiet, peaceful community of New Dresden, about 150 miles north of Minneapolis. The Twin Cities of Minneapolis and Saint Paul were located about two hundred miles south of Tom's former home.

Life had been good, living in his house nestled into a hillside and overlooking a lake. But everything had changed after a close friend and neighbor had been found dead–murdered in his own house. During the investigation, two additional friends of Tom's had been murdered. Because of his closeness to the victims, Tom had been threatened and attacked by the killer. Agility and luck had saved him from the same lethal fate as the others.

He had moved to Minneapolis to leave behind the memories of

his traumatic experiences, and except for an occasional nightmare, his move to the city had worked out well.

After selling his country lake home, Tom had moved into a comfortable high-rise apartment building in Minneapolis and continued to operate and maintain a part-time computer consulting business. His social relationship with Julie Hoffman, a lady he had met on the Internet three years ago, had become closer. She lived in an apartment across the Mississippi River, in St. Paul. That had been her residence for at least ten years. The drive to the Twin Cities to visit her usually took a little over three hours. Her apartment in St. Paul took only one half-hour.

When the bartender came over to offer him another glass of wine, Tom politely refused and asked for his bill. He plucked a credit card from his wallet and tucked it into the bill holder. Later, while signing the ticket, he looked up and saw the man in the sport coat and his lady visitor heading for the door.

The Towers apartment building where Tom Hastings lived was about six blocks from O'Leary's. Walking briskly that evening, he crossed a boulevard and passed a cluster of shops. Beyond them, a street led to the outdoor parking lot at the rear of the Towers. Tom looked up at the stars dominating the clear June sky. A jetliner's lights interrupted the stars as it approached the airport from the south.

Approaching the parking lot, Tom glanced to the right and smiled when he saw the beginning of a bike trail. It paralleled a set of seldom-used railroad tracks and was used by hikers, bikers and in-line-skating enthusiasts. After moving to Minneapolis, Tom had purchased in-line-skates and used the trail frequently. Because it was getting dark that evening, he walked rapidly to the short run of stairs that led to the lighted parking lot. He had his key ready for the lock when he got to the back door of the building.

While waiting for the elevator, his thoughts drifted to what his life had been like living up north. He was more comfortable with country living than city living, but the change had been acceptable, especially since it had brought him closer to his friend Julie. Still, the never-ending clamor of street noise in the city made him long for the quiet of the country. He was amazed by how traffic noises were enhanced at high elevations—the noise drifted all the way up to at least the 20th floor.

———

FERRO WAS RELYING ON A VACANT ELEVATOR AND GARAGE. It was Saturday now—four in the morning. Bloodstains in the apartment carpeting didn't trouble him, but a single drop in the elevator must be avoided. The sheet wrapped around the body was staying put satisfactorily, held in place with packaging rope. Cautiously, he opened the door—there was no one about, as he had hoped. He hurried to the elevator and pressed the Down button. When the door opened, he flicked the Door Open switch. He rushed back to his victim's apartment and lifted the sheet-clad, dead woman's body.

Not too clever of her to invite me in, he thought. Gloria, that's what her name was. They had met at the bar & grill in the Lakes strip mall. After a few drinks, she'd become warm and friendly.

"Oh, you live in the Towers, too," she had smiled and told her new friend.

She had been in no shape to drive, and it had taken very little persuasion to drive her home. Finding the apartment key buried in the bottom of her purse had been the hardest part.

Smiling, he held the bulk firmly and partly dragged, partly carried it around the corner and into the waiting elevator. After releasing the Door Open switch, he pushed the B button to access the lower level. On the way down, his heart missed a beat when the elevator stopped on the seventh floor. As the door opened, his heartbeat increased dramatically—he was expecting to see someone in the hallway.

Ferro held his breath, mentally urging the door to close. Gasping for air, he heard the sound of rushing footsteps. He glimpsed a hand reaching for the slider as the door was closing and his face turned red from the increase in his heart rate. By some miracle, the door closed before the fingers of the hand interfered with the slider. Ferro breathed a sigh of relief, but his strained breathing and racing heart troubled him. He feared having a heart attack in the elevator and being discovered with the body.

The garage was quiet, just as he had anticipated. Releasing the bulk and setting it down by the door, he ran over to her car. His heart calmed a bit when feeling her car keys in his pocket. The car tires squealed for a moment as Ferro hurriedly backed out. Cursing, he straightened and drove ahead, stopping by the body. After opening the trunk, he crudely dragged the body up against the rear bumper, pushed it over the edge and stuffed it into the trunk.

Ferro drove out onto the street that bordered the back section of the outdoor parking lot. He shut off the lights before driving up the bike trail and cruised slowly for a short distance. Far enough, he thought. Turning off the engine, Ferro pressed the Trunk button in the glove compartment and slipped out the driver door. A piece of rope got caught on something as he was removing the body from the trunk. His tension increasing, he worked to free the rope and sheet, succeeding after a few jerks. After lowering the body to the asphalt, he grabbed the shears from inside the trunk and sliced the rope in several places. Peeling away the sheet, he exposed the body.

Grabbing it under both armpits, he dragged it across the tracks into the tall grass. After setting it down, he noticed a shoe was missing. Retracing his path, he searched the ground. Relieved when spotting it, he smiled, stooped down and tossed it toward the body.

He carefully jammed the sheet and remaining pieces of rope into a plastic bag and placed it on the back seat. Once he was convinced no pieces remained, he slammed the back door shut and got back into the car. Placing a stick of gum in his mouth, he turned the car around and drove back, finding a spot in the outdoor lot. Parking her car outside would be less noticeable than in her garage spot, he reasoned.

After dumping the plastic bag and contents into the waste receptacle outside by the back door, he entered the corridor leading to the lobby. *That'll give those dumb cops something to play with*, he gleefully thought.

Lights were on in the lobby office. Peeking through the small spaces of the mailbox wall, he could see that the night person had his legs up on the desk and appeared to be sleeping. There wasn't anyone around to see a lone, sinister person pass through the lobby and enter the elevator.

On the way up, he felt excited, looking forward to seeing what was in her dresser drawers. The idea of doing that when the body was still in the apartment showed no respect.

After finishing in her bedroom, he went back to his apartment. He felt totally satisfied. No one at the Towers had ever heard of Ferro, a name that he had been known by many years ago. The secret of his alias was safe, he concluded as he fell into a deep sleep.

2

SATURDAY MORNING, A FREIGHT TRAIN was snaking its way up the tracks, temporarily blocking access to the bike trail. When the last boxcar passed out of sight, Tom hoped that the bike trail wouldn't be too busy. It was mid-June and the weather looked favorable. Tom dragged the skates backpack from his cluttered front closet. Making certain his apartment keys were in his pocket, he slung the backpack over his shoulder and headed out the door to the elevators.

Getting off at the lobby level, he entered a small foyer. Through its glass door and window, he could see Carl, the building manager, paying astute attention to a finger-waving lady. Leaning back slightly, Carl maintained a smile and appeared relieved that someone was entering the lobby from the foyer door. Tom admired Carl's knack in dealing with tenant problems.

"Hi, Tom. What's up?" asked Carl.

"Not much, just heading out to the bike trail."

"Have a good one," Carl said and headed back into his office.

Carl Borders was a handsome man in his sixties. Hardly any activities in the commons area of the Towers escaped his notice, in spite of his extra-thick glasses. His hair was thinning a little and his mind was extraordinarily alert. Not only did he manage the affairs of the building complex, but he also served as an involuntary, amateur personal counselor.

Tom headed for the corridor that led to the outdoor parking lot. While opening the door, he looked back and smiled because the lady's finger was back in Carl's face. Tom walked across the parking lot toward the stairway that led down to the street.

A flock of mallard ducks swooshed by, all banking at precisely the same moment. They landed in the grass next to the building, feasting on the corn and millet supplied daily by the manager. The flock became airborne when a vehicle approached to enter the garage.

Julie and Tom occasionally hiked some of the miles of trails that cut through the wooded areas of the city. The bike trail by the tracks wound through clusters of trees and along the edges of marshes. It interconnected with other paths leading to and circumventing three lakes, all observable from Tom's apartment window.

After crossing the street, he climbed the short, steep approach to the bike trail. Just beyond the railroad tracks, he sat down on a bench and put on his skates. After skating up the pathway and rounding the first curve, Tom was annoyed to see a cluster of people gathered on the trail. He slowed his pace, hoping to get noticed so they would move aside, but it didn't do any good. The bystanders were determined to remain on the trail.

Tom's initial irritation turned to curiosity when he saw four police officers standing in the tall grass beyond the tracks. The bystanders were gawking at something or someone lying in the grass.

"I think it's a woman," said one of them.

"Whoever it is, must be mighty dead," added another.

Tom stopped and watched as one of the police officers moved away from the others and began talking on a cell phone. Beyond the scene, two police cars were parked in a flat area between the bike trail and the railroad tracks.

"When did this happen?" Tom asked one of the bystanders.

The man pointed and said, "The body was found by that guy over there. He was out for a walk and saw the body lying there. He called the cops on his cell phone. That was only about ten minutes ago."

The sound of a siren stilled the conversation amongst the people on the trail. All heads turned toward the flashing red lights of an ambulance coming straight up the middle of the bike trail. As the sound increased in intensity, the tension in Tom's body grew with each passing moment.

All the observers on the track were forced to stand aside as the vehicle came to a stop in front of the police officers. Leaving the scene, Tom overcame his building curiosity and continued up the trail. He had been through this type of ghastly event before.

After skating the entire distance of the trail, he reversed directions and headed back. As he approached the site where the police activity had taken place, he slowed and came to a stop. Although the obstructive bystanders were all gone, two remaining officers were in the process of wrapping a police tape around a group of stakes spiked into the tall grass.

His curiosity got the best of him, and he stiff-walked in his skates over to the tape. One of the officers looked up and Tom asked, "What happened here?"

"A woman was found dead, right here by the tracks. Do you use this trail often?"

"Yes, I do, almost every day during the summer season."

"Would you mind giving me your name and address—phone number, too, please?"

"No, not at all. I live in that high-rise apartment building right over there." Tom pointed.

"Oh, over there—the Towers, that's what it's called," responded the officer after finishing writing in his notepad.

———

RETURNING TO THE TOWERS, TOM FELT WEAK. A person had died out there, along the bike trail. Walking up the steps to the outdoor parking lot, he thought about the three murders that had changed his life a little over two years ago. *There was a lady lying dead by the tracks. How did she get there?* The scene had had a dreadful appearance, one that would likely spell out the word Murder in capital letters.

Crossing the parking lot, he saw one of the maintenance men.

Andy appeared to be adjusting the hinges on the door to the building. He was a big man with a likable, friendly attitude. Usually sporting a big smile, he towered over most of the residents and his fellow employees. Andy, like others, who maintained the Towers, was dressed in a dark blue shirt and trousers. His hair was thick and dark brown, though he was probably in his mid-fifties.

Seeing Tom approach, Andy said, "Hi, Tom. I saw you out on the bike trail, just cruising right along on your skates. It looked like you were in the middle of some cops and an ambulance. I heard someone was found dead over there."

"Yup, that's what one of the policemen told me," responded Tom.

"Did you see the person who was down?" Andy asked.

"No, I didn't."

"I heard it was a woman," Andy added and removed a package of gum from his pocket.

"Yup, that's what I heard, too," responded Tom, not caring to discuss the matter any further.

"What's wrong with the door?" Tom asked.

"Looks like a couple of these hinges are wearing out. We'll have to replace 'em."

"Don't work too hard, Andy. See you later."

Tom spent most of the afternoon working on a spreadsheet that he had created for a client. Since moving to Minneapolis, he added four clients to his computer consulting business. At about 5:00 p.m. he decided to stroll over to O'Leary's for a beer. On the way down, the elevator stopped on the twelfth floor. When the door opened, Tom felt his heart skip a beat—he was looking at a dark blue sport coat. It was the same man, the smoker, he'd seen at O'Leary's Friday evening.

The man looked at Tom and said, "How ya doing today?"

"Fine, thanks," Tom replied.

After the man got on and the elevator door closed, Tom kept his eyes fixed on the number panel above the door. After they both got off at the lobby, Tom moved through the foyer toward the corridor leading to the rear outdoor parking lot. Before exiting, he stopped and watched the man in the sport coat head out the front door and onto the canopied circular approach to the building. *There's something about that guy, the way he looks at people, the way he struts around...a touch of evil.*

The walk to O'Leary's was interesting. Clever storefronts and window displays along the way enticed Tom to glance inside the shops. Through one window, he watched a Gypsy-like lady wearing a long floral-print dress put her hand on a man's shoulder. The lady edged closer, her shoulder touched his, and he nodded—a sale!

In order to access the Lakes strip mall where O'Leary's was located, Tom needed to cross the boulevardæa challenge because traffic moved at a fast, aggressive pace. Pedestrians beware! A green traffic light does not guarantee safety. The odor of vehicle exhaust irritated his nostrils as he hurried across.

On entering the bar & grill, he was pleased to see that the barstools at the closed end of the horseshoe-shaped bar were available. Since moving to the Twin Cities, O'Leary's had become Tom's favorite hangout. The bartenders and servers were accommodating and friendly. He appreciated the television for watching baseball games, and the lack of loud music.

Sitting down on the middle stool, Tom noticed a man sitting on the stool next to the pillar on the left side. He had a head of tremendously dark hair and wore large horn-rimmed glasses. He was reading a book and occasionally looked up over his glasses and glanced around. His eyes caught Tom's for a moment, then returned to the book.

Two young guys wearing baseball caps were sitting two stools down from the horn-rimmed-glasses man. One of them reminded Tom of his son, Brad, who lived with his wife, Terry, in La Crosse, Wisconsin.

Opposite the two young men with the baseball caps sat a couple Tom had previously met at the Towers. He remembered meeting Carlos and Juanita down in the lobby, where they had been having a discussion with Carl, the manager. Residents of the Towers often stopped in the lobby to visit and chat with the obliging Carl. Sometimes they would wag a finger in his face. Tom grinned.

Carlos and Juanita Valdez resided in an apartment on the

seventeenth floor. They had immigrated from Colombia six years ago, and in December of last year, they had become American citizens. Tom admired their dark features. Carlos sported a thick, black mustache. At their first meeting in the lobby, Tom had noticed that Carlos always kept his left hand in his pocket, out of sight. Juanita was a beautiful lady with full red lips, dark eyes and black, thin eyelashes. Her neck and wrists were heavily populated with attractive jewelry. She was trim and close to the same height as Carlos–about five feet-eight inches, Tom guessed.

The bartender, a young man with an earring in his left ear, sauntered over. Tom ordered a beer and asked for the appetizer menu. He wondered what his mother and dad would have said if he had shown up with an earring. Mother would have looked away with that classic expression of disapproval. His dad wouldn't have said a word about the earring right away. In a couple of days, he would have made a sarcastic remark. Glancing away from the menu, he noticed the eyes behind the horn-rim glasses watching him. Their eyes locked for a moment and the head with the massive bundle of hair turned.

After wiping the bar and carefully setting the beer on Tom's coaster, the bartender asked, "Anything else?"

While explaining his order to the bartender, Tom sensed the eyes behind the horn-rimmed glasses were watching. Jerking his head slightly to the left, Tom stole a quick glance, but he wasn't fast enough—the man's eyes were looking down at the book. Movement behind the man drew Tom's attention. The man with the sport coat was returning. Tom felt a twinge of excitement at seeing him approach the end of the bar. No doubt, it was the same man he had seen there last night and on the elevator at the Towers.

Wedging between the two end stools, the sport-coat man established possession of both. Must be expecting someone, Tom thought. The new arrival appeared nervous and fidgety as he lit up his first cigarette. He set it down carefully in an ashtray, clenched both fists and began tapping one on the bar surface.

Tom's position at the bar allowed for watching the television and people at the same time. Chancing another glance at the horn-rimmed glasses, Tom noticed that the eyes behind the lenses were also watching the sport-coat man. A few minutes passed. The horn-rimmed-glasses man no longer looked at Tom. He was totally focused on his book and the sport coat.

Another flick of a lighter produced more smoke. That's the third cigarette in about five minutes, Tom mentally scolded. The man in the horn-rimmed glasses continued to peek up from his book, ignoring Tom and watching the sport-coat man.

A younger, tall, thin fellow approached the bar. After being greeted by the man in the sport coat, he stood and visited with him for a few minutes. Tom saw the sport-coat man reach inside his coat and remove something. Whatever it was, he handed it to the younger man, who took it and tucked it inside his jacket. Tom noticed the horn-rimmed glasses man lower his book and turn his head slightly to watch the younger man leave O'Leary's.

The sport-coat guy sat down on the end stool and lit up a fresh cigarette. He looked up at the television, then scanned the entire scope of the people at the bar. Tom averted his eyes by looking up at the television screen. The man behind the horn-rimmed glasses was reading a book. As Tom continued to watch the screen, he felt uncomfortable. *Something mysterious and sinister is going on at O'Leary's.*

After the bartender brought his tab, Tom got up from the stool and headed for the door. Pausing before exiting, he turned slightly and noticed the sport-coat guy watching him. Tom shivered as he walked down the sidewalk. He quickened his steps and headed for the Towers.

3

A DENSE FOG HOVERED OVER THE TREETOPS on Sunday morning. From Tom's location on the 20th floor, he could barely make out the streets below. The rumbling sound of wheels on the tracks was audible as a freight train wound its way up the tracks, generating an eerie scene.

The morning was appreciated because of a nightmare Tom had had last night. He was down in the garage and couldn't find the door to the elevators. A man wearing horn-rimmed glasses and a dark sport coat kept blocking his way.

Opening his door, he was glad to see the Sunday newspaper lying on the floor. On certain mornings, it would mysteriously disappear. Sitting on the couch, sipping coffee and reading the newspaper, his attention was drawn to a color photograph of a young lady on the front page.

The headline read, "Woman Found Dead on West Side." As Tom's eyes fixed on the picture, he felt apprehensive. The woman looked just like the good-looking blonde, who had visited the sport-coat guy at O'Leary's two evenings ago. They had left together. Tom felt certain it was she, in spite of not having seen the face of the body by the tracks. The story accompanying the photograph described the location: "next to a railroad track... A hiker made the discovery early Saturday morning." Tom continued to stare at the picture. *Was he really sure it was the same lady he'd seen at O'Leary's? Was it his responsibility to report the sighting to the police?*

Stop this thinking. Involvement in the murders up north had been his reason for moving. It wasn't in his best interest to get involved in this one. Besides, the name Gloria Tingsley didn't ring a bell, in contrast to the murder victims that he'd known in the country.

While watching the Sunday morning news programs, Tom couldn't get his mind off the newspaper picture of the dead lady. He visualized her sitting on the barstool, laughing and partying with the man in the sport coat. Tom felt guilty for not contacting the police.

When he had contacted the police at his previous home, he'd become a target. Memories of a bullet shattering his window, inches above his head, flashed through his mind. A potential assassin had taken a potshot at him from a boat. The bullet had missed and gone through his window.

He decided to visit the lobby later, perhaps on Monday, and find out what the talk was down there.

Forgetting the three people murdered a couple of years ago was difficult enough. Tom had nearly become one of the victims himself. His friend and neighbor Pete had saved his life in spite of efforts to defend himself. Because of the murders, he'd sold his home and moved to the city. *Why should I get involved now, especially after the nightmare I had last night?*

On Sunday afternoon, Tom was apprehensive about using the bike trail. He skated swiftly past the place where the police tape now rustled in the breeze, trying not to think about the body that had been lying there early the day before.

After skating under Interstate 394, he reversed directions and headed back. As he was approaching the police tape area, he noticed two people peering into the tall grass where the body had been found. Tom's curiosity got the best of him. He halted and clumsily stomped on his skates to where they stood. It was a young couple holding hands.

"Hi," Tom said, towering over them. "See anything in there?"

"No, we don't. Was this the spot where the body was found?" the young lady asked.

"I rather think so. Do you use the bike trail often?" Tom asked, attempting to change the subject.

"Yes, we do," said the young man, "about four times a week. How about you?"

Tom gestured toward the Towers high-rise apartment house. "I live up there, in that high-rise, nice and close to the trail. Do you two live near here?"

"Yes, we do," the man answered. "We live there, too."

"I'm Tom Hastings."

The young man said, "I am Richard Fallon. This is my wife, Maria."

After shaking hands, Tom said, "Have you lived at the Towers very long?"

"We moved here two months ago," Maria answered in a soft voice.

"It's the best," said Richard. "We really like that place. The manager is sure good to us. He checks with us often to make sure things are okay."

Richard wore round metal-framed glasses, and his right eye

squinted when he spoke. The narrow, well-defined, whitish streak in his thick, black hair just above the forehead was eye catching.

Maria also had dark hair. It was straight and long, almost touching her shoulders. "I hope this isn't a bad sign," said Maria in her soft voice as she gestured toward the tape. "My mother had cautioned me about being alone in the city at night. I now know what she meant."

"Oh, Maria, your mother overdoes it a little. People get killed in Madison too, you know," said Richard as he looked down at Maria, who was just over five feet tall.

"Maria, the Towers is in one of the safest sections of Minneapolis. That's why I chose this area. What happened over there is probably a fluke," responded Tom.

"Regardless, no way am I going to be on this trail alone. Going down to the car in that dark garage scares me, too," said a concerned Maria.

"Nice meeting you two. I'm sure we'll see each other again," Tom said, maneuvering the skates back to the bike trail.

Nice young couple, he thought. The man wasn't wearing a ring, and Tom wondered if they were married. When Tom returned to the Towers, he took the elevator to the 20th floor, got off and knocked on the door of apartment 2006, home of Greg and Jan Skogen. Just as with the Colombian couple, Tom had met them in Carl's office soon after moving to the Towers. Greg was employed in hospital administration and Jan was a part-time executive secretary in the corporate world.

Tom waited a couple of minutes and no one answered. He knocked again. Same result. Returning to his suite in 2012, he put away the backpack and grabbed a beer from the refrigerator. Cold and delightful, the beer bottle was about half empty when the phone rang.

Jan from 2006 asked, "Was that you who knocked on our door?"

"Yes, it was."

"Hey, Tom, why don't you come over for appetizers and wine?"

"Sure. How soon?"

"How about half an hour?"

"Sure. See you then."

Greg answered the door right after Tom knocked a bit later.

"Come on in," he said. "How ya doin?"

"I'm doing just great, but the murder has caused me to become a little spooked."

"Have a seat in there," Greg gestured, "and we'll bring in some goodies."

Tom moved into their living room and admired the large windows that overlooked a lake surrounded by trees and homes. Greg was a tall man—about six-three. His hair was graying and thin in spots. He had a perpetual smile that complemented his round face.

"You sure have a great view," Tom said.

"Thanks, but there isn't anything wrong with yours either."

"Have you been in my apartment before?" asked Tom.

"Yes, we looked at it when it became available, before you moved here," he replied.

Greg and Tom sat down on the sofa, which faced the television set. Jan came into the room carrying a large tray with an appetizer plate and three empty wineglasses. She set the tray down on the coffee table in front of the couch.

"Would you like red or white?" she asked.

"Chardonnay for me, if you have some," answered Tom.

"Sure do," she said, and returned to the kitchen.

Moments later, she came back with two open bottles of wine, one red and one white. Jan was a perfect match for Greg. They had been married for close to thirty years and had three children, all living out of town. Jan was also tall–about five-eight. Her dark brown, short-cropped hair was neat and attractive. She didn't wear glasses and didn't smile very often–the opposite of Greg, who was always smiling.

"Tom, I know you use the bike trail along the railroad tracks a lot. Were you down there when the body of the lady was, ah, discovered?" asked Greg.

"Well, I wasn't down there exactly when the body was found, but skated past while the police were waiting for the ambulance. Did either one of you know the lady?"

"No," said Jan, "but I think she lived here in the Towers."

"Wow. I wasn't aware of that," Tom responded.

"Yeah," said Greg. "I was talking to Carl yesterday and he

mentioned that she had an apartment on the twelfth floor."

Geez, Tom thought, that's where the sport-coat guy got on the elevator. Torn between sharing the information with Jan and Greg or keeping it to himself, he decided not to say anything.

"I rode down on the elevator with the, ah, lady, about a week ago. Other than saying hello, she was very quiet," Jan interjected. "While getting my hair done last Friday, she—the lady who was murdered— was sitting on a chair reading a magazine. I believe she was waiting for Barb, the stylist. But then, she may have been waiting for James, who was doing a lady from the seventh floor."

"From what I hear, James does a lot of stuff," said Greg.

"Now, what the heck do you mean by that?" retorted Jan.

"Well, rumors are that James has been seen getting on the elevator at several different floors. I don't think one delivers haircuts,,does one, now?" Greg said, erupting in a generous bout of laughter.

"You used the word "murder," Jan. Is that what it was for sure— the dead lady, I mean?" Tom asked.

"'Well, what the heck else could it be? She died of a stab wound, you know. There was blood in her apartment, so that's where it must have happened. I wouldn't think she would have accidentally stabbed herself and made it out to the railroad tracks to die, and not leave a blood trail," responded Jan.

"Where did you hear all this?" asked Tom.

"Down in the lobby. I overheard a police officer talking to Carl," answered Jan.

"News gets around fast in this building," responded Greg.

After helping clean up the appetizer plate and downing a couple glasses of wine, Tom decided to leave.

"Gotta go," he said. "Thanks a lot for the wine and the other stuff. See you guys later."

"You're very welcome," said Jan. "We'll look forward to seeing you again soon."

Tom returned to his apartment and sat down at his computer desk. The window in back of the monitor gave him a view of the railroad track and close to half a mile of the bike trail. Gotta call Julie, he thought. He dialed her number.

Julie Hoffman lived in a high-rise apartment building in St. Paul about ten miles away. The trauma that Tom had experienced while living at his previous home didn't seem to have had much effect on her. Visions of his friend's car being pulled from the lake reoccurred often in his dreams. He was reluctant to tell Julie about the dreams because she had been fascinated with the intrigue and excitement. But then, she hadn't been shot at, or attacked with a knife.

Since Tom had moved to the Twin Cities, Julie had changed jobs. She was now the manager of a data storage department for a large, local corporation. Julie had been disappointed when Tom had decided to sell his home in the country because she'd enjoyed the wildlife and relaxed atmosphere. She understood what Tom had gone through up north—the murders and being attacked. Julie answered on the second ring. After they exchanged greetings, he asked her to join him for dinner on Thursday. "Julie, I have something real special to talk about."

"Oh, what is it?" she asked.

"I'd rather not discuss it right now on the phone. It has nothing to do with you. Your comments and advice regarding something that just happened at the Towers will be appreciated."

"Is it about the murder?" Julie anxiously guessed.

"Yup, you guessed it—but how did you know it was murder?"

"I guess that was an assumption, even though the paper didn't call it that."

"I'll be by to pick you up at six on Thursday."

"Okay," she replied. "See you then."

The next morning, Tom removed a pair of binoculars from his desk drawer and stood by the picture window. The bike trail appeared empty, except for two joggers striding in unison. After glassing the visible half a mile of the bike trail, he set the binoculars down and continued to watch while sipping coffee.

As the two joggers approached the beginning of the trail, Tom noticed a man standing near the bench. *Unusual*, Tom thought, since everyone on the bike trail was usually moving, either on foot or on wheels, if they weren't resting on the bench. Grabbing the glasses, he focused on the man. The man's head was covered with a whitish, long-brimmed baseball cap that was covering most of his face. The back rim of the cap was snuggled onto a generous crop of hair. He was wearing a gray jacket and jeans. His right hand was firmly positioned on his hip as he stood and watched the joggers go by.

After finishing the newspaper, Tom headed down the elevator. It stopped on the fifth floor to pick up Andy from maintenance, who carried a toolbox.

"What's the big project today?" Tom asked.

"Oh, just adjusting some cabinet doors for Mrs. Patton—no big deal. How's your apartment working out?" Andy asked.

"I like it a lot. Everything seems to be working well."

"Good," Andy said.

Tom got off the elevator at the lobby. Andy remained, heading down to the lower level, where the maintenance room was located, along with a large storage area and an indoor parking lot.

———

TOM CHOSE WALKING, OVER DRIVING, to a family restaurant for breakfast. It was located in the Lake's strip mall, three units down from O'Leary's.

Molly's was a popular place for breakfast—ditto for lunch. Molly, the owner, was usually present to greet her customers when they came through the café door. She was also a tenant at the Towers. Tom had shared the elevator with her many times. Molly was built like a truck—tall and wide. Her personality didn't match her build. She was soft and gentle, and her treatment of customers, including Tom, was golden.

"Follow me, Tom. I'll find you a nonsmoking booth or table."

"Okay with me," he replied.

She seated Tom in a booth next to a window overlooking the parking lot. He had already eaten part of his omelet when he glanced out the window. There he was again—the man wearing the sport coat, getting into a car. He backed out of the parking space and drove up the street and onto the boulevard, disappearing from view. Tom wondered what the sport-coat man did for a living. *Sure hangs around the strip mall a lot, always wearing the same type of sport coat.*

————

CLIFFORD AND DALIA JENSEN OWNED AND OPERATED
Jensen's Shirts, an embroidery business located in the Lakes strip
mall across from O'Leary's and Molly's. Tom had a consulting
appointment with Dalia at 10:00 a.m.

Even though Jensen's Shirts was within walking distance of the
Towers, Tom drove because of his heavy briefcase. He found a parking
spot in the lot out front. After getting out of the car, he looked skyward.
An airliner was silhouetted against the background of white puffball
clouds as it approached the airfield.

"Glad to see you, Tom," said Dalia when he pushed through the
front door and entered the shop.

"Nothing like a nice June summer day. Sure nice out there," Tom
replied while laying down his briefcase next to their computer.

On opening the case, he extracted a disk and popped it into the
floppy drive. Tom had been working on a spreadsheet that was
designed to track thread inventory. Dalia brought over a stack of
invoices and laid it down on the desk. Tom sighed. Most of the day
was going to be spent inputting the invoices into the new program.

He admired Dalia's business efficiency. Her filing cabinet was
organized so well that every business paper had a place. She treated
her customers with care and respect. Her brown hair was pulled back
in a business like way into a ponytail held together by a blue plastic
hair-tie. She wore glasses that sometimes were left dangling on her
chest. Tom took a momentary break from his work and noticed her
large blue eyes darting back and forth between a customer and
paperwork lying on the counter. The customer was nodding in
approval.

Tom glanced at his watch. His stomach rumbled slightly when he
noticed the minute hand just moved past twelve.

"See you after lunch, Dalia," Tom said loudly as he headed for
the door.

Dalia waved without looking up.

Walking across a service street, Tom entered Molly's and was greeted by the owner. As she was escorting him to a table, they passed by Carl and his wife, who occupied a booth.

Tom paused. Carl said, "Tom, I want you to meet Sarah, my better half."

Carl's graying hair wasn't quite as thick as Sarah's. He looked down at the menu through metal rimmed glasses perched on the tip of his nose.

"Hi, Sarah, nice to meet you," Tom responded.

"Join us," she said.

Tom raised his hand to signal Molly, who had turned and noticed her guest had abandoned her. She smiled, returned and laid a menu down next to Sarah's on the table of the booth.

After Tom had exchanged niceties with Carl and his wife, their topic of conversation changed to the dead lady.

"It was Gloria Tingsley who was murdered," said Sarah. "She lived on the twelfth floor."

Sarah had a narrow face with a beaked nose. Her graying hair clung to the sides of her head, almost covering her ears, which supported a pair of gold earrings. She wasn't wearing glasses.

"How long had she, Gloria Tingsley, lived in the building?" Tom asked Carl.

"She was with us only six months. I really didn't get to know her very well. She pretty much kept to herself. What are you up to today, Tom?"

"I'm working on a computer project at Jensen's Shirts."

"Cliff and Dalia also live in our building," Carl volunteered.

Sarah added, "That poor girl. I just knew something bad was going to happen to her. She had that wild look."

"Oh, come on, Sarah. You just didn't like her wandering eyes," chipped in Carl.

Before Tom had finished with lunch, Carl announced, "Sarah, I need to get back to work. If you want to stay and visit with Tom, go ahead."

"Oh no, I've got things to do. I'm coming along. Nice meeting you, Tom."

Tom watched as Sarah reached her hand around Carl's elbow and followed him to the exit. Carl opened the door for his wife and guided her through the entryway. They touched each other a lot–always a sign that a marriage was going well.

When Tom returned to Jensen's Shirts, Dalia was on the phone. Her husband, Cliff was just coming through the doorway to the production room.

"Hi, Tom. How's it going?" asked Cliff.

"Pretty good. My goal is to have the program ready for you by this time next week."

"Great. I'm sure Dalia is going to like that. I hate computers–they scare me."

"Computers aren't for everyone, Cliff, but to be successful in business these days, you can't live without."

"Suppose not," he said. "Tom, do you know anything about the woman that was found dead by the tracks behind this building?"

"No, not much, Cliff, except she was a tenant at the Towers."

"That's what Dalia was saying. Speaking of Dalia—she has a problem coming to work alone. She parks behind the building, not far from the tracks, you know," said a concerned Cliff.

Cliff's small shoulders were just wide enough to support the pair of suspenders that held up his blue jeans. Underneath was an oil-stained blue T-shirt that had the title "Jensen's Shirts" embroidered across the back. He didn't wear a belt, allowing his generously sized stomach to expand freely. His soft green, lazy-looking eyes appeared enlarged behind a pair of lenses that were framed in brown plastic. Cliff's gray-haired crew cut and round face reminded Tom of someone he had seen in television sitcoms.

Tom had a productive afternoon and decided to put aside the project at 4:00.

"I'll call you next week, Dalia, and we'll spend some time together going over this spreadsheet. I think it's almost ready—shouldn't take you long to learn it."

"Okay," she said, rushing to answer another phone call.

Cliff had remained in the production room all afternoon. Tom placed a backup copy of the spreadsheet in his briefcase, closed the cover and snapped the latches.

"See you next week."

"Okay, Tom. Have a nice evening."

Tom Hastings walked out the door and headed for his car. He was looking forward to getting home and readying for his date with Julie.

An hour later, he drove his car onto an entry ramp to Interstate 94, heading for St. Paul. There were a lot of spaces in the parking lot at Julie's apartment house. He felt the jolt of a tire falling partially into a well-disguised pothole in the pavement.

Tom buzzed her number and waited for the loud clang that released the lock on the inner door. He took the elevator to the eighteenth floor and knocked on her door. When it opened, he was treated with a pleasant view: a gleaming smile and a sexy blue dress. Julie was ready for the evening.

"Hey, you look great," Tom said.

"Well, thank you, Tom. I feel that way."

"Where would you like to go for dinner? How about Lands End?" he asked.

"Sounds good to me."

The parking lot at Lands End was congested with vehicles. Tom found a parking slot in the far corner, thanks to his date. One of Julie's talents was finding close-in parking spots, but not this time. On entering the restaurant, they noticed about a dozen people milling around in the waiting area. Julie worked her way over to the hostess.

She returned and said, "About a half an hour wait. How does that sound?"

"Fine," Tom said and steered Julie toward a couple of unoccupied stools at the bar. The bartender, sporting a huge black mustache, approached his newest customers. They satisfied his inquiry by ordering two glasses of wine. When the bartender returned, Julie took one sip from her glass and looked up. Tom knew what was coming out of that pretty mouth next.

"Well, Tom, what about it? What's going on at the Towers? Who was she? What mysterious news do you have for me?"

"Julie, this is just between us. I have to tell someone what I saw."

"Oh, this is exciting. Let's have it before I go stark raving mad."

"Okay, here it is. I saw the murdered lady the evening before she died. She was sitting at the bar at O'Leary's with a guy. She joined him after he smoked up the place for about half an hour. I especially noticed him because he was dressed in a sport coat—only one in the place. They sat together for close to an hour, smoking cigarettes. Now get this—they left together, and the very next morning, the lady's body was found dead by the tracks.

"The following day, I saw him again. He got on the elevator with me on the twelfth floor of the Towers."

"Was he wearing the sport coat?"

"No, first time I've seen him without one. Later, that evening, he did wear the sport coat, at O'Leary's again. He sat on the same stool, fidgeting as if he were nervous. Later, a younger man shows up. They talked for awhile and he accepts something from the sport-coat guy. Even though I only got a glimpse of the something, it appeared to be a small package. The younger man leaves after getting the package, or whatever it was."

"What happened next?"

"I think the sport-coat guy was getting wise to me, noticing me watching. I didn't hang around—got out of there fast. I could feel his eyes on me when I was going through the door."

The hostess approached and asked Tom and Julie to follow. She led them to a booth with a nice view of the parking lot. After explaining the specials, the hostess announced the pending arrival of their waitress, Cindy.

After the hostess left, Tom smiled at Julie. "I have more. The lady who was murdered was also a tenant at the Towers. Plus, hear this— she also lived on the twelfth floor. If you remember, that's the same floor that the sport-coat guy got on the elevator."

"Golly, Tom, aren't you going to the police with that information?"

"Geez, Julie, I don't think I dare. You surely remember all the problems I ran into up north a couple of years ago. I think I'll just sit on this for awhile and see how it plays out. Of course, if the police come over and start asking me questions, I'll have to tell them what I saw. Meanwhile, I'll stay out of it."

"Yeah, sure, Tom, but this is different. The police would certainly be interested in knowing what you saw–especially seeing the two of them together at O'Leary's. Later seeing the sport-coat man get on the elevator at the twelfth floor. I think the connection is worth a mention."

"Well, I'll give it some thought. I just hate to get involved in another murder at my new home."

Julie and Tom talked about a lot of other things, but the topic always returned to the murder and the man in the sport coat. They had a great evening.

At close to 2:00 a.m., Tom returned to the Towers. He drove his car into the usual spot in the lower-level parking lot. When he pressed the elevator button, the door opened. James, the barber, got off. He awarded Tom with a sly glance and quickly moved through the elevator door and into the lobby.

James appeared to slice through the air when he moved—his fit and slim build was partially responsible. He had long, skinny arms and narrow, manicured fingers. His blond hair was trimmed high and it stood up about three inches above his scalp. Tom thought about James's green eyes and how they had narrowed when the elevator door had opened.

4

FRIDAY WAS A FREE DAY FOR TOM HASTINGS, with no scheduled appointments. Julie had mentioned the idea of a movie that evening. After spending some time reading the morning newspaper, he put on a jacket and headed down to the elevator. When he got off at the lower-level garage, Emil from maintenance was waiting to get on.

"Good morning," Emil said.

"How are you doin' today, Emil?"

"Just fine, but I've a tough job. I'm heading up to twelve to clean up the apartment where the lady was killed."

"Oh, was she killed in her apartment?" Tom asked.

"Yup, it appears so—all that blood on the carpeting."

When the elevator door closed, Tom was left standing with the obvious question in mind. *If she was murdered in the apartment, why was she dumped out there by the tracks?*

He felt guilty for not telling the police what he had seen at O'Leary's the night before the murder. The need to talk to someone was gnawing at his brain. Shopping at a department store mall was not his favorite thing, but that's exactly how he spent part of the day. While trying on clothes, his elbows brushing against the walls of the small fitting room, his thoughts were about the lady who had died and the man in the sport coat.

Greg and Jan may know what's going on? Tom made a mental note to call them; he needed to talk. Returning home, he had a phone message waiting from Julie and another from his daughter-in-law, Terry. Julie offered to pick him up for a movie that started at 7:00. Terry asked if the weekend two weeks away was available for a visit by her and Brad.

He returned Julie's call and left a message. "I'll meet you down in the lobby at six forty-five."

Terry was home when Tom called their home. The weekend Terry had requested was open for Tom and he welcomed their visit.

The movie was long and dreary, but they managed to stay in their seats until it ended. The dialogue in the story was saturated with four-letter words and violence.

"Let's stop for something to eat—how about O'Leary's?" Tom asked.

"Sure. Great spot," Julie replied.

The parking lot in front of O'Leary's was completely full except for a space directly in front of the door.

"Hey, must be our lucky day," Tom chuckled.

"It's a Julie spot," she joked.

Julie swung her red convertible into the parking slot and they entered the bar & grill. The hostess led them to a booth overlooking the busy boulevard. After sitting down and looking at the menu, Tom glanced in the direction of the bar area. He was not entirely surprised to see the sport-coat man sitting on a stool on the opposite side of the bar from where he usually sat.

"Don't look know, Julie, but the sport-coat guy is here. He's sitting at a barstool at the far end of the bar."

Tom watched Julie's sly eyes shift to the left and lock on the man in the sport coat.

"Slick-looking guy," she said.

"What's he doing?" Tom asked. "I didn't dare look after the stares I got the other day."

"He's smoking and fidgeting with a small package."

"Anyone next to him?"

"No, he seems to be alone. Wait—a guy in a leather jacket just came over."

"Is he real tall?" Tom asked.

"No, he's quite short. Uh-oh, the short guy took something from his hands and he's leaving."

Tom looked up at the door and saw the shorter man in the leather jacket walking out.

"You're right. He's real short. Geez, he sure got out of here in a hurry. Did you see what it was they exchanged?"

"No, not for sure. It was too low and too quick."

"Say, Julie, it may not be too wise to look over at the sport-coat guy too often. I think he got a little suspicious of me the other evening."

They placed an order for two appetizers and two glasses of wine. "We've got to find out who the guy is," said Julie.

"I'm not sure if I want to," Tom responded.

Julie had that adventurous look in her eyes. She wasn't going to leave this one alone. "Let's stay until he leaves and then I'll check it out with the bartender," she suggested excitedly.

"Whoa! That sounds like trouble to me," Tom blurted out.

"Oh, come on. Let's play detective."

They were on their third glass of wine when the man in the sport coat finally left. Julie excused herself and Tom watched as she headed for the lady's room. As she was returning a few minutes later, Tom saw her stop and talk to the bartender. Geez, Julie is going to get us in trouble, Tom thought.

When Julie returned, she had an accomplished look on her face as she slid into the booth.

"Vito," she said. "The sport-coat guy's name is Vito."

"What, no last name and social security number?" Tom asked.

"Next time," Julie laughed.

"I wonder what Vito gave the smaller guy. Drugs, perhaps?" Julie added.

"Well, I have to admit, passing packages—if that's what it was— at a bar is a little suspect," Tom responded.

Tom imagined talking to the police and how interested they would be in the information he possessed about the man in the sport coat— not only seeing his meeting with the victim, but also the suspicious traffic. They waited for about five minutes before leaving. Julie drove them back to the Towers in her red convertible.

"I need to get home and get some sleep," said Julie.

"I was thinking of luring you to my apartment, but since you're tired, and I'm not so peppy myself, perhaps it's time to call it a day," responded Tom.

It was almost midnight when Tom got out of the car and closed the passenger side door of the red convertible. He watched as she drove onto the boulevard and disappeared from view. Tom entered the Towers via the back door. After arriving at his apartment door, he noticed a small piece of paper wedged under the door. *Greg and I need to talk to you. Give us a call soon as you have time. Thanks.* The note was signed by Jan.

5

VITO MANCHINO WAS SITTING AT A DESK in the showroom. He was looking out the window, watching an elderly couple scrutinizing window stickers. His ex-wife's lawyer, a source of perpetual harassment, was on the phone demanding more money. *Will they ever be satisfied?* He thought. *Damn! They're driving me into the poorhouse.*

"I'll do the best I can," he told the attorney and hung up.

When reviewing his sales for the current year, he was impressed— they were up twenty percent. So, why are all my bank accounts overdrawn and three credit cards maxed? He wondered. Jesus, where did all that money go? I need more of it. The risky side of the business isn't doing too badly. Some of my customers are slow in coming up with the money. That Tingsley lady can be scratched from the list. She won't be around any more. Twelve hundred bucks out, gad for a loser.

Perhaps a different delivery place is in order, he thought. O'Leary's is a nice place, but there's a guy who regularly sits at the end of the bar. He's been watching me—maybe a cop. Vito remembered sharing an elevator with him. The guy lives above me, at least the thirteenth floor. Then there's that other fella, the one with the big glasses. He was watching me, too.

He knew the police were going to question him about Gloria Tingsley. His alibi possibilities had interrupted his thoughts all day long at work, and it had been difficult to focus on selling cars. Vito was confident that Melissa would come through. "I was with her all night," he whispered to himself.

Oh crap, there goes Farnsworth. That elderly couple was looking at Lincoln cars, and they probably have cash. Damn that lawyer, he thought. Those two should have been mine.

Vito Manchino enviously watched Farnsworth shake hands with the gentleman, then grasp the lady's hand in both of his own. She was eating it up. They were going to drive out with a new Lincoln Town Sedan, he was sure.

Vito needed a cigarette. Getting up from his chair, he walked over to the scheduling board. After dumping a gum wrapper in the wastebasket, he flicked his marker to the Out column.

Big-lipped Myrtle, sitting behind the reception counter, was on the phone. "Be gone for the rest of the day," he told her.

Vito smiled when Myrtle peered over her glasses and nodded.

———

TOM HASTINGS' PHONE RANG SHORTLY BEFORE EIGHT the
next morning. He was happily surprised to hear Julie's voice.

"Have you read the paper?" she asked.

"No, I'm still in bed. What's the big news?"

"There is an article about the Towers murder in the *Star Tribune*.
You may find it interesting."

"Thanks for calling. I'll get up and make some coffee and check
it out."

"Would you call me after you read it?" she asked.

"Okay, but it may not be for a couple of hours."

"Sorry I woke you up. Talk to you later."

Tom tried going back to sleep, but to no avail. Julie's mention of
the word "murder" was imprinted on his mind. The longer he remained
in bed, the more he wanted to get up and read the article. Within
minutes Tom was up, filling the coffeemaker with water. He opened
the apartment door and stooped down to pick up the newspaper.
Coincidentally, his next-door neighbor was doing the same thing.

"Good morning," she said.

"Same to you neighbor. I'm Tom Hastings. Since we live next
door to each other, it's time we meet."

"Yes, it is. I'm Joan Collison. Just moved in at the beginning of
the year. You haven't been here very long either, have you?"

"No, I haven't—moved in last fall. We'll have to have coffee some
day. Nice meeting you."

"Yes, meeting for coffee would be great. Some other time, though.
I need to get ready for work. Have a nice day."

Her smile had an effect on Tom's demeanor. He unconsciously
returned the smile before stepping back and closing the door. Tom
laid the newspaper down on the table next to his lounger and walked
to the kitchen in search of that first cup of coffee. He was glad the
next door neighbor was attractive. Geez, even before makeup, he
thought. Well, back to the lounger and the newspaper.

"Gloria Tingsley, age 35, was found dead lying next to a railroad
track in the Downy neighborhood. Her apartment, a few blocks away,

had been ransacked...Though the motive for the brutal murder has not been determined, the crime may have been a combination of burglary and murder."

The article was confusing. What had happened first? Was she killed in her apartment and dumped by the tracks, or was she killed by the railroad tracks and then her apartment burglarized? The article continued: "Police are questioning Miss Tingsley's ex-husband and her current boyfriend...thus far, no arrests have been made."

The writer of the article explained the information was based on an interview with Detective Anderson of the Minneapolis Police Department.

The phone rang a second time. The caller was Jan from down the hall.

"Have you read the paper this morning?" she asked.

"Yes, I'm reading it now, all about the Gloria Tingsley murder."

"Isn't that scary, a murder right in our building? The police are going to be all over the place, maybe even television cameras."

"That's all we need, Jan, noise and publicity. I'm for peace and quiet," commented Tom.

"Would you like to meet Greg and I for lunch at Molly's?"

Tom felt good about her proposal. He needed to talk to somebody.

"Okay, I'll be there at noon."

"See you then, Tom."

After dressing, Tom called Julie. "I've read the article," he told her.

"What do you think happened?" she asked.

"I don't have a clue, but I'm meeting Greg and Jan for lunch. They will likely have the latest—more than the newspaper—at least Jan will."

"Will you call me tonight? I'm anxious to hear more," said Julie.

"Sure will. Meanwhile, have a great day."

Tom got on the elevator and headed down. It stopped on the twelfth floor and two uniformed police officers got on.

"Good morning," one of them said.

"Yeah, should be a great day. Are you fellows here because of the murder?" Tom asked.

"Yes, we sure are," replied the taller officer.

"Is there any news on who did it, or any major suspects?" asked Tom.

The shorter officer frowned. "That's not for us to say. You'll have to talk to Detective Anderson for answers to those questions."

Tom's eyes were locked on the smaller officer until the elevator stopped at the lobby. The two officers proceeded out the front door to a waiting squad car. Tom watched the car leave before making his way to the mailbox wall.

His watch showed two minutes short of noon when he entered Molly's. Glancing around, looking for his two neighbors, he spotted an arm waving above the top of a booth across the room. Greg and Jan both smiled as Tom approached.

"Lots of room on my side," said Jan.

Tom took a seat.

Greg continued smiling. "Things are heating up at the Towers. The lady on the twelfth floor, Gloria Tingsley, must have really had something going. Why do you suppose she was dumped back there by the railroad tracks?"

Tom frowned. "The two officers I met on the elevator earlier today sure didn't have much to say."

Jan tapped Tom on the shoulder. "Did you read the article in this morning's paper?"

"Yeah, I sure did."

"The whole thing doesn't make sense. If the killer hauled the lady out to the railroad tracks, it may have taken more than one person."

Tom imagined the hunchback look of Dracula crossing the street in the dead of night with a lady draped over his shoulder. He was tempted to share his secret of seeing the sport-coat man, Vito, with the Tingsley lady at O'Leary's, but decided against it.

Instead, he asked, "Do either one of you know of a person, name of Vito, that lives in this building?"

"No, sure don't. What's he done?" asked Greg.

Jan interrupted, "Vito. Hmm...I've heard that name mentioned before. Perhaps Carl mentioned it. Why do you mention the name?"

"Oh, there's this guy I've seen at O'Leary's a lot. He lives in the building—twelfth floor, I think," responded Tom.

"Twelfth floor—isn't that where Gloria lived?" asked Greg.

Jan's eyes darted from Greg to Tom. Her lips tightened together, and she was about to speak when the waitress arrived.

After the waitress took their orders, Jan asked, "So, Tom, what's the deal on this Vito guy? Does he hang around alone—at O'Leary's, I mean?"

"The man seems to draw a crowd. He's always dressed up—sport coat and tie—probably a salesman."

After they finished lunch, Jan nudged Tom with her elbow. "Would you and your significant other like to come over for cocktail hour this evening?"

"I'll check with Julie and give you a call. What time do you have in mind?"

"Five-thirty would be fine. So Julie is her name."

"That's right, you haven't met her yet, have you?"

"No, I haven't."

"Oh, by the way, have you met Joan, my next door neighbor?"

"Yes, I sure have. She's the broad messing around with the barber," responded Greg.

"Come on, Greg, you don't know that for sure," retorted Jan. "I had her over for coffee a couple of times. She's an interesting person—works for an activist group—People for Equality, or something like that."

"Hopefully, see you two about five-thirty," Tom added, and left Molly's.

The grocery store was his next stop. Calling Julie on his cell phone from the parking lot, he was pleased when she was receptive to the invitation by Greg and Jan.

"I'll be at your house about five."

"Okay. See you then."

There wasn't anyone around in the maintenance area of the Towers when Tom loaded his grocery bags onto a cart and proceeded up the elevator. After depositing the bags in his kitchen, he pushed the cart back into the elevator and headed down. The elevator stopped on the twelfth floor. The mysterious sport-coat man, whom Julie had recently identified as Vito, got on. He was wearing a leather jacket and jeans. A denim shirt was partially exposed under his jacket.

Without uttering a greeting, the man looked up and watched the floor numbers changing on the way down.

As the elevator rushed to its destination, he said, "You like O'Leary's, don't you?"

Tom's eyes narrowed. "Yeah, I like that place. Lots of sports to watch. I'm Tom Hastings. Have you lived at the Towers long?"

The elevator door opened to the lobby. Vito said, "I'm Vito. See ya," and got off while Tom continued down to the maintenance area.

———

JULIE'S CALL WAS RIGHT ON TIME, as expected. He buzzed her in. She was dressed for the evening.

"You look great, Julie."

"Thanks, Tom."

"I saw your man Vito on the elevator today. It's apparent he lives on the twelfth floor. That's where he got on."

"Was he wearing a sport coat?"

"No, he was wearing a scrubby leather jacket. Well, if you're ready, let's head over to Greg and Jan's."

They walked down the hallway and Tom knocked on 2006.

Jan opened the door. "Hi, Tom. Hi, Julie—nice of you guys to come. I want you to meet some people."

She led them into the living room where two strangers were sitting on the couch.

"This is Candice Tellburt—Tom and Julie. Mr. Handsome sitting over there is Jack Billings."

Candice and Jack rose from the couch and exchanged handshakes with Tom and Julie.

"Candice and Jack live in our building," Jan announced. "Both live on the seventeenth floor."

Tom's initial thought about Candice and Jack was that they were a couple. Since Jan used the plural "both live," perhaps they lived separately. Jack was indeed a handsome-looking guy. He had a full head of dark, wavy hair, combed straight back. Mixed streaks of gray in the temple areas lent to a distinguished appearance. His small, dark eyes had a penetrating effect on whomever he was talking to.

Greg entered the room, hugging Julie and accepting Tom's handshake. Jack set his drink down on a coffee table and sat down. Tom noticed Jack was about the same height as Greg.

After all the visitors had sat down, they busied themselves with cheese and crackers that Jan placed on the two coffee tables. Greg and Jan sat down on chairs facing the couches. Greg stretched his body forward, extending his arm to grab his share of the food. After exchanging the usual pleasantries, the topic of discussion switched to the murder.

Candice added a new observation. "I was going up the elevator about midnight on the day of the Tingsley murder when it stopped on the twelfth floor. After the door opened, two men were standing in the hallway, apparently waiting to enter. They didn't get on, perhaps because I was going up. Their attire was unusual for this building as both of them were dressed rather shabbily."

Tom asked, "Candice, did you talk to the police about this?"

"No, I haven't. Do you think I should?"

Candice was a very attractive lady. She showed a lot of leg when sitting on the couch. Her hair was short and dark—sort of bunched up on top of her head. Her eyes were a pretty brown and her skin was very dark, hinting at time spent in a tanning salon.

Candice glanced from person to person, but no one answered her question.

Jan's voice broke the silence. "I had a talk with a detective down in the lobby area, just yesterday." The firmness of her voice drew everyone's attention. "Yes, he took my name, my apartment number and phone."

"Are you sure it was a policeman?" asked a serious-faced Greg, drawing a generous amount of laughter.

"Oh, get out of here, you clod," smiled Jan.

She continued. "I told the detective about the handsome-looking man in a sport coat who got on at the twelfth floor on the day of the murder. "Darn—I wasn't certain as to the time, being I was up and down about five times that day. However, I did find out the name of the man dressed in the sport coat. It's Vito Manchino."

Jack grinned. "Well, looks like I'll have to hide my sport coats. Heaven help me if I wear one on the elevator."

Greg asked, "What's the big deal about a sport coat?"

Tom glanced at Julie, who showed a bank of teeth, trying to hold back a smile. He was tempted to tell the group what he'd seen at O'Leary's the night before the murder.

After about an hour and a half of conversation, Tom stood up. "Julie and I need to go. We have some plans."

"Nice to meet you two," said Candice.

Jack got up from the couch and there were more handshakes.

Jan walked Tom and Julie to the door. "Thanks for coming—too bad you have to go. See you soon."

Tom gave Jan a hug and thanked her for the treats. He looked back toward the living room and watched as Jack put on his Texan-like hat.

Julie and Tom walked down the hall back to 2012. "Wow, was that ever interesting. All this stuff about people on the twelfth floor!" Julie exclaimed.

"Where should we go for dinner?" Tom asked.

6

DETECTIVE BILL ANDERSON HUNG UP THE PHONE and looked up, a gentle tap-tap on the glass door getting his attention. Lieutenant Rod Barry was standing behind the door, peering in with excited eyes. Rod was built like a railroad tie with no waist and a square head. He had large blue eyes and light brown hair.

The detective waved and Barry entered.

"Have a seat, Rod. We have a new assignment," said Anderson stoically. He was beginning his final year on the force, having started as a rookie cop twenty-eight years ago.

"What's up, Bill?"

Bill Anderson was a big man, about six-three, his middle was moderately expanded, causing his belt to be partially covered. His full head of gray hair glistened in the rays of the overhead light. His ruddy face furrowed slightly when he spoke.

"The chief has dumped the railroad-tracks murder in my lap. He's freed up your slate so you can assist me. Are you interested?"

"Yeah, I read about it in the *Trib*—a lady by the name of Tingsley. She lives in that nearby high-rise apartment building. Bunch of weird characters live there, I hear."

"Well, I don't know about that, but we need to get over to the lab and see what they have come up with. After that, we'll meet with the manager of the Towers high-rise."

"The Towers—is that what it's known as?"

"Yup, exactly."

———

SUNDAY MORNING'S NEWSPAPER DIDN'T HAVE a single article about the Towers murder. Old news already, Tom thought. He was sitting in front of the window overlooking the bike-trail. A freight train was slowly making its way up the tracks and interrupted access to the trail. Geez, there must be fifty cars, Tom thought. He had always wondered what was in the boxcars. Where were they going? After the final unit passed from view, he focused his binoculars on a person standing on the bike trail. It was the same man he had seen earlier in the week.

Perhaps more stuff for the police, Tom thought as he watched for another ten minutes. When the man walked across the tracks toward the Towers and disappeared from view, Tom lowered the binoculars and walked out onto the balcony. He waited and wondered if the man he had been watching would show up crossing the parking lot.

About three minutes later, Tom saw the whitish cap emerge onto the stairway connecting the street to the parking lot. The man took a few long strides while crossing the parking lot and headed toward the entry to the Towers.

––––

MARCIL HUGGINS WAS LYING ON THE COUCH in his fifteenth-floor apartment, thinking about Susan Buntrock—her alluring smile and beautiful teeth. Feeling lucky about meeting her at a party, he thought about that evening and how he'd decided to attend at the last minute.

Getting up early on Sunday morning, he anxiously headed out to the bike trail. Susan walked or jogged the bike trail often, Marcil remembered. Standing at the edge of the trail, he peered at the joggers and bikers as they approached and passed by. After spending an hour watching and waiting for Susan to appear, he was disappointed that she hadn't shown. His enthusiasm picked up when he saw a young lady on skates approaching, wearing tight shorts. Even though it wasn't Susan, Marcil felt satisfied after she'd passed and returned to the Towers.

He entered the lobby from the outdoor parking lot. Carl is engaged in conversation with that lady again, he thought. She's down here every day. He wondered if they were talking about him, since they quieted when he entered.

After arriving at his apartment on the fifteenth floor, Marcil returned to the couch. He fell asleep, pleasantly dreaming about an encounter with a tall blonde. Marcil was disappointed when he woke.

Getting up, he looked out the window overlooking the balcony. There goes that in-line-skater guy again—lives on the twentieth floor, he thought. Marcil had overheard it down in the lobby. He watched as Tom Hastings walked down the parking-lot steps and across the street toward the bike trail.

Financially comfortable, Marcil knew he couldn't afford a serious relationship after what had happened to his wife. Living alone at the Towers was not by choice. Thrice, he'd been turned down.

That Tamara Oxley lady isn't a bad one, he thought. A few days ago, Marcil had been going down the elevator when it stopped on the sixth floor. When she got on, her perfume generated feelings that frightened him. Fighting off the urge to grab her, he intentionally stumbled when exiting, reaching out with his hand and grasping her by the leg for a moment. When she turned and smiled, feelings of exhilaration radiated through Marcil's body.

———

TAMARA OXLEY LIKED LIVING IN THE TOWERS. It was quite the change after living in a small town in western Minnesota. Her parents had been against the move. The marriage had lasted only six years. She wanted children, but couldn't have any. Her husband was abusive and said that kids would get in his way. The broken cheekbone was the last straw and she went to the police.

Some of the men who lived in the building attracted her. She would love to get to know Jack Billings better. He was one handsome guy, she thought. That dark, wavy hair with the graying temples, the dark eyes...lots of money, too. *I loved that hat.*

Tamara wasn't certain where Candice Tellburt fit in. Candice and Jack were seen together, but they weren't married. At least that's what Jack had said when they met for lunch. More encouraging was the fact that Jack and Candice had separate apartments, even though they were both on the seventeenth floor.

Then, there was Vito, handsome Vito—very good-looking, but a little too sly for her taste. Never trust a car salesman, she'd been taught. Smiling, she reflected on the evening she'd spent at the Manchino apartment. Vito had said other people were invited. Well, they never showed up, only Vito and her. She didn't care for his gum-chewing habit.

Her dad owned and ran a small town car dealership. Two of his young male employees had vied for her affection. Craig had been so cute, but with only one thing on his mind, she later discovered. Marvin sold more cars and she foolishly married him instead of Craig, strictly from her Daddy's influence. After eight years of abuse by that big lug, her dad finally had admitted he was wrong.

The man she wanted to get to know the most at the Towers was the Colombian, Carlos. He was very married though—off limits. Still, they'd had lunch and two glasses of wine. One never knows, she thought. The hug she'd experienced out in the parking lot had been awesome.

A real smooth operator that Richard, the slick-talking boy with the silver streak in his hair. He, too, was married, to sweet little Maria. Poor little thing, she didn't have a chance. Richard was a mover, Tamara could tell.

She rushed to the door when hearing the knock.

"Hello, Tammy," her visitor said.

Feelings of excitement passed through her body at the peak of the hug.

———

FERRO HAD THAT FEELING AGAIN, much too soon. After being satisfied with Gloria, he'd been confident she was the last one. Shockingly, the feeling had come back within hours, the first time ever that soon. Previously, he'd been able to count on at least four to six months.

Getting into Tamara Oxley's room had been as easy as pie. She'd fallen for his line—amazing, he thought. Gloria Tingsley had taken a lot of convincing before she'd agreed to let him in. If it hadn't been for the booze, she wouldn't have been that careless.

He now sat with Tamara on the couch, sipping wine and watching television for a couple of hours. The wine helped reduce the snakelike feeling his innards were experiencing; he almost gave up on his objective.

After Tamara excused herself for a trip to the bathroom, he stood and stretched. Reaching in his back pocket, he lifted out a pair of surgical gloves and put one of them on. Walking to the bathroom door and leaning against the wall, he waited. After the door opened, it was over in minutes. Holding his right hand over her mouth, he penetrated her heart with the knife. She died quietly—the best way. Causing people to suffer was not his intention.

He went into the bathroom and washed the blood off his gloved hand and the knife. Returning to the living room, he carefully wiped off the outside of both wineglasses. After spending the next ten minutes in her bedroom, he was ready to leave.

Making sure the keys for both her apartment and car were in his pocket, he silently stole through the corridor and up the elevator to his apartment. Being close to exhaustion, he plunked down on the couch with his clothes on and fell asleep. The penetrating sound of the alarm clock jolted him up off the couch at 4:00 a.m. The snake-like feelings in his stomach were gone.

Returning to Tamara's apartment, he pitied the lifeless body lying on the floor. Noticing it had stiffened some, while wrapping her in the sheet, he tied four loops of rope around the body. Each time he went through this procedure, it became easier. During an earlier incident, he had tied only three loops, and there had almost been a disaster when the body had begun to slip out of the sheet.

She was a bit heavier than the Tingsley lady, but without incident he moved her into the elevator and exited on the lower level. Struggling with the weight, he moved to the far wall, escaping the surveillance camera mounted over the door. He knew the chance of a vehicle entering at this time of night was remote. After finally arriving at her car, he opened the trunk. He held his breath when he heard the garage door apparatus engage. Quickly closing the trunk, he cradled the body and ducked down. Headlights shone across the back-wall, meaning the car was going to park somewhere in the rear two rows. By dragging the body between two cars and staying low, he avoided being spotted.

After hearing the slam of two car doors, he stayed as low-as possible and partially covered the body. Two sets of footsteps approached and they came within a few feet. His heart was beating so rapidly that it sounded to him like a drum. To his immense relief, the two persons continued walking toward the door leading to the elevators.

The intrusion had unnerved him. Making sure no one else was in the garage, he removed the rope and sheets. Instead of placing the body in the trunk, he successfully stuffed it into the front seat. A push, a tug here, another there, and Tamara appeared to be sitting behind the wheel, asleep. After locking and closing the door, he picked up the pieces of rope and wrapped them in the sheet.

Returning to his apartment, he stuffed the sheet, the rope and his outer clothes into a plastic bag. Stepping into the utility room, he sent it down the garbage chute. *It was more useless ammunition for the police.* He smiled when visualizing them digging through the dumpster. The rummage sale he'd visited in St. Paul had had good used clothes. Exhaustion ensued when he reentered his apartment. Ferro slid under the blanket in his bed and fell into a deep sleep.

7

DETECTIVE ANDERSON HATED WORKING ON SUNDAYS, but here he was in the office, going over the current evidence in the Towers case. Both victims had been killed in their apartments. The apartments hadn't been totally trashed, but in both cases the contents of the drawers where the ladies kept their jewelry and personal stuff had been strewn about. The only other clue had been the gum wrappers found on the floor—two of them. They weren't identical, but both had been crushed to approximately the same size. Neither lady had had gum in her purse. Their billfolds, credit cards and other items hadn't appeared to be tampered with.

Digging through the trash in the dumpsters had been a miserable job for his men, but they came up with what could be a significant clue–a plastic bag containing strips of synthetic rope, a white sheet, a shirt and a pair of trousers. All items were stained with blood. Forensics was working on them, and as sure as he sat there, the detective knew the blood was going to belong to the most recent victim.

When his partner in the investigation came through the door, Anderson looked up. "Good morning, Rod. Nice way to spend a Sunday, eh?"

"Yeah, I can't wait," replied the burly lieutenant.

"Rod, it looks like we have a serial killer on the loose. MO appears to be the same in both killings. This can't wait until tomorrow. We need to begin our interviews today."

"Who have you talked to so far?"

"Well, the building manager, Carl Borders, mainly. There was this lady down there in the lobby, name of Jan something or another. She had something interesting to say."

"What was that?"

"An older guy, apartment on the twentieth floor, saw the first victim the night of the murder at a bar—O'Leary's, it says here."

"What time was that?"

"Don't know. That's what we have to find out today. His name is Tom Hastings, number twenty twelve. According to this Jan, Hastings saw the lady visiting with a man. The man's name is Vito Manchino and he also lives at the Towers. Now get this—same floor as the first victim."

"Wow, you may have something there."

"The building manager, Carl, is going to let us in, about an hour from now. Let's get going."

————

LATE SUNDAY MORNING, TOM WAS ON HIS WAY to the bike trail. The gray clouds didn't appear to be threatening. When the elevator halted on the sixth floor, a lady carrying a briefcase got on.

"Good morning," she said.

"Same to you. Looks like work for you this Sunday morning," Tom replied and wondered why she was carrying a briefcase on a Sunday morning.

"I'm Susan—do you live here?"

"Yes, I'm up on the twentieth floor. My name is Tom."

"Nice to meet you," she said as the elevator stopped at the lobby, Tom's exit. Susan remained on the elevator, as her destination was the lower-level garage.

When Tom pushed through the door accessing the lobby, he saw several people milling about—something was wrong. Carl was talking to Greg, Jan and two other people. They all turned toward Tom as he approached.

"Have you heard the news?" asked Jan.

"No, what's going on?"

"We've lost another tenant," said Carl. "Tamara Oxley was found dead in her car last night—down in the garage, of all places."

"Not another murder," Tom responded.

Carl shrugged his shoulders. "Don't know for sure. I got this frantic call from her sister—Tamara hadn't been answering her phone all day. When the sister came over, we checked Tamara's parking spot in the garage. Tamara was in the car and appeared to be sleeping— too dark to tell for sure. Her sister pounded on the window. No one could sleep through that. In desperation, we called the police. She was dead." Carl looked down at the floor and added, "They came and took her away—the ambulance people."

Jan placed her hand over Carl's shoulder. "There, there now, Carl, it wasn't your fault."

"Cousins. They were cousins—first cousins—Gloria and Tamara. Now they're both gone. They were such sweet girls," Carl bemoaned.

Jan remained close to Carl, consoling him while he lamented the loss of two friends and tenants. Tom stood next to the door a few steps away from Carl and Jan, absorbing some of their sorrow. A feeling of awkwardness overwhelmed Tom, so he excused himself, and was about to proceed out the back door toward the parking lot when he heard Jan call.

"Oh, Tom—wait up a second. Can we talk for a moment?"

"Sure, Jan."

They walked into the corridor leading to the parking lot, and Jan said, "Tom, it was murder. Carl is in denial."

"How do you know that for sure?"

"I overhead the detective say so."

"Oh well, I better get on with my day. I'm headed out to the bike trail."

"Yeah, go ahead. We'll talk more later."

———

TOM'S LEGS LOOSENED QUICKLY and he moved up the trail at a strong pace that morning, attempting to think about happy things and not the dreadful news he'd received in the lobby. It was a typical Sunday morning in the summer. There were an above average number of people using the trail. He recognized Carlos walking toward him in the other lane. They exchanged waves. The Colombian sure looks down this morning, Tom thought. *Perhaps he heard about the second death.*

Skating nonstop to the end of the trail where it merged with a city street downtown, he searched his mind for which tenant Tamara Oxley was. He guessed she was the one who got on at the sixth floor, her perfume overwhelming.

After returning to the beginning of the trail, he decided on another round-trip. His thoughts were constantly on the two murders and the people who could be involved—mainly, Vito and the man Tom had seen watching the bike trail. Tom knew it was only a matter of time until the police contacted him. His better judgment told him to not get involved, but deep down, he knew differently. The second murder was going to heat things up and the police would come calling.

Tom was nearing the completion of a second lap when he passed by Candice Tellburt biking in the opposite direction. Waving, she brought her bike to a halt. He recognized her from the party at the Skogen's yesterday. He looked back and saw that she had stopped. Tom reversed his direction and skated over.

"Good morning, Mr. Hastings. Have you heard the ugly news?" Candice asked.

"Yup, I sure did, just a few minutes ago in the lobby."

"I probably shouldn't be out here alone, but then it's Sunday and lots of people around," Candice moaned sorrowfully.

"Life has to go on, Candice. We can't all go into hiding," Tom responded confidently.

"You're right. Did you have a good time at the Greg and Jan party the other day? I enjoyed talking to your friend, Julie."

"Please call me Tom. Yes, there was a lot of interesting discussion, including your story about the two men on the twelfth floor."

"Oh, could be just a coincidence, except they didn't belong. Most maintenance and delivery people are usually dressed neat."

"Have the police contacted you yet?"

"No, they haven't, but if they do, I'll tell them about the two men on the twelfth. Did you notice the police tape down in the garage, closing off the stall that Tamara Oxley used?"

"No, I haven't been down there this morning. I just heard about it in the lobby. Another person from our building, dead." Frowning, Tom asked, "Did you hear if it was a murder, too?"

"I'm assuming it is—what else could it be? I suppose it could be suicide. After all, the other victim was her first cousin."

Tom was looking down at the asphalt when Candice added, "I suppose this means an all-out alert for the rest of us. I mean, we will have to be careful about moving about the building alone at night, especially down in the garage."

"You know, Candice, life at the Towers will never be the same until the murderer is caught. I've gone through this before. It's like living a nightmare, over and over again," Tom added.

"Before? What do you mean?"

"A couple of years ago, I was caught up in the middle of three murders where I lived up north. Every single day meant being extra cautious for survival. Ah, sorry. Didn't mean to scare you," Tom responded as he watched Candice's expression change to fear.

"I appreciate your being candid. We'll have to be very careful."

"Well, Candice, I need to be on my way. Nice talking to you."

"Good-bye, Tom. See you again, and thanks for the warning."

When Tom was nearing the end of the bike trail, he was looking for the mysterious man in the white baseball cap. There wasn't anyone around. Probably doesn't matter, he thought. *Vito is the number one suspect.*

Returning to the Towers, Tom hoped Carl and Jan would not be in the lobby. His wish was granted. Instead, two police officers were standing next to the front door. They didn't pay any attention to him as he moved toward the elevators. The calm, peaceful community that Tom had selected for his new home was currently a bed of turmoil. The presence of police officers generated a hollow feeling in the pit of his stomach.

When Tom returned to 2012, his answering machine was beeping. "Hi, this is Jan. Greg and I are anxious to talk about the Oxley deal. Would you call me back?"

Tom wasn't in the mood to talk about either one of the Towers deaths. Instead, his thoughts focused on escaping the Towers for the remaining hours of the day. Dialing Julie's number, he was disappointed when she didn't answer.

"Julie, this is Tom. How about getting together today? Give me a call," he recorded on her voice mail.

While he was spending time at his computer during the next hour, his phone rang. He anxiously picked up the receiver, expecting Julie. Instead, it was a man's voice.

"Mr. Tom Hastings, I presume?"

"Yes, that's me," answered Tom.

"I'm Detective Anderson of the Minneapolis Police Department. Please don't get alarmed, Mr. Hastings, but I need to talk to you. Someone in the building brought up your name. You may have some information that could help us in the investigation. Surely you are aware that two of your fellow tenants have lost their lives."

After listening to the detective's statement, Tom Hastings knew that he could no longer remain on the sidelines. His thoughts reverted to a couple of years before when police officers had been at his home frequently, investigating three local killings. Moving back to the country—perhaps it was an alternative? Not now, at least not until the murders were solved. The police would take a dim view of him leaving.

"Oh sure, Detective. When and where would you like to meet?" Tom responded.

"Actually, I am down in the lobby and would like to come up right now."

"Okay. Come on up."

Tom soon heard the knock. When he opened the door, two men were standing in the hallway.

"I am Detective Anderson and this is Lieutenant Barry."

"I'm Tom Hastings. Come on in."

Before they stepped into his apartment, Detective Anderson said,

"I apologize for interrupting your Sunday—this shouldn't take very long."

Lieutenant Barry walked over to the window and commented, "Wow—nice view!"

Tom invited the two men to sit on the couch in his living room, taking a nearby chair.

Detective Anderson looked at Tom. "We heard through the grapevine that you had seen Gloria Tingsley at O'Leary's bar & grill on the night before she was murdered."

Uh-oh, Tom thought, someone has spilled the beans.

"Yes, it's true. I saw her visiting with a gentleman at the bar. At least, it may have been her. The picture in the newspaper the next day sort of—there was a resemblance."

"Had you ever seen them together before?" asked Barry.

"No, I hadn't. That was the first time. I haven't live here very long though, you know."

"Do you know who the gentleman was?" asked Barry.

"No, I didn't recognize the man—never saw him before, but I think I know his first name."

"And what would that be?"

"Vito."

"What did they appear to be doing?" continued Barry.

"I really wasn't paying much attention. The one thing I did notice was the smoke coming from the cigarettes."

"So, both of them were smoking?" asked Anderson.

"Yes, they sure were. The smoke drifted all the way to my end of the bar."

"Did they leave together?"

"I'm really not sure, because my back was to the door."

"Well, did they leave the bar together? Did they get off the barstools at the same time?"

"Yes, they did, Detective."

"Would you be able to recognize the gentleman if you saw him again?" asked Barry.

"Yes, I believe so. Actually, he must either live or work in the neighborhood. I have seen him at O'Leary's on other occasions."

"Was this before or after you saw him with the lady?" asked Anderson.

"After. The evening with the lady was the first time."

"Ah, how many times did you see him after the lady?"

"Ah, about four times in or around O'Leary's, and a couple of times here at the Towers."

"Where did you see him at the Towers?"

"The elevator. He gets on at the twelfth floor."

"Okay, thanks, Mr. Hastings. We may need to contact you in the future. Don't get up—we'll find our way out," said the detective.

"Oh, yes, one more thing—are you acquainted with a Towers tenant by the name of Jack Billings?"

"Ah, I know a man by the name of Jack that lives on the seventeenth floor. His last name may be Billings."

"Where and when have you seen him—the latest, I mean?"

"At a cocktail party down the hall."

"Whose place was that?"

"Yes, ah, at Greg and Jan Skogen's"

"When was that?"

"Just this Friday evening."

"Okay, thanks again, Mr. Hastings. Here's my card if you need to call us."

"Oh, by the way, do you chew gum?" asked the detective.

"No, I don't. Why do you ask that?" responded Tom.

The detective raised his chin, smiled and said, "Oh, just curious."

Tom was tempted to ask them about the Tamara Oxley lower-level garage death, but decided against. Their visit had been uncomfortable as it was, and he was glad when they left.

An hour later, Julie called. "Why don't you come over?" she asked.

"I'll be there in an hour," Tom happily replied.

———

ARRIVING AT JULIE'S APARTMENT, Tom Hastings felt good about escaping the Towers for a few hours, even though he knew Julie was going to pump him for information.

"I thought you'd never get here. I'm anxious to hear the latest," she said as he entered.

Julie became excited when hearing about the visit from the police. She was anxious to know what they had talked about.

"Julie, I only answered their questions. I didn't volunteer anything. They were mainly interested in my observations at O'Leary's the evening before the murder. Someone must have told them I was there."

"Didn't you tell them the name of the man that was with her? How about the fact they both lived on the same floor?"

"Yes, I did mention his first name—but then, they likely already had that information. I didn't mention what floor the sport-coat man lives on. Whoops, I may have mentioned seeing him get on at twelve."

Tom sat in silence for a minute, hesitating to announce the second death. His facial expression grew more serious. "Julie, there's been another death at the Towers. A lady was found dead in her car in the lower-level indoor parking lot."

"Oh my God. You've got to be kidding."

"No, I'm afraid not."

"Was she murdered?"

"I really don't know for sure. Jan claims she overheard a detective say it was another murder."

"When did this happen?"

"Last night—Saturday, only two days after the other lady."

"So, what do you think is happening? Is there a serial killer on the loose?"

"Geez, I'm afraid so. I can't believe this is happening to me again. Three neighbors and friends murdered when I lived in the lake country, and now serial murders in my apartment building. Is there a black cloud following me around?"

"Tell you what, Tom, I've some fresh salmon and a couple bottles of chardonnay cooling in the fridge. Why don't we go out and find a good rental to watch after dinner?"

"Sounds great to me," Tom replied, smiling.

———

JACK BILLINGS WAS ON HIS WAY to the airport on Monday morning. The eastern sky was beginning to show some light. His mind was mixed between focusing on the business in Colombia and on the events at the Towers.

International Oceanic was an impressive company name. His friends at the Towers would never know what type of exporting he did. The exception would be Vito Manchino, of course—but then, he'd never talk. He's in it as deep as I am, Jack thought. Then there is that Colombian, Carlos. How convenient that he has so many connections.

While reaching out the window and taking a ticket to the parking lot, he thought about the naive Tamara Oxley. It hadn't been so easy convincing Candice that he had no interest in Tamara. She had nodded but hadn't believed him. Well, who cares, he thought, I'll soon be with Carlita. Four days and nights of bliss—good times ahead. After taking the ticket, he needed to reset his large hat, dislodged by the reach. Placing a fresh stick of gum in his mouth, he continued into the airport parking lot.

An hour later, he looked out the plane window and noticed the upper floors of the Towers projecting above the sea of green and blue. The plane banked and headed for Colombia.

———

"COME ON IN, ROD," Bill Anderson said as he waved his arm. The detective was sipping on a fresh cup of coffee just supplied by one of the office staff.

He took a long swig and looked into Rod Barry's eyes. "I talked to the chief this morning. He was firm. 'Need some action,' the man said. The second murder really brings on the media. He said the mayor's office called."

"Have the lab guys finished with the second victim yet—ah...the Oxley lady?" asked the lieutenant.

"Yes, they have, but the report is preliminary. Here's what we have so far: MO was the same. Both died from a precision stab wound penetrating the heart. Both had their bedrooms ransacked—mainly the dresser where they kept jewelry and personal stuff."

"How about the rest of the apartment?" asked Rod.

"Nothing seemed to be touched. Of course there are tons of fingerprints. It's going to take some time for the lab guys to sort those out. My guess is that none of them belong to the killer."

"Yeah, it all fits. This monster is slick. He knew we would find the junk he dumped in the waste container and dumpster. All the stuff is untraceable and no prints."

"Why would the creep move their bodies after the killing?" asked a puzzled lieutenant.

"Beats the hell out of me. Creep may be a good word for the killer, but not nearly strong enough. Then, there are the gum wrappings—more calling cards."

"Oh, we've got a criminal profile expert coming over tomorrow. The state guys are sending her—she's with the Bureau of Criminal Apprehension."

"Her?"

"Yeah, a her. Let's see here—my notes—her name is Kate Purley."

"Fresh out of college, I bet," muttered the Lieutenant.

"We shall see."

"How about the surveillance cameras down there? Did they record anything that could help us?" asked the lieutenant.

"Naw, the guy is too smart—went around it. Oh, by the way, Rod, we're going to need to set up a patrol schedule for the Towers. I talked to Marty at West Side Precinct. He said there weren't enough men to patrol the building around the clock. However, he can spare two men that would check out the building about eight to ten times a day."

"Yeah, that's good, but the manager isn't going to be pleased," responded Rod. "I guess if Carl wants more, he's going to have to hire some people. Would you coordinate the patrols with Marty—say, every two hours starting at four in the afternoon?"

"Shall do."

8

THE ROAR OF AIRCRAFT JET ENGINES greeted Tom Hastings as he was readying for his appointment on Monday morning. Glancing out the open window, he saw the airliner banking and turning southward. His watch showed almost ten, time to go down for his haircut with James.

The barber was waiting when Tom Hastings entered the barbershop, located in a suite one level below the lobby.

"You know, Jim, the barbershops were all closed on Monday where I used to live," Tom said.

"Uh-huh, Mr. Hastings, things change. Demand is good on Mondays here. I'll take it when available. Besides, I'd rather have time off during the weekends."

"No problem with me, Jim. I like the Mondays." Tom referred to the barber as Jim, rather than James. Lady clients usually called him James.

The only sound in the room over the next few minutes was the intermittent snipping noise generated by the scissors. James's associate, Barb, was cutting a lady's hair.

Her client interrupted the silence. "Two murders in the building— isn't that awful?"

"I'm afraid to go into the parking lot alone. It's worse than awful," responded Barb.

"Yeah, we almost need armed guards. I hear there's a guy living on the twelfth floor that the police are checking out. Something about being with Gloria the day before she died."

"You don't say? I heard that Tamara and the other lady, Gloria, were cousins," responded Barb.

"Yes, not only were they cousins, they worked in the same place."

"Same place. Now, where would that be?"

"They both worked at one of the big car dealerships, I hear," responded the client.

Noise from the power clippers that James had just started prevented Tom from hearing any more of the ladies' conversation.

Barb finished with her client, who left before James got done with Tom.

Tom wrote out a check and handed it to James, who responded, "Thanks a lot, Mr. Hastings. Come back and see us again."

"You're welcome. What do you think of the two murders, Jim?"

"Makes me afraid to be alone in the building. There's a lunatic on the loose that hopefully doesn't live in this building."

That Monday afternoon, Tom parked in the lot in front of Jensen's Shirts. He looked up at the sky and watched a flock of mallards set their wings as they approached the lake. He was committed to another computer session but secretly wished he were walking amongst the wildlife at his former country home.

Cliff was working in the back room while Dalia and Tom spent time reviewing her recent data entries in the spreadsheet.

"How am I doing?" she asked.

"Hey, you're coming right along. Looks like you're getting the hang of it."

"Well, thanks. I'm trying real hard. Lately, I'm finding it darn hard to concentrate—the murders at the Towers and all that. Why don't the police arrest someone? I could give them a couple of names—actually more than two."

Tom looked up from the spreadsheet, his eyes wide and his mouth partially open. Does Dalia know something? he thought. He looked back down at the computer screen. "Uh-oh, I see a problem with the "D" column—the totals are wrong. Needs fixing—my problem."

Tom worked alone for about an hour until satisfied that the sub-total and total formulas were correct.

Cliff came out of the back room. He stretched, walked over to the window and looked out into the street. A customer came in the door and Cliff directed her over to Dalia, who was working behind the counter.

"How's it going with the production, Cliff?" Tom asked.

"Not bad—did ninety-two shirts today."

"Wow, that sounds terrific! You needed a break."

Cliff didn't answer and continued to look out the window.

Tom completed his work on the spreadsheet at 3:30 p.m. He felt an annoying stiffness in his hips while rising from the chair. After a few seconds of moving around, his stiffness left. Before leaving, Tom copied the spreadsheet file to a floppy disk and placed it in his briefcase.

As he was putting on his jacket, Dalia asked, "Are you all done for today?"

"Yes, I am. Give me a call if you find any bugs in the spreadsheet—I can come over almost any day," Tom replied as he watched Cliff place a fresh stick of gum in his mouth.

By the way, do you chew gum? That's what the detective had asked Tom. *Why did the detective want to know if I chewed gum?* He wondered.

Dalia appeared pleased with the progress of the new program. Tom was confident that the spreadsheet, which was designed to track thread inventory, would be a big time-saver. Cliff was in the production room when Tom left the building. Driving in the direction of the Towers, Tom felt satisfied with the work he was doing for Dalia.

I could give them a couple of names—actually, more than two. Dalia knew something.

————

JAN WAS SITTING ON THE COUCH when Tom had entered the lobby. She looked up. "Oh, there you are. I was trying to reach you today."

"What's up?" Tom asked.

She went into the details about an interview that she and Greg had had with a detective.

"How did this come about?" Tom asked. "Did the detective call you?"

"No, Greg and I were sitting here in the lobby when these two plainclothes officers came out of Carl's office. One thing led to another and the next thing we knew, they were up in our apartment asking us questions."

Oh, so that's how the detective got my name, Tom thought. Well, if it wasn't her, it would be someone else, even Carl.

"Well, I gotta get home," Tom said.

"They were cousins, you know," Jan stated, firmly.

"Jan, I heard that. A coincidence, perhaps?"

"Yes, first cousins. Tamara Oxley and Gloria Tingsley were also brought up in the same town—some western town in southern Minnesota. They both worked for Great Plains Ford."

"Jan, did the detectives say how Tamara died?"

"Both girls were stabbed—some type of knife blade. Both were killed in their apartments and hauled out. Vito works there, too, you know, at Great Plains."

"Vito? You mean Vito Manchino?"

"One and the same. He lives on the same floor Gloria did," she added.

———

THE TOWERS WAS REALLY QUIET for the next couple of days. Tom hardly talked to anyone. Emil visited Tom's apartment, coming to fix a hinge on a cabinet door in the kitchen.

Emil usually didn't talk when he worked, but as he was packing up his tools, he said, "I'm off to an apartment on the sixth floor—second bloody mess in a week. I wonder what's going on around here, anyhow—two dead ladies, both murdered?"

"Thanks for fixing the cabinet, Emil."

When Tom closed the door behind Emil, he visualized a pool of blood on the carpet floor. *They both worked for Great Plains Ford...Vito worked there, too, you know.*

His thoughts went back a couple of years to when he'd been attacked in his home by an intruder. Tom had won and the intruder had paid with his life. That hadn't been true for Gloria Tingsley and Tamara Oxley. They'd both lost.

Tom called Julie and they decided to go out for dinner on Friday. She accepted his offer to come over at 5:30.

Tom checked the sports television schedule for Thursday evening, targeting a baseball game starting at 6:30. At about six, he changed into casual clothes and headed for O'Leary's on foot. Two uniformed police officers gave him a stare as he left the building.

9

TOM'S FAVORITE STOOL WAS OCCUPIED, but that wasn't a problem. He found an empty one on the right side, opposite from where the sport-coat man usually hung out—Manchino was the last name according to Jan. The sport-coat man was missing that evening.

The three stools nearest the server station across from where Tom sat were empty. He ordered a beer and asked the bartender to change the channel to seventeen, to the baseball game. She courteously granted his television request. The game between the Braves and the Cincinnati Reds was in the bottom of the first inning with no score.

Tom was on his second bottle of beer when his suspect, Vito Manchino, arrived, heading right for the end stool directly across from Tom. A couple of minutes later, the smell of smoke penetrated the air as Tom continued to watch the television. The feeling of those dark eyes watching him was overwhelming for Tom. He turned his head slightly to look at the new arrival. Vito Manchino, wearing the notable blue sport coat, nodded at Tom—a respect of recognition, *or a warning*. Between sips of wine, sometimes during commercials, Tom glanced at Vito. Not surprisingly, Vito was still smoking. The difference this evening was the absence of fidgeting.

The Reds were batting in the top of the fourth with two men out when Vito received a visitor—a lady. Her arrival preoccupied him, allowing Tom to glance across more frequently. The lady's long blonde hair, draping down to her shoulders, covered most of her slim face. Her red blazer contrasted with Vito's dark blue sport coat. Even though

Vito was above average in height, close to six-feet, she appeared to be taller.

The fingers of her left hand were saturated with rings—large, gaudy ones. Her blouse was open at the neck, displaying a double-rowed pearl necklace.

"Another one?" asked the bartender.

"Yes, I'll have another," Tom responded.

The Braves were batting in the bottom of the eighth when Vito and his lady friend got up to leave. Tom's eyes followed them to the door, watching as Vito held it open while the lady passed through. Tom stretched his neck and looked out the window. He saw them walking together in the parking lot before disappearing from view.

Tom knew he could recognize that lady if he ever saw her again. He remembered the detectives' questions about the first one, the Tingsley lady.

Leaving the restaurant a few minutes later, before the game ended, he began the walk home. By taking the long way, he avoided dark alleys and streets. Just before getting to the Towers, he had to walk a short distance that wasn't lighted and had little traffic. He hurried through the area and arrived at the back door of the Towers as quickly as possible.

At exactly 5:28 p.m. on Friday, the next day, Tom parked in the lot next to Julie's apartment building. Julie was ready with a series of questions when he entered her apartment.

"Whoa, young lady. I understand that you need to know," Tom said, "but we can talk about all this stuff at dinner. Where would you like to go?"

"Ramono's," she replied. At Ramono's located only three blocks away, they waited for half an hour before gaining a table.

"So, what's the latest?" Julie asked anxiously.

"Well, I saw Vito Manchino at O'Leary's yesterday evening and he was joined by another lady. They left together."

"Wow! Is the lady going to have her picture in the newspaper tomorrow?"

"Geez, I hope not. Julie, do you remember the other day when I told you about the dead lady found in her car?"

"Yes. What's the latest on that one?"

"Well, the word is out she was murdered—in her apartment. The body was dumped in her car—different than the Tingsley lady—not by the railroad tracks."

"Do you have a name?"

"Yes. The dead lady's name was Tamara Oxley."

"Oh my gosh—I met an Oxley woman at a party during the Christmas holidays. I wonder if that was the same person."

"Sure could be. I don't recall ever hearing that name before, ah...Oxley."

"Did the police officers that visited your apartment mention anything about a reason for the murders?"

"No, they didn't talk about a reason and I wasn't about to ask. However, I don't recollect anyone saying anything about a forced entry. That could mean the victims knew their attacker."

"Sure sounds like someone that lives in your building," responded Julie.

Tom nodded. "I think we need to visit Greg and Jan later. They usually have the latest news."

Ramono's Restaurant was a quaint, quiet place—a perfect spot to engage in private conversation. The waiters were dressed formally and the tables were topped with white linens. A "single red rose" in a fancy vase adorned the middle of the table. Complementing the atmosphere was the tasteful, subdued sound of classical music in the background.

The two deaths at the Towers occupied most of their conversation as Tom and Julie dined. The subject was so intense that afterwards, Tom hardly remembered eating. When dropping off Julie at her apartment, he asked her to come over the next afternoon.

"Perhaps we could get together with Greg and Jan and find out what's going on."

After a long embrace, Julie said, "Good night, Tom. See you tomorrow."

10

MARCIL HUGGINS' HEART WAS BEATING RAPIDLY. He needed to get out and go somewhere. Haunted by his prison tenure of twenty years, his mind flashed back to his young wife, then only eighteen years old. He'd never forget answering the door and seeing the accusing eyes of two detectives—deadpan faces, just standing there. *Are you Marcil Huggins? Your wife, Marny, was found dead in an alley, stabbed to death.*

He'd been the only suspect. *You have the right to remain silent...*It had been the beginning of a living nightmare.

The jury hadn't believed his explanation. The lawyer, damn his soul, had said there was nothing to worry about. Twenty years in the pen had been Marcil's reward for trusting that jerk. Marcil's memory of his mother sobbing in the courtroom was the worst part.

Marcil rose from the couch, reached up into the closet with his stubby fingers and put on his cap, covering his thick, dark head of hair. He slipped on his jacket and headed down the elevator. Getting off at the lobby, he paused and looked through the glass at Carl and a lady deep in conversation. *It's that snoopy one from the twentieth.* She bothers me, Marcil thought as he moved through the door and lobby without disrupting the conversation.

––––-

TOM WAS LOADING THE COFFEEPOT the next morning and the phone rang. Julie was on the line.

"So, Tom, are we going to visit with Greg and Jan today?"

He managed a raspy laugh. "Julie, you are really on top of things this morning. I bet you have been awake half the night thinking about this."

"Yeah, I sure have. The stuff you have going on over there is fascinating."

"Tell you what, young lady, you just go about your business this morning and I'll see what I can do. It's too early to knock on their door yet. On the serious side, messing with murders could be extremely dangerous."

"Okay, Tom, I've got the message. Have a nice morning."

Pausing at the elevator door a few minutes before noon, Tom delayed heading down for the mail. Instead, he knocked on Greg and Jan's door.

Greg opened the door. "Good morning, Tom. Glad you don't have a knife in your hand."

"Hi, Greg. That's not very funny. I'm in a generous mood—how about you and Jan coming over about five for some snacks and vino?" asked Tom.

"Sounds great to me. Hold on a second and I'll check with Jan. Step in a moment."

Tom entered their apartment.

When Greg returned a minute later, he said, "We'll be happy to come over. Is Julie going to be there?"

"She sure is. I'll see you at five."

Tom took the elevator down to the lobby. There was a bunch of mail in his box. He was sifting through some of the junk stuff when Emil came in from the back parking lot.

"Hello, Mr. Hastings. How's it going today?"

"Don't know yet, Emil—too early to tell. Boy, looks like you are working overtime this morning."

"Yeah, I didn't finish cleaning the parking lot yesterday, and the boss put the pressure on me—get it done by Monday or else."

Tom went back up to his apartment and reviewed the mail. After finishing, he looked out the window overlooking the bike trail. The man in the gray jacket and white baseball cap was standing along the edge. Tom got out his binoculars, verifying the man was the same one he'd seen the other day—The one with the black hair bunched up behind a baseball cap. Tom watched for a few minutes, but the man didn't move much. The guy·was looking directly up the trail.

After dialing Julie's number, Tom listened to all the rings. She didn't answer. Instead, a taped message softly said, "Please leave a message."

"The Skogens are coming over at five. Why don't you come over at four and we can get some food together? I'm heading to the grocery store right now. Thanks!"

An hour later, Tom returned, carrying two grocery bags. The elevator stopped on the sixth floor. A lady got on and their eyes locked.

"Hey, we've met before, remember? My name is Susan."

"Yes, I remember. You were carrying a briefcase."

"Good memory. Your name is Tom, isn't it?"

"Yup, my name is Tom. You have a good memory, too."

"I'm going up—you need to go down, don't you?"

"Yes, but I'll ride along. No briefcase today?"

"No, today is my day off and I'm heading out to the mall. I need to do some shopping."

The elevator jerked to a stop on the twentieth floor.

Tom got off. "See you again, Susan. Have a good day off."

Susan was an attractive girl. Her generous smile exposed a perfect set of front teeth—likely crowns, he thought. Her long blonde hair reminded him of a movie star from the fifties. He couldn't remember the name.

Tom was getting a bunch of snacks together when the phone rang. It was Julie calling on her cell phone. "Come on up. I could use some help," he told her.

A minute later, Julie anxiously walked through his door.

"What time are they coming over?" she asked.

"About five. Maybe you could help me with this and make the plates look a bit more presentable."

Julie laughed. "Yeah, it sure looks like you could use some help."

At close to five o'clock, Jan led Greg over to unit 2012. She gently rapped her knuckles on the door.

Tom swung the door open. "Hi, guys, come on in," he said, gesturing toward the living room.

"Hi, Tom. Hi, Julie," said Jan, giving Tom a big hug. Greg shook

Tom's hand and greeted Julie with a lighter hug.

"Hey, that looks real good," commented Greg, noticing the two plates of appetizers.

Greg sat down by one of the plates and began nibbling. Julie returned from the kitchen with a bottle of white wine. She filled all four glasses and joined the others on the sectional sofa.

Julie spoke first. "What's the latest on the two ladies getting murdered here at the Towers?"

Jan said, "Life will never be the same here, at least not for a long time. I'm hanging on to my guy wherever I go."

Jan continued. "Both of the girls were stabbed in the heart with a small knife. There was lots of blood—a big mess, I hear. Sounds like the work of a psycho."

Greg added, "The killer weirdo burglarized their apartments—well, maybe not. The cops don't really know what, if anything was stolen. Who knows—could have been jewelry! I did hear all the dresser drawers were pulled out and their things were scattered about."

Julie's eyes had been dashing back and forth between Greg and Jan during the latest exchange of conversation. She anxiously looked at Jan and asked, "Do you think the killer lives in the building?"

"Without knowing for certain, I would say yes," answered Jan. "It would be a natural for a guy like Vito Manchino—but then, I heard he had an airtight alibi for both murders."

Greg got up from his chair, walked over to the window and said, "The bike trail sure looks calm today—not so calm here at the Towers. Two cousins murdered. Both lived in this building. Even though they both worked with Vito Manchino, I don't think he's a psycho killer. Manchino appears much too slick—to trash a bedroom, I mean."

"Would you like another glass, Greg?" asked Julie.

"Sure," replied Greg while returning to his seat.

Tom sipped on wine, crunched on some crackers and cheese, and listened to all the banter and theories about what may have actually happened.

After they finished two bottles of wine and two plates of appetizers, Greg rose from the couch. "We gotta go. Thanks for the wine and all the food. It was real nice. Thanks."

A couple of handshakes and hugs later, Greg and Jan left.

"Wow, we sure cleaned up the appetizers, didn't we?" Julie said.

"Not much left. How about a movie?" Tom asked.

"Hey, great idea—maybe we can get our minds off the murders. Where's the paper? I'll see what's playing. What do you think of the small knife thing? Sounds gruesome to me, Tom."

"I don't know what to think. However, we better take this seriously. I don't want you alone in the parking lot at night. In the future, you'll be getting an escort from the parking lot to my apartment.

"Aw, come on, Tom, I can take care of myself."

11

LATE SUNDAY MORNING, TOM GRABBED HIS BACKPACK from the closet and headed down the elevator with Julie. He insisted on escorting her to the parking lot, in spite of her attitude of invincibility. Tom watched while Julie drove off and gave him her usual last wave. He saw her left arm go up and blow him a kiss.

After standing there for a few moments, Tom headed for the bike trail. As evidenced by the number of vehicles parked on the street next to the tracks, it was going to be busy that morning.

Rollerblades had come into Tom's life as a result of his meeting Julie. She was a frequent participant when they met, which challenged him to give the in-line-skating a try. Catching on quickly, he experienced a great deal of satisfaction being outdoors and exercising. Tom was always cautious during the first few strides, respecting the possibility of a fall and injury. After gaining confidence and body mobility, Tom would then increase his speed.

That morning, Tom experienced skating rhythm sooner than usual. His strides felt strong and secure. About ten minutes up the bike trail, he met Susan speed walking. Their eyes locked for a moment and her thin lips and attractive front teeth formed a friendly smile. They exchanged waves. Tom's smile was too late for her to see as they were going in different directions.

The bike trail extended for about four miles toward the downtown area. Tom did the entire length. On the return trip, he was moving along at a slower pace when he saw Jack Billings and Candice Tellburt advancing. Neither of them looked up to see Tom wave as they passed. Their faces were splattered with beads of sweat and their eyes were focused on the asphalt below in total concentration.

Taking one's eyes off the trail for any length of time was risky when in-line-skating. With strong strides, Tom rolled past the final curve. His eyes spotted a gray jacket and white baseball cap at the end of the trail. Slowing his pace, he remembered having seen a person from his apartment window–had been dressed in similar clothing.

He picked up the pace, anxious to meet up with the man. When Tom looked up again, the man was leaving, walking across the railroad tracks. The white baseball cap dropped out of sight before Tom reached the end of the trail. While Tom was sitting on the bench changing to street shoes, he noticed a dark-colored SUV pull away from the curb.

During his walk back to the Towers, he was entertained by a flock of waxwings flitting in and out of a patch of trees. Stopping, he studied the birds. They reminded him of his former country home. As a consolation, living at the Towers did not seriously compromise his appreciation of nature. Its location and surroundings were a haven for wildlife.

After showering, he drove his car to the Lake's strip mall and parked near Molly's Restaurant. Tom grabbed the Sunday morning newspaper from the backseat and locked the doors. A gray rabbit scooted across the lot, stopping under a pickup truck. Tom smiled and headed in for breakfast.

"Hi there, Tom. Nice to see you up so early," said Molly, smiling.

"Hi, Molly. It's really not that early. What looks good today?"

"Everything is good today. You must know that by now."

"Of course. How about a nice, quiet booth so I can read the paper?"

"Follow me."

The second page of the *Star Tribune* had a piece about the murders at the Towers. This article was just as confusing as the first one. Tom read it twice and wondered if Jan had it all mixed up. Burglary wasn't even mentioned. Was it possible the police were deliberately providing misleading information to the press? When the waiter came, Tom looked up and spotted the man in the white baseball cap and gray jacket sitting alone at a table across the aisle.

"Ah, yes. I'll have the Aztec salad and a glass of iced tea."

"Okay, gotcha. Thanks," replied the waiter.

As the waiter scooted off, Tom glanced across the aisle. His view was mostly of the man's back. The man's head was tilted down, and he was apparently studying the menu. The white cap lay on an empty chair. Tom's scrutiny of the man was interrupted by a soft female voice.

"Hi, Tom. Good morning."

Looking up, he was pleased to see his new friend Susan from the Towers. Molly was leading her to an empty booth down the way.

"Oh, hi, Susan. Are you alone? Please join me if you are."

"Well, thanks, Tom. I'd be happy to."

When Tom stood up, Susan extended her hand and he grasped it warmly. She placed her purse on the seat across from him and sat next to it.

Molly laid a menu down on the table and said to Susan, "I'll get you some silverware."

"Did you have a nice walk this morning, Susan? I noticed you were moving right along," said Tom.

"Yes, I was really rolling, but not as fast as you were."

"Susan, there's a guy sitting across the aisle and two tables down. I saw him standing next to the bike trail this morning. I was wondering if you know who he is. It's okay to turn and look because he isn't facing our direction."

Susan turned her head to the right. "You mean the man in the gray jacket?"

"Yup, that's the guy."

"His name is Marcil Huggins. He lives at the Towers—I think on the fifteenth floor. I met him at a party a couple of months ago. He gives me the creeps—the way he looks at me and all that."

"Have you ever see him on the bike trail?" Tom asked.

"Yes, I have. He stares and sometimes smiles at me. I pretend not to notice him and just keep on joggin', I hear he's a girl-watcher."

Tom frowned. "I've seen him hanging around the bike trail a couple of times. I'm wondering what he's doing there. He doesn't walk, jog or seem to do anything else."

Susan smiled and looked at some people at the nearest table. "Well, he appears harmless. Lots of men girl-watch."

Tom chuckled and asked, "So, what kind of work do you do, Susan?"

"I'm in graphics and design. I work for a small company downtown, and we're heavy in the creation and maintenance of websites. I find it real exciting. What do you do?"

"Well, for starters, I'm retired. However, I do some consulting for small businesses—computer accounting, mostly."

"Oh, that sounds interesting. Do you have a card? My boss is looking for someone to help select a new accounting system."

"Aw, shucks, Susan, I don't have a card on me at the moment. I'll drop one off for you later."

"Yeah, that'll be fine. I live in apartment six-twelve. I'll be home all afternoon. Got lots of work to do."

They chatted until breakfast was finished.

"Well, Tom, I've got to go—nice talking to you."

"Sure, Susan. Have a nice day."

Susan got up, rested her hand on Tom's shoulder for a moment, hoisted her purse and headed toward the door. Tom watched Marcil Huggins turn, stretch his neck and stare at Susan as she walked away. After she disappeared from view, Marcil returned to his original position. Tom had gotten a good look at his face and hadn't recognized him. Tom left Molly's and drove back to the Towers.

After parking in the lower-level garage, Tom walked toward the door leading to the elevators. After pausing about four vehicles down, he noticed a dark-colored SUV—it looked like the one he had seen leaving the bike trail earlier. Marcil Huggins lives on the fifteenth floor, he thought. He's the man I see hanging around the bike trail a lot.

When Tom entered the lobby, he noticed Vito Manchino and Jan sitting on the couch. Vito was talking and Jan was listening. They looked up when they heard Tom enter.

"Hi, Jan," Tom said.

"Tom, I want you to meet Vito Manchino. He lives on the twelfth floor. You've probably seen him around."

Tom didn't make any attempt to approach the couch. He was shocked that Jan was visiting with the person he thought was the murderer. The smile Vito had displayed while talking to Jan had disappeared.

He scowled and asked Tom, "What do you do besides watch baseball games?"

"I guess that's my business—free country, you know," Tom responded sternly.

Leaving them, Tom passed through the door leading to the elevators. He didn't look back and wondered what the devil was up to.

That Sunday afternoon, Tom reserved time for finalizing the spreadsheet for Jensen's Shirts. His appointment the next morning was set for 10:00 a.m. After entering his apartment, he went to the desk and fetched one of his business cards. He proceeded down to the sixth floor and worked his away along the hallway until coming to six-twelve. He knocked, it opened and Susan stood there dressed in a robe.

"Hi again. Here's the card I promised you."

"Oh, thanks, Tom. I'll pass this on to my boss tomorrow. Would you like a cup of coffee?"

"Ahh, no, thanks, Susan. I have work to do. Have a nice afternoon."

"I sure will. See you again."

Later that afternoon Tom received a phone call from Jan.

"Sorry to disturb you, Tom, but what did you think of this Vito guy?"

"Well, Jan, I guess I wasn't there very long. What did you find out?"

"He sells cars. He's been divorced three times. What else do you want to know?"

"Does he kill people?"

"Well, I sure hope not. Actually, he seems like a nice guy. I'll have him over next time when Greg and I have a party, maybe next weekend. Would you and Julie be available on Friday?"

"Don't know right now, but I'll give Julie a call."

"Let me know, Tom. I think I'll go ahead with the plans for Friday—how does about five sound?"

"Sure will, Jan—thanks. Talk later," responded Tom, even though he wouldn't look forward to being in the same room as Vito Manchino.

12

TOM CALLED JULIE THAT EVENING, relaying Jan's invitation for Friday evening's party.

"Tom, I was hoping to hear from you. Sure, I will be delighted to come out on Friday. My seminar ends on Thursday and I'm taking the next day off. I can be at your place mid-afternoon. Pretty good timing, don't you think?"

"Hey, I'm real glad you can come. There's one hitch. Jan is going to invite your number one murder suspect, Vito Manchino."

"Wow. That should be interesting. I'm shaking already."

"That's not funny, Julie. He really could be the one."

They talked for another ten minutes, mainly about what Julie was learning in the seminar.

"Time to get ready for bed. Have a nice night," said Julie.

While preparing for bed, Tom suddenly remembered talking to Terry about their visit the next weekend. Oh well, he thought, the party at Jan and Greg's won't last long, especially if Vito Manchino is there.

MONDAY MORNING AT 10:00, TOM HASTINGS WALKED promptly into Jensen's Shirts.

"Hi, Tom. You've come just in time. Business is booming," said

Dalia.

"The program is all set to go. I have some more testing to do. By the time I leave today, you'll be inputting inventory. How about that?"

"Oh, that sounds exciting. Isn't that awful about the two ladies from the Towers—murders in our building, I mean. I don't like the idea of going home and being alone in the lower-level garage—especially at night."

"Yeah, I don't blame you. Hopefully, the police will solve the murders before too long."

"Boy, I don't know. I was down in the lobby the other day and there were two detectives in Carl's office. They had Andy and Emil in there. Sounded like they were getting questioned pretty well. Mrs. Gray was in there, too. She didn't look any too happy."

"The murders are tearing away the confidence of everyone. The staff must be under severe pressure, and in her case, danger. She works alone in all sections of the building," added Tom.

Dalia swallowed and cleared her throat. It was apparent she didn't want to proceed with the conversation.

"Well, I guess I better get to work," added Tom.

By 12:00 noon he had the spreadsheet formulas finalized. Dalia had just gotten off the phone.

"Hey, Dalia, I'm taking a break. If you have some time about two this afternoon, I can show you how to run this thing."

"Great. I'll drag Cliff out of his hole in the back to answer the phone. See you after lunch."

Monday lunch breaks were usually busy at Molly's. She was surrounded by a pack of people, pressuring to get a table. Molly was frantically writing names on a list and Tom wasn't looking forward to waiting. Leaving Molly's, he walked a few steps down the sidewalk and entered O'Leary's. A crowd was gathered in the lobby in numbers about the same as the crowd in Molly's. Tom wondered what was going on—why were there so many people. He thought about the quiet main street in New Dresden, his small town up north.

Wedging past the hostess, he found an empty stool next to the server station on the far right side of the bar.

"What'll you have, sir?"

"The special looks good to me. Would you bring over a cup of coffee, too?"

"Sure thing."

Vito Manchino was not in his usual spot. Instead, there was a middle-aged man perched on the end stool. The top of his head was bald, but he had an abundance of brownish gray hair around his ears and down the back of his neck. He had a narrow chin, exaggerated by a long goatee terminating in a sharp point. His small, narrow eyes were busy scanning the room.

Their eyes locked for a moment and Tom quickly glanced away. A few minutes later, Tom looked over at the end of the bar again. The goatee man was staring at him. Tom looked away again. He was relieved when the bartender placed his lunch platter down in front of him. The goatee man's plate arrived at the same time.

Tom finished eating first, and as he was leaving O'Leary's he noticed that the man was still sitting there. I wonder why that person drew my attention, he thought. Occupying the same stool Vito usually does may have been the reason or perhaps it was the unusual goatee.

After Tom returned to Jensen's, he spent close to an hour entering data into the spreadsheet.

"Dalia, I'm ready for you—are you available?"

"Okay, I'll fetch Cliff."

She retreated through the rear door and returned in a minute with Cliff right behind her.

"So, what am I supposed to do?" Cliff asked.

"Answer the phone if it rings. Wait on whoever comes in. If you need some help, I'll be right over here with Tom."

"Well, okay. But darn it, I was pretty busy back there. Someone has to do the real work, you know."

"Blow it out," Dalia replied.

The phone only rang twice while Tom was working with Dalia.

"Hey, Tom, I think I've got it. This won't be so tough. It's sure going to be nice to know where we are with the threads. Running out would be a disaster."

Tom worked with Dalia for about another hour. "Well, looks like you've got it, Dalia," he said. "I'll be on my way, and if you have any questions or need some help, give me a call."

"Okay, Tom. I'll do that."

"Oh, by the way, Dalia, have you ever heard of a guy by the name of Marcil Huggins?"

"Boy, have I! He's a real pest. He stops in here every once in awhile. And you know what? I think he's flirting with me. I'm glad that Cliff doesn't hear some of the things that guy said."

She looked at Tom and smiled. "Imagine, Tom, two guys fighting over me. Well, anyhow, I don't mind this guy stopping in to visit once in awhile, but I have so darn much to do all the time. He gets in the way. I haven't the heart to tell him to leave. He looks lonely."

Vito Manchino was my number one suspect. What about Huggins? Could he be the killer? He's all over the place—out on the trail— lives in the Towers.

Tom left Jensen's and headed for his car in the parking lot. The large liquor store sign at the end of the mall reminded him of his low beer supply. He walked the short distance and entered. Tom was in the back part of the liquor store when he spotted the goatee, unmistakably the same long, pointed drab of chin hair he'd seen at O'Leary's. The man was meandering the wine aisles.

Tom made his selection and headed for the checkout. Only one person was in line ahead of him. He heard a little shuffle behind him and turned. The man with the goatee was next in line. He was holding two bottles of wine, one in each hand.

"Hey, didn't I see you at O'Leary's at noon today?" he asked.

"Yeah, I think you did. I was sitting across from you."

"I'm Phil Bartron."

"Tom Hastings here. Nice to meet you."

"You must live at the Towers. I've seen you over there," Phil added.

"Yes, you are right. I do live there. What floor are you on?"

"The twenty-second. Have you lived there long?" asked Phil.

Tom wasn't too pleased about being asked these questions by someone he had just met. "About a year," he reluctantly answered.

Phil continued with the conversation. "I've lived there for five years. It's a great place. Do you have a wife?"

Tom was getting irritated, but he answered. "No, I don't."

Phil added, "I've never been married and don't ever intend to be."

Tom was relieved when the checkout clerk finished with the person in front. Ignoring Phil Bartron, he quickly signed the credit card slip and picked up his bag.

"See you again," said Phil.

Tom nodded and left the liquor store, heading for his car. He felt tired and was anxious to get home to a relaxing evening ahead.

13

PHIL BARTRON RAN AWAY from his sixth marriage a couple of years ago. He moved to a part of the country foreign to him, intentionally. He was desperate to escape the lawyers, every one of his former wives had one. Minneapolis, Minnesota looked good to him, he found a nice apartment in a high-rise—the Towers, they called it. Phil didn't like heights, but he'd been forced to settle for the twenty-second floor.

Phil hated the thought of looking for a job. The money he'd snatched from Rita's estate would last another three years. If it hadn't been for her son, Bruce, Phil's take would have been a lot bigger.

Her mysterious death had aroused suspicions. Phil smiled when thinking about the inquest decision. He was standing in front of the panel when they announced his vindication. How could he ever forget Bruce's intense glare? If looks could kill, I would be a dead man, Phil thought, smiling.

Three weeks after the inquest, Phil was served papers. Bruce wasn't giving up and had his attorney file a wrongful death suit. The legalities took close to a year. Phil was shocked when the jury ruled in favor of Bruce.

Phil managed to move money into a secret bank account in Minneapolis of all places. He was prepared in the event of a loss in the courts. His car was packed—to leave town at three in the morning was brilliant, he thought. The look on Bruce's face after learning of Phil's disappearance the very next day would have been rewarding to Phil.

Finagling a new social security number wasn't easy. Stealing the number from his dead friend was a good plan—no taxes to pay. The downside was the loss of retirement income, forever. I'll have to find a new source of money in a couple of years, he thought.

The Towers was a home to a number of single women—several future possibilities for Phil. He had his eye on Candice Tellburt. She apparently had a man, but that didn't look to Phil as if it was going to last.

He didn't think there was a chance with Susan. She's too young, he thought. Besides her eyes are on that Hastings guy from down below on twenty. Tom, that's his first name. We met at the liquor store.

Phil Bartron had first noticed Hastings at O'Leary's on the other side of the bar, sitting alone. The glances from Tom had worried Phil, and he wondered if Tom was an agent of some kind, perhaps a private eye. His worry had diminished after meeting Tom at the liquor store. Perhaps all those glances had been just a coincidence.

———

THE NEXT THREE DAYS PASSED QUICKLY for Tom Hastings. Dalia called on Thursday, informing him that the inventory program was working well. She asked Tom to stop by the next week and check out her data entries. He readily agreed, and they set aside time on the next Tuesday afternoon.

Julie was arriving from Dallas the next morning at 10:00. Her seminar concluding with a breakfast at 6:30. The Braves were scheduled to play the Mets at 7:00 that evening on television. Tom decided to watch the baseball game at O'Leary's. Riding down the elevator, he thought about his advice to Julie about being alone at night in the parking lot. Instead of walking as usual, he decided to heed his own words and drive to the restaurant.

On entering the garage, he was startled to come face-to-face with two police officers.

"Good evening, sir," one of the officers said.

After realizing they were on patrol, Tom relaxed. "Hey, glad you're here. This garage is a little spooky."

One of the officers nodded and smiled.

After entering O'Leary's, Tom glanced at the bar area, noticing his favorite stool was available. When the bartender approached, Tom pointed to the television and asked him to change the channel to the Braves game.

"No problem. What'll you have?"

"Sam Adams, please."

"Bottle or tap?"

"Bottle."

Tom watched as the bartender flicked through the channels until the Braves versus Mets game appeared. Phil Bartron, the man he'd met at the liquor store on Monday, was sitting on the right side, about six stools away. Before Tom had a chance to look away, Phil glanced in his direction and raised his glass. *Was that a toast to me?* Tom wondered. There was something about that man—a weirdo, perhaps. Tom wasn't anxious to establish a friendship with him.

When Phil looked at him, Tom felt like he was getting sized up for something. Just what that might be, he couldn't imagine, but Tom's instinct was guiding him.

A couple of innings went by. The Braves were at home and they had a five-run lead going into the seventh. Glavine had just struck out Piazza to open the inning. Tom was the only customer watching the game.

Carlos and Juanita Valdez entered O'Leary's behind him and, took the last two barstools on the right side, next to the fancy gold pipe separating the customers from the fold-down gate to the bar.

They'd hardly been seated when a skinny guy wearing a baseball cap and sporting a long goatee sat down between them and Phil Bartron. As the two goatee men glanced around, they reminded Tom of camelhair paintbrushes working the surface of the bar. Tom smiled and shifted his gaze from the two goatees to Carlos and Juanita.

Juanita smiled and waved with her fingers. Carlos nodded his head and pointed toward the television set with his right hand, sending a message that he, too, was interested in baseball. The bar area was too noisy to converse with anyone.

In a few minutes, Phil Bartron got up from his stool, reached down and picked up a small leather bag. Extending the strap, he hoisted it over his shoulder. Slowly, he made his way around the pillar.

Tom felt a gentle tap on his shoulder. Turning his head, his eyes came even up with the goatee, alarmingly close to his face.

"Hello, Mr. Hastings. Are you enjoying the baseball game?"

"Yeah, Phil. I have the name right, don't I?"

"Yes. You have a good memory."

"You're leaving, I see," Tom firmly stated.

"Yeah, it's pretty dead around here—no one to look at."

Tom turned away from Phil, back toward the television. He heard the irritating sound of snapping gum. The smell bothered him—it was like cheap perfume. The sound of shuffling feet behind him suggested a message that Phil Bartron hadn't left yet. Tom continued to look up at the television, not wanting to talk to him anymore. Adding to Tom's irritation was the feeling of an occasional brush of hair against his jacket. Phil Bartron remained for another five torturous minutes before making his way to the front door.

After Bartron left, Tom glanced at Carlos and Juanita, who were both laughing. *At me*, Tom thought. The Mets were batting in the top of the ninth. Two runners were on base, there were two outs in the inning and Nelson was at bat. The Braves were leading by four. Tom felt another tap on his shoulder and was relieved when he turned his head to face Juanita. She and Carlos were on their way out.

"*Como esta uster, se´nor Tom?*" asked Carlos.

Tom looked up with a confused expression.

In her thick, Colombian accent, Juanita said, "Say, Tom, did Phil give you bad time? We saw you brush him off and we think it was very funny."

"So, you guys were laughing at me. That's exactly what I thought," Tom laughed. "I didn't take it too serious. Better take your wife home, Carlos. She is too funny."

"Certainly, se´nor Tom. I hope your team wins."

"Do you like baseball?" Tom asked.

"*Me encanta*," answered Carlos.

Tom didn't respond as he watched the Colombian natives wander toward the door. His team did win. The pinch hitter, Nelson, grounded out, and the Braves beat the Mets. Tom paid his bill and headed out to the parking lot.

When Tom got on the elevator at the Towers, James the barber was getting off. "Good evening, Mr. Hastings. Did you score this evening?"

"No, I am afraid not, Jim. How about you?"

"Sure did," he responded as the elevator door was closing.

14

ON FRIDAY MORNING, TOM SCOOTED OUT OF BED EARLY. He'd previously agreed to pick up Julie at the airport and he needed to get out there by 9:00. He was pleased that he had remembered to call Brad and Terry. Their arrival later that evening wouldn't be until about 9:00. He would be home from the party by then.

Even though his car was parked in the lower level, he exited the elevator on the first floor to check the mail. First, he saw Carl standing by the front door, looking out. Then, he saw Jan, a cup of coffee in her hand, standing by the office door.

Carl turned his head when he heard Tom approach. "Oh, it's you, Tom. I'm glad is isn't that weasel of a Phil Bartron."

"What happened?" asked Tom.

Jan piped in. "I'll tell you what happened. I was coming down on the elevator and that weasel, the nerve of him, tried to take my clothes off."

"What about the police? Surely, you reported him."

"Sure did, but a lot of good *that* did. They went up to talk to him and he denied everything—my word against his."

"Worse than that, I can't force him to give up his apartment. The creep's lawyer has already called," added Carl, frowning.

Tom wasn't surprised by the news—He hadn't liked the man from the get-go, now he had another reason for disliking him. He looked at his watch. "I'm picking up Julie at the airport. She's coming in early today."

"What a gentleman you are! Where has she been?" snipped Jan.

"Seminar in Dallas all week. Well, I better get going. See you at five, Jan. I don't imagine Phil Bartron is on your guest list."

"Are you kidding? Get out of here. Go pick up your Julie."

Tom had never seen Jan so upset and at just the mention of Phil Bartron. Could Phil be the killer? He visualized the small man dragging a body into the elevator, into the garage, into the car...it was possible.

"Do you chew gum?" the detective had asked.

Bartron sure does. The killer does, Tom thought.

———

AFTER PARKING AND ENTERING THE AIRPORT TERMINAL, Tom looked at the arrival screen. Julie's plane was delayed for one hour. Darn the luck, he thought. Tom went through the security gate area and headed out onto the main concourse. Off in the distance, he noticed a large gathering of people listening to a speaker perched on a box. Next to the speaker were young men and women carrying banners.

Each banner was blue and had the words *Equality for Everyone* embossed on it in white. One of the people holding a banner was Tom's next-door neighbor, Joan Collison. He listened for a few minutes until the speaker began talking about money. Then he turned to leave.

"Just a minute there, neighbor," he heard.

Stopping, Tom saw that Joan had left the group and sought his attention.

"Hi, Joan. What's going on?"

"We are raising money for the unfortunate in Tanakia. Perhaps you would care to hear about it?"

"Well, not now. I have a plane to meet. Perhaps some other time?"

"Okay. I'll knock on your door."

"See ya," Tom said and turned to walk toward the nearest security check-in.

Boy, I don't need a lot of that, he thought. Just before reaching his destination, he heard loud voices and the sounds of commotion.

Airport security officials had surrounded the Equality group, attempting to break up the rally. Tom could see some scuffling taking place. Two uniformed police officers had arrived and were assisting. My heavens, he thought, my next-door neighbor is an activist.

A few minutes later, Julie emerged from the ramp leading from the plane. Laden with a bulky, heavy shoulder bag that pinned down one arm, she waved with the other when seeing Tom on the concourse. After she passed through the security gate, they embraced and Tom insisted on taking the shoulder bag.

"Welcome home. How was the seminar?"

"Oh, just great, Tom. It seems there's always more to learn. One of the many speakers introduced a new method for information management. I couldn't keep up taking notes."

"Well, let's head over to baggage pickup."

Tom grabbed Julie's hand and they exited the gate area and took the elevator down to the baggage retrieval.

"It's that one—the large green case with wheels."

Tom lifted it off the revolving conveyer and they were on their way to the airport parking lot.

"Anything new at the Towers?" asked Julie.

"Yup, there sure is, and I'm sure you'll hear all about it at Jan and Greg's later today."

"I can't wait."

Tom parked in Julie's apartment building parking lot.

After he'd helped her carry her baggage to the elevator, she said, "Give me a few hours. I'll get to your place about four."

"Okay, see you then. Remember to call me from the parking lot. I'll come down and get you," Tom replied and their lips touched for a moment.

Tom headed home to prepare his apartment for company. When he was going up the elevator, it stopped on the ninth floor. Mrs. Gray, the Towers housekeeper, got on.

"Hello, Mr. Tom. Hope I'm not slowing you down," she said while pushing her cart into the elevator.

"Not at all, Mrs. Gray. I could sure use you today. I am expecting company later today and my apartment is a mess."

She laughed and in an Irish brogue replied, "Got too much to do as it is."

Tom remembered hearing Carl say that, "aside from himself, Mrs. Gray had lived here longer than anyone else." She must know her way around and probably knows everyone in the building, Tom thought. Her information would be valuable at Jan's party if she were invited.

At close to four that afternoon, Tom's phone rang. Julie had arrived. "My cell phone doesn't work."

"I'll meet you in the lobby—you stay right there until I get down."

He pressed number Four on his telephone to buzz Julie in, and hurriedly took an elevator down, expecting to meet her in the lobby.

When the elevator door opened, he momentarily panicked. Julie was nowhere in sight. Rushing to the corridor that leads to the rear door, he looked, but no one was there. Then he felt a little tap on his shoulder. He turned so quickly he almost knocked Julie to the floor.

"Geez, you really scared me. Where were you?"

"Just went to the washroom. No big deal."

"Let's go up. I've got some news—then you'll understand why I'm so jumpy."

As the elevator hummed upward, Tom told her about Jan getting attacked in the elevator by Phil Bartron.

"Maybe she's exaggerating."

"Perhaps a little, but I don't think so. I've never heard Jan talk that way."

After they'd entered his apartment, Tom smiled and said, "Julie, I've got a treat ready for you."

After a big hug, Julie asked, "Now, what could that be, Tom?"

"A glass of vintage—should we give it a try?"

"Sure, why not."

Reaching in the refrigerator, he lifted out a bottle of wine and filled the two glasses sitting on the counter. Handing one to Julie, he offered a toast that generated an appreciative smile. After their wineglasses met, generating a loud clink, Julie's expression changed to a frown.

"This Phil Bartron, what does he look like?"

"He's a small guy, quite bald—but the most noticeable feature is the long goatee."

"Tom, when I pulled into the parking lot, there was a guy standing by a car—down at the other end. He had a goatee."

"That's likely the guy. You need to stay as far away from him as you can—I mean no riding on the elevator with him, after what Jan accused him of.

"I met him for the first time at a liquor store a few days ago. Then, he bugged me at O'Leary's yesterday. He was standing right behind me when I was watching the game. I could feel the brush."

"The brush—you mean the goatee?"

"Yeah, the brush."

"Weird man. Thanks for the warning."

"Jan was pretty upset, but hopefully she'll calm down by the time her party starts. Speaking of Jan, I guess we better get over there."

15

APARTMENT 2006 AT THE TOWERS WAS READY. Standing in the kitchen, Jan was waiting for the first knock. Greg was sitting on the couch watching television. He got up and joined Jan in the kitchen.

"Are you calmed down?" he asked his wife.

"Yup, I think so. This should be interesting. I'm anxious to hear what everyone has to say."

"Maybe we'll get a confession."

"Oh, go on, Greg. Nothing like that is ever going to happen here."

"Nevertheless, I'd bet my money on that Vito guy. He's a slick one, that boy," added Greg.

Jan's body jerked slightly when she heard the knock.

"I'll get it," Greg eagerly announced.

Jan and Greg's first guest of the evening were Aaron and Kit Alhaya. They were escorted into the living room by Greg. Jan came into the room, greeted them and had them sit on the couch.

The next knock came from Tom. Julie was standing behind him and looked back when one of the elevator doors opened. She saw Jack Billings escorting Candice Tellburt. She remembered that even though they often were seen together, they lived in separate apartments on the seventeenth floor.

Tom turned and said, "Hi, Candice. Hi, Jack. You two remember Julie, don't you?"

"Oh yes. We met right here, didn't we?" answered Candice.

Jack's left arm was draped around Candice's shoulder and he extended his right hand to Julie.

"How are you two?" asked Julie.

The door opened. "Well, what do we have here?" asked a smiling Greg.

"Trouble, for sure," answered Jack.

After the usual exchange of greetings, Jan appeared. "Come on in, how are you all?"

She led her guests out of the foyer and into the living room. Greg followed but remained back a pace while Jan introduced her guests to Aaron and Kit Alhaya, who got up from one of the couches.

Aaron and Kit were African-American.

"Please sit down, everyone," Jan announced.

"Come on, Greg, let's get these people something to munch on and perhaps something to drink," said Jan.

Greg followed her into the kitchen while Tom sat down next to Aaron and Kit on one couch. Julie sat down with Jack and Candice on the other.

"So, do you two live in the Towers?" asked Tom.

"Yes, we moved in a couple of months ago," replied Aaron.

"I hear you live just down the hall," said Kit. "We live on the nineteenth floor just below you. Jan says you are a computer consultant."

"That's right, Kit—only part-time. I'm actually supposed to be retired. What do you two do for a living?"

"Aaron teaches science at the university. I work for an insurance company. My job is to arrange seminars and meetings."

"So, Aaron, how long have you been at 'the U'?"

"Close to ten years now. It seems like just the other day."

"Do you two have any children?" Tom asked.

"No, we don't," responded Kit. "Guess it's a little late for that now."

Jan and Greg arrived with two trays of appetizers and six empty glasses. They set a tray down in front of each couch and returned to the kitchen.

"Does everyone want wine? How about you, Jack?" Jan asked.

Jack Billings cleared his throat. "How about some Scotch?"

"Stay put, Jack. I'll mix you one," answered Greg.

Moments later, Jan returned with two bottles of wine, one red and one white. She moved from person to person, smiling and filling glasses on request. Greg returned from the kitchen with a tall glass of scotch and soda for Jack.

Julie began a conversation with Jack, who raised his glass and took a generous mouthful. Candice was talking to Greg. Tom continued to chat with Aaron and Kit. Half an hour passed before a loud knock on the door attracted everyone's attention.

"I'll get it," said Jan.

Tom watched Julie's eyes narrow as she observed the entrance of the newest guest. He'd thought Jan had been kidding about inviting Vito Manchino—she hadn't.

"Hey, everyone, I would like you all to meet Vito Manchino," Jan announced.

"Don't get up," said Vito as his dark eyes canvassed the room.

He moved along the two couches, paused at each person, bent over slightly and shook their hands.

When he came to Tom, he said "You're everywhere, aren't you,

Hastings?"

Tom didn't extend his hand, nor did Vito. Instead, the latest arrival straightened up and moved to where Jack Billings was sitting and sipping his scotch.

Jack broke the ice by asking Vito, "How are car sales holding up this year?"

"Couldn't be much better. Cars are selling—that's what really counts for me."

When Vito approached Julie, she raised her head. "How are you, Mr. Manchino?"

Vito sat down in a chair next to Jan.

Another knock on the door drew Greg's attention. He left his chair and headed for the door. Tom heard a familiar-sounding lady's voice. Turning, he saw Greg escorting Susan into the room. All the guys, Tom included, stood up. Greg took Susan by the hand and introduced her to each person. Once again, Tom noticed Julie's eyes narrow as Susan and Greg approached.

"I think you two have met," Greg quipped.

"Oh, hello there, Tom. Nice to see you again," Susan said softly.

Tom glanced at Julie and noticed her head tilt slightly.

"Yes. Susan and I have met. Nice to see you again," he responded.

Greg gestured toward Julie. "Julie, meet Susan."

With a frown on her face, she said, "Hi, Susan. I hear you do websites. That must be interesting and exciting."

Susan didn't answer and sat down on a chair that Greg placed next to the couch where Tom was sitting.

"Would you like some wine?" Greg asked.

"Thanks, Greg. I'll have some white, please."

"Say, Tom, I talked to my boss about your consulting business," said Susan. "He's interested in talking to you about a new accounting program. Why don't you call me at work next week and we'll set up an appointment?"

"I'm glad to hear that, Susan. I shall do that—thanks."

The evening moved on. Arms extended to and retracted from the appetizer plates. Jan returned to the kitchen three times to replenish. After Tom's delightful conversation with Aaron and Kit, he focused on Susan, talking with her about her work and boss. When Susan excused herself, Tom moved, sitting down next to Jack.

Communication skills were a strong trait of Jack Billings. He spoke slowly and chose his words carefully.

"Tom, I hear you are in computer consulting," said Jack.

"Yes, that's true, Jack, but only part time. What sort of business are you in?" Tom had guessed that Jack was a businessman.

"Exports, Tom, exports. I'm part owner manager of *International Oceanic*. Ever heard of it?"

"No, Jack, I have not—but then, I haven't lived here very long. Do you travel a lot?"

"Yes, I sure do. I'm gone most weeks, Monday through Friday." They continued the conversation for a few minutes until Candice came over.

"Jack, it's time for me to go. Are you coming?"

Jack stood up. "Nice talking to you, Tom. Let's have lunch sometime."

"Yes, I would like that," answered Tom.

Jan and Greg followed Jack and Candice to the foyer. At that moment, Aaron and Kit stood up and stepped over to Tom.

"Nice meeting you, Tom. Hopefully we will see you again," said Aaron. "Where did Julie go?"

Tom got up and shook their hands. "I enjoyed talking to both of you. Julie is in the washroom. I'll say good-bye to her for you. Have a nice evening."

The Alhayas proceeded to the foyer and front door, where Greg and Jan had just said good-bye to Jack and Candice.

Tom headed for the kitchen. He found a glass and helped himself to a long drink of water. When Tom returned to the living room, Vito was standing next to Susan and looking down at Julie on the couch.

"Do you need a new car?" he asked her.

"No, I don't—but of course if the right deal came around...."

"I've always got the right deal. Come and see me sometime," responded Vito, as he removed a card from his shirt pocket and stooped down to hand it to Julie.

"Don't I get a good deal, too?" asked Susan smirking.

"Just about as good as Julie would get," answered Vito.

Tom saw the empty place next to Julie and sat down. He'd been afraid Vito was going to sit by her. "Now, what's this about all these good deals?" Tom asked Julie.

Vito turned, looked at Tom and responded, "The good deal is only for the ladies. "Speaking of ladies, I have one waiting for me." After that announcement, Vito left the living room and headed for the door in the foyer.

Tom noticed Vito shaking Greg's hand and clasping both of Jan's hands.

After Vito had left, Susan waited for about five minutes before leaving. She didn't say so, but Tom thought it was deliberate, to allow Vito time to go down the elevator.

Tom went and sat down on the couch by Julie. "Well, Mr. Hastings," she said. "Nice to see you again."

He burst into laughter. "This should be interesting—the wrap-up."

Jan came in. "Want any more wine, either one of you?"

"No, thanks," said Julie.

"I've had enough, too," Tom responded.

"How about some coffee then?" asked Jan.

"Yes, that'll hit the spot," said Julie.

"Me, too," added Tom.

Jan left for the kitchen.

"Well, what did you learn, Julie?" asked Tom.

"That Vito guy is one slick, smooth character. I wouldn't trust him to cross the street. He's one heck of a flirt besides."

"Yeah, I know what you mean. I sure liked Aaron and Kit. They are both intelligent, classy people. What did you think of Susan?"

"Well, that's another matter. I noticed you spent some time with her."

"Yes, I did. Her boss is interested in hiring me to help with their accounting. She joined me for lunch at Molly's one day this past week. It wasn't scheduled. She just happened by."

"Yeah, I'll bet."

"Oh, come on, Julie. It's only business."

Jan and Greg both came into the room. They brought in four cups of coffee.

"Well, what do you guys think?" said Greg as he took a sip of coffee.

"Nice party," Tom said.

Jan piped in, "Well, now you two have had a good look at this Vito person. Do you think he could be the killer?"

"That's a startling question, Jan. I don't know what to think," said Julie.

"Well, I noticed he gave all the girls plenty of eye, including you, Julie. Don't think I'd want to be alone with him anywhere, much less in the garage down below. He has plenty of slick talk. I say, beware of that man," snapped Jan.

"Oh, I don't know," said Greg. "He's just the usual car salesman. If he was alone in a dark room with you, Vito could be the one in danger."

"Oh please, Greg—none of your funny stuff tonight. I wonder what Vito does besides sell," retorted Jan. "Candice was sure quiet tonight. I wonder what was on her mind. I'm not so sure that thing she has going with Jack is going to last. He's gone so much. She must be lonely. I wonder if he isn't one of those guys who has a girl in every port."

"There you go again, Jan. We guys don't have a chance. Give us a break," lamented Greg.

Julie said, "Well, Tom, it's time to go—remember, your son will be here about nine." She directed her attention to Greg and Jan, and added, "Thanks so much for the evening. Your guests were delightful."

They all stood up and Julie and Tom made their way to the front door. A couple of hugs and handshakes later, Julie and Tom headed back to his apartment.

Julie sat down on the couch and said, "You know, Tom, I think I need a glass of wine. Will you join me, if I pour?"

"Sure. Brad and Terry should be buzzing any moment."

"That was brave of Jan to invite the number-one suspect," said Julie and lifted the glass to her lips.

Tom was about to reply when the door buzzer engaged.

"I suppose we'll have to tell them all about the murders," said Tom while pressing a key on the phone to let his son and daughter-in-law in.

"You've got to be kidding," responded Brad after his dad had told them about the double murders. "Looks like you may have to move back to the country. That's why you moved here, wasn't it? To get away from the violence up north?"

"Oh, I'm not ready to give up yet. The police are all over this place. They should solve this soon."

"I don't think there's been a murder in La Crosse for years. Maybe you should move there."

16

JULIE HOFFMAN AND TOM SAT NEXT TO THE WINDOW overlooking the bike-trail on the morning after Greg and Jan's party. They were sipping coffee and reading the *Star Tribune*. Brad and Terry were still in bed.

She was browsing through the front-page section when she exclaimed, "Tom, there's a story on the murders. Guess what? Gloria Tingsley's ex-husband has been detained."

"For her murder or both of them? The Oxley lady, too?"

"Nothing mentioned about the second one at all—very strange."

"Well, Tom, I have to get ready and head for home. Being gone all week, I have tons of stuff to do."

"I have a hair appointment with Barb at ten. She's going to take a little gray out. I'll be heading down there pretty soon.

"Weren't you surprised last night that there was no discussion about the murders?" asked Tom.

"I thought James was your hair person."

"I take whoever is available. Jim had a full book today."

"Oh. Getting back to the party...Jan, Vito and I talked about the murders."

"Really? So what did Vito have to say?"

"He doubted the murderer lived at the Towers. Vito thinks that both ladies were involved with drugs and that's why they got murdered. Jan didn't agree with that. She said the murders were committed by a fanatic psycho of some kind."

"I was a little surprised that Jan didn't bring up the incident involving the goatee guy—she was probably too embarrassed to bring it up," added Tom.

Julie packed her things and they went down the elevator together. Tom escorted her into the parking lot.

"Talk later, Julie. Hope you have a good day."

"Same to you, Tom. Thanks for everything."

Tom watched the red convertible leave the parking lot. The window opened and Julie's hand appeared—a parting wave.

Just before 10:00, Tom left a note for Brad and headed down the elevator to the barbershop. Mrs. Gray came aboard on the fourteenth floor. She was delivering packages.

"Top of the day to you, Mrs. Gray. I hope all is well with you."

"My goodness sake, Mr. Hastings. I hope you don't mind, but I have a couple more stops."

"Not at all. You have your job to do."

The elevator stopped on the twelfth and seventh floors for two more deliveries.

When Tom arrived at the barbershop, Barb was just finishing a gentleman—the young man Tom had met on the bike trail.

"Be with you soon, Mr. Hastings. Have a seat."

Tom sat in a chair next to a young lady.

"Hello, there. I think that we have met before—on the bike trail. You are Maria, aren't you?"

"Yes, I remember you. You were on those skates. I seem to have forgotten your name."

"I'm Tom Hastings. Is that your husband getting his hair done? Richard is his name, right?"

"You are correct, Mr. Hastings."

"Okay, Tom, I'm ready for you," said Barb.

Tom took off his glasses and snuggled into the barber chair. While

Barb was coloring his hair, Maria changed places with her husband, Richard. He gave his wife a peck on the forehead, waved to Tom and left.

After James cleaned the floor around his chair, he spent the next few minutes surveying Maria's head and walking around the chair several times. Appearing confused, he brought out a pair of scissors and began nicking here and there.

"I hear the murderer has been caught," said Barb.

James started, backed away from his chair and stared at her.

Tom replied, "Yeah, Barb, that's what the *Star Tribune* said this morning. But only one of the murders was mentioned."

"Well, I think we can assume both of them were committed by the same person," said Barb after clearing her throat.

James paused again, glaring at Barb. "Now how can you assume that? Have you been talking to the detective? Huh?"

"So what if he was up in my apartment. He was in a lot of others, too."

James laughed and added, "Okay, Barb. I'll be quiet."

No more words were spoken for the next few minutes, until Barb said, "Okay. All done, Tom."

Hastings pulled cash out of his billfold, paid for the service and thanked Barb.

"You're welcome," she responded.

When Tom passed through the lobby on his way to the elevator, Phil Bartron was sitting on the couch. In a cool and deliberate voice, Phil said, "How are you today, Mr. Hastings?" The tone of his voice suggested that he was getting the message that Tom didn't want to be his friend.

"I'm getting by," responded Tom.

The elevator opened and Tom entered.

He spent the balance of the weekend doing things with his son and daughter-in-law, until they left for La Crosse on Sunday afternoon.

On Monday, just before the noon hour, Tom called Susan at work, asking her to set up an appointment to talk computer accounting. They agreed to Tuesday at four in the afternoon.

"Thanks, Susan. I'll see you on Tuesday."

"Looking forward to it," she sang out softly.

17

TOM DROVE TO THE STRIP MALL ON MONDAY EVENING. He parked near O'Leary's, entered the bar & grill and gained possession of his usual barstool at the closed end of the bar. After he'd sat down, the bartender wandered over and Tom ordered a beer. Marcil Huggins was parked on a barstool on the right side of the bar. Joan Collison, Tom's next-door neighbor, was sitting at a table facing the bar, directly across from Marcil.

The gentleman sitting at her table had his back to the bar. Tom noticed his thick dark hair, a large ring on the little finger of his right hand, and his dark brown shirt. Tom wasn't sure, but the shape and features resembled a man he had noticed at the bar the night Gloria Tingsley had been with Vito.

Tom glanced at Marcil. The beak of the white baseball cap was pulled down partially over Marcil's eyes. On occasion, he would glance up at the television, but most of the time he was looking in Joan's direction. Both of his hands were grasping a drink. Tom remembered that Jan didn't care for him—Marcil gave her the creeps.

Dalia had had a different view. *Marcil occasionally visits the store. He's a pest but I feel sorry for him. He's lonely.*

The bartender took Tom's order: a sandwich to go with the beer. Returning to the server station area, the bartender laid down a napkin for a new customer. Vito Manchino, wearing his dark blue sport coat, had arrived. Surveying the room, he waved at Joan Collison, who returned his greeting. He glanced in Tom's direction and their eyes locked for a moment. Vito moved onto the end stool as Tom responded with a conservative nod.

Manchino lit a cigarette before the bartender brought him a beer. A little bit later, a skinny man joined him, sitting down on the stool next to him. Tom was quite certain it was the same person who had visited him a couple of weeks ago. The skinny man also lit a cigarette, contributing to the cloud that was drifting toward the closed end of the bar.

After Tom's sandwich arrived, he ordered a second beer. When he was finished with the sandwich, he noticed the skinny guy got up from his stool. Something fell out from inside his coat. The man stooped down and came up with a small package. Tucking it under his left arm, he hurried out. Why would they do this in public and be so obvious if it were a drug exchange? Tom wondered.

Tom glanced at Marcil, who had watched as the skinny guy was leaving. Marcil's eyes suddenly darted back toward the table where Joan was sitting. His brow furrowed and his eyes narrowed, arousing Tom's curiosity.

Glancing at Joan's table, Tom saw Joan and her man friend rise. They shook hands and Joan headed for the door. Marcil's eyes followed her all the way. The man returned to his chair and put on a pair of horn-rimmed glasses.

Vito stubbed out a cigarette, lighting another immediately. Focusing on a stack of papers lying on the bar surface, he retrieved a pen from his shirt pocket and began writing. Flipping up the top sheet, he studied the next. Bringing it up closer to his eyes for a moment, he laid it down, gathered all the sheets together, folded them and placed them in the pocket of his jacket.

The bartender retrieved a slip from the register and laid it on the bar in front of Vito. After reviewing the slip, Vito reached into the inside pocket of his jacket and brought out a billfold. He peeled off some bills and laid them on top of the slip. After getting up from his stool, Vito Manchino headed for the door. Tom waited until Vito was outside and then did the same.

When entering his apartment, Tom heard his phone answering machine beeping. Julie had called and left a message.

Tom returned her call. "Anything new going on at the Towers?" she asked.

"No, except I saw some of my neighbors at O'Leary's this evening." Tom told her about seeing Joan, Vito, Marcil and the skinny guy. "So, was Vito wearing a sport coat?"

"Yes, he was. He also passed something—couldn't see what it was—to same guy as before, the one who was there the day after the first murder."

"I wonder what he's passing to those people," said Julie.

"Yeah, I'm wondering, too. Maybe it has something to do with car sales. The skinny guy could be his messenger."

Julie responded, "Messenger boy, perhaps, but not likely about cars. I wonder if any of those characters carry a knife."

"Julie, wouldn't surprise me if the police showed up in force at O'Leary's. They could have the killer and a drug ring all wrapped up in one box."

"Tom, I envy you being in the middle of all that activity. Be careful on the way home. It's time for me to go to bed. Talk to you tomorrow."

"Okay, Julie. Have a good night."

18

FERRO FEARED INSANITY WAS OVERTAKING HIM, stealing his very soul. He was sitting in his car in the garage, waiting and watching. His feeling of need for another woman was intense. A car came through the garage door, turned left and flashed its headlights against the windshields of the first row of cars. After it had parked, Ferro sat up enough to see who was getting out of the car.

It wasn't a woman. He slumped back down behind the steering wheel. Looking at his watch, he could see that both hands were slightly past twelve. Yawning, he thought about giving up, but then another car came. It turned left and parked at the far end. Ferro sat up and waited. A woman, walking briskly, came up the aisle between the two rows of vehicles.

He watched as she fumbled in her purse, searching for a key. After she went through the door, he got out of his car and gently closed the door. Moving quickly across the lot, he had his key ready and caught up with the woman as she was entering an empty elevator. Before the sliding door closed, Ferro stepped inside.

"Good evening," he said, stopping at arm's length from her.

The lady looked up at him and was relieved to see a smile. Reaching up, she pressed the 20 button.

"What floor do you want?" she asked.

"Twenty Four," Ferro replied.

As the numbers flashed by, he became conscious of his steadily increasing heartbeat. Looking at the woman, he feared she could hear the pulsation that was battering his inner ears. Her attention was glued to the changing numbers on the display panel. He grabbed onto the bar in the rear of the elevator as nausea grew and dizziness began to overtake him. *Stay cool*, he mentally commanded.

Number 20 appeared. The elevator stopped and the door slid open.

The woman said, "Good night," quickly stepped out and hastened down the hallway.

Ferro put a hand on the door slip, keeping it from closing. The woman didn't look back as she rounded the corner.

All the nausea symptoms disappeared as Ferro stepped out and reached in his coat pocket. He pulled out a plastic bag and quickly and quietly followed the woman. Peeking around the corner, he saw her fumbling in her purse again, just as he had hoped. The cloth inside the plastic bag was soaked well enough.

Hearing the apartment door open, he dashed in behind the woman and brought the cloth around her face pressing it firmly over her mouth. She gasped and resisted, forcing them both to fall to the floor. Ferro's head struck the frame of the door, but his hand remained over her mouth. In minutes, her body went limp.

Tom was reading in bed when he heard a thumping sound. Tipping his head up for a moment, he listened. There was no further sound. Setting the book down, he got up, walked to the kitchen and opened the fridge. After taking a drink of water, he hesitated returning to the bedroom. Instead, he stole to the door, turned the latch and opened it slightly. There was no one there and all was quiet. He returned to his book.

Half an hour later, the door of 2010 opened a sliver. Seeing no one, Ferro tiptoed toward the elevator.

Finding it impossible to concentrate, Tom put the book down. He got up again and walked to the door. While peeking out, it was only a flash, but he saw the back end of someone turning the corner, headed for the elevators. He opened the door wider and listened.

Ferro held his breath, waiting for what seemed forever. At last, an elevator door opened. Tom heard the swishing sound of the door closing. Minutes later, Ferro was in bed and sinking into a deep sleep. Tom was sitting up in bed thinking.

BILL ANDERSON WAS STILL IN HIS PAJAMAS, a cup of coffee in one hand, and a page of the newspaper in the other.

"Honey, the call is for you," his wife reported.

Grabbing the phone from the cradle, he said, "Yes? Bill Anderson here."

"Good morning, Detective. There's been another one."

"Another what?"

"A killing at the Towers."

"Oh, for God's sakes. That's all I need. When did this happen?"

"We got the call early this morning."

"Okay, I'll be there as soon as I can," said the detective before hanging up the phone.

"Holy smites, Marci, I won't have time for breakfast—got to get to the office right away. Remember the serial killer stuff that I was telling you about? There's been a third one."

Detective Bill Anderson turned off the ignition of his Land Cruiser in the underground parking lot at headquarters. While waiting for the elevator, he thought about the pressure that was going to come from his boss. Three murders in one building—the media was going to explode in his face.

While walking through the central lobby, he was in an ugly mood. The staff people at the desks ignored him—they knew from his past that a "good morning" or "how are you" was not the thing to say.

Approaching his office, he wasn't surprised to see people in it. Chief Larum was partially sitting on the desk, and Lieutenant Barry was sitting in the visitor chair. Their heads turned toward the door when the detective entered.

"Thanks for coming right over, Bill. We've got a major problem on our hands. When the word gets out, probably within the hour, the media is going to be all over me. I hope you understand that. The Towers is your baby full-time as of right now. All your other cases are going to be reassigned. Rod is going to be your assistant. We need results and fast."

"So, who was the latest victim, and where?"

"It happened last night—time is not certain—in apartment twenty-ten. We've got some of our people over there—the medics are there, too. I think you better get down there right away and take over," answered Chief Larum anxiously.

"Let's go, Rod. Ah, Chief, talk to you when we get back."

The two officers got together their needed equipment and headed for the elevators.

"Mackerel, Bill, this one is going to be tough—some weird nut on the loose, wiping out part of the female population. My guts are hurting. Catching this guy isn't going to be easy."

———

NOISES OUTSIDE HIS DOOR STARTLED TOM THE NEXT MORNING. He had been sipping coffee while reading the newspaper. Rushing to the door, he swung it opened. He was stunned to see two men wearing whites and carrying an empty gurney into Joan's apartment. A uniformed police officer followed the procession. He glanced at Tom and hesitated before entering the apartment.

Tom stepped out into the hallway and asked, "What's going on? What happened?"

"There's a dead lady in there," said the officer.

"Oh my God—could it be Joan?"

"Well, I don't know the lady's name, but whoever it is has been murdered."

Tom stood in shocked silence. In a few minutes, another group of people came down the hallway from the direction of the elevator. Two men were dressed in suits. Two others were wearing blue jumpsuits and carrying bags. They all entered Joan's apartment. The police officer closed the door and remained in the hallway. Tom returned to his apartment.

Shocked by the thought of Joan getting murdered next door, Tom was in a state of mental confusion while getting dressed. *How could this be happening, and right next door?* He remembered his appointment at Susan's office at 4:00. *I need to get a hold of myself.* Tom's immediate mission was to learn more. After leaving his apartment to head for the elevator, he paused. A shorter police officer was holding Joan's door open and two men in white were busy working a gurney through the doorway. Tom backed off a step, allowing them their needed space. After staring at the white sheet that was covering the remains, Tom waited in the hallway for a couple of minutes, allowing time for the attendants to place the gurney in an elevator.

He asked the police officer, "Do you know what happened in there?"

"I don't know a thing—only that a stiff was found." He gestured toward the door.

How crude, Tom thought. He didn't ask him any more questions but walked toward the elevator.

"Sir, would you hold up?" said a voice coming from the direction of Joan's apartment.

Tom turned and saw a man in a suit. Looks familiar, he thought. Could be one of the two detectives who visited my apartment earlier.

The man walked over to Tom. "You're Tom Hastings, aren't you?"

"Yes, I am. We've met before, haven't we?"

"Yes. I'm Detective Anderson of the Minneapolis Police Department. If you remember, we had a little visit in your apartment three or four weeks ago."

"Yeah, I remember."

"If you don't mind, Mr. Hastings, I would like to ask you some questions. It appears as if your next-door neighbor has been murdered."

Tom gasped as reality surfaced. His neighbor Joan had been murdered. Searching for a response, he answered, "Okay. Hopefully

I can help you—right now is fine."

"Good. I want you to understand that I'm not demanding this interview right now; we could do it later."

"No, now is fine. I have something to say."

Tom unlocked his apartment door, and the detective followed him inside. Motioning the detective to sit on the couch, Tom sat on a chair.

"Did you hear any noises last night?" the detective asked.

"I was in bed last night when I heard this thump. I got up, looked out the door and saw nothing. About half an hour later, I got up again and peeked out the door."

The detective leaned forward.

"I saw a flash of a person turn the corner toward the elevators."

"Was it a man or woman?"

"Couldn't tell for sure—man, I would guess."

"What type of clothing? A cap?"

"Dark—everything looked dark. Not sure about a hat—dark top, though."

"Could you tell me where you were yesterday evening and what time you got home?"

"Yeah, I had dinner at O'Leary's—got home sometime between nine and ten."

"Were you alone?"

"Yes, I was, but there were people at O'Leary's that know me. Do you want to see a copy of my credit card tab?"

"Ah, no, that won't be necessary—not right now anyhow.

"Was a Vito Manchino one of the people at O'Leary's last night?"

"Yes."

"Was he with anyone?"

"There was this tall, skinny guy. They visited for awhile."

"You don't know his name, huh?"

"No, but I've seen him there more than once."

"Oh. How well did you know the lady next door? —Joan Collison, I believe was her name."

"I didn't know her well at all. We talked about, say, three times, since I moved here."

"Did you know what she did for a living?"

"I believe she worked for some sort of activist group. I saw her out at the airport a couple of weeks ago. She and her group put on a rally on one of the concourses—apparently against the rules, since they were broken up by airport security."

The detective looked up from his notepad, his face showing curiosity, and asked, "Was there any resistance—ah, violence—shown by your neighbor or anyone else?"

"No, there didn't appear to be any, but then I left before the incident was finished. Oh, Detective, I just thought of something."

The detective looked up from his pad, "Yes?"

"Joan Collison was at O'Leary's last night. She was sitting with a guy that I don't know."

"Was he wearing horn-rimmed glasses?"

"Yeah, he was," Tom answered with a puzzled look on his face.

"Last time we visited, I asked you if you knew Jack Billings. You said you did, is that correct?"

"Yes, it is."

"Did you happen to notice if he chews gum?"

"No, I didn't, but then I haven't seen much of him."

"How about a Marcil Huggins—do you know him?"

"Yes, I do. He lives on the fifteenth floor, I believe—hangs around the bike trail a lot."

"Does he chew gum?"

Tom's face contorted slightly and his eyes narrowed. "I think he does."

"Okay and one more: Do you know a man by the name of Phil Bartron?"

"Yes, he lives here, too. I see him around once in awhile, especially at O'Leary's. He chews gum also. May I assume gum has something to do with the murders?"

"It could. Okay, thanks. That's it for now. Likely you'll be hearing from me again."

"Can I ask you a question?" asked Tom.

"Sure, go ahead."

"Ah, was Joan...stabbed, like the others?"

"Yes, she was."

"Was her bedroom messed up?"

"Yes, it was."

"And there was a gum wrapper on the floor, right?"

"You have it right," said the detective, standing up. "I've got to go. Thanks." Tom opened the door for the detective, who hurriedly walked down the hallway toward the elevators.

Tom went back into his apartment and sat down on a chair overlooking the bike trail. His thoughts were confused. *Joan—gone, hard to believe.* Tom thought about the upcoming meeting with Susan at four that afternoon. It wasn't going to be easy getting up for that.

His need to talk to someone drove him to the elevator. He didn't care to knock on Jan and Greg's door during the morning hours. Instead, he headed down for the mail—there would be people down there talking about what had happened.

When Tom reached the lobby, he wasn't disappointed. Numerous people were meandering about. Jan was sitting on the couch. The others he didn't recognize. They were likely Towers residents shocked by the news. No one was saying much, they were all just pacing around. Tom walked over to the couch and sat down by Jan.

"Tom, that wasn't Joan, you know."

"What do you mean, Jan? Did you see her?"

"No, but it wasn't Joan. I could tell by the shape. The person under the sheet was much bigger than Joan."

"Well, maybe it was padded or something?"

"No, Tom, I just know it wasn't Joan."

"Geez, I hope you're right. I need some air. I think I'll go up and get my skates."

Jan continued to sit on the couch. Tom got his mail and headed back up the elevator, encouraged by what Jan had said about Joan.

On Tom's return trip, he had his backpack strapped over one shoulder. The elevator stopped on the twelfth floor. Vito Manchino got on.

Tom looked into his eyes. Vito stopped chewing and looked away. Tom looked at his hands—they were anything but steady. *At least they weren't bloody.*

The sport coat that Vito was wearing looked new. He's probably got a whole bunch of 'em, Tom thought.

"I've got a pale blue Mercedes in the lot with your name on it," Vito said, smiling.

Tom looked at him, surprised. "That's way over my head. Haven't you heard the news?"

"What news, sport?"

"Another murder."

Vito's head tilted downward toward the floor. He mumbled, "Oh crap. Was it Joan Collison?"

"I saw the ambulance guys carry a body out of her apartment—not sure it was hers."

"Whew, that's three of 'em now. Someone is bent on cleaning us out," Vito said, smiling.

Tom didn't think that last crack was very funny. When the elevator door opened on the main floor, the lobby was empty. Tom wondered where everyone had gone, and followed Vito out of the elevator. Manchino went out the front door, and Tom headed down the hallway leading toward the outdoor parking lot.

When Tom got to the bike trail, Marcil Huggins was sitting on the bench. *Another gum chewer.*

"Do you mind if I sit here and put on my skates?" asked Tom.

"No, help yourself. Great morning for it," responded Marcil as he moved over.

While Tom was changing from tennis shoes to skates, he noticed that Marcil's hands were trembling. Beads of perspiration were clinging to Marcil's forehead beneath the brim of the white baseball cap. There was a dark stain on the rim of his gray jacket cuff.

"Have you heard about the third murder?" asked Tom, while glancing at Marcil's eyes.

Marcil was looking up the trail and responded in a few moments, his voice cracking. "There was some mention in the lobby—a body was carried out. Nobody said she was dead."

Tom stood up after buckling up the skates. He gave Marcil a stern look, placed his arms through the straps of his backpack and proceeded up the trail.

19

GORDON BEARD WAS ON THE PHONE, legs up on the desk, talking to a bank officer. Gordon fully owned SkyWeb, an Internet graphics company, he'd originated. Receipts during the first month of business, just over two years ago, were outstanding. The most recent six months showed revenues declining by seventy percent. He wasn't sure why business had taken such a major downturn.

Larry, the vice president of the bank, was concerned about SkyWeb having missed the last three payments.

"Look, Larry, the downturn is temporary. Orders are starting to come in again—got two new clients just yesterday."

"Mr. Beard, the board has made it clear: no more missed payments or we will have to take action. I'm sorry but it's not my decision. Your next payment is due in two weeks."

"Should be no problem, Larry. I'm expecting some big checks any day now. You need to remember that Internet businesses took a hit when the economy went south. We are tied to the economy, you know."

"Well, I understand that, but it doesn't change things. Just remember: no payments and we will be forced to take formal action."

"Get lost, brother," Gordon muttered after hanging up.

He got up from the chair, opened the door and walked out into the waiting room.

"Trish, anything come in the mail today—payments, I mean?"

"No, Gordon, nothing today."

"Ah, bull. They promised, didn't they—the Carson people?"

"Yes, they did, Gordon. I talked to Bill, the boss. He promised us a check by today."

Gordon returned to his office and slammed the door. *Vito is going to have to wait for his money—there's no other way*, he thought while dropping down in his chair. Taking a small packet out of his pocket, he laid back and brought it up to his nostrils.

——

SHORTLY BEFORE 3:30, TOM CARRYING HIS BRIEFCASE left for Susan's office, located in a brick and stone office building downtown. Before getting on the elevator, he checked the directory. SkyWeb-Designs, the name he was looking for, was listed sixth from the top. After getting off the elevator on the third floor, he walked down the hall and saw their sign on a glass door.

Tom entered a small waiting room and his attention focused on an attractive young lady sitting at a desk. She was on the phone but looked up at Tom and gestured toward a sitting area. Tom took a chair, laid the briefcase down on a table and looked around. The walls were decorated with large, contemporary, framed posters.

The young lady finished on the phone and asked, "Can I help you?"

"Yes, I'm Tom Hastings. I have an appointment with Susan."

"Oh, yes—she is expecting you. I'll tell her you are here." She disappeared through one of three doorways, returning a few seconds later.

"You can go right in, Mr. Hastings."

Tom picked up his briefcase and walked through the door. Susan looked up from behind her desk, smiled, stood up and walked around to the front, extended her hand and Tom was impressed by her firm handshake.

"Hi, Tom. Glad you could make it. Won't you have a seat?"

Tom set the briefcase on the floor and sat on a chair next to the desk. Susan returned to her position. The walls in Susan's office were generously decorated with graphic designs of websites. A nineteen-inch flat-screen monitor sat on her desk.

"Gordy is coming in as soon as he gets off the phone. He's my boss, the one I told you about, and he's interested in a new accounting system."

"So, how many people work here?" Tom asked.

"Just the three of us. Trisha handles the front desk, I design the websites and Gordy does the selling."

"Any idea on how many clients you have?"

"Not sure. Gordy should know."

A young skinny guy entered the room. Tom couldn't believe his eyes. It was the same person he had seen at O'Leary's—the one who'd gotten something under the counter from Vito.

"Hi, I'm Gordon."

Tom stood up and shook his hand—the grasp wasn't nearly as firm as Susan's was.

"I'm Tom Hastings. Susan tells me you are looking for a new accounting system."

"Yeah, we sure are. Could you give us some idea on how much this will cost us?"

"I need to learn more about your company before I can answer that. But, I can tell you right now that my fee will be reasonable. How many clients do you currently serve? Are you presently doing your own payroll?"

"We have about two hundred and fifty clients that hire us to originate and maintain websites. No, we don't do our own payroll but would like to, especially since there are only three of us. I have confidence that Trisha would be capable of handling that. She has some previous accounting experience."

For the next ten minutes, they continued to discuss the company operations.

"Gordon, I have an accounting software in mind called BizWorld. If it's okay with you, I'll come up with a written proposal that will include the cost of the software, and details of my fees and support."

"Ah, yeah. That'll work. When can you do that?"

"I can be back here with a written proposal by Friday."

"Could you make it by noon on Friday?"

"I'll be here at eleven. How does that sound?'

Gordon looked at Susan and said, "How will that work with you?"

"Fine—eleven sounds good."

"Nice meeting you, Tom. You live at the Towers, don't you?"

asked Gordon.

"Yeah, I do. How about you?" responded Tom.

"I'm up on twenty one, nice view."

"Oh, I'm just below you on twenty."

"See you Friday," said Gordon.

Tom watched as Gordon walked to the door and had a little trouble getting it open. After jerking a couple of times the door released. After going through, Gordon slammed it shut.

Susan looked at Tom, raised her arms and opened her palms. "I think he's under a lot of pressure," she said.

"Does your boss have a last name?"

"Beard—his name is Gordon Beard."

"How long has he been in this business? When did SkyWeb-Designs originate?"

"Actually, we have been in business only two years, but our growth has been fabulous. I fully expect we will double the number of clients by this time next year."

"A change in subject, Susan, but the Towers has had another murder."

Susan's eyes opened wide and she put one of her hands to her mouth.

"Oh, Tom, what happened?"

"Next door to me—in 2010. A Joan Collison lived there. Did you know her?"

"Oh no, not Joan."

Her head dropped down and her chin rested on her clasped hands. When she raised her head, he could see tears had flooded her eyes.

"When did it happen?" she asked.

"Last night or this morning. Susan, I don't want to get your hopes up, but there is a possibility the victim was not Joan. The body had not officially been identified. I personally heard a Tower's resident say she didn't think the dead person was Joan."

"Oh God, please make that be true," Susan meekly whimpered.

"I'm sorry that I am the bearer of such depressing news. I guess you would have found out by the end of the day anyhow."

Susan got up from behind her desk. Tom stood up and they hugged

lightly. "Thanks for coming, Tom, and for bringing me the news."
"I'll see you on Friday at eleven. Let's hope the news gets better.
So long for now."

20

DURING TOM'S DRIVE BACK TO THE TOWERS, his thoughts
were about Susan and how she had reacted to the news. He wondered
how well she'd known Joan. They must have been friends. Her boss,
Gordon, had looked like a basket case—something was really wrong
there. Tom parked in the outdoor lot and entered the lobby.

Carl was standing with his back to Tom, talking to two ladies
seated on the couch.

Hearing someone approach, he turned and said, "Hi, Tom."

Tom didn't reply. His mind was experiencing confusion and relief:
one of the two ladies sitting on the couch was Joan Collison.

Tom thought of Jan and what she had said earlier: *But it wasn't
Joan. I could tell by the shape.* She'd been right. Carl was looking at
Tom and waiting for a reply. Joan was looking at him also. He was
speechless.

Carl broke the silence. "Well, Tom, you haven't lost your neighbor
after all."

"Joan, I'm so glad to see you sitting here. It is you, isn't it?" Tom
smiled and asked.

Joan smiled, "It's me, alright. I suppose I owe you an explanation.
The lady in my room was one of the people from the rally at the
airport. She was from out of town and I gave her a place to stay. I
really didn't even know her. She was staying at my apartment while
I was visiting a friend."

"Well, the lady that died—what happened?" Tom asked.

Joan shuddered and replied, "The police haven't told me anything,
but Jan said she was murdered like the other two."

"Well, I'm going up," Tom said.

The elevator door opened and Tom stepped in, his mind in total confusion. He was thinking about calling Susan and telling her Joan was okay. Things were happening fast and Julie would be upset if he didn't let her know what's happened. Tom decided to have a drink, settle down and relax before making any calls.

When Tom entered his apartment, the answering machine was beeping. Jan had left a message asking him to stop by between five and six. I'll have the drink first, before going over to see Jan and Greg, he thought.

He mixed a strong scotch and water and the first couple of gulps removed some of the tension that had been building in his stomach. He sat down and called SkyWeb. Trisha informed him that Susan had gone for the day.

Tom refreshed his scotch drink and headed over to Jan and Greg's. Greg opened the door within moments after Tom knocked.

"Come on in, Tom. I'm glad you're alive. Jan and I have survived the day so far. I see you already have a drink. Have a seat in the living room."

"Thanks, Greg, I will," Tom replied.

The television was tuned to the news. Tom took a seat on one of the couches and took another gulp of his scotch.

Jan peeked in and said, "Tom, I see you've survived the day."

"Well, Jan, it isn't over—plenty of things happening so far."

"Didn't I tell you that the person under the sheet wasn't Joan? Didn't I tell you?"

"You sure had it right, Jan—right away, you said, '*It's not Joan.*'"

"Tom, the lady in Joan's apartment died the same way as the other two: a clean, knifelike penetration of the heart—Bedroom was trashed, same as the others. According to what I heard the detective say, it happened sometime between eleven and one. Did you hear anything over there?'

"I sure did. At eleven, I heard this thump. I checked out the hallway. No one was around. About half an hour later, I checked again and caught a glimpse of someone leaving—just a glimpse of the back of a person as they turned the corner."

"Wow, Tom! Do the cops know that?"

"Yup, they sure do. I already told the head detective. He came over and asked me a lot of questions."

"He did, huh? If you had to guess right now who the person was, who would you say? Marcil Huggins, perhaps? Did he have a sport coat? Was the person big? Was it a man?"

"Jan, your questions are too overwhelming. The detective already asked me all that.

"Oh, I just remembered," he added. "This afternoon I told Susan that Joan was dead. I tried to call her a few minutes ago but she had left work."

"No problem," said Jan. "I talked to Susan about half an hour ago. She already knows that Joan is still alive—almost flipped when I told her on the phone. I asked her to drop by after work. She wasn't sure if she would come or not."

"Need another drink?" asked Greg.

"No, I don't think so. I think I'll go home, shower and head over to O'Leary's just to unwind. I suppose I should call Julie. She's going to be ticked if I don't clue her in to what's happened here."

"Thanks for coming by, Tom. We should know more tomorrow," said Jan

"Okay, thanks. I'll see you guys later."

Tom's glass was half full when he arrived back at his apartment. The phone was ringing when he entered.

"Hi, Tom. What's new?" asked Julie.

"Oh, just another murder, that's all."

"What? You're kidding!"

"No. Some lady got herself killed in Joan's apartment, next door. It happened last night. This whole place is in total chaos—police all over the place. It's another murder, MO similar to the other two. Hey, if you can come over after work on Friday, I'll know more. Even Jan doesn't know what's going on. Well, she did say that the lady was killed with a knife."

"Tom, that's just like television. I can't believe what's happening over there. When I come over, I'll call from my cell in the parking lot. Would you come and get me?"

"Yes, that's a darn good plan. Brave little Julie is starting to get wise."

"Well, at first, the two loose ones getting murdered didn't seem like a threat to me. But now, an ordinary lady gets murdered. I think I got the message."

"Julie, I'm getting cleaned up and heading over to O'Leary's. I need to clear my mind."

"Okay, talk to you later."

O'Leary's was quiet. Tom's favorite stool was available, along with the other four stools at the closed end of the bar. When the bartender came over, Tom ordered a beer and asked him to change the channel to the Twin's station. They were playing the Red Sox in Boston.

Tom saw some familiar-looking faces in the smoking section on his left. Sitting at a table were Vito Manchino and Gordon Beard. They were hunched over and facing each other, a smoke cloud forming over their heads.

Two attractive young ladies were sitting on stools on his left, almost directly in line with the table Gordon and Vito were at. Both had nice figures. Tom wondered how long it would take before they attracted Vito's eye.

He had his answer in a couple of minutes when Vito and Gordon got up from their table. After Gordon walked toward the door, Vito remained standing and glanced around, his face showing anger. Within a minute, Vito was talking to the two ladies. Both broke out in laughter, which must have resulted from a successful Vito Manchino joke.

Attired in his sport coat, Vito took a stool next to one of the girls and stubbed his cigarette in an ashtray. While lighting a new one, he looked up and saw Tom Hastings. He frowned, displayed his foxlike smile and refocused on the girl next to him.

The Twin's third baseman stroked a base-clearing double, putting them ahead of the Red Sox three to two. One of the guys in a group of people gathered on the right side of the bar clapped. Beyond them, on the same side of the bar and sitting next to the server station–Phil Bartron.

The four empty barstools concerned Tom. Phil might come over and join him. At the moment, his potential pest was occupied with watching the two young ladies visiting with Vito Manchino.

The Red Sox tied the game in the seventh inning. Tom decided to leave to watch the rest of it in his apartment. He noticed the ashtray in front of Vito was filling up quickly. Vito appeared fidgety that evening, very much as he had the first time Tom had seen him. The impact from the drinks was having its effect. The two ladies and Vito were getting noisy. It was time for Tom to leave.

21

THE LADY ENTERING THE ELEVATOR on the eleventh floor looked scared. It was Thursday morning and Tom Hastings was leaning against the far corner inside the elevator heading down for the mail. She said, "Good morning," but eyed him rather suspiciously. Tom knew the lady was relieved when the elevator opened on the lobby floor. To her, Tom was a potential murderer.

Mrs. Gray was vacuuming the carpet of the lobby area. Tom noticed two police cars parked out front. There wasn't anyone milling about, but he could hear voices in Carl's office.

Tom pressed the Up elevator button for the return trip. When the door opened, Susan was exiting.

"Oh, it's you, Tom. I'm scared as hell to get on this elevator by myself. When will this nightmare end?"

"Well, I'm still in a daze after what happened yesterday next door to me. Jan told me that you were informed about Joan not being the victim."

"Yes, and I was so relieved to hear that Joan was okay. I wish the police would get with it—find the evildoer. None of us are safe around here anymore."

"You're not the only one, Susan."

"Are you coming over tomorrow?"

"Yup, sure am. I've got the proposal almost ready—guess we're all set for about eleven. Shouldn't take long—probably be done by lunchtime." Susan nodded and proceeded into the lobby.

Tom took the elevator up and entered his apartment. The *Star Tribune* had a story about the recent death. The writer didn't use the word *Murder.* They should interview Jan—she knows, Tom thought. *"The victim died as the result of a knife wound."* Hmm...the writer opened the door for a possible accident or suicide. Tom wondered what Jan would think when reading the article.

Tom spent the next hour working on the proposal for SkyWeb. The wording was perfect and it was time to print a couple of copies. His preparation for the next days meeting was complete.

Looking out his balcony window, he could see the bike trail, vacant except for a lone person with a dog. Tom grabbed his skates backpack and headed down.

Greg was in the lobby visiting with Carl. "Heading out to the bike trail?" asked Carl.

"Yup, that's where I'm going. What's up, Greg?"

"Jan has the flu. I've grounded her."

"Yeah. I bet you have. Well, I'm off. See you later."

"When is Julie coming over again?" asked Greg.

"Tomorrow evening. We may take in a movie."

"Have a good run, Tom," said Carl.

The cool breeze on Tom's face felt good as he slowly made his way up the bike trail. The bike trail was not busy that morning—he liked that. A rhythm developed and his speed increased. Tom did the entire four-mile trek, turned and began the return trip.

A locomotive pulling a long line of boxcars was approaching. The engineer was sitting in front of the controls with one arm resting on the window ledge. He glanced at the skater and waved. Tom returned his wave and wondered what it would be like driving a train— there would be no red lights to wait for at intersections. You'd always have the right away, and there would be no parking lots.

Climbing the steps to the rear parking lot of the Towers, Tom paused to watch a hawk circling over the small grove of trees. He wondered if Joan was going to continue to live next door. He crossed the parking lot and headed for the back door. No one was in the lobby. Tom filled a Styrofoam cup with coffee and headed up the elevator.

An hour later, Tom was on his way to lunch at Molly's. En route, he stopped at Jensen's Shirts. Dalia was busy as usual. Cliff was standing by the counter with his hands in his pockets.

"Hi, Cliff. Taking a break?"

"Yeah, I'm all caught up for a change."

"Hi, Tom," said Dalia. "Hey, I really like that program. It's beautiful. No more scribbling notes all over the place. We should have done this long ago."

"Well, I'm really glad to hear it's going well. I guess that's why I stopped by, just to see how you're doing."

"Thanks for coming by. I'll let you know if I run into any problems. Oh, by the way, I hear we lost another tenant—well, not really a tenant, but someone visiting."

"Dalia, did you know the most recent murder occurred right next door to me, on the twentieth floor?"

"No. Did you see or hear anything?"

"Sure did."

Tom told her about his experiences of that night.

"I imagine there were police all over the place."

"They sure were. A Detective Anderson asked me a bunch of questions."

"Now, that's really being involved. Hopefully, he didn't think you did it."

Tom chuckled and replied, "I don't think so, but he sure put a scare into me. I won't let Julie enter by herself anymore, coming from the outdoor parking lot."

"Who's Julie?"

"Oh, she's my friend. She comes to visit once in awhile."

"I've got Cliff to protect me—right, handsome?"

"Protecting you? I thought you were protecting me," responded Cliff.

Tom left Jensen's and entered Molly's. The hostess, Molly, was standing toe-to-toe with a big guy who'd apparently had a problem with lunch.

"I'm sorry you didn't like your food." She tore up the slip and let it slip through her fingers. The little pieces of paper floated in the air and eventually sprinkled the floor. One of the pieces landed on the guy's foot. He turned and grumbled something and walked out the door.

"Oh, I don't like that guy. If it wasn't against the law, I'd belt 'im one."

Tom tried to keep from laughing but just couldn't hold back at least a little chuckle.

"Oh, you think that's funny—huh, Mr. Tom?"

"Yup, I think that was funny—the way you tore up the slip and sprinkled his foot. He may not come back, you know."

"Well, good riddance. I've had it up to here with that slob." She leveled her right hand and placed it up even with her nose. "Follow me. I've got a table by the window for you."

While Tom was studying the menu, he caught a glimpse of a white cap and gray jacket approaching the restaurant door. Marcil Huggins was on his way. The few relaxed moments he'd had visiting with Molly were gone.

Tom quickly opened the newspaper and held it high, not caring for any company on that day. When Tom peeked around the edge of the newspaper, he noticed Molly was leading Huggins to a table on the other side of the room.

Feeling that his position was secure, Tom Hastings set the paper down.

"Can I take your order?" asked a waitress. "Whoops!" She exclaimed as her pencil dropped to the floor.

Tom spent the next half an hour enjoying lunch and reading the paper, occasionally glancing at Huggins. The hunched Marcil was facing the other way and hadn't noticed Tom.

"How was lunch?" Molly asked as Tom was leaving.

"Do I dare complain?" asked Tom, jokingly.

Molly laughed deeply and loudly. She was still laughing when Marcil approached.

"Hello, Hastings. I saw you out on the bike trail this morning."

"Yeah, Marcil, I was out there for a bit. Didn't see you, though."

Marcil Huggins firmly and clearly said, "I wasn't there but could see you out my window."

22

TOM HASTINGS WAS REVIEWING HIS SKYWEB PROPOSAL
on Friday morning. After placing it in his briefcase, he picked up the
Star Tribune. A small headline on the fifth page caught his attention:
"Serial murder at the Towers." The article established the latest
victim's name. It was a woman by the name of Gretchen Miles from
Indianapolis, Indiana. Tom read the article twice, searching for
mention of a cause of death. He read the words "foul play" and
"jewelry was stolen."

Before leaving, Tom called Julie's apartment and left a message
asking her to come over after work and perhaps take in a movie. He
was aware that Julie liked movies and felt she would be pleased.

By 10:30 he was headed downtown, arriving at the SkyWeb
parking lot twenty minutes later. When he drove around the block a
third time, a spot opened up at the far end.

Greeted by Trisha when entering the SkyWeb reception room, he
said, "Good morning, Trisha. I'm here to see Mr. Beard and Susan."

"Mr. Hastings, how nice to see you again. They're expecting you.
Why don't you go right in?"

She pointed toward a door other than the one to Susan's office.
Tom entered and saw Gordon Beard and Susan huddled behind a
computer screen. They looked up when he entered.

Without saying a word, Gordon pointed to an empty chair across
the desk. Tom didn't know what to make of his demeanor. For a
moment, Tom felt like leaving.

Forgetting his emotions, he said, "Hello, Mr. Beard. Hi, Susan.
I'll get right down to business. I know you're both very busy."

Tom retrieved a folder from his briefcase and plucked out two
copies of a single one-page document. He handed one to Mr. Beard
and the other to Susan. He waited in silence while they scanned the

document.

"It's a deal," said Gordon. "When can you start?"

"How about next Tuesday? I need some time to purchase the accounting software and plan final strategy."

"Okay, Tuesday it is. If there is anything you need to get ready, see Trisha at the front desk, " said a testy Gordon.

"Yes, I will. The new software will take some training. Included in my fee is training for Trisha and either of you two, if you care to sit in."

Gordon Beard wasn't interested in the details of accounting. He was mainly concerned about the balance of their checking account. "Please, Tom, do what you have to do to—install, train, whatever. Trisha will be your priority."

Susan added, "I really don't have much to do with our bookkeeping end of things, thank God."

"We're not going to get this done in one visit. My goal will be to spend about three hours on each visit—perhaps only two hours, depending on attention spans. I'll be over at one, right after lunch on Tuesday," added Tom.

"See you guys on Tuesday," Tom said as he clicked his briefcase shut and left the room

Trisha had a worried look on her face when Tom sat in the chair by her desk. "Here's a list of what I'll need by our first visit," Tom told her.

She studied the list and said, "Okay, Mr. Hastings, I'll do the best I can."

"Can't expect more than that, Trisha. See you on Tuesday," Tom said, getting up from the chair.

"I'll be looking forward to it," Trisha said, her usual smile turned to a frown.

I don't think I will be, Tom thought as he headed out the door and made his way to the elevator. Arriving at his car, Tom noticed the parking place next to his was empty. He also noticed a small dent just behind his rear door. This job is not starting out well at all, he thought—a dent in my car and a disturbed client.

He returned to the Towers and parked in the outside lot, making sure there was plenty of room·between his car and the adjacent vehicles. After getting out of the car, he gazed around the lot, wondering if any of the vehicles belonged to the murderer.

Andy and Emil were standing next to the walkway leading to the back door.

"Anything big happen today?" Tom asked.

"Well, this pavement should have been patched last week, but instead we've been busy in the apartment next to you. That was some job, the carpet cleaning—worse than the others."

"Was the place a mess, other than the carpet?"

"There were some drawers pulled out in the bedroom—other rooms were fine," Andy answered.

"And some jewelry scattered on the floor," added Emil.

Andy said, "Well, by tomorrow the holes should be no more—eh, Emil?"

Tom heard a grumble from Emil while he headed toward the door. After arriving back at his apartment, he found a message from Julie on the answering machine. She was looking forward to the movie.

23

RICHARD FALLON LEFT HIS DESK, needing a coffee break. From his position in the lunchroom, the door partially open, he could see Jane sitting at her desk, her tight skirt up over her knees. The red dress she was wearing today made it almost impossible for Richard to concentrate. Next time Maria visits her parents in Madison, *I'll try,* he thought.

Outside the lunchroom window that looked out over the office building corridor, he saw a neat blonde walking by. Julie, that's her name, he was sure. He remembered seeing her with that Tom Hastings at the Towers.

Returning to his office, Richard paused to read a note placed on the desk. *Fallon, I need to talk to you.* Ellen Hayley, his supervisor, signed it.

What the hell does she want? He mused. Gathering up some dander, he stomped down the hall to her office. Knocking gently, he waited for a response.

"Come in," he heard her say.

"You wanted to see me?" Richard asked.

"Yes, please close the door and have a chair, right there," she said pointing.

"Ah, Mr. Fallon, I've received two complaints about you. They concern two young ladies who claim you have been verbally sexually abusive in the lunch room."

"Aw, jeez, I was just joking."

"Mr. Fallon, we take accusations like that seriously around here."

She pushed a paper across the desk. "I want you to read what they said to me. It's all on that paper."

Richard grabbed the paper and held it up to the light. Before he had finished reading it, his face formed into a scornful frown. He set the paper down.

"Missus Haley, I think they are exaggerating, ah—"

She interrupted and firmly said, "As far as I'm concerned, the issue is over. However, I don't want to hear any more stories such as those about you. Do you understand?"

"Yeah, I understand. Sorry. It won't happen again."

"Very well, Mr. Fallon. You may go."

Sheepishly, Richard Fallon left the supervisor's office. He drew a few stares from some of the other employees while sauntering back to his office.

———

JULIE'S RING CAME AT 6:30 P.M. She knocked on Tom's door a couple of minutes later.

"Did you see anyone on the way up?" Tom asked.

"Yup, I saw Jan down in the lobby."

"Wow, that's surprising. She was supposed to have the flu."

"Well, she did look a little pale and her voice was raspy. However, she seemed alert and anxious."

"What do you mean by anxious?"

"Well, she was standing and looking out the front door as if she was expecting someone. When I opened the lobby door she turned quickly to see who I was."

"Did she say anything about the murder of the woman next door to me?"

"No, we really didn't talk."

"Here's the list of movies in the area. Why don't you look them over? Let's make a decision."

They decided on a movie called *Late Shift*. The movie theater was located in a shopping mall about five miles away. Tom stood in line for tickets while Julie did the same for popcorn. The man buying tickets at the ticket window looked familiar. When he turned his head, Tom recognized the goatee. It was Phil Bartron's—long and pointed.

Tom watched as Phil headed for the ticket takers. Instead of passing into the theater, Phil moved off to the side and stood looking around. Tom's turn came at the window, and after purchasing two tickets, he headed over to the counter to join Julie. Phil had disappeared.

After half an hour of previews, the movie finally began. It was a story about factory workers who worked the midnight shift. Some of the people in the story lived two separate lives. About an hour into the movie, a shriek was emitted a few rows from the front. A woman got up, said something to the person next to her and stormed out. Moments later the man who'd been sitting next to the lady also got up and left.

"Did you see who that was?" whispered Julie to Tom.

"No, what happened?"

"It was the little man with the goatee. He must have done something to the lady next to him."

A minute later the woman returned with an usher.

"Too late—he's gone," a person sitting next to the two empty seats said to the usher.

"Sorry, folks. Please get back to the movie," said the usher as the woman returned to her seat.

———

THE NEXT MORNING, SATURDAY, Tom and Julie gathered their tennis apparatus and headed for the courts. The elevator stopped on the twelfth floor. Vito Manchino got on.

Tom could almost hear Julie's heartbeat speed up. He wondered why Vito was in and out of his apartment so much. *Was he making deliveries?*

"Hello, Vito," Tom said.

"Good morning, lovebirds—looks like tennis today. Wish I had the time for stuff like that—tennis."

"You should give it a try," responded Tom. *Beats killing people,* he thought.

"I'm just too damn busy—too many irons in the fire. Maybe it's time for a change. Meanwhile, I'm off to St. Paul for breakfast with a friend."

Vito watched as Tom and Julie got off at the lobby.

"He sure looked me over," said Julie. "We'll have to watch the paper tomorrow. If a certain lady from St. Paul dies, we may have a solution to the murders."

"Geez, that guy makes me uncomfortable. There's something about him that I don't like. Whether he is the murderer or not, he gives me the creeps."

Julie drove her car to the tennis courts. All but two of the courts were busy that morning. Claiming one, they sat down and changed to tennis shoes.

After playing a couple of sets, Tom and Julie were sitting and resting, pondering whether they should play a third set, when a familiar-looking couple walked by on the other side of the fence— Richard and Maria Fallon.

"Julie, see those two—they live at the Towers, on the nineteenth floor. I've seen 'em on the bike trail a couple of times."

"Oh, I know that guy. He works in my building. Let's see...what is his name anyway?"

"Try Richard."

"Oh yes, that's it...Richard...Richard Fallon. The girls in the office talk about him a lot. It seems as if he is quite the hustler. I haven't met him...never even talked to him. One of the girls in the office goes out to lunch with him a lot. Are they married? He doesn't wear a ring at work."

"Yes, that's his wife who's playing tennis with him right now. Well, Julie, have you had enough, or do you want to play another set?"

"I think I've had enough for now, but one of these days I'm going to whip your butt. Let's get back, get cleaned up, and I'll take you out to lunch."

"Sounds perfect, Julie."

An hour later, they entered Molly's.

"Hi, you two—nonsmoking, right?"

"You remembered," Tom responded.

Molly led them to a table by the wall. Seated at the adjoining table were Carlos and Juanita.

"Hi, neighbors," Tom said. "Are you enjoying the weekend?"

"Yes, we are, Mr. Tom. Did you do the in-line-skating this morning?"

"No, I didn't, Juanita. Julie and I just got off the tennis court."

"Oh, you two play tennis—how sporty."

"Carlos and Juanita Valdez, this is my friend, Julie."

Carlos stood up and extended his right hand to Julie. His left remained in his jacket pocket. Julie took his hand for a moment and then released. Carlos returned to his seat.

Juanita bowed her head. *"Creo que a Julie le gusta Tom."* Yes, Julie does like Tom, she thought.

"Carlos and Juanita are originally from Colombia. They have recently joined us as citizens."

"How interesting," responded Julie. "I spent some time in Colombia when I was in college. It's a beautiful country."

"Thank you for saying that," said Juanita.

The waitress interrupted and Carlos and Juanita returned to their lunch. After Julie ordered, she said, "Carlos and Juanita seem like such a nice couple. Maybe we should get to know them better. I would like to hear more about Colombia."

"Next time we have a cocktail party, let's have them over," Tom said.

"That's a great idea. When are we going to do it?"

"How about next weekend—say, Friday? Jan should be over the virus by then."

"Yes, let's do it. I'll help you get stuff together for the party. Who are we going to invite?"

"Well, for starters, we have Carlos and Juanita. Then there's Greg and Jan, perhaps Candice and Jack, and how about the tennis couple, Richard and Maria?"

"How about Vito and your other two favorites, Marcil and Phil?" chided Julie.

"Surely, you jest."

Julie laughed. "Let's make some calls tomorrow before I leave."

"How about dinner at O'Leary's tonight? We can talk about it then. I'm buying—strictly casual. We can people watch—see who's around."

"Yes, that sounds exciting. O'Leary's is getting to be a real hangout for you, isn't it? I'm all for that. I'd like to meet more of your suspicious friends."

On Saturday afternoon, Julie and Tom decided to go shopping. Her birthday was approaching and she needed a new outfit. The elevator stopped on the seventh floor.

James the barber hopped on, looked at Tom, and said, "Hi."

"How are things with you today, Jim?" Tom asked.

"Could be better—I could win the lottery," he replied.

"Do you have an apartment on the seventh floor?" Tom continued.

"No, I don't," he replied.

The elevator stopped at the lobby, Tom and Julie got off, and James remained.

When Tom got into the red convertible and closed the door, Julie asked, "If James doesn't live on the seventh floor, where does he live?"

"I really don't know. Does it matter?"

"Only if he kills ladies," replied Julie.

"I don't know if he even lives in the building. I've seen him get off the elevator a few times down at the lobby and garage, but he probably just has a bunch of friends. He works in the barber shop, down a level from the lobby, you know."

It was a beautiful day and Julie speed-guided the red convertible, top down, through the traffic with ease. Since it was a Saturday, the mall parking areas were packed with vehicles.

"Finding a parking spot in this maze is quite the task," Tom said.

Julie began by driving her vehicle as close as possible to their destination building. Right next to the handicapped spaces was a single parking spot.

"Look, a Julie spot," she said. Skillfully, she outmaneuvered her competitors and captured the lone space. The driver of one of the other vehicles didn't look too happy.

"Hey, Julie, I think you have a new friend. She waved to you. Hmm...missing four fingers."

Julie was too busy gloating over her victory to notice. Tom doubled up in laughter.

After Julie made her selections at a department store, they carried two large bags back to the car.

"Hey, Julie, maybe you can wear that nice new black dress next Friday if we have the party."

"I sure will."

Shopping had taken its toll. They both napped before readying for dinner at O'Leary's. Julie dressed sharply—she wasn't wearing the new black dress but did have on a nice gray skirt.

"Hey, I thought we were going casual," Tom said.

"This *is* casual. Just wait until Friday."

"I'm ready. Let's head out," said a gleeful Tom.

When the elevator door opened, Phil Bartron's goatee was tilted upward. His hands were bracing the rail along the inside back wall.

"Good afternoon, folks," the little man's high-pitched voice uttered, getting around a wad of something in his mouth.

Tom almost pulled Julie back to wait for the next one. Reluctantly, he followed Julie into the elevator, not responding to Phil's greeting.

"Hello," said Julie. "Nice afternoon."

"Yeah, and it's going to get better. Who's your friend, Tom?"

Tom really didn't want to introduce Julie to Phil, but he was trapped. Rather, he would have liked to grab a hunk of that hair and pry the weasel off the wall.

"Julie, this is Phil. He lives up above me somewhere."

"On the twenty-second floor. Nice to meet you, Julie."

They shook hands and the three walked out together into the parking lot. Julie and Tom split off from Bartron and got into her red convertible. As they were leaving the lot, Tom noticed Phil Bartron walking down the stairway that led to the street and the mall.

As expected, O'Leary's was busy. Tom and Julie took chairs in the tiny waiting area, lucky to find two. They'd been waiting for about five minutes when Phil Bartron came through the door.

He looked down at Tom and Julie. "Hey, if I'd known you were coming here, I woulda hitched a ride."

Neither Tom nor Julie responded. Tom pressed his elbow against Julie's ribs, hoping she'd get his silent message. Tom had the feeling Phil was expecting an invitation to join them for dinner.

Julie received the message, remaining speechless. Lacking an invitation, Phil moved on toward the bar where they saw him take a stool on the far side, not far from the server station.

Tom and Julie were seated in the nonsmoking section, some distance from the bar area. From his position at the table, Tom could see Phil's back. Sitting across from him, next to the gate, was Marcil Huggins.

"Don't look now, but there's a pair to draw to," Tom said.

"You don't like those two guys, do you?" Julie asked. She laughed. "Maybe we should invite them to the party on Friday. They would add a lot."

"I don't think so, young lady. Well, I really don't know either one very well, but they both give me the creeps. Those two guys invented the word *snoopy*. It seems as if they are always looking for someone to latch on to. I hate that."

"Oh, Tom. People are people."

"By the way, Julie, what about the new couple we met at Jan's— Aaron and Kit? I really liked them."

"Sure, they are interesting."

"I'll get their number from Jan."

When Tom and Julie left O'Leary's, Marcil and Phil were still at the bar. Tom had rushed through dinner, fearing Phil was going to ask for a ride back to the Towers.

"How about some skating tomorrow?" Tom asked Julie.

"Sounds great to me. Mine are in the trunk." Julie parked in the outside lot. Tom exited the car and looked in all directions. Relieved that no one was about, he escorted Julie through the back door and into the Towers. He didn't see anyone in the lobby while they waited for the elevator. Just as the elevator door was closing, a uniformed police officer entered the lobby.

24

TOM AND JULIE DIDN'T LEAVE THE APARTMENT on Sunday morning until about eleven. Loaded with backpacks, they walked out into the parking lot and down the steps to the bike trail. When they arrived at the bench, a young lady had just changed into her skates. She stood up, fastened her backpack and scooted up the trail.

"Wouldn't it be nice to be that agile?" Julie said.

"Oh, we don't do so badly. When we were her age, in-line-skates weren't even invented. Have you done any more thinking about the party on Friday?"

"Well, let's see...who did we put on our list? Greg and Jan for sure. Then there's the young couple, Richard and Maria. They are so cute— and besides, I think he's interesting. I would like to learn a little more about him. All that stuff I hear about him at the office is likely loose, jealous gossip. Oh, and since you're so stubborn, we'll have to pass on Vito Manchino, even though Jan invited him to their house."

"You're not serious, Julie. Everything about him makes me uncomfortable."

She laughed. "Only kidding. Okay, that's four on our list."

"Don't forget about Jack and Candice," added Tom.

"Yes, they're a real nice couple. What floor do they live on?"

"The seventeenth. One problem we may have inviting them— Jack is usually gone during the week. Well, maybe he'll get home on time on Friday. Then there is Susan and the two Colombians. I almost forgot— how about my next door neighbor, Joan? But then, she isn't my neighbor any more."

"I think we should pass on that last one," said Julie.

"Okay. How about Carlos and Juanita? I think we decided on them earlier."

"Sure, that's fine."

"And Susan?"

"Well, okay, but I'll have to keep an eye on her."

Tom laughed. "Julie, my dealings with Susan are strictly business."

After changing into skates, they slowly made their way up the trail. Since the bike trail was busy, Tom and Julie skated in single file. They cruised by the second bench. There was one conveniently located about every half a mile. When Tom saw the fourth bench appear in the distance, he motioned for Julie to stop.

"I need a break. How about you?"

"Yes, I agree," said Julie.

They sat for a few minutes. A familiar-looking man and woman on skates were approaching in the return lane. The white streak in the dark hair of the guy was unmistakable. Richard and Maria slowed and pulled over.

When Richard's skates left the hard surface and made contact with the sod, he stumbled. "Whew, that was close. I'm new to in-line-skates and haven't fallen yet. You almost witnessed the first one."

After a few minutes of discussion on the art of in-line-skating, Julie asked, "Would you guys like to come to our party on Friday?"

Maria responded, "Yes, I would like to come. How about you Richard?"

"I like parties. What time?"

"Anytime after five," answered Julie.

"See you on Friday. Come on, Richard. Let's get going."

"Well, that was easy," Tom added after the couple had left.

Julie and Tom got up from the bench and continued on their way. They stopped and rested at one bench on the return trip. Feeling relieved to remove the skates after completing the eight miles, Julie said, "That was fun."

"I cannot ever imagine tiring of this," Tom responded.

Later that afternoon they went over the party list. Julie began by calling Greg and Jan's apartment.

After being on the phone for about ten minutes, she reported, "Jan's flu is getting better each passing day. Should be fine by Friday. Jan gave me Candice and Susan's phone numbers. Do you want to call them or should I?"

"Go right ahead. You're doing just fine."

In a few minutes Julie announced, "Jack is expected to be home by noon on Friday. They accepted our invite. Also, regarding Susan, she wasn't home but I left a message."

After completing their plans for the party, Julie said, "It's time for me to go home. I hope none of our guests get murdered before Friday."

After a pause in their conversation, Julie added, "Now that wasn't funny, was it?"

"Not really, but I like your sense of humor. I'll check with Carl and see if he'll give me Carlos and Juanita's number. Also, I'll check with Jan about the phone number for Aaron and Kit."

"Oh yes, I forgot them," said Julie. "You'll take care of them, won't you?"

Tom watched the red convertible exit the parking lot and turn onto the boulevard. The top was down and Julie's hair was flowing with the wind.

————

FOUR PLASTIC BAGS LAY ON THE DETECTIVE'S DESK. The police lab technicians had finished their analysis. The first bag had been discovered in a trash container the day after Gloria Tingsley's body was found. The second one was found in a Dumpster following the Oxley murder. Each of the other two contained a gum wrapper—one from each crime.

Detective Bill Anderson was reading the report that described and analyzed the contents.

"This doesn't tell us smithies, Rod. Whoever disposed of that stuff knew damn well that we'd find it. Assuming the killer is a man, he didn't give a hoot, either. Gum wrappings at the first two, but not the third. Different brands, similarly crumpled."

"Bill, I'm positive we can conclude the first two murders were committed by a man. No way any lady would have the strength to move those bodies that far."

"Yeah, I think you're right. Strange that he would move the first two bodies and not the third—certainly a warped mind. Also, whoever is behind the killings lives in the Towers."

"Why do you think that?" asked Rod.

"Because the manager, Carl, tells me no one has noticed any strangers moving about the building. The killer is likely someone he knows—a tenant."

"Yeah, that makes sense because our surveillance team hasn't come up with squat so far. Everyone they have questioned in and about the building had been tenants."

"By the way, Randy's background checks on all the males living at the Towers are almost done—should be ready tomorrow, he says," the detective reported.

"I'm looking forward to seeing the list," he added. "Soon as it's ready, we'll set up interviews. Miss Kate Purley insists on going with us. Nothing much I can do about that. The chief is going along with her."

"I think she's way off track—saying the murderer is a happily married man—she must have got that right out of a textbook," jeered the lieutenant.

The two officers were interrupted by a knock. One of the desk sergeants was at the door. "Detective, the TV station called again. They really want that interview."

"We've got a lot of loose ends at the Towers. Until those are resolved, I can't talk to the media. I need another twenty-four hours."

"Okay, I'll tell them," replied the lieutenant.

25

TOM HASTINGS' BUSINESS ACCOUNTING STRATEGY for SkyWeb was ready. He called early Monday morning to verify their appointment time for Tuesday. When Trisha answered, Tom sensed a tad of apprehension in her voice. Like most front-office employees, she wasn't too keen about making changes.

Tom felt tempted to use this Monday as a day of simple leisure, then thought of Dalia and their new software. Better check her out, he thought.

Greg was sitting on the couch in the lobby when Tom stepped off the elevator and picked up the mail. Tom sat down by Greg. "How's Jan and her virus?"

"Getting better every day. She should be normal for your party on Friday."

Greg was sipping coffee and shuffling through some papers extracted from his briefcase.

"An office away from my desk," he said. "Sometimes I can think better here in the lobby than I can at work."

"What's new in the hospital business?" Tom asked.

"Well, costs are going up and we are forced to continually streamline operations to keep our head above water. Dealing with the insurance companies is a nightmare."

Hearing Tom and Greg talking, Carl walked in from his office and poured a coffee.

"Sounds like big business going on out here," he said.

"Not much business for me today, Carl. I've got most of the day off," answered Tom.

"Some guys have all the luck," Carl replied.

"Say, Carl, I need to contact Carlos and Juanita Valdez. Is there some way I could get their phone number?" asked Tom.

"Sure, come in my office. I'll get it for you."

As Carl was writing the number on a notepad, Tom asked, "Anything new on the murders?"

"The cops don't say much. The good news is that they are all done in the apartment—the one next to you. I'm getting it cleaned up and you're going to have new neighbors."

"What's happened to Joan?"

"I moved her down to an apartment on eighteen. She had a problem with remaining in twenty-ten after what happened."

"Hmm...sure can't blame her for that," responded Tom.

Carl paged through a small booklet until he found the phone number. After writing it down on a notepad, he handed it to Tom.

"Thanks, Carl. I really appreciate this. I know you trust me."

Carl remained seated at his desk when Tom left the office. Greg was still working out of his briefcase on the lobby couch as Tom headed for the elevators.

Tom spent the rest of the morning hours surfing the Internet and working on his own personal accounting. He checked his e-mail and there was a message from Julie. She was anxious for Friday's party and jotted down a list of supplies they would need. Looks like I'm in for some shopping, he thought.

Gazing out the window, he was mesmerized by the sea of treetops that were interrupted only by streets and buildings close to the Towers. The downtown skyline emerged as a mountain bursting up through the sea of green. Splashes of blue represented three small lakes, one of which was located just beyond the bike trail and the railroad tracks. Waterfowl, searching for food, moved freely above the treetops.

The bike trail was abandoned, except for one person sitting on the bench. Tom was not surprised to see Marcil Huggins as the lone occupier, after focusing on him with the binoculars.

Tom took the elevator all the way down to the lower-level garage. It was quiet and lonely down there, and the sound of the click of his car doors unlocking bounced off the dank walls and ceiling. Police surveillance did not began until 4:00 p.m., according to Jan. He drove his car out onto the boulevard and turned into the Lake's strip mall parking lot. He found a spot right in front of Jensen's Shirts and he entered the shop.

Dalia was busy with a customer but turned, saying, "Good morning, Tom. How are you today? I'll be with you in a minute."

"No problem, Dalia. I have plenty of time."

Dalia remained busy with her lady customer for about ten minutes. After the lady left, Dalia turned to Tom, "I can't believe how much fun it is working on the spreadsheet. I've even taught Cliff how to enter inventory items from invoices. Anything I can do for you today?"

"No, Dalia, I just stopped in to make sure everything was going okay. I'm off to Molly's."

"Have a nice lunch."

Before Tom entered Molly's, he rifled through his briefcase and selected an investment magazine. After being seated, he began thumbing through the magazine. Looking up, he saw Juanita sitting two booths away. She smiled and waved. Tom couldn't help but notice that her hand was glittering with an abundance of jewelry.

Tom remembered Friday's party—he could save a phone call. He rose from his table and approached Juanita. To his surprise, there was a lady sitting opposite Juanita.

"Sorry to bother you ladies, but I need to talk to Juanita for just a moment."

"What is it, Tom? Oh yes, this is my friend, Anna."

"Hi, Anna, nice to meet you. Juanita, I would like to invite you and Carlos to a cocktail party at my apartment on Friday. Anytime after five."

"That sounds like fun. I'll check it out with Carlos this evening."

"I live on the twentieth floor—number twenty-twelve." Removing a business card from his shirt pocket and handing it to Juanita, Tom continued, "My phone number is on the card. Would you call and leave a message after you talk to Carlos?"

"Thank you very much, Tom. I shall do that. *Me gustas*—my pleasure."

"Nice meeting you, Anna," Tom said and returned to his table. He continued reading until lunch arrived.

"Can I get anything else for you?" asked the waitress.

"No, thanks. That will do."

After lunch, Tom drove back to the Towers and parked in the outside lot. When he entered the lobby, Carl was standing and talking to a man dressed in a suit: Detective Anderson. Tom recognized him from their two visits.

"Hello, Mr. Hastings," the detective said.

"You have a good memory, Detective—remembering names," responded Tom.

"It's part of my job. I'll be calling you again for another interview, probably tomorrow."

Carl said to the detective, "Why don't you come in my office, and I'll get the stuff you asked for."

"Okay. Talk to you later, Mr. Hastings."

When Tom arrived at his apartment, he looked out the window overlooking the bike trail. The bench was empty—no Marcil or anyone else. Tom rested on the couch for a few minutes and watched the business news. Later that afternoon, he grabbed his skates backpack and headed down the elevator, getting off at the lobby. Carl and a lady were standing next to the front door.

"You're a busy guy, Tom. Have fun," Carl said.

The bench was still empty when Tom arrived at the bike trail. Skating up the trail, he passed the place where the body of Gloria Tingsley had been discovered. The grass was partially recovered from the trampling it had received during all the activity. Nature's healing powers were at work out there, while the Towers remained in turmoil. It was less than two months since the first murder, but Tom thought it seemed longer.

On the return trip, while approaching the beginning of the bike trail, Tom noticed someone on the bench. Getting closer he wasn't surprised to identify Marcil Huggins. Tom slowed and was pleased when Marcil left the bench and headed across the railroad tracks.

After sitting and changing his footwear, Tom stared at a gum wrapper in the grass, close to the bench. He picked up the wrapper with the tips of his fingers and held it up in front of his glasses. Rather than disturb the wrapping to see the brand name, he gently placed it into his shirt pocket.

After returning to the Towers, his answering machine was beeping with a call from Juanita. Her message was sweet and simple: "Carlos and I will be delighted to come to your party on Friday."

Tom placed the gum wrapper in a small freezer bag.

26

SQUEALING TIRES AND THE LOUD BLAST of a horn greeted Tom Hastings on Tuesday morning as he arrived at the SkyWeb parking lot. The horn was a response to a black Mercedes that had charged from the parking lot into the fast moving traffic. Tom looked at his watch. It was five minutes to ten—he was on time. There was no doubt the driver of the Mercedes was Gordon Beard.

When Tom entered the reception room of SkyWeb, there wasn't anyone at Trisha's desk. He took a seat and could hear giggles and laughter coming from Susan's office. This went on for a couple of minutes until Trisha emerged.

"Oh, there you are, Tom. I didn't hear you come in. Am I in for it today?"

"Good morning, Trisha. I promise to make the learning process as smooth and easy as possible," Tom said, while watching Trisha take her seat. "For starters, I need to borrow your computer for about half an hour."

"No problem. I can work out of Gordy's office. He's gone for the day."

She got up from her chair, being careful to manage her tight, short skirt.

Tom set his briefcase down, opened it and fished out a CD-ROM. The software installed without incident.

Tom walked into Gordon's office and asked Trisha, "Do you have the documents I requested when I was here last time?"

"Sure," she said, while leading him back to her desk. She opened a drawer and pulled out a large folder. "This should be what you need. Let me know if anything is missing."

"Thanks, Trisha."

"If anyone comes in, just let me know," Trisha said.

The creation of a skeletal chart of accounts in the accounting software took up most of the first hour. Tom got up from Trisha's chair and entered Gordon's office.

"I'm all done at your desk for now, Trisha. Could I have access to Gordon's computer?"

"Sure, Tom. Help yourself."

Twenty minutes later, he emerged from Gordon's office and knocked on Susan's door.

"Come on in," she responded.

"Hi, Susan. I guess I'll need to borrow your computer for a few minutes."

"Well, hello, Tom. How are you this morning? I'll take a break right now, so help yourself. Say, thanks for inviting me to your party on Friday."

After finishing with Susan's computer, Tom joined Trisha at her desk and showed her how to enter banking transactions and vendor invoices.

After another hour passed, she said, "My head is spinning, but I think this is going to work."

Susan came out of her office. "Hey, you guys, how about some lunch?"

Trisha replied, "You saved me Susan, thanks."

Tom laughed. "You're doing great, Trisha. We'll spend another hour or two after lunch and call it a day."

Trisha locked the front door and they rode the elevator down to the main floor. Walking two blocks, they entered a small Chinese restaurant. Both the ladies were attractively dressed. Susan wore black slacks and a gold jacket. Trisha's short, tight red skirt turned a few heads.

Their conversations related mainly to the weather, traffic and the accounting program they were working with. There was no mention of the Towers or the party on Friday. Trisha appeared relaxed and in no hurry to return to work.

Susan appeared to be slightly apprehensive. "I have to get back. If you two want to sit longer, go ahead."

"I think it's time for me to get to work also," Tom replied.

Susan used a company credit card to pay for the lunch. Upon returning, Tom noticed the black Mercedes convertible had returned to the parking lot.

When they entered the front office, Gordon's door was closed. Susan proceeded immediately to her office and Trisha and Tom got back to work on the accounting program.

They were working close to half an hour when the door of Gordon's office opened. Much to Tom's surprise, it wasn't Gordon who came through—instead Vito Manchino, obviously upset. He slammed Gordon's office door shut and briskly stepped through the room and out into the hallway. Tom looked at Trisha. She smiled and shrugged her shoulders. There weren't any comments as they continued their work.

Half an hour later, Gordon emerged from his office, his face noticeably pale.

"How's it going, Hastings?" he asked.

"Hello, Gordon—so far, so good. Trisha makes an excellent student. We're about done for today. If we give Trisha a few days to catch up on data entry, I can come back in about a week to review the progress."

"Good going, Trisha. I'll be gone for the rest of the day. Thanks for coming over."

Gordon left. After a few minutes, Susan came out of her office.

"What was that all about?" she asked.

Trisha responded, "Vito was in there with Gordon. They apparently had a little disagreement."

"Oh, so it was Gordon and Vito. I heard the door slam. I didn't think it was Tom."

"No, Susan. It wasn't me."

"How are things going out here?" Susan asked.

"Well, we're about finished for today. As a matter of fact, we are done. Trisha, if you could catch up on the banking transactions, I'll come back next week and we'll set up payroll. If you run into any problems, just give me a call."

"Okay. I'll do the best I can."

Susan returned to her office. Tom packed his briefcase, snapped it shut and left. The black Mercedes was gone when Tom strolled into the parking lot.

On returning to the Towers, he parked in the outside lot and entered the lobby through the rear door. Carl and Jan both turned and looked when they heard the door open.

"There he is. Are you staying out of trouble, Tom?" Carl asked.

"Just out on a job. What's going on around here? Hi, Jan."

"Well, there were some cops around here for awhile this morning. Two detectives went up and met with some of our neighbors. The one in the uniform hung around in the lobby. They're all gone," said Carl.

"Going up?" asked Jan.

"Yup, soon as I pick up the mail."

As Jan and Tom were riding up the elevator, she said, "I think the police are close to an arrest. As nearly as I could make out from their conversations, they were tying up some loose ends."

"Did you talk to any of them?"

"Yes, I talked to Detective Anderson. He didn't say as much, but his body language had that look—the kind you see on TV."

They reached the twentieth floor.

"Glad your flu is better, Jan. See you on Friday, if I don't run into you sooner. Oh, by the way, Jan, do you have Aaron and Kit's phone number?"

"Yes I do, Tom. Hold on a bit and I'll get it for you."

She unlocked her apartment door, entered and left the door open. In a minute, she returned with a small piece of paper.

"Here's their number, Tom. Have a nice evening."

After Tom entered his apartment, he got a beer out of the fridge, twisted off the top, and took a seat overlooking the bike trail. He could see a convoy of mothers and little children making their way up the trail.

Two small push-carriages and four small children dressed in bright colors decorated the landscape. A man walking in the opposite direction had to restrain his dog from intermingling with the children. That's what's missing, Tom thought—hardly any children. The Towers lacked children. When Tom had finished his beer, he couldn't resist the temptation. In a few minutes he was moving up the trail.

Before reaching the second bench, he passed the colorful convoy. Making a slight swerve, Tom avoided a little fellow in a red cap who had wandered off the walking section of the trail.

One of the mothers yelled, "Troy, get back over here."

Tom skated three miles, in about twenty minutes, then pulled over and rested on a bench. On his return trip, the procession of children was gone.

While approaching the Towers end of the bike trail, he noticed someone was sitting on the bench. It wasn't Marcil Huggins—this man had a goatee. Slowing, Tom considered skating over the tracks, not using the bench, and avoiding Phil Bartron. Too dangerous, he thought, and worked his way over to the bench.

"Hello there, Mr. Hastings. I see you're doing your thing."

"Hello, Phil."

"I've got a bad knee or I might give that a try. I heard the most recent Towers murder was next door to you."

"Yes, it sure was. Getting pretty close."

"Did you know the lady that died?"

"No, but I know Joan, the one who lived there."

While strapping on his backpack, Tom looked down at Phil whose face was expressionless. His eyes were glazed, looking beyond Tom toward the sky. There was something sinister about the man. Tom wasn't sure what it was. He felt moments of pity for him.

After walking a few steps from the bench toward the Towers, Tom looked back. Phil was still sitting on the bench, his head down and nestled between his arms—his hands were covering the top of his head.

While Tom was showering, he thought about the expression on Phil's face. That man was dealing with something inside—something **not** very pleasant, he thought.

27

TWO NARROW BLACK EYES, scarcely visible under the brim of a large black hat, greeted Tom Hastings when he sat down on a stool at O'Leary's. The front and rear brim of the hat were turned down. Tom was pleased to see four empty stools at the closed end of the bar on that Wednesday evening, because he wasn't in the mood for visiting. The man wearing the big hat was sitting on the end stool, next to the right pillar.

Tom had seen him at O'Leary's previously—he was the man that wore horn-rimmed glasses, and today, no glasses, but instead a hat. The man turned and looked at Tom. Their eyes locked for a few moments. Tom slowly turned away, not interested in starting up a conversation.

When Tom got the bartender to switch channels to a baseball game, the hat man sitting by the pillar became irritated. He gestured by throwing up both his hands. Tom chose to ignore him and proceeded to eat from an appetizer platter that had just arrived. A couple of innings went by and the hat man got up from his stool.

Tom and he exchanged a strained glance.

The man paused next to Tom when leaving. "Hope you're enjoying the game," he said sarcastically.

The bartender came over and asked Tom, "Do you need a refill?"

"Yeah, I could use one more. Who was that guy sitting over by the pillar?"

"Oh, that's Mr. Crank. Well, that's not his real name, but most of us that work here call him that."

Tom watched the game until the final out in the top of the ninth. The Cubs won another close one. The next day the standings in the Central Division would show the Cubs leading by four games. Almost an entire century had passed since the Cubs had won a World Series. *Could this be the year?*

The lower-level garage at the Towers was quiet when Tom emerged from his car. He looked at his watch. It was 10:45. Tom had just pressed the lock button on his key chain when he spotted movement down at the other end. Remaining in the same position for about a minute, his eyes searched, his ears listened not hearing a sound. He was hoping to see uniformed policemen emerge, but no one did.

Tom quickly moved toward the elevators, continuing to look at the far aisle. Tom had his key ready when he reached the door leading to the elevators. He was pleased to find one of the elevator doors open and waiting. Stepping in, he pressed the 20 button. As the elevator door began closing, the sound of running footsteps outside the elevator caused Tom to hold his breath. A hand reached out to stop the door from closing—it belonged to James.

"That was close. Good evening," James said.

"Hello, Jim. Was that you out in the garage," Tom said and gasped for air.

"No, I came in from the other door."

James pressed number 7. When the elevator stopped, he got off without saying another word.

———

ON THURSDAY MORNING THE PHONE RANG in Tom Hastings' apartment.

Julie said, "Good morning, Tom. Tomorrow's the big day. You didn't forget, did you?"

Tom chuckled. "No, Julie, I didn't. When are you coming over tomorrow?"

"If you're free, I'll come over about noon and take you out to lunch."

"I'll look forward to it."

"Anything new at the Towers?" she asked.

"If there is, I'm not informed. After tomorrow evening we should both know a lot more."

"I talked to Richard in the hallway yesterday. He and Maria are anxious for our party. Well, I need to get back to work. See you tomorrow."

Tom had been seeing Julie for close to three years. They had a warm relationship, sharing their love for nature and other things, such as in-line-skating and tennis. The word *marriage* had never been brought up. They both appeared to be satisfied to live independent lives and enjoy each other's company at frequent intervals.

After Tom hung up, the phone rang again. It was Trisha from SkyWeb. She had some questions about the use of classes in checking transactions. They discussed the particulars of when and where to apply classes.

After ten minutes, Trisha said, "By darn, I've got it. Thanks."

"I'll see you next Tuesday, and we can review the classes and get going on payroll. Have a productive day, Trisha."

Tom hung up and grabbed a coffee. The bike trail looked inviting out the window. Half an hour later, Tom was heading down the elevator carrying his backpack. When he arrived at the lobby, no one was around. He made his way out the back door and out to the bike trail.

While he was changing into skates, a warbling sound drew his attention. Looking up into a tree just behind the bench, he saw a pair of myrtle warbler's flitting amongst the branches—a sign of peace. They held his attention for a couple of minutes, eventually flying away.

Tom had skated the entire four miles of the main trail, stopping to rest at the first available bench during his return. The sensational view of the downtown skyline and the sounds of birds were compromised by the turnpike and the highway noises.

When he reached the beginning of the trail, the bench was empty—no Marcil watching the girls go by, no Phil. Tom sat for a few minutes, enjoying the sounds of the birds and the beautiful sky. Large, billowing white clouds moving silently across the blue background. After changing into tennis shoes, he walked back toward the Towers.

The lobby was deserted—a nice change, he thought. Tom didn't see anyone during the trip up to the twentieth floor. Were the residents on a holiday?

He popped the cap of a beer bottle, grabbed a financial magazine and moved onto the balcony. Daylight was vanishing when Tom heard the first roll of thunder. The spirits must have pulled a lever as daylight converted to darkness in a matter of minutes. Low, fast-moving dark clouds swept in from the west. Down below, he could see swirls of paper debris and dust.

Tom put down his reading and looked off into the distance. A spike of lightning creased the sky, seeming to hang as the bolt struck bottom and lit up like a sparkler for a second or two. Again and again, the lightning shot down from the blackened clouds, pounding the earth. At times, the thunder alternated between gentle rolls and ear-shattering cracks.

The Towers held fast, as it had so many times in the past. Tom imagined the building splitting in two from the electric barrage. With warm feelings, he watched the storm crescendo to a climax and eventually diminish as it moved to the east. Tom was experiencing his first major thunderstorm since living in the high-rise.

One final stab of lightning attacked the bike trail, and it was all over. Daylight returned, and the skyline of downtown Minneapolis glowed in reemerging sunrays. Lightning flashes in the distance continued until a popcornlike white thunderhead appeared. As darkness was imminent, Tom left the balcony and took a position in front of the television.

The next morning, Tom was up early. There was no mention of the storm in the *Star Tribune*. He had a big day ahead, especially with the party coming up. There was plenty of time for a bike trail session, he reasoned. When exiting the elevator at the lobby floor, he saw Jan talking to Carl. They both turned when Tom came through the foyer door.

"Well, there's Mr. Tom, off to the bike trail again, I see," said Carl.

"You're going to wear it out, Tom," chuckled Jan.

"You should try it—not only is it fun, it's healthy."

The trail was littered with twigs and leaves. Tom skated slowly and cautiously. While approaching the second bench, he saw a huge tree, downed by the last night's storm, lying over the trail and extending well onto the railroad tracks.

Stopping in front of the tree, he could hear the sound of a motor approaching from the other side of it. A city maintenance truck came to a stop and three men got out to survey the tree. They started their chainsaws, generating the crackling, whining sounds that Tom had been accustomed to while living up north. He watched for a few minutes, feeling nostalgic while absorbing the aroma of freshly cut oak. His skating session was finished for that day.

On his way back to the Towers, he detoured and called on Jensen's Shirts. There wasn't anyone at the counter when he entered. Cliff came out of the back room. "Can I help you?"

"Hi, Cliff. Where's Dalia?"

"Oh, it's you, Tom. I didn't recognize you at first." He lowered his head and said, "Dalia's in the hospital."

"Oh no," Tom said. "Hopefully, nothing serious."

"We don't know for sure. She had severe pains in her side and they're doing some tests. I'm going over there in about an hour. Hopefully, she can come home."

"Well, give her my best. I hope everything is okay."

"Thanks, Tom."

28

JULIE CALLED AT 11:00 ON THE MORNING OF THE PARTY.

"Hey, did you have a storm over there last night?" Tom asked. "I sure had one over here. The wind knocked down a tree over the bike trail."

"No, Tom, but I could see some lightning flashes over your way. I plan on leaving the office at about eleven-thirty. I should be at the Towers by twelve."

"Okay. See you then. I'll be out in the parking lot. We can take your car over to Molly's."

"Sounds good. See you then."

Tom went down the elevator at 11:50. There wasn't anyone in the lobby as he made his way out to the parking lot. While he was standing and waiting for Julie to arrive, a black Cadillac turned off the boulevard and pulled into the lot.

———

JACK BILLINGS'S PLANE HAD LANDED at Minneapolis-St. Paul International Airport Friday in the morning, a day earlier than originally scheduled. Accustomed to first class, he was irritated with the crowded aisle when getting off the plane. He hated economy class.

The money he'd been expecting from the most recent transaction hadn't been there. He'd argued with his connection in Colombia, but it hadn't done any good. The short man with the mustache had held his ground. U.S. immigration had confiscated the shipment and there'd be nothing for another month—too risky.

Jack didn't think he would have any trouble paying personal bills, it was the inconvenience he dreaded. Moving in with Candice was an option if the money didn't come in the next month. Better be nice to her this weekend, he thought.

His headache returned when he reached the concourse. Jack ducked into a rest room, dropped a pill in his palm from a small bottle, and chased it down with a plastic cup of water. He thought about the first two hours of the flight. It had been excruciating until the medications had deflated the aching in both temples.

He wasn't looking forward to the meeting with Carlos. The Colombian was not going to appreciate his story.

The tall blonde he had met on the jet was waiting for her luggage at the carousel.

"Hello. Did you have a pleasant flight?" Jack asked as he tipped his hat.

"Why, yes. How about you?"

Jack's face reddened, as he hadn't expected a charming, soft response. The lady reached onto the carousel and retrieved her bag.

"Have a nice evening," she said.

Moments later, Jack lifted his suitcase off the carousel. Grabbing the handle and proceeding toward the gate, he passed the taxicab station and spotted the same blonde. She was standing in line, waiting her turn.

He paused next to her and said, "Need a ride? I'm headed north."

"Why, yes, thank you. I hope it won't be too far out of your way. Where do you live? I'm over in the Lake area."

"So am I. My name is Jack."

"Oh, I'm Bette. Nice to meet you."

They chatted during the long walk to the short-term parking lot. After placing the lady's luggage in the back seat, he dropped his own in the trunk.

————

TOM WATCHED THE BLACK CADILLAC slip into a parking slot and come to a stop. The lone occupant sat in the car for a couple of minutes. When the person stepped out and headed for the door, Tom recognized Jack Billings wearing a wide-brimmed Texas-style hat.

As he approached, Tom said, "Hi, Jack. I'm glad to see you arrive in time for our party."

Just then, Julie's red convertible made its appearance in the parking lot. She pulled up to where Jack and Tom were standing.

"Hi, Tom. Hi, Jack," she said.

"You look pretty sharp in those red wheels," Jack said.

Julie laughed and asked, "Are you and Candice coming over for our party later today?"

Jack placed his hand against his right temple. "Well, I think we are. I haven't been home all week. I'll check with Candice to make sure. If you don't hear from us, count us in."

Tom got in the passenger seat of the convertible. Julie circled the lot, made a turn and headed out to the boulevard.

"Take a left at that light," Tom said as a black SUV sped right through the red light.

The wheels of a vehicle coming through the intersection from the other way squealed and smoked as the driver slammed the breaks to avoid the SUV. All other vehicles at the intersection stopped and allowed the second vehicle to clear.

"Boy, that was close. Darn those red light hackers," an irritated Tom expressed.

Julie said, "Tom, I think that was Vito Manchino in that SUV. Did you see him?"

"No, I didn't notice who was driving."

Julie pulled up into an empty space right in front of Molly's. They went inside.

"Hey, nice to see you guys. I've got just the booth for you," boasted Molly proudly.

Following her, Julie and Tom were delighted at her choice. After getting seated, Tom glanced around and recognized Gordon Beard sitting at a table across the room. Seated with him were two men, both strangers to Tom. Julie and Tom each ordered coffee and a salad.

"Julie, I have been trying to get a hold of Aaron and Kit. So far, no luck."

"That's too bad. I was looking forward to seeing them again. Maybe it's not too late to try them again when we get back," said Julie.

"Well, Tom, I heard earlier today that someone is going to be arrested for the Tower murders," she added.

"That's news to me. Where did you hear that?"

"I talked to Richard in the hallway at work today. He sounded serious when he told me."

"Who's going to be arrested?" Tom asked.

"I don't know. He didn't say."

"Well, Richard should be at the party today. Maybe we will find out."

Their salads arrived. "Anything else I can do for you?" the waitress asked.

"No thanks," Tom answered.

As they were nibbling on the salads, Tom lifted his coffee cup for another sip and glanced at the table where Gordon Beard was sitting. One of the two strangers had left. Gordon had both elbows firmly planted on the table while he was talking. The man sitting across from him was shaking his head. Gordon's right elbow lifted and slammed down on the table. The loud bang caused a few heads to turn.

Gordon quickly glanced around the room and put both hands under the table. His visitor across the table shook his head slowly from side to side, got up and left.

"What are you watching?" Julie asked.

"Susan's boss is at a table across the room and appeared to have some sort of fit. Both his guests have left—not a friendly visit."

Julie grabbed the ticket. "That was a great salad. I'm buying the lunch. I'll get this taken care of so we can get on with our shopping."

"Gee, thanks. I don't have the heart to turn you down."

After Julie paid the ticket, they headed out toward her car. Behind the wheel of a vehicle next to her car was one of the men Tom had seen lunching with Gordon Beard. As Julie steered her car away from the parking lot and headed for the boulevard, Tom noticed the man's face was red and he was talking on a cell phone.

The small red convertible dashed into a parking spot at the grocery store. The couple busied themselves adding items to the shopping cart, and Tom was amazed how full it was after Julie had made her final selection.

"Julie, I wonder what our guests will drink. Wine, for sure. How about some gin or scotch?"

"Gin tonics would be good. I would think a guy like Jack probably drinks scotch," she answered.

Weighed down with six bags, they headed for Julie's car and put the bags in her trunk. After they had added three more bags from the liquor store, Julie was turning onto the street, bound for the Towers. She parked the car in the unloading area at garage level and they loaded the bags in a cart. As they were getting the elevators, Jack was approaching from the garage.

"Hi, Jack. Get aboard. I think there's just enough room for all of us," Tom said.

"Wow, looks like quite the load."

"Jack, it took me and three other guys to drag Julie out of the grocery store. Once she gets going, there is no stopping her."

Jack laughed. Julie didn't.

The elevator stopped on the seventeenth floor.

"This is where I get off. See you about five," Jack said.

After the door closed, Julie said, "Now, is this going to be a 'pick on Julie' evening?"

"Naw, just kidding. I appreciate the help."

After rolling the bags into the kitchen, they unloaded the boxes and packages. Tom steered the empty cart into the hallway and into an elevator.

While heading down, the elevator stopped on the seventh floor. James got on—his eyes were glassy. Something was wrong. He was stiff like a sleepwalker, as if some sort of trance.

James didn't seem to be aware of anyone else in the elevator. On the trip down, Tom glanced at him three or four times, but James didn't acknowledge his presence. After James got off at the lobby, Tom continued down to the drop-off area, wondering what was wrong with his barber.

When Tom got back up to the apartment, Julie was well underway with preparing plates of appetizers. The time was approaching 4:00 p.m. and they had one hour remaining before company would begin arriving.

Tom dialed Aaron and Kit's number.

"Julie, no one home at the Alhayas."

29

THE FIRST KNOCK OCCURRED JUST AFTER 5:00. Julie and Tom were sitting on the couch. Both got up and went to the door.

Tom swung it open to Juanita and Carlos. "Hello, Tom. Hello, Julie," said Juanita, smiling and extending her right hand. Tom grasped it and said, "Hi, Carlos. Hi, Juanita. Come on in."

Carlos responded with a greeting in Spanish. He shook Tom's hand while keeping his left hand in his trouser pocket.

"Hello again, Julie," Carlos said and grabbed her right hand with his right and kissed it. "Me gusta, Julie." I like Julie, he thought.

"Come on in and have a seat," Julie said.

Juanita was wearing a stunning black dress. A triple strand of large pearls embraced her neck, and she wore matching bracelets and earrings. The earrings must have been at least two inches long. Carlos's ring finger on his right hand sported an enormous red ruby on a gold ring. Tom wondered how much a ring like that cost.

Julie led them into the living room. Tom proceeded to the kitchen, reached in the fridge and brought out a bottle of white wine. A full bottle of red was already open.

"Anyone care for some wine?" he asked when entering the living room.

The two guests looked at each other, and Juanita said, "Yes, we'll both have some red."

Tom poured them each a glass of cabernet and returned to the kitchen. Moments later he was back in the living room with a bottle of chardonnay. After filling two of the empty glasses on the coffee table, he reached down and handed one to Julie. Sitting next to Juanita, Julie was making it apparent her own travel experiences in Colombia were going to be an interesting topic of discussion with the first guests.

Another knock on the door got Tom up from his chair. "Stay put, Julie. I'll get this one."

Smiling Greg and his serious-faced wife, Jan appeared in the doorway. Tom received and returned a big hug from Jan.

"Hi. Guys. Nice to see you again," Tom said while shaking Greg's hand.

After sending them into the living room, Tom returned to the kitchen for more red wine. Julie took care of the introductions. The neighbors from down the hall were dressed rather casually compared to the first two guests. After filling two glasses with red wine—Greg and Jan always drank red—Tom returned to the living room.

Greg sat down next to Carlos, while Jan walked around looking at the art on the walls. Tom sat in a chair across from the sectional couch and near the front door. After completing her tour of the artwork, Jan returned to the group.

Greg asked Carlos, "What kind of work do you do?"

"As little as possible," he replied, laughing. "No, se´nor Greg. I do medical research associated with the university."

"How about Juanita?"

"Oh, she travels a lot, especially on weekends—She's an airline stewardess for Northwest."

Jan suddenly announced, "Has anyone heard? The police have made an arrest. The murderer has been caught at last."

The room went deadly silent, all eyes on Jan.

She continued, "Just as I suspected, it was Vito Manchino. The police picked him up, and he's in the slammer."

"Geez, when did that happen?" Tom asked.

"This morning," she replied.

Tom caught a glimpse of Carlos's left hand when it pulled partially out of his pocket. A glint of silver, was that what he saw? *Does Carlos have a steel hand?*

Juanita said, "Well, that's a relief. I've been very afraid in the garage by myself. Now I can park and come up the elevator without fear."

The conversation about Vito being arrested was interrupted by a knock on the door. Tom got up from his chair to answer. Candice, Jack and Susan were standing in the hallway. After more greetings, Tom led them into the living room. He introduced the three new guests to Carlos and Juanita.

"Susan, what would you like to drink?" Tom asked.

"Oh, some white wine would be fine. Make it a tall one. I can't believe that Vito was arrested for the murders. I don't know why he would have to kill to get what he wants."

Tom looked into her eyes and frowned. Susan was wearing a short red skirt and a white blouse. Tom noticed Carlos's dark eyes darting back and forth between the two new lady guests. Candice also wore a skirt, a brown one. Jack had on a tan sport coat and black slacks. His belt buckle sparkled with shining stones. An auctioneer would have a field day marketing the buckle, along with Carlos's ring, Tom thought.

"How about you, Candice? What would you like?"

"Same for me."

"And you, Jack?"

"Do you have any scotch?"

"Sure do. Water or soda?"

"Neither—on the rocks will be fine," answered Jack, who was visibly uplifted by the announcement of the arrest.

Julie got up from her position on the sectional and said, "Tom, I'll get the wines. Would you get Jack's scotch?"

"Sure will," Tom replied.

While turning, before approaching the kitchen, Tom noticed that Jack had sat down by Susan on one end of the sectional. Candice, Jan, Greg and Juanita were clustered on the other end. Carlos was sitting alone between the two groups.

Julie was opening a bottle of wine when Tom reached the kitchen. He gave her a gentle tap on the butt. She looked over her shoulder and smiled. "Not now," she said while pushing up against him. "Later."

When Tom got back to the living room, all the wineglasses had been filled. Jack gazed at Tom, apparently anxious for his drink.

"Here you are, Jack," Tom said, handing him the scotch and ice. "Hey, Carlos, are you doing okay over there?"

"Yeah, Tom, I am. Good wine."

Jan explained something to Candice, when she said in a firm, loud voice, "Oh, that's impossible, Jan. Vito couldn't have done all the killings." All conversation ceased, and Candice had the floor.

A knock at the door broke the silence. Tom got up and opened it to Maria's warm smile—a firm handshake from Richard, who was wearing a black shirt and tan trousers. Maria had on a blue denim dress. Cute girl, Tom thought.

"Welcome to my home. Come on in and meet some people."

Tom introduced Maria and Richard to the guests in the living room. Jack, Julie and Susan were in the kitchen. The most recent arrivals sat on the sectional: Maria next to Juanita and Richard next to Candice.

Tom left the room and moved into the kitchen, where Jack and Susan were engaged in conversation. Jack's glass was full to the brim. He'd apparently mixed himself another scotch. Julie was working on a second batch of appetizers.

"How are you doing?" Tom asked Julie.

"Just fine, Tom. I'll have the goodies out there in a minute. I see Richard and Maria arrived."

"Yeah, they just got here. Need any help carrying the stuff?"

"Oh, thanks, Tom. These two plates are ready."

Tom returned to the living room and set the plates down, one on each coffee table in front of the sectional. Richard was talking to Candice, and they were sitting embarrassingly close to each other. Carlos had gotten up from his original position and moved over next to Jan on the other side of the sectional. Juanita was alone and raised an empty glass toward Tom.

"I'll be right back, Juanita," Tom said, heading to the kitchen. He grabbed a half-full bottle of red wine and returned to the living room. Juanita was missing—probably in the bathroom.

Jack entered the room and said, "Oh, there you are." He sat down next to Candice, who was in the process of moving away from Richard. Maria and Juanita walked in from the direction of the bathroom.

"Here's your glass, Juanita," Tom said.

"Thanks, Tom."

"How about you, Maria—do you need anything?"

"No, I'm fine, Tom. Thanks."

Richard got up from the sectional, stepped over to Maria and gave her a light hug. She shied away from him, saying, "Richard, maybe we should go."

Greg had gotten up from the couch. "Oh, come on, Maria, the party has just begun."

Richard turned toward Maria and smiled, adding, "Yeah, Maria, we don't get out that often."

"Well, I certainly don't, but you sure do." Maria shrugged her shoulders and walked away. She sat down on the far end of the sectional and raised her wineglass to her mouth. Tom watched as she gulped most of the wine down. Richard sat down by Juanita.

Jack looked at Carlos. "How's the research business, Carlos?"

Carlos's face flushed when he responded, "It's slowed down for me recently. How about you?"

"That's the way it is with exports and imports. Have you ever heard of International Oceanic?"

"No, se´nor, I have not heard of it. What do you import from Colombia?"

"Coffee, sir. Coffee."

Tom glanced toward the balcony where Greg and Jan were standing. They had separated from the group and appeared to be engaged in conversation.

Tom noticed their wineglasses were almost empty so he poked his head through the door leading to the balcony. "Hey, either one of you need any more wine?"

"Sure, Tom," said Greg. "I could use a little more red, thanks."

"How about you, Jan?" Tom asked.

"No thanks, Tom. I've had enough for now."

Tom backed up a step into the living room and turned. He noticed Carlos was talking to Richard in the corner of the room, beyond the sectional. Richard's defensive facial expression caused Tom to wonder what Carlos was telling him. The Colombian's penetrating, shiny dark eyes were locked on Richard, who was listening intently to a barrage of fast talk.

Jack got up and headed for the kitchen. He was helping himself and didn't need Tom's help with drinks any longer.

Candice got up from the sectional and walked over to Tom. "Nice party, Tom. What do you think of Vito being arrested for the murders?"

"Well, Candice, I really don't know what to think. The police must have pretty good evidence to arrest him for all three. How do you feel about all that? I heard you express some doubt earlier in the evening."

"Well, Tom, without going into details, I can tell you for sure that Vito wasn't anywhere near Tamara Oxley when she was killed."

"Gee, Candice, if you are so sure, why don't you go to the police?"

"I just can't—just can't. Not now."

Tom stood there with a puzzled look as Candice slowly walked away. She walked into the kitchen and came out moments later with Jack.

"We have to go, Tom. Thanks so much."

"Glad you could make it. Get enough to eat, Jack?"

"Oh yes, Tom. Too much."

Tom watched as the two of them headed for the door. He noticed that no one was sitting. Susan and Jan were standing by the television, and Richard was in the process of joining them. Càrlos was in the kitchen talking to Julie and Greg and Maria were standing oñ the balcony. Tom looked at his watch—it was almost eight.

Carlos came in from the kitchen and joined Tom, who was talking to Juanita.

"*Te gusta el libro?*" Juanita asked Tom.

Tom looked at her, rather puzzled.

Juanita laughed. "The book, Tom—did you like the book we were talking about?"

Carlos smiled and butted in. "We'll be leaving soon, Tom. I would like to thank you for inviting us. You have some interesting friends."

"Glad you could come." Tom shook Carlos's right hand and guided the two toward the door. When he turned around, Richard and Maria were approaching.

"My wife is dragging me home," said Richard.

Maria looked irritated. "Well, if you would just keep your hands to yourself, there wouldn't be a problem."

Tom cleared his throat, somewhat embarrassed by what Maria had said. He lifted his chin. "Thanks for coming."

They left.

Susan was the next to leave. As she made her first step into the hallway, a thumping noise beyond the corner of the hallway drew their attention. Tom watched with interest as Susan walked toward the noise. After rounding the corner, she raised a hand to her mouth, and her knees bent slightly. Tom knew something was wrong. He quickly ran to her side and saw Richard lying on the carpet. Maria was holding his hand and crying.

"What happened?" Tom asked.

"He hit him. Jack hit Richard, then he went down the elevator," sobbed Maria.

Tom knelt down by Richard and saw blood oozing from a cut in his lip. "Are you okay?" he asked Richard.

Richard laughed. "Wow, thin skin—Jack has a thin skin."

Tom helped Richard to his feet. Maria fetched a napkin from her purse and gently blotted Richard's lip. Susan escorted Richard and Maria onto the elevator.

When Tom returned to the living room, Jan, Greg and Julie were sitting on the sectional.

"What did Candice tell you about Vito?" asked Jan.

"No more than what she told the group," Tom answered.

"Well, I think there is something fishy going on there," responded Jan.

"Oh, come on, Jan. Give her a break," said Greg.

Irritated, Jan said, "Let's go home, Greg."

Tom was surprised that the commotion by the elevator went unnoticed by those remaining in his apartment. He made no mention of the knockdown incident to either Greg or Jan.

After their last two guests had left, Julie and Tom sat out on the balcony.

"Julie, there were some fisticuffs out by the elevator."

She looked at Tom with wonderment. "What do you mean, fisticuffs?"

"Apparently, Jack decked Richard. He was lying on his back on the carpet when I got out there."

"Who was lying on his back?" asked Julie.

"Richard. He had a cut in his lower lip. There was some blood."

"Too close—he got too close to Candice."

"Yeah, I noticed that—and Jack had a lot of scotch. The bottle is half empty."

Julie said, "It's four to three."

"What's four to three?" asked Tom.

"The vote on Vito's guilt."

30

JULIE AND TOM HEADED OVER TO MOLLY'S on the morning after the party. They had just gotten seated and were studying their menus when Greg and Jan entered the restaurant. Jan spotted Tom and put her hand on Molly's shoulder to get her attention.

Leading Greg to Julie and Tom's table, Jan asked, "Okay, if we join you two?"

"By all means. Sit down you guys," Tom replied.

Julie said, "Well, did you learn anything at the party yesterday?"

"Yeah," said Greg, "I learned that everyone is a suspect—even me. You definitely are one, Tom."

"Oh come on, Greg. That's not nice," said Jan. "How about you, Julie? What did you learn?"

"Well, I had long talks with both Jack and Richard. You can cross those two guys off your list. They may have agendas, but murder isn't one of them. Richard is too busy hustling ladies to even consider reducing their numbers."

Jan sneered at the last statement and added, "Richard is a rookie compared to Jack. Did you notice the small, beady dark eyes, and how they looked all us girls up and down? I thought his eyes were going to burn a hole in Susan's red dress."

Tom said, "Geez, guys, were we all at the same party? I didn't notice any of that stuff."

Julie smiled. "You're getting old, Tom."

When their breakfasts arrived, conversation ceased for a few minutes.

"Julie, how do you feel about playing some tennis this afternoon?"

"Tom, that sounds like a nice idea, but I need to get my apartment cleaned up before Alice comes over. We have tickets for a concert tonight."

Jan asked, "Who's Alice?"

"We went to college together. She recently lost her husband and I try to spend some time with her now and then."

After the waitress returned their signed credit card slips, they got up from the booth and headed for the door.

"See you later, Molly," Tom said.

"Thanks for coming, guys."

Greg and Jan split off from them and headed for their car, parked at the opposite end of the lot. Julie and Tom left in the red convertible. The tennis courts were busy, but they found an empty one and played a couple of sets.

"Well, Tom, I think it's time for me to get home. Thanks for the party. I was impressed that you didn't mention the Richard-Jack incident."

"No, they'll find out soon enough. Thank you, Julie. You did most of the work."

Julie dropped Tom off at the Towers and watched as the little convertible streaked onto the boulevard.

Back in his apartment, Tom checked the newspaper sports page and noticed the Braves were playing in Florida. Game should be on television this evening, he thought. O'Leary's will have the game.

At seven, Tom got on the elevator and pressed the B button for the lower-level garage. There was plenty of light in the entry area, but farther down, especially in the corners, it was dimly lit.

If Vito Manchino did commit the murders, then the place is safe, thought Tom. If he didn't...Tom felt a stab of fear. Quickly, he moved into his car and drove out into the street.

The parking lot in front of O'Leary's was full. Going to be crowded in there, Tom thought. After circling the lot twice, he found an empty space.

On entering O'Leary's, Tom excused his way past a number of people waiting to be seated. Without hesitating, he occupied an empty stool at the closed section of the bar. When the bartender came over, Tom ordered a beer and asked for the remote control.

"Sure, Mr. Hastings. Help yourself."

Tom clicked until the baseball game appeared. The Marlins were leading the Braves two to one in the second inning.

The gentleman sitting next to Tom was reading a folded newspaper. He looked up and asked, "How are the Twins doing?"

The man's eyes behind the thick, horn-rimmed glasses looked small. Tom realized immediately it was the same person who had given him a bad time when he'd changed channels before.

"The Twins played this afternoon. I'm watching the Braves and Marlins," Tom answered, and continued to look at the television.

"Oh," the man replied, and continued reading the newspaper.

Glancing down the left side of the bar, Tom could see Phil Bartron visiting with a lady seated next to him. On the other side, Carlos Valdez was sitting on a stool and looking in Tom's direction. Tom gestured by raising the palm of his right hand. Carlos smiled. Tom wondered where Juanita was. It was the first time he'd seen Carlos alone. Oh, yes, she was an airline stewardess—likely out of town a lot.

The third inning ended and was followed by a series of commercials, allowing Tom to divert his attention away from the television. The lady sitting next to Phil had gone. Probably couldn't handle the rhetoric, thought Tom. Phil was now focusing his attention on the man sitting to his left. The man honored Phil with a nod now and then, and before the fourth inning started, he, too, got up and left. Tom was glad he hadn't an empty stool next to himself.

The man to Tom's right put away his newspaper and asked, "Your team winning?"

"Actually, the game is tied. We got a lucky run in the top of the third to tie the score at two each."

"Well, it's time for me to head out—pretty quiet around here this evening." He left, leaving an empty stool. Minutes later, Tom felt a slight nudge on his right elbow. It wasn't Phil—it was Carlos.

"Good evening, se´nor Tom. I see you like your baseball."

"So, is Juanita flying this evening?"

Carlos laughed. "Yeah, Juanita will be gone all weekend. She's on an overseas flight."

"Does she always do the overseas flights?" asked Tom.

"Yes, she does."

The next inning started, and he refocused on the television. Without looking at Carlos, he asked, "Don't they have baseball in Colombia?"

"Oh yes—very good."

The Braves dodged a bullet in the bottom of the fourth. The Marlins had the bases loaded with nobody out. Somehow they managed to escape without giving up a run. Tom did a little clap when the inning ended with a pop-up to the second baseman.

"Time for me to go," said Carlos.

"Hello to Juanita when she gets home. Thanks for coming to the party yesterday."

"Thank you, Tom. See you later."

After Carlos had gone, Tom glanced to the left and noticed that Phil Bartron's stool was empty. Hastings' turn to leave came after the seventh inning, with the score still tied at two.

While Tom was walking to his car, the parking lot seemed darker than usual, and an eerie feeling came over him. Was he being watched? Probably my imagination, he thought. A couple of minutes later, Tom pulled into his parking spot in the lower-level garage. While walking toward the exit door, he noticed a red sports car across the aisle. Someone was sitting in the driver's seat.

Tom hesitated, wondering why someone would be sitting in the car. He stopped, turned and looked back.

Whoever was in the car wasn't moving. Cautious as a highway patrolman, he approached the car from the rear. Tom thought of the flashlight in his car, but it wasn't worth the effort. When Tom reached the front, driver's side window, he bent over slightly to get a better look. The lone occupant appeared to be asleep. It was a man—Richard.

31

TOM KNOCKED ON THE WINDOW, getting no response. Pulling on the handle, he felt the resistance of a locked door. As feelings of panic emerged, he looked around the parking area, hoping to see someone to ask for help. Tom was alone.

Leaving Richard in the car, he readied his key while hastening to the door leading to the elevators. After he negotiated the corridor, the wait at the elevator seemed extraordinary, at the least. When the door finally opened, he punched M, for the lobby.

Tom looked at his watch on the way up—it was almost 10:00. When the door opened to the lobby level, he was hoping to see a police patrol, but the lobby was empty. He dashed over to Carl's office door. There was no one sitting at the desk.

He was at a loss for what action to take. There always seemed to be patrol officers around, but not this time, when they were really needed.

Tom got back in the elevator and went up to his apartment. He called Greg and Jan.

"Hello," Tom heard a sleepy Jan say.

"Jan, this is Tom. There's something weird going on in the garage."

"What is it, Tom? What's wrong?"

"Do you remember Richard, who was at our party?"

"Yes, the hustler who got what he deserved by the elevator."

"He's down in his car and appears to be asleep. I just came from the garage."

"Hey, that sounds like an emergency. Did you notify the office?"

"There wasn't anyone there. The patrol guys weren't around either."

"I'll get Greg up. Give us a minute to get dressed."

"Okay, I'll be waiting in the hallway."

Should I call Carl? No, I'll stay with Greg and Jan first. The three of us will decide what to do. Tom looked up at his clock. Only one minute had passed since calling Jan—time was moving slowly. After two minutes had passed, he proceeded down the hallway and waited by their door.

Soon, the door burst open. Jan, her face excited, led a sleepy-looking Greg out of the apartment.

"This better be good," said Greg, dazed.

Tom had pressed the Down button on the elevator wall on his

way to Jan and Greg's. He saw the elevator door opening as Jan asked, "Did you try wake him?"

Tom turned and rushed to the elevator to keep it from closing. Jan and Greg followed, and they all got into the elevator.

"Yeah, I rapped on the window and he didn't respond. Do you suppose...Naw, it couldn't be."

"Couldn't be what?" said Jan. "Another murder?"

"Geez, what do you think I should do? Call Carl? What do you guys think?"

"Why don't the three of us go down and have a look?" suggested Jan.

"Yeah, that's what I had in mind. Maybe we can wake him up," responded a more confident Tom. "Oh, thanks for getting dressed so fast. I didn't really know whom I should call first—Carl, or perhaps the police. I've been hoping to see the patrol show up. Maybe they're down there now."

When the elevator door opened, Tom led the way, proceeding to the garage. He led them to the red car. Tom was about to say, here he is, when he stopped himself. He wasn't sure whether to feel shocked or relieved. Richard was not in the car.

32

"SO, HOW DO YOU EXPLAIN THIS?" asked Jan firmly. She raised her chin and tilted her head.

"Hey, I was sober when I came home. I'm not whacko. Richard was sitting right there just a few minutes ago. There is no way I could have imagined something like that. His eyes were closed and he looked asleep."

"Could you see if he was breathing?" asked Greg.

"No, I couldn't tell—but then, I really wasn't looking for that. Well, I suppose there is no point in calling Carl—or anyone else. It's a good thing I didn't get Carl down here. He wouldn't have appreciated being woken up for no reason. Bad enough that I have to face up to you guys."

Greg said, "Why don't we go up to the lobby. The night attendant has to be around somewhere. Maybe the patrol guys will show up."

Nothing more was said as they made their way to the lobby. To their irritation, there wasn't a soul around.

"Where do you suppose everyone is?" asked Jan anxiously. "Heck, let's head home. I don't like the looks of this."

Willingly, Tom and Greg followed her into the elevator. When it reached the twentieth floor, Jan said, "Why don't you come in for a few minutes, Tom?"

"Perfect idea. I need to unwind a bit before going home."

"Well, I imagine there's a perfectly good reason why Richard would have been snoozing in his car," said Greg.

"Like what—being drunk maybe?" retorted Jan.

"Or perhaps—drugs can do that, you know," Greg added.

"What bothers me is the fact I rapped on that window pretty hard. He didn't budge. Not the slightest movement," explained Tom.

"Somehow, I feel Richard owes you an explanation, Tom. So, what are we to do about this? Should one of us knock on Richard and Maria's door tomorrow morning? I believe they live on the nineteenth floor."

"Ah, nineteen-thirty if either of you two are interested," said Tom. "Or maybe, we can post Greg down in the lobby and wait for either Maria or Richard to make an appearance."

"Oh sure—great way to spend a Sunday," sneered Greg.

"Well, guys, I feel a bit better now. Think I'll go home. If there is anything to this, I am sure we will hear about it," responded Tom.

"We'll check with you tomorrow," said Jan.

"Good night guys. Thanks for going down with me, and for the coffee," Tom said and headed back to his apartment.

Tom called Julie. She had just gotten home. "Up kind of late, aren't you?" she asked.

"I have another story."

"What is it? For heaven's sake, spit it out."

Tom explained going to O'Leary's and later discovering Richard sitting and sleeping in his car. "There wasn't anyone in the office or anywhere so I talked with Jan and Greg. Then, when we got down into the garage, Richard was gone."

"So he fell asleep for a bit and then woke up and went home. Considering his lifestyle, that sort of fits, doesn't it?"

"Well, perhaps, but it's the first time I've run across anyone asleep in the garage. The last person who was discovered asleep in that garage was Tamara Oxley. She was asleep for good, remember that?"

"If I see Richard prancing up and down the hallways on Monday, as I fully expect, the joke will be on you."

"Actually, Julie, some of my neighbor sleuths may find out what's going on long before Monday. They have a whole day for sleuthing tomorrow."

"Hey, I was thinking about driving up for some tennis tomorrow. Will you be up for it?"

"Oh, you're darn right. Come on out mid-morning and I'll beat your butt."

"How about eleven?"

"Sounds good to me. See you then," said Tom. If Richard were still in the car when they got down there last night, he would have called 911—he was sure.

33

TOM HASTINGS WAS GREETED WITH SPLATTERING RAINDROPS on the bedroom window on Sunday morning. After waking, he lay there thinking about Richard, and feeling a building guilt for not calling 911 the night before. It wasn't my fault, he attempted to convince himself. The attendant wasn't in the office— no police officers, either.

The tennis outing he was planning with Julie was on the back burner at the moment. His insides were telling him to check with Carl about Richard. Whoops, today is Sunday, he thought. Carl may not be down in the office. It's worth a try, anyhow.

After getting dressed, he called Julie. "How's the weather over there? It's drizzling here."

"It's raining here, too."

"According to the forecast, it's supposed to clear up early afternoon. Why don't you come over about four? Should be okay to play tennis by then. By the way, the new *Pearl Harbor* movie is on tonight. How about taking it in?"

"Great idea, Tom. I've heard a lot of good things about that movie. See you at four. Oh, have you heard anything more about what happened to Richard?"

"No, but I'm going to check it out in the lobby when I go down. Hopefully, nothing big happened."

The rain bought Tom some time to deal with the Richard incident. He decided to walk to Molly's for a late breakfast and visit the office on the way. Tucking the Sunday newspaper under his left arm, he grabbed an umbrella from the closet.

Glancing in the lobby office, he was glad to see Carl sitting at the desk.

After knocking on the door trim, Tom said, "Hi, Carl. Working on Sunday, huh?"

"Yeah, Fritz left us last night. It won't happen again. I fired him. Should have a new person for tonight."

"Carl, I came home last night about ten. After parking in the garage, I noticed Richard Fallon sitting in his car. He appeared to be asleep. Since there was no one in here, I brought Jan and Greg down. We went down to check him out—he was gone. Is that any big deal?"

"Ah, not as far as I know, Tom. There's been nothing reported. He may have fallen asleep and then left before you guys got down there."

"Well, I hope that's what happened. You know, Carl, everyone is pretty nervous around here. Anything beyond normal is going to get reported."

"Yeah, Tom, I understand. I've been trying to talk the detective in to increasing the patrols. So far, he said they're stretched and can't do any more right now."

"Thanks, Carl. I think I'll get on with the day," responded Tom, and he left the office.

Tom snapped open his umbrella before leaving the building. The rain was lessening in intensity and the birds were chirping up a storm as Tom walked toward the Lake's strip mall. The sky should be clear by four, he thought.

The boulevard separating the Towers area from the strip mall was as busy as ever. Crossing on foot was a challenge. Reliance on pedestrian green lights was no assurance of safety. Tom noticed six vehicles speed through the intersection after the light had changed to red. Tom rushed across the boulevard, barely beating the roar of motors and squeal of wheels. Tom's mind was preoccupied with thoughts of Richard, asleep in his car—or another victim.

"Good morning, Tom. Just one?" Molly greeted him, smiling.

"Yup, just me."

She led him to a booth in the nonsmoking section. He was well into the business section of the newspaper when a waitress brought him a pot of coffee. "Anything I can get you?" she asked.

"Yeah, I'll have number five."

"How would you like your eggs?"

"Over and medium."

"Thanks." She quickly picked up the menu and left.

When the waitress returned with his food, he set the newspaper down and looked around the room. Marcil Huggins was sitting by himself at a table next to the entry. His face was buried in a book.

After finishing his breakfast, Tom headed for the door. Marcil looked up and said, "Hello, Hastings."

"Too rainy on the bench this morning, Marcil?"

Marcil's face tightened and seemed confused by Tom's comment. Setting down his book, Marcil said, "A novel by Mercer. It's a fascinating story about a serial killer, based on a true story—took place in New Jersey."

"Sounds like the Towers," commented Tom.

"Is your girlfriend Julie coming over today?"

Tom was surprised that Marcil knew Julie's name. "Yes, she is. Say, Marcil, you live on the fifteenth floor, don't you?"

"Yes, I do. Is that a problem?"

"I was wondering if you know the Fallons, Richard and Maria. I think they live on the nineteenth."

Marcil looked out the window. "No, I don't. Why do you ask? Why are they important?"

"Ah, no special reason—just wondered."

Marcil returned to his book. Tom left his table and walked out into the parking lot. He glanced back at the restaurant windows, seeing Marcil through one of them. Even though Marcil's remained up, it didn't appear as if he was reading. His eyes appeared closed.

When Tom arrived back at the Towers, he entered through the front door. Jan and Carl were standing in the lobby. She was talking and he was listening. Tom had a pretty good idea what they were talking about.

Carl looked at Tom. "Well, hello, Tom. You haven't seen Richard around, have you?"

"No, sure haven't. Anything new?"

"No, but I'm not blowing the whistle on that one just yet. I called the Fallons' apartment this morning, but no one answered. I'll wait a bit before checking out their apartment."

Tom had experienced an agonizing thought: *What if Richard was the serial killer?* He may have been resting after committing another— faking sleep when I was looking at him through the window.

Jan piped in, "If he was dead, how could he have been moved that quickly? Why, we were down there within ten minutes of when Tom saw him."

"Yeah, he probably went right up to his apartment," Carl responded. "Well, I've got to get back to work."

"Are you going up, Tom?" Jan asked.

"Yup, want to ride along?"

"Sure," she responded, and they entered an elevator.

Partway up, Jan exclaimed, "That couldn't have been Richard in the car last night."

"Why not?"

"I just remembered. Richard and Maria drove to Madison yesterday morning to visit her parents."

"Who told you that?"

"Not sure. I heard it somewhere, probably in the lobby."

34

TOM'S PHONE RANG A FEW MINUTES SHORT OF FOUR. Julie had arrived. After pressing six on the phone to buzz her in, he regretted not meeting Julie downstairs, even though it was midafternoon.

A few minutes passed before he heard the knock on his door. Eagerly rushing to the door, he was relieved to see Julie standing in the hallway with an excited look on her face.

"Hi, Julie. You have that look. What's up?"

Julie entered and took a seat on his couch.

"I rode up the elevator with one of your favorite people, Marcil Huggins. As he was getting off on the fifteenth floor, I asked him if he knew the Fallons. He held the elevator door opened and said, 'Oh, you mean Richard and Maria'."

"Strange, when I asked him the same question at Molly's this morning, he denied knowing either one of them," Tom replied.

"Well, that's not all. He also said the Fallons aren't going to be around for awhile because they're out of town."

"Geez, what do you suppose that means? How the devil could he conclude that, unless he knows something that we don't know?"

"If I were the cops, I'd pull Marcil in right away. He'd be my number one suspect," Julie sharply retorted.

"So, you don't think Vito is guilty?"

"No, I don't, not after hearing what Candice had to say."

"Well, it's not up to us. Are you all set for tennis? We better get going before it rains again."

"Okay, Tom. I'm all set. My racquet and shoes are in my car."

They headed down the elevator. It stopped on the seventeenth floor and the door opened. Jack Billings was standing there waiting.

He looked pale. He got on and said in a weak voice, "Hello, lovers. You two stay real busy, don't you?"

Julie replied, "Yup, we're headed out to the courts. How about you?"

"Oh, I'm just going for a walk. I need some fresh air."

Everyone got off at the lobby level. Jack headed out the front door. Tom and Julie strolled up the hallway leading to the outdoor parking lot.

When they got outside, Julie said, "Did you see how pale Jack was? He must have had a tough night."

"Yeah, I noticed," replied Tom.

"I wonder what the deal is between Jack and Candice. I think they have separate apartments," responded Julie.

"All kinds of people out there, Julie," Tom replied.

The parking lot at the tennis courts was almost full. After Julie found a spot, they slipped on their court shoes and walked along one side of the fence looking for an empty court. The sound of tennis balls getting stroked across the net enhanced their enthusiasm. After passing by two pairs of occupied courts, they claimed an empty one at the far end.

The problems at the Towers were temporarily put aside during the first set. Julie cashed in on a series of short drops just over the net to keep the game close. Tom's consistency held her to winning three games during the first set. She failed to return a deep serve and lost six to three.

After returning to the bench for a break, Julie asked, "I wonder what's really happened to Richard?"

"Boy, I sure don't know. The whole thing is really weird. I think we will know a lot more tomorrow when they supposedly return from Madison."

"Did you notice if Richard's car was down in the garage?"

"No. I haven't been down in the garage since last night with Greg and Jan."

"After tennis, let's go down and check."

"Okay. Are you ready for another set?"

"Sure am," Julie replied, and they charged back onto the court.

After a second set, they returned to Julie's car and she drove back to the outdoor parking lot at the Towers.

"Let's go up and shower. I have some stuff to nibble on before we go to the movie."

"Okay, but let's take your car to the movie, Tom. Then we can check out Richard's car."

An hour later, they were on their way down the elevator to the lower-level garage. Tom wasn't sure what they were going to find, and he was afraid. After turning a corner and heading toward his car, Tom eyed the red sports car.

"Richard's car is still here, Julie," he anxiously muttered.

He led Julie to the red sports car parked across the aisle from his. Bending down, he peaked into the driver's side window.

Julie was right behind him, and she exclaimed, "Look, Tom, the keys are in the ignition!"

Tom was tempted to try the door handle. "I don't think we should touch anything, Julie. You never know where this is going to lead."

Julie drew a napkin from her purse, and using it as a glove, she carefully pulled on the door handle. It opened.

Tom stepped back from the car while Julie stuck her head in and glanced around.

"Hey, Tom, look here. Not only are the keys in the ignition but there is a briefcase on the floor on the passenger side."

Julie stepped away, allowing Tom to look inside and see.

"Geez, this doesn't look right at all. We didn't notice this last night. Jan really took a look in there. You would think she would have noticed the keys."

"This is weird. Who leaves keys in their car, especially with a briefcase in there?" asked Julie.

Both Tom and Julie were startled when a beam of light appeared from between two cars.

"Okay, you two, hold it right there," said a voice coming from beyond the beam.

Tom and Julie froze. Julie's mouth was partially open, her arms out front, not far from Tom's.

The flashlight was lowered, and they could see two police officers approaching.

"Can we see your identifications, please?" asked one of the

officers. Julie began fumbling in her purse. "Can I have that?" the officer asked.

"Yes, sure," replied Julie and handed it to him.

Tom had pulled out his driver's license and was holding it in his outstretched hand.

The second officer examined it. "I see you live here. Is that your car?"

"No, it isn't—it's rather a long story."

"Story, huh? Well, let's hear it."

Meanwhile, the first officer had ended his examination of Julie's purse. He asked her, "Would you find your ID for me?" he asked.

While Julie was looking for her wallet, Tom began explaining why they were standing by the red sports car. When he'd finished, the officer said, "Okay, let's go up to the office."

The other officer was shining the flashlight on Julie's license. "So, you don't live here—he does?"

"That's right. We were out playing tennis."

Tom and Julie walked ahead of the officers. They took the elevator up to the lobby level. When the elevator door opened, Phil Bartron, toothpick in mouth, was waiting. His frown and narrow eyes made his goatee appear longer than ever.

The four occupants brushed past him on the way to the office. Carl looked up from his chair and laughed, "Aha! I see you've snared someone. What evil deed were they doing?"

"Mr. Hastings, would you explain to us and the manager what you were doing hanging around the red sports car?" said one of the officers.

"Well, as I told you before, we were checking out our friend, Richard Fallon. He was in his car last night, asleep apparently. Later he disappeared, and now we noticed the keys in the ignition and a briefcase on the floor."

"What? What's this about the keys and a briefcase?" asked Carl.

"That's what we'd like to know, Carl. Julie spotted them when she looked through the window. We were curious. Remember how we talked about that earlier—about Richard, and how he may have fallen asleep and then went to his apartment?"

One of the officers interrupted. "You two will need to explain all of this to Detective Anderson."

Tom was becoming agitated and he responded, "Look, if you two guys were here last night when you were supposed to be, we wouldn't be in this office right now."

"Now, don't get huffy, mister. We're just doing our job," replied one of the officers.

"Ah, I can vouch for these two," said Carl. "Why don't you call your detective, and we'll go up and check out the Fallon apartment."

"Let's go check it out right now," replied the officer.

The lock clicked as Carl's key turned in the door of nineteen-twenty-two.

"You three stay here and we'll take a look around," said one of the officers.

There was only the sound of heavy breathing in the hallway as the two officers did a preliminary search of the apartment.

"Hmm...no one at home and nothing seems to be out of place," reported one of them when they returned.

"Is it okay if we go back to our apartment?" asked Julie. "I need to go to the ladies room."

"Yeah, sure. We're done with you two for now. You can expect a call from Detective Anderson, and soon."

Julie and Tom got on an elevator going up, leaving the two officers and Carl standing in the hallway.

"Well, whose idea was that anyhow, to go check Richard's car out—huh, Julie?"

"I'm sorry, Tom, but we didn't do anything wrong," answered Julie contritely.

"Oh heck, what can we do about it anyhow. Let's head for the movie regardless," responded Tom.

There was a line at the ticket counter. Tom joined the end of it while Julie headed for the popcorn counter. As Tom was advancing in the ticket line, he was thinking of Richard's car and the briefcase. The smell of movie theatre popcorn brought him back to realizing he was in a movie house. He glanced toward the inside lobby and could see Julie, who was cradling a tub heaped with popcorn in both arms.

"Two for *Pearl Harbor*," Tom told the dark-hair lady working the ticket counter.

He joined Julie in the lobby, passing the tickets to a red-jacketed usher, who tore them in two and returned the stubs to Tom's hand. Julie was carrying the tub of popcorn as they entered the sparsely lighted movie room.

After Tom and Julie had endured six unsolicited previews, the main feature finally started. It took Tom and Julie back into history as they watched small propeller-driven airplanes swooping and dropping bombs. Tom had been only a little boy when the war started, Julie hadn't even been born. The little people on the ground were running in all directions trying to find shelter. Most American fighter planes went up in flames, hit while they were parked on the ground. Tom wasn't sure what Julie was thinking, but his thoughts kept drifting back to Richard's car.

After the movie ended, they drove back to the Towers. Tom drove the car through the garage door, turned onto the aisle leading to his parking place.

Julie exclaimed, "Look, Tom, the car is gone!"

Tom slowed his car to a stop. They stared at the empty parking spot where Richard's car had been sitting just before the movie. Tom parked, grabbed Julie's hand and moved quickly toward the exit.

"The plot thickens," said Tom as they stood and waited for an elevator. "Where do you suppose the car has gone?"

"Maybe Richard came home and drove it off," answered Julie, "or maybe something else happened, and the cops drove it off."

"In either case, I'm as thirsty as could be—it's the salty popcorn," said Tom.

"Yes, I am thirsty, too. I'll come up and have something to drink, and then I should really be getting home. Tomorrow morning is going to be busy."

When they got off on the twentieth floor, Tom noticed a sliver of light under Greg and Jan's door. Perhaps they will still be up after Julie leaves for home, he thought. When they entered Tom's apartment, the answering machine was beeping. It was Jan—she was excited and needed to talk.

"Come on, Julie. Let's get over there and find out what's going on."

35

JAN OPENED THE DOOR WITHIN MOMENTS OF TOM'S KNOCK.

"Come on in, guys. Have you heard the news?" asked Jan.

"No," Tom said. "What's going on?"

"Richard has disappeared, for real this time. Maria returned this evening from Madison. She was expecting him to be home, but he wasn't. After going down to check on his parking spot, she became alarmed. Richard's car was there, but no Richard. She consulted with Carl and found out he had Richard's keys and briefcase. The police sealed them and put them in his safe, pending Richard's return."

"Oh my goodness," said Julie, "the plot thickens."

Greg added, "Oh well, Richard will probably show up. Who knows what tricks he may have been up to during the weekend. I wonder why he didn't go with Maria to see her parents."

"So, what did the police have to say, Jan?" asked Julie.

"According to Carl, they have put him on the missing persons list—what do they call it—an all-points bulletin? One officer was overheard saying that Richard could turn out to be another Towers victim. Imagine: three people murdered, all from this building, and now this Richard thing." Jan's voice trailed off.

The room became silent for a few seconds. Then Julie asked, "What do you guys think of Candice's statement about Vito? — I mean, when she said Vito could not have committed all three murders."

Greg answered, "Yeah, I caught that, too. Does that mean Candice and Vito were together when Miss Oxley got it? I don't remember her explaining the reasons for what she said about Vito."

Julie said, "Well, it appears Candice knows something we don't know. I wouldn't necessarily conclude there is something going on between Vito and Candice; however, it's possible—that Vito is quite a looker."

Jan piped in, "I don't think either Vito or Jack could be the murderer."

"Why is that?" asked Tom.

"Because according to Carl—and the police—other than the mess on the floor of all three, the only disturbance was in the bedroom. Most of the drawers of their dressers were pulled out. Their jewelry was strewn about. I can't see Jack or Vito doing something like that."

"Geez, that's news. I heard something about the first murder and missing jewelry. All three—that's something," responded Tom.

"In the case of the first two, the police don't know how much, if any, jewelry was missing. However, Joan Collison reported several valuable pieces missing," added Jan.

"Well, kid, let's get going," Tom said to Julie. "It's time to move on."

"Thanks for coming over. It's good to talk. Be careful, you two," responded Jan.

Julie and Tom left Jan and Greg's apartment and returned to 2012.

They visited for a few minutes, and Julie said, "Well, Tom, I've got to get home. Early to work tomorrow morning."

"Okay, Julie. I'll see you down to your car."

They were alone in the lobby after going down the elevator, except for voices emitting from Carl's television in the office. Tom heard the sound of a person shifting positions in a chair. Likely the security night attendant, Tom thought.

Tom and Julie walked out into the parking lot and Julie pressed the unlock button on her key chain. Tom gave her a hug and a smack on the lips. "See you soon, Julie. I hope you have a good day at work tomorrow."

"Thanks, Tom. I'm looking forward to our next visit."

Tom watched Julie's car as it headed toward the exit ramp. The bright red taillights blinked as she slowed before rounding the corner of the building. He scanned the parking lot. There was no one about.

The stillness reminded him of the country home that he'd left.

Threatened by a faceless killer, Tom had been forced to carry a gun to protect himself. Now here he was, standing alone at night in a parking lot, in a city. Three murders have been committed, and my gun is in my closet, twenty floors away, he reflected. He quickly left the parking lot and reentered the Towers.

A police officer greeted him in the lobby.

Back in his apartment, Tom probed the far corner of a shelf in his bedroom closet, feeling for the bulk of a .32-automatic pistol. Carefully, he continued to probe until his fingers felt the metal. After withdrawing the gun, he pulled out the clip and verified that it was empty—no bullets in the barrel either. Where had he put the box of shells? After rummaging through likely places, Tom found the box in a junk drawer of a hallway closet. The box was nine short of being full—six had been used for target practice and the other three had gone into the chest of the intruder who'd threatened his life a couple of years ago.

Tom took the box of bullets back into the living room and sat down on the couch in front of the coffee table, where the empty clip lay. Each bullet made a clicking sound as he pressed it into the clip. After filling the clip, Tom pushed it into the handle. He set the gun back down on the table and stared at it for about two minutes. Before going to bed, he placed the gun back on the shelf in his bedroom closet. Hesitating for a moment, he reached in the far corner, removed a baseball bat and set it by the front door.

36

MONDAY MORNINGS WEREN'T ALWAYS BAD. Detective Bill Anderson was studying a piece of paper lying on his desk. Lieutenant Rod Barry was sitting on a chair, snuggled up to the desk. His elbows were spread out on the surface, his chin resting on the his stacked fists.

"Even though we had to let Manchino go, he's staying on this list," said the detective.

"I see you have the Hastings guy down there. Isn't that a little remote?" asked Rod.

"Yes, it is, Rod, but I'm not quite ready to take him off there just yet. I'm going to have a talk with him sometime this week. Hopefully, by tomorrow. I want to hear his explanation of why he and his girlfriend were down in the garage standing by the Fallon car."

Rod chuckled and added, "Yeah, the way officer Stills tells it, he looked guilty as hell. You know, Hastings and the broad could have put both the keys and briefcase in the car before the officers noticed them."

"Well, Rod, I'm really not expecting Hastings to confess or to become a serious suspect. What I really want is to learn more of what he's seen in the building and over at the pub—O'Leary's."

"So, who's left? Billings, the barber, Huggins, the goatee guy and?"

"And who?" asked Bill, looking up at his assistant.

"Maybe the manager, Carl Borders. He sure has the run of the place."

"Do you think he's strong enough to move the two bodies?"

"If he used a dolly, he could have been," answered Rod.

Bill looked up at Rod and shook his head. "Would you like to look at the list?"

"Sure," replied the lieutenant. "See if you agree with the underlines:"

Vito Manchino
Tom Hastings
Marcil Huggins
Gordon Beard
Carl Borders
Phil Bartron
James Brabinski
Jack Billings
Greg Skogen
Carlos Valdez

"Yup, you have it about right. Have you heard from our undercover agent lately?" asked Rod.

"Oh, you mean Cal?"

"Yup, Cal."

"Well, he's been hanging around O'Leary's a lot. The last time I talked to him, he said there's something being passed between Manchino and his visitors. The most interesting one is Gordon Beard, the one who's on your list."

"Does he have enough stuff for an arrest?"

"He might have, but then, we're sort of holding off—the serial killer could be one of them, and that's a priority."

"Oh, there's one more thing. He was hanging around the parking lot at O'Leary's one night, and guess who Vito Manchino was having an argument with?"

"Gordon Beard?" guessed the lieutenant.

"No. Carlos Valdez."

———

TOM LOOKED OUT HIS WINDOW on an overcast Monday morning and muttered, "All weather is good, really. Living in Minnesota, you have to expect this."

He dressed and took the elevator down. Surely, updated news of Richard's disappearance would find its way into the lobby, he thought.

Not surprisingly, Jan was sitting on the couch. "Good morning, Tom. Time for some coffee?"

"Yeah, Jan, just what I came down for." He filled a Styrofoam cup from the dispenser and sat down next to her.

Carl emerged from his office. "Good morning, Tom—Jan. Does anyone have any answers today?"

"Nothing from me, but that's what I came down here for. Find out what's new on Richard's disappearance?" asked Tom.

"Not a single thing," answered Carl.

One of the elevator doors opened and Marcil Huggins emerged. He pushed through the lobby door, paused and glared for a moment, then walked off toward the back door without saying a word.

"I wonder what's with that guy?" whispered Jan. "Most of the time he pesters me and won't go away," she added in a loud and concerned voice.

Their attention was drawn to a police car pulling up in front of the front door. An officer emerged from the passenger side and leaned over to open the back door. Vito Manchino stepped out of the back seat. He looked up at the sky, stretched and said something to the police officer. The officer got back into the car, and the wheels squealed slightly as the car left the loading area.

Tom continued to sit on the couch next to Jan. Carl had not moved from his standing position in the lobby, and his arms were hanging down away from his body. His mouth was partially open and remained that way as Vito pushed through the second door and entered the lobby.

"Hi, people. I'm back," Vito cheerfully announced.

"Well, Vito, what's going on?" spurted Carl.

Vito stopped, gave Carl a challenging look and made quick, long strides that carried him through the door leading to the elevators.

The lobby became dead quiet—not a word was spoken for at least a minute.

Jan broke the silence. "Candice was right. She knew Vito wasn't guilty."

Carl and Tom had not moved. They didn't say a word.

Jan stood. "If Vito didn't do the murders, someone else must have."

Tom stood up and softly said, "I'm going back to my apartment to get the skates and get some fresh air."

Jan placed her hand on his shoulder. "Wait, I'll go up with you. Please hold the door while I get my mail."

Jan and Tom rode the elevator up. They said good-bye and Tom returned to his apartment. After fishing the skates backpack from his front closet, he laid it down and retrieved his gun from the shelf in the bedroom closet. The gun fit into the zippered pocket of the backpack.

On the way down, the elevator stopped on the seventeenth floor. Candice got on.

"Hi, Tom. Thanks for the nice party last weekend."

"You're entirely welcome, Candice. Julie and I were glad you and Jack could both come. Do you have the day off today?"

"I don't work on Mondays. How about you?"

"My part-time computer business doesn't demand a Monday schedule. Have you heard about Vito Manchino?"

"You mean his release from jail?"

"Yes. I was down in the lobby about an hour ago when a police car dropped him off."

The elevator reached the first floor, and Tom followed Candice through the door leading into the lobby.

"See ya', Candice," Tom said.

She turned and looked into his eyes. Tom realized at that moment that she knew something—she had some information to share. He searched her eyes trying to decipher what it was. Without saying anything, she turned and hurried out the front door. Tom Hastings headed for the rear parking lot.

To Tom's relief, Marcil Huggins was not at the bench on the bike trail. Tom reached into the small, zippered pocket of his backpack and placed his fingers around the .32-automatic. The gun felt cold, but he continued to grasp it until the metal warmed. Tom removed his hand and re-zipped the pocket.

After putting on the skates, he slung the backpack over his shoulder and was about to begin. A man suddenly appeared on the slope leading to the railroad tracks. It was Marcil Huggins. Tom paused.

"Hello, Mr. Hastings. I see you're ready to go."

Tom thought about the gun in the backpack. How in the world would I ever get to it back there? I do have a holster somewhere in the apartment, he thought.

"Oh, hello, Marcil. Are you out girl watching again today?"

The look on Marcil's face wasn't appreciative as he responded. "I can think clearly out here on the bench."

"Oh, okay. I'm off—see you later."

Passing by the site of the Tingsley murder, Tom noticed the tall grass had been almost totally restored to normal height. Visions of the stooped over policemen and onlookers were still fresh in his mind. Tragedies always drew a crowd.

Tom's stint on the trail was physically and mentally rewarding. When Tom returned to the bench, Marcil was gone. After changing out of his in-line-skates, Tom walked back to the Towers.

He saw no one during the elevator trip to the twentieth floor. After showering and dressing, he grabbed the baseball bat on his way out and went back down the elevator to the lower-level garage. After placing the bat in the trunk of his car, he drove to the Lake's strip mall.

Tom's first stop was Jensen's Shirts. He was delighted to see Dalia back at her post behind the front desk.

"Hi, Dalia. I missed you during my last visit. Hope you're feeling better."

"Oh, I'm just fine, Tom. I'm glad you stopped. Your program is working just fine except for one small problem—the total in column five of sheet six is not quite right."

"Should be easy to fix, Dalia. Is the computer available right now?"

"Sure is, Tom."

He sat down at her computer and spent about ten minutes searching for the errant formula that was causing the problem.

"Aha. There it is, Dalia. It should work fine now."

"Thanks, Tom."

"If you find any other bugs, please give me a call."

"Sure will."

Tom left Jensen's and strolled over to Molly's for lunch. Looking at his watch, he saw it was close to 1:00 p.m.

The place was almost empty.

"Sit anywhere you want," said a lady who was filling in for Molly. Tom took a booth overlooking the parking lot and unfolded his newspaper.

A waitress brought over a pot of coffee, set down a cup and asked, "Coffee, sir?"

"Yeah, I'll have a cup and a fish sandwich with some chips."

As expected, the service was a little slow because most of the noon hour staff had left for the day. Tom continued to read the newspaper and was startled by a tap on his shoulder. He looked up and saw Carlos smiling down at him.

"Good afternoon, se´nor Hastings. Nice to see you again."

"Well, hello, Carlos. What brings you to Molly's on this Monday afternoon?"

"Se´nor Hastings, I decided to take the day off. Juanita decided it would be a good day for me to clean up our lower-level storage area. She doesn't like it down there—says it gives her the creeps."

"Yeah, I know what she means. It's rather cryptic. I need to get my storage area into shape, too. Right now, it looks like a pile of junk. I'm planning on putting up some shelves, when I get around to it. What do you think of Vito Manchino being released from jail?" asked Tom.

Carlos's eyes narrowed and his brow furrowed. "I wasn't aware. Did this happen lately?"

"This morning, Carlos. I was down in the lobby when the police dropped him off."

"Your lunch has arrived, se´nor, I'll see you again."

As the waitress placed the plate down, Tom looked up and watched Carlos briskly head for the door. Carlos's right hand pulled the door open and his head turned to look back. His eyes locked on Tom's for a moment, then quickly he turned away and exited.

37

RETURNING TO HIS APARTMENT, Tom had two main projects on his mind. One was to prepare the next day's visit to SkyWeb, the other to improve his storage area. He spent the next two hours working on his preparations for SkyWeb—mainly examining their new accounting database and making notations. After placing his notes and disks into a briefcase, he took the elevator down to the garage. Tom drove his car to a home improvement store and picked up three shelving boards, six brackets and a box of special screws.

After parking at the delivery area of the Towers, he removed the supplies from his car. The Towers storage area was located on the same level as the garage. It was a large room with rows of fenced cubicles that reached to the ceiling. Each cubicle was secured with a wood-framed wire fence and a padlocked door.

Lining up the three boards, he cradled them into both arms and made his way to the door that led to the storage area of the building. After manipulating the boards through the door, he entered a long, concrete corridor that led to a door accessing the cubicles.

The corridor had concrete blocks for walls and a gray painted concrete slab for a floor. The ceiling was saturated with long pipes that conveyed heating and cooling to the building. The area reminded Tom of his youthful, religious school days, when teacher nuns had read stories about catacombs: dark, long passageways used to store remains of human bodies. Shuddering, he entered the storage room with the three long boards and proceeded down the middle corridor to his cubicle.

After unlocking the padlock, he propped the three shelving boards against an internal wall of the cubicle. Returning to the elevators, he rode back up to fetch his tools from his hallway closet.

On his way back down, armed with a toolbox, he got a suspicious look from a lady on the elevator. Her haste in exiting at the lobby level resulted in a slight stumble. Tom smiled while watching her hurry through the foyer.

Installing the three shelves took about an hour. After rearranging the boxes and other contents on the new shelves, he was pleased with the result.

While gathering his tools and placing them back in the toolbox, he heard a noise that sounded like a door slamming. Tom remained still and listened, his apprehension building by the second. In the background, he could hear the hum of the air conditioning units, sounding like distant World War II airplanes. Quietly, he finished placing the tools and stray screws into the toolbox. He closed it and set it on the floor just outside the cubicle door. After stepping out into the side corridor and squeezing the padlock shut, he paused and listened. There were no unusual sounds.

Calm down, he mentally commanded. *It could be another tenant.* Deciding not to chance a defenseless confrontation, he reached down, opened the toolbox and grabbed a hammer. He peeked around the corner. The corridor was visible the entire distance to the door and not a person in sight. Remaining in his partially secluded position, tucked into the side aisle, he patiently waited.

His level of apprehension increased when he heard a clanging metallic sound coming from the door area. Firming up the hammer in his right hand, he was about to step out into the main corridor when the overhead lights went out.

He felt a wave of agonizing tension and his stomach knotted. A terrifying image emerged regarding an incident that had happened three years ago in his country home. After an intruder had threatened his life with a knife, Hastings had been fortunate to deter and injure him with a tennis racquet, eventually killing the intruder with a pistol. He now thought about the .32-automatic resting on a shelf in his front closet.

The toolbox remained on the floor, the hammer secure in Tom's right fist. He remained dead silent, his ears straining for sounds. After about five minutes, he peeked around the corner, thanking the heavens for the emergency light in the main corridor ceiling. His eyes were adapting to the darkness, and the door at the end of the corridor was visible again.

Tom picked up the toolbox from the floor with his left hand, the hammer firmly grasped in his right, and cautiously began to step toward the door.

About half the distance to the door, he heard something. Tom stopped, and his heart jumped into his throat when he heard heavy breathing coming from somewhere near the door. His trembling left hand was losing control of the toolbox. An annoying clunking sound echoed through the room when he set it down on the concrete floor.

Staying close to the cubicles on his left, he elevated his right arm above his head, the hammer ready. He proceeded slowly toward the door. Only a few steps away from it, he stopped to listen. The heavy breathing sound was gone. His right hand began to tremble. *It was now or never*, he thought. After counting to three, he made a dash for the door. His left hand initially fumbled with the knob, the door finally opened. Moments later he was running down the long corridor toward the steel exit door. After opening it, he glanced back and was relieved to see no one pursuing.

Tom dashed up the stairs and down a hallway, then slashed through the door leading to the elevators and lobby. Jan and Carl were standing there when he entered.

"Tom, what the heck are you going to do with that hammer?" exclaimed Jan, alarmed.

"Yeah, Tom—for God's sake, what's going on?" asked Carl.

Gasping for air, Tom blurted, "Carl, someone down in the storage area scared the hell out of me. I was down there putting up some shelves when the door slammed. There was another noise and then the lights went out. I heard someone breathing, and feel damn good to be standing right here, right now."

"You sit down, Tom, and I'll call the cops." Carl said, and hurried into the office.

"Why don't you set the hammer down, Tom?" said Jan, hoarsely.

Tom looked down at the hammer in his right hand and noticed his fingers were white.

"Oh sure, Jan," he said, dropping the hammer on the couch.

They waited and finally a police car pulled up in front. Two officers got out and entered the foyer. Carl opened the door to allow them to enter the lobby.

"What's going on, Carl?" asked the first officer.

Carl pointed to Tom. "That gentleman sitting over there said he was threatened by someone in the storage area."

Tom stood up and nervously said, "I'm Tom Hastings from the twentieth floor. I was down in the storage area putting up shelves in my cubicle, when I heard these strange noises. Then the lights went out. While sneaking out, I heard someone breathing."

"Did you see anyone?" asked the second officer.

"No, but someone was down there. I can tell you that for sure."

"Okay. You lead the way, Mr. Hastings, and let's take a look."

Tom led the two officers, followed by Carl and Jan, through the foyer, down the stairwell and through the steel door leading to the long corridor. When they arrived at the door leading into the storage area, Tom paused and looked back at the officers.

"It was in there," he said.

Both officers drew their guns and one of them opened the door. To Tom's surprise, the light was on. Holding his gun in both hands, the first officer crouched and slowly advanced. The second officer was holding the door open with his body, his gun in both hands and pointed toward the ceiling.

When the first officer got to the last row of cubicles, he stopped and looked back. "There's no one down here. It's all clear."

While the second officer continued to hold the door open, Tom, followed by Carl and Jan, advanced to the last row where Tom's storage unit was located. Reaching down, Tom picked up the toolbox from the corridor floor.

"This is where I was when the lights went out," he said.

"Where did you hear the breathing?" asked one of the officers.

"It was over there, about half way to the door. The breathing seemed to be coming from between the last two rows."

Walking over to the aisle that separated the last two storage rows, one of the officers shone his flashlight into the area.

"What's that on the floor over there?" Tom asked.

The officer with the flashlight walked in about two steps and stooped to pick up an object.

"Looks like a gum wrapper," the officer said.

"We better put that in a plastic bag," said the second officer.

"Yeah, you're right," agreed the first officer, putting his gun back in its holster.

"Would you lead the way back to the lobby, please?" asked one of the officers.

Carl advanced to the door and led the way back.

"Mr. Hastings, could you step into our car for a few minutes? We need to file a report."

"Sure thing," Tom said.

Tom was in the police car for about ten minutes, answering some questions and eventually signing a statement. A number of residents amassed in the lobby while Tom was busy with the officers.

Marcil Huggins and Carlos Valdez were standing with their backs to the door, looking down at Jan, who was sitting on the couch. She stopped talking when Tom opened the door.

Carl said, "Well, Tom, I'll talk to the owners, and perhaps we can do something about that storage area."

"Going up, Jan?" Tom asked.

"Yes, I'll ride up with you," she answered.

As they were riding up, Tom asked Jan, "Do you think the police believed me?"

"I'm not so sure. I think Carl believed you, though."

"How about you, Jan?"

"Of course, Tom. Why would you make up something like that?"

The elevator stopped and the door opened. Tom stepped through the door with the toolbox. "Thanks for believing me, Jan."

"Of course, Tom. Let's talk later."

After getting back to his apartment, Tom put the toolbox away. He reached up onto the shelf in the bedroom closet and brought out the .32- automatic. He placed it on the kitchen counter and returned to the closet to retrieve the holster. After snuggling the gun in the holster, he stood there and stared at it, thinking, *do I have to go through that again?*

38

FERRO WATCHED TOM HASTINGS CARRY three boards through the door leading into the storage area. He had been hanging out there for the past hour, yearning for that special feeling. Not being certain what it would take to satisfy his needs, he found some satisfaction in just hiding in the storage area.

He was hoping a woman would come in, alone. Harming Hastings would not be gainful. Ferro reached in his pocket and drew out a stick of gum. Removing the wrapper, he allowed it to drop to the floor. Another hour went by and Hastings was about finished.

Acting on instinct, Ferro moved over to the door and opened and closed it rapidly, generating a slamming sound. He smiled, thinking it would scare Hastings and he'd get out fast. The intended result did not happen. Instead, his unwelcome visitor did not move.

A few minutes went by—Hastings was holding fast. Ferro reached up with his hand and banged once on the outside wire-fenced cubicle wall, fully expecting Hastings to grab his tools and leave. More time elapsed and Hastings continued to hold his ground. Next, Ferro reached around the corner and flicked the light switch off. Sadistic feelings of accomplishment excited Ferro. He continued to expect Hastings to bolt for the door and leave. For a moment, Ferro thought of giving up and leaving—there was no point in taking it any further.

He was about to do so when he heard Hastings tiptoeing toward the door. Hoping that his victim didn't have a flashlight, Ferro pressed his body tightly against a cubicle. The sound of rushing feet and the opening door brought him satisfaction. Ferro laughed out loud for a few moments after hearing Hastings' running footsteps dissipate at the end of the long corridor.

How Hastings reacts to this should be interesting, he mused. After hearing the next door open and close, he calmly left the storage area and took the elevator up to his apartment.

———

RUNNING WAS NOT ENOUGH. His attacker was at both ends of the corridor. Tom Hastings sat up in bed, awakening from a startling nightmare. His nightshirt was wet with perspiration. Reaching and groping on top of the night table, he felt the leather of the holster. Sitting up, he imagined Robert Ranforth chewing on a stick of gum, smiling while terrorizing his victim a few feet away near a storage cubicle.

Robert Ranforth was more than a dream: he was a real murderer from the past. He'd been the reason for Tom Hastings move to the city. Tom had killed Ranforth's hired gun during a confrontation in Tom's house. Ranforth, the person behind all the murders had been caught and sent to prison, but cruel memories remained.

Getting back to sleep was impossible. Tom made a pot of coffee and pressed the start button on his computer. He needed a distraction from the terrorizing incident in the storage area. By playing a soft-music CD on the stereo and concentrating on a game of chess on the computer, he was able to tire and eventually go to sleep.

On Tuesday morning, just before leaving for SkyWeb from his apartment, Tom paused by the door. The holster, containing the gun, was lying on the kitchen countertop. Returning to the kitchen, he placed it in his jacket pocket before heading down to the garage.

After exiting the elevator at the lower level and walking by the hair salon, he looked through the barbershop windows, noticing that James and Barb were both working.

Tom entered the garage, paused and gazed around. Seeing no one, he hurried to his car, got in it and locked the doors. Placing the holster into the glove compartment, he backed the car out and left the garage.

Promptly at 10:00 in the morning, Tom entered through the main door of SkyWeb.

"Good Morning, Tom," said Trisha cheerfully.

"Hi, Trisha. Are you ready to go to work?"

"Sure am. I've got all the invoices entered. Sort of proud of myself. Would ya check'em out?"

"Good girl, Trisha. We'll do it together."

Tom had been working close to an hour when Gordon Beard came out of Susan's office, passing by without making any comment. Tom's head tilted upward from the keyboard when he heard the door close to Gordon's office.

"Just two corrections, Trisha—you're doing real good. Let's check out the vendor list, the payables and the bank accounts."

"It took me all last week to do the invoices, Tom. Also, I entered about a dozen bills and wrote some checks," responded Trisha anxiously.

"Good, let's take a look."

After clicking through the checks and the bills, it became evident to Tom that Trisha needed more training. Spending the next hour correcting most of the errant bills and checks, he worked in silence while Trisha tended to the phone.

Susan came out of her office and smiled. "Hi, Tom. Nice to see you again."

"Greetings, Susan, " Tom said, while looking up and returning the smile.

Susan paused for a minute, then moved by them and out through the main office door.

Tom returned his attention to Trisha and her data entries. After another hour of work, Trisha's confidence returned and she successfully input a dozen bills.

"Trisha, I think you've got it. I want you to complete the data entries for that stack of bills, keeping in mind what you learned today. After you finish those, I'd like you to go ahead and write checks for the payables that are due.

"I'll return next Tuesday about the same time and we'll focus on statement charges and receiving payments."

"Oh great, Tom. Thanks. This is starting to be fun."

Tom packed his briefcase, snapped it shut and was standing by Trisha's desk when Gordon Beard's office door opened. Gordon stepped into the room, hands in his pockets and chin almost touching the buttons of his shirt. Pausing, he looked up and noticed Tom standing by Trisha's desk. After making eye contact, Gordon's expression changed from a frown to a smile.

"Oh, hello there, Mr. Hastings. How's it going today?"

"Just finished. I think Trisha has a good handle on the new accounting system. I'll check in again next Tuesday for another review. Is that okay with you, Trisha?"

"Yes, Mr. Hastings. Thanks for your help," said Trisha, smiling.

Gordon's facial expression changed back to a frown as he quickly stepped across the room and reentered his office.

"So long. See you next Tuesday, Trish," Tom said after hearing Gordon slam his door.

While riding down the elevator, Tom was thinking about the relationship between Gordon Beard and Vito Manchino. They appeared to be buddy-buddy at O'Leary's. It's not so here, at SkyWeb, he thought. *Who was selling to whom?*

The traffic was slow and tedious on his drive back to the Towers. After reaching his apartment, Tom slipped the SkyWeb backup diskette into his computer's floppy drive, restoring the file onto his hard drive. He spent the next hour studying the current SkyWeb data entries, making some notes. When he was about to close the program, a specific number attracted his attention.

Tom ran a profit/loss report for the current year, noticing a net loss of close to two million dollars. Thinking about the Mercedes that Gordon was driving, he scanned the expense items and balance sheet. It was apparently a business expense.

Tom didn't want to be snoopy, but he ran a customer list. To his surprise, there was a Vito and a Carlos. Both had been the recipients of a large amount of money.

39

BEER AND CIGARS WERE TOOLS USED FOR RELAXATION by Tom Hastings. He sat on the balcony for close to an hour that evening, thinking about Gordon Beard, Vito Manchino and Carlos. From Tom's observations and the SkyWeb books, he knew they had something going. How about the packages that Vito slipped to Gordon at O'Leary's? Vito coming to visit at Gordon's office? Were they in business together? Was Vito selling drugs to Gordon? Was either one involved in the murders? Why was SkyWeb paying Carlos Valdez?

He couldn't visualize any of the three men terrorizing anyone down in the storage area. Thoughts of that incident contributed to his feelings of tension.

The Internet! Excitedly, Tom brought up a search engine window on his computer. He typed in *FBI Wanted List* and pressed the Go button. He selected Minneapolis as a region and a list of names with pictures appeared. About halfway through the list, he lifted his finger to his lips. The man in the picture looked familiar. No, I guess not, he concluded. The name, Ferro, under the picture was unfamiliar. Tom made a mental note to bring it up with the detective on his next visit. After pressing the Print button, he reached for his beer.

It was empty. There were none left in the fridge, but O'Leary's would have some. After dressing and putting on his jacket, he paused.

The gun! Putting it in his jacket pocket, he considered the risk of carrying the gun, especially without a permit. Minnesota had strict laws. The heck with them, he thought. Protection was needed in the garage.

On the way down, the elevator stopped on the seventh floor.

James got on, smiled and said, "Hello, Mr. Hastings. Going out for the evening?"

Wow, green shoes and three large turquoise rings on the fingers of his right hand. Splashy—weird, Tom thought.

"Yeah, I'm headed over to O'Leary's. How about you?"

"Not much going—just visiting a friend."

No more was said until the elevator reached the lobby. As James was getting off, he laughed nervously and said, "See ya."

The barber didn't look dangerous or strong enough to move bodies around.

There wasn't anyone around when Tom stepped out of the elevator on the lower level. While walking toward the garage, he put his right hand in his jacket pocket and felt the cold steel of the automatic. Upon entering the garage, he paused and looked around—no one was in sight. Tom's parking spot was twelve places up the right aisle. Walking to the car, he kept his right hand in his pocket. Before backing out of his spot, he transferred the gun to the glove compartment.

After backing out into the aisle, Tom saw a car approaching from the opposite end. Its speed is excessive, he thought. Arriving at the exit first, Tom recognized Phil Bartron as the driver. The car turned and bullied its way to the garage door, ahead of Tom. By the time Tom's car exited the building, Phil's car was nowhere in sight.

When Tom arrived at O'Leary's parking lot, he noticed Phil entering. Mighty anxious to get there, that Phil Bartron, Tom thought.

Scanning the barstools on entering, Tom didn't see any sign of Phil Bartron. All five stools at Tom's favorite end of the bar were available. He took a position adjacent to the left post. When the bartender came over, Tom ordered a beer and asked to change channels to the Braves baseball game.

"No problem," the bartender said while turning and heading for the beer cooler bin.

He returned with a bottle of beer and the television remote. "Here you are, sir. You're in control."

"Thanks a lot," Tom gratefully responded.

The game was in the third inning with no score. Two innings later, Vito Manchino entered and sat down in his usual place, next to the server station on the left side of the bar. He was wearing his dark blue sport coat. He reached in the side pocket and brought out a pack of cigarettes and a lighter. He laid the pack on the bar, pulled over an ashtray and lit up. A large billow of smoke emerged from his nostrils before he noticed Tom Hastings. Vito stared at Tom for a few moments. Tom noticed Vito's glare out of the corner of his eye as he continued to watch the game.

The mysterious Phil Bartron appeared from out of nowhere and sat down on the stool next to Vito Manchino. Tom watched with interest as Phil's head bobbed up and down when he talked. Manchino retracted his shoulders and leaned back in an attempt to distance himself from Bartron, frequently taking drags from a cigarette. What—him too, thought Tom. Does everyone use drugs around here?

While observing Bartron and Manchino, Tom detected an annoyed look on Vito's face. A few minutes later, Phil Bartron brought up both fists against the sides of his head, while turning away from Vito.

Focusing on the baseball game was increasingly difficult for Tom because of the interactions between Vito Manchino and Phil Bartron. Finally, Phil got off the stool and left the bar and grill.

During the next two innings of the game, Vito Manchino sat alone, smoking cigarettes. He was glancing toward the door, as if expecting someone.

The bartender stepped over in front of Vito and replaced the ashtray, by this time heaped with a pile of tangled butts. Tom's mind was tiring. He waved to the bartender, requesting his bill. After signing the credit card slip, he glanced over at Vito Manchino and was astounded by what he saw.

Phil Bartron had returned and handed something to Vito. Vito's head and hands lowered. Whatever he received from Phil went into his coat's inside pocket. Vito fumbled around in the other side pocket for a moment and then handed something to Phil beneath the bar surface. Phil smiled, got off the stool and headed for the door.

Tom left the bar and grill, walked into the parking lot and watched Phil Bartron's car turn a corner. Driving down the street leading to the boulevard, it stopped for a red light. When the light turned green, Phil's car turned left, heading away from the Towers at his usual rate of speed. The sound of a siren and the flashing of lights signaled that Phil was in trouble.

Sitting at a booth overlooking the boulevard at O'Leary's, a man wearing horn-rimmed glasses was talking on a cell phone and smiling.

"You got him—good job," he muttered into the mouthpiece.

———

PHIL BARTRON WAS ALSO SMILING. He knew a speeding ticket was coming, but they wouldn't find the stuff—not even a sniffing dog would. Vito had a fail proof plan for this kind of occurrence.

"Step out of the car, please," Phil heard an officer say.

"Can I see your driver's license?" the officer added.

Phil was ready with the license, and the officer shone his flashlight on it.

"Okay. You come back with me to the squad car. We're going to search your car."

"You, ah...have no right. What's the charge?" stammered Phil.

"Reasonable cause," said the officer as he escorted Phil and assisted in placing him in the back seat. The officer didn't notice when Phil touched the side of his left leg, and a gray cloth packet dropped from inside his pant leg, silently coming to a rest in a pile of scattered debris next to the curb.

A second squad car had pulled up behind the first. Two officers got out and proceeded to search Phil Bartron's car.

About half an hour later they returned. One of them said, "Bob, there was nothing in the car. How about his clothes and shoes?"

"He's clean," replied the officer from the car.

"We better let him go," added the officer who was standing watch over Phil.

"Okay, Mr. Bartron. You're free to leave but I need your signature right there. You were doing fifty-plus in a thirty-five zone."

Phil was smiling when he signed the complaint. He knew the packet would still by lying by the curb when he felt safe to return. The release mechanism inside his pant leg had worked again. Vito is a genius, he thought.

———

TOM HAD WALKED FIVE STEPS FROM HIS CAR when remembering the gun. Returning to his parked car, he retrieved the gun and placed it in his jacket pocket. After locking the car doors, Tom strode toward the door that led to the elevators. He felt secure while his right hand was resting on the automatic.

On the way up, the elevator stopped at the lobby. Carlos and Juanita were waiting, along with Joan.

"Good evening, se´nor," said Juanita.

"Hello, Juanita," responded Tom. He hesitated for a moment and added, "You, too, Carlos. Hi, Joan."

"Did the evening treat you well?" asked Carlos.

"Yes, it certainly did. I had a nice time at O'Leary's, and I'm alive. What big adventure did you two have?"

"Si, not much. We visited relatives in Saint Paul," answered Carlos.

"Are your relatives from Colombia?" Tom asked.

"Yes, they are from Colombia. They are here on working visas. We are trying to talk them into applying for citizenship," added Carlos.

The elevator stopped on the seventeenth floor, and Juanita said, "Have a nice night, se´nor Tom. Have you heard anything about what happened to Richard?"

"No, I haven't, but he'll probably show up one of these days," Tom responded. He put his hand on the door slide to prevent it from closing.

Tom released the door, and just before it smacked shut, he overheard Carlos tell his wife, "That's a bad one, that Richard. He's never coming back."

As the elevator zoomed upward, Tom wondered what information

Carlos had about Richard that no one else did. *"He's never coming back"* sounded so conclusive. Tom's thoughts drifted to one of the pictures he saw on the Internet. *Ferro*, that's the name listed under the face.

When the elevator door closed, Joan's attempt to talk was muffled by her trembling lower jaw. Tom looked over at her, puzzled.

"Tom—her jewelry. One of the bracelets looks like one of mine."

"You mean Juanita?"

"Yes, she had three of them on her left wrist."

"Could you be mistaken? Maybe she has one identical."

"Possible, but unlikely—it's one that's been in my family for over fifty years."

The elevator stopped on the eighteenth, Joan's floor. She held the slide, and her voice crackled slightly, "Tom, do you think I should report what I saw to the police?"

"Sure, if you're certain the bracelet is yours."

"I'll call the detective tomorrow morning."

After returning to his apartment, Tom settled into comfortable lounging clothes, poured a glass of wine and sat down by the phone.

Carlos—could it be Carlos? Naw, he's happily married, has a good job. He seems like such a nice guy. Tom thought about the possibility for a few minutes. He decided to make it a priority to talk to the detective.

Tom dialed Julie. The phone rang three times before she picked it up, and he was pleased to hear her voice. "Hello," she said.

"Hi, Julie. This is Tom. How are you this evening?"

"Oh, just fine, Tom. I'm anxious to hear the latest from the Towers. I have some things to tell you from work, about Richard."

"Geez, that ought to be interesting. Can you tell me anything now—like has he been at work?"

"No, he hasn't, and neither has someone else. Perhaps coincidence, but there is a young lady missing also from about the same time."

"Julie, how about lunch tomorrow? I want to hear more. I'll come downtown and try to get lost in the skyways. How about taking an extra hour for lunch?"

"Sounds great, Tom. I'll do that. Why don't you come at about eleven and we'll go from there?".

"Okay. Now as I remember, you are on the twenty-sixth floor of the Cleaver Tower. Is that right?"

"Yes, it is, Tom. I guess I'm real tired tonight. Let's call it a day and I'll see you tomorrow at eleven."

"I can't wait," responded Tom.

That night, he lay in bed, thinking what Joan said – *one of the bracelets looks like one of mine*.

40

A GURGLING COFFEEPOT HAD WOKEN TOM THE NEXT MORNING. Timers sure come in handy, he thought while opening the hallway door and stooping down for the *Star Tribune*. The front-page story about a shoot-out in downtown Minneapolis caught his attention. It happened between the police and three persons near the Cleaver building. All three suspects were killed.

"Geez," Tom said out loud, "what next?"

In a couple of hours, Tom was on his way downtown. Traffic was brisk as usual. Parking in a familiar public parking lot about two blocks from the Cleaver building, he looked at his watch. He was early for the appointment and decided to roam the skywalks.

Tom didn't pay attention to his route while following the series of walkways. Half an hour later, he paused in an unfamiliar area, not knowing for certain the return course. Attempting to find his way back to the Cleaver building, he stopped to study a skywalk wall map. His attention was drawn to a man who was rapidly walking away. *My God, that man resembles Richard,* Tom thought. Instinctively, he followed, hurrying to catch up, but the distance between them lengthened. Tom lost sight of the man as he turned a corner.

He glanced at his watch. It read ten minutes to eleven. Looking around at the shops and not recognizing any of them, Tom felt a low-level panic. Walking rapidly, he began retracing his original path, hoping to reestablish his bearings.

After passing through the nearest skywalk and into an office tower building, Tom was relieved to spot a skywalk map. The map didn't solve his problem because it was confusing. *Aha*, he thought as a security guard came around the corner.

Tom approached him. "Could you tell me the direction to the Cleaver building?"

"Sorry, sir, but I am not familiar with that building. Let's take a look at that map."

The guard studied the map for a few seconds. "Ah, there we are. I think you go back that way and take a left at the next skywalk. Then go straight ahead through two more skywalks and take a right."

"Okay. Thanks a lot."

"No problem."

Tom followed the security guard's directions, eventually spotting a Cleaver Building sign. Taking the elevator to the twenty-sixth floor, he arrived in the waiting room of Julie's workplace only fifteen minutes late.

The receptionist eyed him suspiciously and asked, "Are you here to see Julie?"

"Yes, I certainly am—late, but here."

The receptionist picked up a phone and her lips moved for a few moments. She looked up at him. "She'll be here in a minute."

"Thank you," Tom said, and took a seat.

He stood up when Julie entered the room. "Oh, there you are," she said. "Did you get lost?"

"Geez, I sure did. The skywalks darn near did me in."

Julie laughed. "Well, let's get going. How about Devon's, down on the main level?"

"Sounds good to me," Tom said, even though he hadn't ever heard of the place.

Grabbing Julie's hand, he led her out the door and down the hall toward the elevators.

Devon's was a classic office building restaurant. The windows had white curtains that matched the tablecloths, which covered deluxe-looking mahogany tables with matching chairs.

A sharply dressed hostess greeted them. "Smoking preference?" she asked.

"Non," responded Julie.

The hostess led them to a delightful table next to a window overlooking the sidewalk. Tom bumped the hostess slightly while hurrying to pull a chair out for Julie. Tom wasn't sure what to make of the scowl on the hostess's face as she placed two menus on the table. "Whoops, sorry," he said.

She sternly responded, "Your waitress will be with you shortly."

"What a grouch. So, what's the latest from the Towers?" asked Julie anxiously.

"Two things. Richard is still missing and Vito is back. I saw him at O'Leary's last night, and he was passing out stuff again."

"Passing out something. What in heaven's sake does that mean, Tom?"

"I saw him receive a white envelope from a Towers resident by the name of Phil Bartron. I'm not sure if I ever talked to you about him before."

"Oh yes, Tom—remember? He rode up the elevator with us one time. He's the guy we saw at O'Leary's—he gives me the creeps. How could I forget that weird goatee?"

"Yeah, that's right, you have met him. Well, anyhow, he was the person who passed the white envelope to Vito Manchino. Then, guess what? Vito slips something to Phil, who then leaves."

"Drugs, do you think?" asked Julie.

"Hmm...I surely don't know, but what else could Phil be paying him for—if it was money in the white envelope? It's probably what you suspect, Julie, and that would make Vito a drug dealer. Apparently, the police are so busy trying to solve murders around here, they aren't messing with lesser law violations. But get this—when I was leaving, I saw Phil Bartron being pulled over by a patrol car. I didn't hang around—traffic was too thick. Maybe it was only a speeding ticket."

"Tom, the stories in this building about Richard are getting out of hand. Who knows what's true and what isn't, but there is something we all don't know. I was having lunch with one of the girls from the office next door, and she heard that Richard ran off with one of the secretaries."

"You're kidding, Julie. But then, maybe you're not."

"A Pearl Morse...I think she works for an accounting firm on tenth. She didn't show up for work about the same time Richard disappeared. No one has been able to reach her. Her parents were upset—they called the police."

"Speaking of Richard, the reason I was late today is because of someone, who I saw in the skyway. While studying a skyway map, a man walking fast, his back to me drew my attention. He looked liked Richard—same size, similar features—even walked like Richard."

"Did you see where he was going?"

"No, he was walking so fast, I couldn't keep up and lost sight of him when he rounded a corner."

"I wonder if the police would be interested in what you just told me," said Julie.

"Huh. I don't think so—only seeing him from the back, not being sure—I'd probably be wasting the police's time."

"There's more stuff about Richard," Julie whispered and her eyes widened.

"What?" Tom asked, leaning forward and propping his elbows on the table.

"A rumor has been spreading that the firm Richard worked for is missing eighty thousand dollars. So far nothing in the paper, but I have heard it from three different people."

"You know, Julie, even though this isn't my job or problem, I'm planning on hanging around the skywalk for a couple of hours. Maybe the Richard-like man will show up again."

"Tom, it sounds like you're going to play detective. That's exciting, just like the stuff you did up north a couple of years ago."

"There's one more thing."

"What?"

"I was riding up the elevator yesterday with Juanita and Joan. Joan's the lady who lived next door, until her friend got murdered. She moved down to eighteen."

"Well, what?"

"She claims that Juanita was wearing one of her bracelets."

The waitress brought the bill. Julie stared at Tom while he gave the waitress his credit card.

"Another turn—is it accurate?"

"Don't know. She's going to tell the detective. I know you have to get back to work, so let's get going," Tom said.

Julie gave him a *you're-up-to-something* look. He gave Julie a tight hug and a smack on the lips just before she entered the elevator. The door closed and Julie was gone.

41

THE SKYWALKS ATTACHED TO THE CLEAVER BUILDING connected to a building across the street that hooked up with three other skywalks, which fanned out in different directions. Tom followed the middle one toward the area where he had seen the phantom, Richard-like person. People traffic was down. There was a little coffee shop just across the walkway from the wall map. Tom purchased a cup of espresso and a newspaper, and sat down at a small table by the window.

His view was directly in line with a corridor about half the length of a football field. Glancing up from the newspaper often, he was making sure no one passed without being noticed. He looked at his watch and memorized the time. He set a goal to keep up the vigil for one hour.

Twice, approaching men piqued his curiosity, but both of them were false alarms. He looked at his watch. The hour was almost up and Tom was about to leave when spotting two familiar persons walking in his direction.

One of them was Susan from SkyWeb, the other Vito Manchino. Tom held the newspaper up, hiding his face. When Susan and Vito slowed and entered the coffee shop, Tom could feel an increase in his heart rate. Susan and Vito approached the counter, continuing to chat while placing their orders. Tom's elbows remained propped on the table, his face buried in the newspaper. They took a small table, two windows down. Vito Manchino's back was to Tom and blocked Tom's view of Susan.

Tom lowered the newspaper and turned his head slightly to the left, attempting to listen with his right ear, the one with better hearing. Just like his eyes, one ear was better than the other. Bits and pieces of the conversation at the next table were audible.

Tom heard Susan say, "But Vito, what if they find out?"

Since Manchino was facing away, Tom couldn't hear his response but did see him raise his right arm after saying something.

Susan said, "Gordon isn't going to like this one bit. Couldn't you just hold off for another month?"

Vito shook his head and rose from the table. Tom quickly elevated his newspaper. Manchino moved over to the service counter and had his cup refilled. While he was gone, Susan gazed out the window. When Vito returned and blocked Susan's view again, Tom lowered the newspaper a little.

"What about Bartron?" asked Susan as she put both hands on the table and leaned forward.

Tom held his breath, waiting for an answer that he couldn't hear. His mind was racing.

Geez is Susan involved with Vito? Why would she bring up Phil Bartron? Hmm...Vito passed something to Phil at O'Leary's—is Phil in jail? Gordon Beard has to be involved.

At that moment, the Richard look-alike appeared, coming down the skyway corridor toward the coffee shop. The interruption caused Tom to lower the newspaper farther, peeking over the top and hoping Susan would not notice. As the man got closer, Tom realized it was not Richard. There was a physical resemblance, but the face was different. Susan and Vito rose from their chairs, not noticing their observer, who was hidden behind the newspaper. They left the coffee shop.

Tom had no problem finding his way back to the parking lot near the Cleaver building. Although the mystery of a Richard sighting was cleared up, a new one had been created. Susan and Vito being seen together was bothersome to Tom. After locating his car, he headed back to the Towers.

42

PARKING IN THE LOWER-LEVEL GARAGE didn't appeal to Tom. He pulled into a vacant slot in the outdoor parking lot.

Carl was visiting with a lady when Tom entered the lobby.

"Hello, Tom. What's new?" asked Carl, as he asked so many times before.

"I am happy to tell you there is nothing new, and you and I are both alive," Tom answered, and headed through the door to the elevators.

Arriving at his apartment, Tom had three phone messages. One was from Jan, another from Dalia Jensen and the third from Trisha at SkyWeb.

His first call was to Jensen's Shirts. Dalia answered. "Oh, thanks, Tom, for returning my call. I don't have any problems with your program, but there is something else I need to talk to you about."

Now, what could that be all about, Tom thought. "When would you like me to stop by?"

"I really don't want to talk here, so how about lunch at Molly's tomorrow?"

"Okay, Dalia, I'll see you at Molly's, noon tomorrow." After hanging up, he sat in front of the phone, his curiosity growing. *What does Dalia want to talk about? Is it about Marcil?*

Next, Tom dialed the SkyWeb number.

Trisha answered.

"Hi, Trisha. This is Tom Hastings. You called?"

"Thanks for calling back, Tom. I got stuck with some stuff here and I was wondering if you could stop by before next Tuesday. My problem appears to center around classes—something is missing."

"Sure, Trisha. How about tomorrow after lunch?"

"That will be just fine. See you then."

His final call was to Jan.

"Well, good afternoon, Tom. Greg and I were wondering if you would like to have dinner with us this evening. We plan on going to that new restaurant down the street—Maningo's is the name."

Tom was tired and had planned on spending the evening at home, but knowing Jan and Greg, there was likely some news.

"Sure, Jan. What time do you have in mind?"

"Why don't you come over about six?"

"Okay, I'll see you then."

As Tom was getting ready for dinner with Jan and Greg, he debated whether or not to share the events that he'd experienced in the skywalk. Still not certain at six when he left for Jan and Greg's apartment, he tentatively decided not to mention seeing Vito and Susan at the coffee shop.

Greg responded to his knock. "Hey, come on in, Tom. How about a drink?"

"Yes, I'll have a glass of white wine, thanks."

"Make yourself at home in there. I'll bring it out."

Tom moved past Greg and met Jan on his way to the living room.

"Hi, Tom. Glad you could make it."

After they'd hugged, Tom sat down on the couch while she joined Greg in the kitchen.

Greg came in and set a glass of white wine on the low table in front of Tom.

"Thanks, Greg. This is going to hit the spot—it's been a long day."

"What did you do today, Tom?"

"I spent some time downtown, doing the skywalks—got myself lost real good. The maps and directional arrows are sure confusing. Well, actually, I went downtown to have lunch with Julie."

"And how are things with Julie?"

"Just fine, Greg," Tom said as Jan came into the room and seated herself at the opposite end of the couch.

"Tom, do you remember Maria?" asked Jan. "She is, or was, Richard's wife," asked Jan.

"I sure do. What happened?"

"Maria moved out of the building and back to her parents home in Madison. I think she is convinced that Richard isn't coming back."

"What did she say about Richard?"

"She thinks he left her for another woman."

"Oh my gosh. How could he possibly leave a sweet person like Maria?" responded a contrite Tom Hastings.

Greg coughed and cleared his throat. "It wouldn't surprise me a cow's udder if Richard's body shows up in the river."

"Oh, come on, Greg. You don't really believe that," retorted Jan. She added, "Have you heard that Jack and Candice split? They both still live here, but don't see each other anymore."

"No, Jan, I didn't know that. What's the scoop?"

"Well, it may have something to do with Vito Manchino. Remember when she said that Vito couldn't have committed one of the killings? At least, that's what I thought she said at your party."

"Yeah, I remember Candice said something like that. Have you seen Vito around?" asked Tom.

Greg cut in. "Vito Manchino really gets around. I saw him at my bank the other day—Monday it was, I believe. It looked like he was wheeling and dealing with one of the loan officers—sexy lady, she was." Turning his head slightly and throwing a sly grin at Jan, he added, "Nice legs."

Jan responded, "Sexy, you say, Greg. How would you recognize that?"

"I have my ways," Greg quickly answered, chuckling.

Tom absorbed the last sip from his wine glass, set it down and said, "Well, let's see what that new restaurant is all about."

"Yeah," said Greg. "I'll drive."

Tom remembered his car was parked in the outside lot. "Hey, guys, I'll go down the elevator to lobby level and drive my car down into the garage. I'll meet you down there."

The elevator stopped on the twelfth floor. Vito Manchino joined the group. He sneered. "Hello, you guys catching any criminals today?"

"Do you know of any we could catch, Mr. Manchino?" answered

Jan, irritated.

Vito didn't answer and the elevator doors opened to the lobby. Tom, Greg and Jan got off, and Vito continued to the garage level.

"Hey, Jan, why did you get off here? We need to go down."

"I couldn't stand riding with that creep another moment longer," responded Jan.

After driving his car around to the garage entrance, Tom swiped the smart card and the big door opened. Greg and Jan had their car running and stopped near the entrance. Tom drove into his slot, walked briskly to their car and got in the back seat.

Maningo's was a cozy, small Italian restaurant located two blocks from the Towers. Greeted at the host station by a tuxedo-attired host, Tom thought, *uh-oh, this is going to be expensive.* The host led them to a table.

After sitting down and studying the menu, Tom said, "These prices don't look so bad after all."

"Don't look now, but it looks like Candice in the far corner," said Jan.

The waiter arrived with a bottle of Italian red and interrupted them. "Who is going to do the tasting?"

Tom gestured toward Greg, who was eyeing the far corner.

"Greg, we don't have all day," Jan announced.

Greg shifted his gaze, took a sip from the splash of dark wine in his glass and nodded. "Nice wine. Pour some for my friends."

After their glasses were filled, the dark-skinned waiter asked, "Are you ready to order?" The three diners nodded, and the waiter took their orders.

After he left, Jan commented, "Wow—is that man handsome, or what?"

"We better not let Jan decide on the tip," laughed Greg.

Jan said in a hushed tone, "Those dark eyes remind me of Carlos."

Tom and Greg stared at Jan, waiting for her to say more.

"So, where did you see Carlos?" asked Greg, curiously.

"Just this past Monday, I was at the strip mall shopping for groceries and met Carlos in the produce area. I've seen his dark eyes before, but this time they seemed so much more penetrating."

"What did you talk about?" asked Greg.

"Oh, the usual stuff—weather and the Towers. He mentioned how much Juanita likes living in the Towers, but it was a little too cold for him, especially his left arm. I didn't ask him what he meant about that. As usual, it was hidden in his left pocket. I've always wondered why he does that."

"Maybe his left hand is missing," said Greg, smirking.

Tom thought about his party. "Remember the party—Julie's and mine? I caught a glimpse of something silver. Perhaps he has a steel claw, or something like that."

Jan continued. "Anyhow, I began to feel uncomfortable because he kept inching close and closer to me. He seems to like talking right into your face. I didn't have a grocery cart to hide behind, so he got pretty close."

It was Tom's turn to talk. He clenched his teeth. "We're likely going to have some news tomorrow. That goatee guy, Phil Bartron, was picked up by the cops today out on the boulevard, not far from O'Leary's. He picked up something from Vito Manchino at the bar. We left about the same time—he was really going fast. He didn't go through the red light, but when he turned to head toward downtown, he goosed it and the patrol car stopped him. Whatever Vito passed to him may be in police hands."

Greg responded, "I bet it wasn't cigars."

"Besides the serial murders, it sounds as if we have a major drug thing going on, right here in our building," fumed Jan.

"Tomorrow will be interesting," said Tom. He decided not to mention the bracelet.

The entrees arrived, ending the conversation about Phil and drugs. After they'd finished dinner, Greg drove the car back into the Towers lower-level garage. The elevator door opened at twenty and Jan asked Tom if he wanted to come in for a glass of wine.

"I'm a little tired and have a big day tomorrow, but thanks anyhow," answered Tom, thinking about Dalia and their lunch date the next day.

43

Fᴇʀʀᴏ ᴡᴀꜱ ʀᴇᴀᴅɪɴɢ ᴛʜᴇ *STAR TRIBUNE* ᴏɴ ᴛʜᴜʀꜱᴅᴀʏ ᴍᴏʀɴɪɴɢ. He chuckled when reading the article about the unsolved murders at the Towers. That Detective Anderson—a nice guy, but not very skilled. They don't have a clue, he thought, throwing the newspaper in the trash.

Ferro's feelings were back to normal after his satisfaction on the twentieth floor a couple of weeks ago, and later scaring Tom Hastings down in the storage area. The tension in his stomach had been relieved.

However, he had a new problem. That lady over at the embroidery shop knows something. She has been watching me, Ferro thought. Dalia—that's her name. Her stares bothered him. She suspected, he was sure.

The elevator stopped on the sixth floor. Susan Buntrock, dressed in a business suit, briefcase in hand, got on.

"Good morning. How are you?" she asked.

"You look very nice this morning," Ferro answered.

"Thank you," Susan responded.

Ferro got off at the lobby and Susan continued down to the garage level.

There's that snoopy lady from twenty, talking to the building manager. They're probably talking about that creep Richard. He deserved what he got. Womanizers like that don't deserve to be around—not in my territory, he thought.

Ferro's car was parked in the outdoor lot. He got in and drove out onto the boulevard, then turned onto the lake road. After parking alongside a curb, he remained in the car for a few minutes, watching the hikers and bikers. It's time, he thought, exiting the car and walking toward the strip mall.

Crossing the boulevard on foot wasn't desirable, but he didn't want his car parked in the mall lot. Walking to the alley behind the stores, he noted that only one Jensen car was parked in the places reserved for the embroidery shop. Her husband, Cliff, as hoped, wasn't there.

Pausing by an outdoor ATM machine, he stood and watched the front door of the shop for a few minutes. A man had just left, but a lady carrying a shopping bag who'd parked in front was about to enter. Ferro walked slowly by the shop window, caught sight of Dalia and the lady customer busy at the counter, and continued down the sidewalk.

Walking to the end of the block, he stopped, turned and waited. Finally, the lady left the shop. Quickly, Ferro headed for the Jensen's Embroidery shop door and entered.

Dalia's expression when she first saw him was going to be the trigger for whether he did or didn't. The reaction in those big brown eyes would give her away. If she knew something, the eyes would show fear. If she didn't, they would be friendly.

Intense waves of pressure flowed through his body as he approached the counter. Dalia looked up, her eyes initially showed fear, but they calmed. His paranoia was overwhelming; there was no turning back—not now.

"I'd like to check out some of your new embroidery items. Do you have time to show me?"

"Oh sure. They're in the back room," Dalia eagerly responded.

She led the way through the production door and to the far wall where stacks of finished product were stored on shelves. His hand missed covering her mouth, and she shrieked when the blade sliced into her heart. Ferro was glad he didn't have to look into her eyes while she was dying.

Hearing the front door open, he refused to panic, gently releasing her body, allowing it to drop to the floor. He got behind one of the embroidery machines and waited.

NOON HOUR WAS APPROACHING AS TOM HEADED for the elevators. Phil Bartron was in the elevator when the door opened on the twentieth floor.

Tom was stunned, expecting him to be in jail. "What was all that business out on the boulevard last night, Phil? The sirens and flashing lights."

"Nothing much—got a speeding ticket, that's all. Are you headed out for lunch," Phil asked.

"Yes, I have a date," Tom responded, wondering if he should believe the little guy.

"That must be nice—to have a date—with a lady, I mean," Phil Bartron added.

"Yes, it's a date with a lady, but only business, darn," Tom chuckled.

Phil Bartron's doubtful expression when getting off on the ground floor amused Tom Hastings. After exiting the elevator and moving through the door to the garage, Tom felt insecure without his gun. Even though it was daylight outside, the only lights in the parking garage were pale yellow overheads. They never light enough in the garage, he thought. Arriving at his car, twelve stalls down from the entry area, he got in quickly and drove off without incident.

Tom found an empty parking spot right in front of Jensen's Shirts. Carefully opening the car door so as not to scratch his neighbor's red car, he stepped out and headed for the front door. Since his date with Dalia was for lunch and not business, he wasn't carrying his briefcase. A cluster of small bells clattered to announce his arrival when he pushed open the door.

On entering, his senses warned him something was wrong. Along with the room being unusually quiet, he detected a strange odor. Walking to the counter, he peeked over the top. There was a sheet of paper lying on the floor, but otherwise the desk appeared to be in order. He touched a partially filled cup of coffee sitting on the desk by the computer—it felt cold. Looking around, he noticed the door to the rear production room was slightly ajar.

"Hello," he sang out in a loud, determined voice.

There was no answer. After waiting for about two minutes, he sang out another hello and got the same negative result. He walked over to the production door, put together a fist and rapped a couple of times.

"Hello. Anyone home?" he called for a third time.

His raps pushed the door open enough to expose the upper works of an embroidery machine in the dimly lit room. Grabbing the doorknob in his right hand, he pushed on the door, opening it enough to lean into the room. Glancing about, he could see the embroidery machines loaded with miles of yarn. Down on the floor at the far end of the room lay a pile of fabric. No one appeared to be in the room, so he returned to the reception area.

"Where is Dalia?" he whispered. We had a lunch date. She is always reliable—always here when expecting me. The pile of fabrics—the unusual smell. Apprehension choked his breath. Something was wrong, he feared anxiously.

Clearing his throat, Tom again said strongly, "Hello!"

The feeling of finality was overwhelming, so he pushed the production door completely open and approached the pile of fabric. About three steps away from the pile, Tom Hastings found himself staring at a large pool of blood, glistening from the dim overhead lights. It extended out from underneath the fabric.

The reason for the strange smell was now apparent. He was overwhelmed with the choice of lifting the fabric or running and calling the police.

A swishing sound coming from the other end of the room sent feelings of fear and panic racing from his mind to his stomach. Jerking his body sidewise, he saw a shadow move across the far end of the room toward the back door. Straining to see who it was, Tom heard the door open and close. Without disturbing the pile of fabrics, he ran back to the door that led to the reception room. Promptly, he advanced to Dalia's desk and picked up her phone.

"I need police and medical help immediately at Jensen's Shirts in the Lake's strip mall."

"What seems to be the problem?" a woman's voice asked.

"There's a large pool of blood, and there may be a body."

"Okay. Stay on the phone. I'll get you some help."

There was a pause for about thirty seconds before the lady's voice returned. "Would you give me your name, please?"

Tom gave his name, address and phone number.

"Please stay on the phone. A police car should arrive there momentarily."

Amazingly, within a minute a police car approached and parked in front of the building next to his car. Two officers got out quickly and approached the door.

"Two officers are here. Can I hang up?"

"Yes. Thanks for calling."

Tom noticed both officers had their right hands resting on their weapons.

"What seems to be the problem, Mr. Hastings?" The first officer asked.

"There is a pile of fabric in the production room—back there—in there." Tom pointed toward the door. "The pool of blood is next to it."

One officer stayed with Tom, the other grabbed his gun from his holster and advanced into the back room.

Within moments, the officer returned. "There's a body back there and a lot of blood. I didn't feel a pulse—we need the paramedics and a call to the precinct. You stay right here. Make sure no one touches anything."

While watching the first officer dash outside, the other got out a notepad and began asking Tom questions. After getting the spelling correct on Tom's name, he wanted to know what he was doing there.

While the officer was writing down his answers, Tom heard a siren. His thoughts returned to his morbid experience of being attacked by an intruder in his house in the country. He remembered getting a batch of questions that day. *I've been through this before*, he thought. Calm returned.

He looked at his watch. It showed close to 1:00. Tom told the officer, "I need to make a phone call. Can I make it from that phone or the cell in my car?"

"Better do it from your car, but you better plan on being around until we're finished here. I'm sure the detective will want to talk to you."

"I'll be right back," Tom said.

The police officer nodded in approval.

Tom strode out to his car. He dialed the SkyWeb phone number and Trisha answered.

"Hi Trisha, this is Tom. I am going to have to change our appointment because of an emergency. How about tomorrow, right after the lunch hour?"

"That's okay, Tom. I have lots to do today anyhow. See you tomorrow."

"Thanks, Trisha," Tom replied, and hung up.

While he was on the phone, a paramedic emergency vehicle had pulled up in front. Two medics hurried into Jensen's Shirts.

The policeman remaining in the main room was watching Tom as he reentered the reception room. The officer said, "Have a seat over there by the window, Mr. Hastings. This is going to take awhile."

Tom sat on one of the chairs in the customer waiting area, attempting to recover from the shock of finding what likely was a dead body, perhaps Dalia's.

He looked up at the officer. "Did you see what was under the pile?"

"Yes, it was a woman. Likely killed within the past two hours."

"Oh geez, I hope it isn't Dalia," Tom weakly responded.

"Dalia—she's the person you came to see, right?"

"Yes, Dalia and her husband, Cliff, own this business."

The door to the back room opened wide and the medics and the other police officer came through it. The medics exited the building while the officer approached Tom. "I'm expecting a detective to arrive at any moment. I suggest you wait right here. He may have some questions."

Tom got up from the chair. "Do you have any concept on what happened, and who was under the pile?"

"Well, we're not certain, but it's a female with a wound in the chest. I suspect it is the owner and operator of this place—Dalia Jensen, I think you mentioned was her name. We'll know more soon."

Tom's overwhelming grief mixed with a surfacing fear. He brought his hand up to his forehead and stared at the floor. Not Dalia, he thought. The officer watched as Tom staggered slightly and slumped into the chair.

A second police car entered the parking lot and pulled up in an empty slot. An uniformed police officer, who was driving, and Detective Anderson emerged.

Tom recognized Anderson from the interview at the Towers. The detective came through the door and was greeted by one of the original officers. They talked for a short time and the officer pointed at the door to the back room, then toward Tom Hastings. Detective Anderson glanced at Tom before heading through the door leading to the production room.

Tom stared out the window for the next five minutes, patiently waiting for the detective to return. One of the original officers remained in the room with Tom while the other was in the back room with the detective.

When the detective returned from the production room, he walked directly to where Tom was sitting. "So we meet again, Mr. Hastings."

Tom looked up at him. "Yes, I guess we do, detective. Looks like another murder, doesn't it?"

"Yes, the lady lying dead in there is the owner of this business. As you probably know, her name is Dalia Jensen."

Tom raised both hands to support his head, his biggest fear confirmed. Dalia was the victim.

"What brought you here today, Mr. Hastings?"

"She called me a couple of days ago—said she needed to talk to me. I'm not sure why. There was no mention of the inventory spreadsheet program that we were working on—I don't think this was about business. I was supposed to pick her up for lunch."

"Did you see anyone else here today? How about her husband, Clifford?"

"Strange, Detective Anderson, I felt something was wrong right away, after entering. There was no one here—dead quiet—also a strange smell. I called out about three times and knocked on the production door—no response. After checking out the room back there, I noticed the pool of blood by the pile of fabric."

"Did you touch anything?"

"No, except perhaps the doorknob."

"How about the phone at the desk, or anything on the desk?"

"Well, yes...I used the phone to call you guys."

"Oh, okay. Look, you can leave for now. I have your phone number and will likely get in touch soon. I may have some more questions," said the detective, closing his book and moving away.

"Wait, I forgot something," added Tom.

The detective stopped and turned to hear Tom say, "When I was looking at the pool of blood, I heard a noise behind me. Glancing back, I caught a glimpse of someone, a shadow of a person, leave through the back door."

"What's that? You saw someone?" the detective exclaimed.

"Yes, but not well enough to see what it was or who it was."

"Could you tell whether it was a man or woman?"

"No, I couldn't, but gut feeling tells me it was a man."

"Why do you say that?"

"Because of the bulk of the person and the speed. Whoever it was moved very quickly."

"The rest of the day, I want you to think about what you saw go through that door. Perhaps more will come to you later. I expect to get over to your building to interview Mr. Jensen later today. I will give you a call then also."

"Is that all, then?"

"Yes."

44

LEAVING THE DREADFUL SCENE WAS A RELIEF for Tom Hastings. He drove back home and parked in the outdoor parking lot.

As Tom stood, waiting for an elevator, Marcil Huggins entered the lobby, coming from a doorway that led to a stairwell and the lower level. As Marcil approached, Tom noticed his baseball cap was off-center and his clothing had a disheveled appearance.

Tom stared at Marcil as they entered the elevator.

He said, "Hello, Marcil."

Marcil looked up at Tom with glassy eyes, said nothing and punched his floor number. When the elevator door opened on the fifteenth floor, he exited without saying a word.

The elevator continued upward. Marcil's appearance and behavior had stunned Tom. *Would Detective Anderson be interested?* He remembered Dalia talking about Marcil, how he would hang around and pester her. Could this seemingly docile individual be the killer of four women? A chill went through his spine when he got off the elevator. Nodding, he thought. *I'll have to report this to the detective.*

Expecting a call from Detective Anderson sometime during the afternoon hours, Tom focused on finding things to do in his apartment. The phone rang at four, but it wasn't the detective. Jan was on the line.

"Tom, I heard what happened over at Jensen's. You were there and it must have been awful...you need a hug. Why don't you come over about five? Greg and I are both anxious to hear your story."

"Jan, I'm expecting a call and a visit at any moment. I'll come over right after. It may be later than five."

"That's okay, Tom. Please come over as soon as you can."

"See you later, Jan," Tom said, and hung up the phone.

Five minutes later, the phone rang again. It was Detective Anderson, calling from the lobby.

"Come right on up," Tom responded.

Three minutes later, Tom heard the expected knock on the door.

"Mr. Hastings, do you remember Lieutenant Barry? He was here with me a couple of months ago."

"Yes, I do remember."

After shaking both men's hands, Tom gestured them to the couch in the living room.

The detective brought out a notepad and leafed through a few pages before speaking. "You said earlier that Jensen's Shirts was a client of yours. You had made about six visits to their place of business?"

"Yes, that's true. I visited there exactly six times."

"During your visits, Mr. Hastings, did you notice or hear of any strange happenings? Persons hanging around and such?"

"Well, there was this one person that Dalia mentioned hung around and pestered her."

"Who would that be?"

"A man by the name of Marcil Huggins. He lives in this building on the fifteenth floor."

"Are you acquainted with that man?"

"Yes, I am. I have seen him at O'Leary's on occasion. Also, he hangs around the bike trail by the railroad track."

"Anything else about Huggins?"

Tom sighed deeply. He hated the thought of being a tattletale, but in this case there wasn't much choice. "I rode the elevator up with Marcil earlier today after returning from Jensen's."

The detective leaned forward, anxiously waiting for Tom's next words.

"Marcil Huggins never said a word, His clothes appeared to be in disarray and his cap was off-tilt. His eyes were glassy."

Lieutenant Barry asked, "Is he usually that quiet when being around you?"

"No. Most of the time he was very chatty."

The next question came from the detective. "The person you mentioned glimpsing while in the production room—has this become any clearer?"

"No, it hasn't."

"Could it have been Marcil Huggins?"

"Yes, it could have, but it could have been anyone...any man."

"So, you are quite certain it was not a woman?"

"The bulk of the person—that's all."

"Ah, Mr. Hastings, I have a report here stating that about three weeks ago you were involved in an incident down in the storage area. Is this true?"

"Yes, it is true. After I told the manager, Carl, he called you guys."

"You told the police officers about hearing someone breathing, but didn't see the person."

"Yes, someone was breathing in that room besides me...very deeply."

"Do you think the person could have been Marcil Huggins?" asked the detective.

"I have no way of knowing, but I do have a gum wrapper," responded Hastings.

"A gum wrapper?"

"Yes. I picked it up from the grass next to the bench, down by the bike trail."

"Did you see someone toss it?"

"No, but it was lying there right after Marcil Huggins left. He had been sitting on the bench."

"Ah, we'll take it with us, if you have it. However, its value is questionable because you didn't see him drop it there."

The detective closed his notebook and stood up. Lieutenant Barry also rose.

Tom went into the kitchen and returned with the freezer bag.

After taking the bag, the detective said, "Thanks for your information, Mr. Hastings. We'll be in touch."

Tom looked up at the detective. "I have a question."

"What is it?"

"I was looking at FBI wanted pictures on the Internet the other day. I noticed one of the persons resembled a tenant at the Towers."

"Yeah? Who's that?

"Carlos Valdez."

"Thanks. We'll check it out," responded the detective.

The two police officers headed out the door without saying another word. Even though it looked bad for Marcil, Tom wasn't convinced he was the killer. If he was the killer, then it was all over, and Tom could put the gun away.

————

THE POLICE STATION DOOR OPENED. Detective Anderson went directly to his office, Lieutenant Barry close behind. There was one written message on his desk. One was from the drugs division and the other was from the FBI. *Detective Anderson, please call Captain Barkley from Drugs and Captain Townsend from the FBI.*

Rod Barry sat and listened while the detective made the calls. Captain Barkley told him that their informer at O'Leary's had goofed somehow. He'd been sure about a drug transfer, but the guy they'd stopped, Phil Bartron, had been clean. Either he hadn't had the stuff on him in the first place, or he'd dumped it somehow.

Captain Townsend of the Minneapolis FBI branch volunteered their services when Detective Anderson told him about the fourth murder. Two agents were assigned to the case and would arrive at the station in the morning.

After Detective Anderson got off the phone, he said to his assistant, "Barry, this thing is getting out of hand. We're having the FBI over tomorrow to help. Meanwhile, the apparent drug bust fell through. That's not our cookie, but the man they set up is also one of our murder suspects—Phil Bartron."

"Ah...I remember him...the weasel with the goatee," responded the lieutenant.

Detective Anderson took the plastic bag out of his pocket and dumped the gum wrapper on the desk. "Bring me the other two, would you, Rod?"

When they were all laid out, he said, "Hmm...not exactly the same, are they?"

"No, they could be a waste of time, Bill. Most of our suspects chew gum."

"Yeah. Maybe that Hastings has something. Let's check out the FBI list. I feel rather embarrassed about not doing that sooner."

45

TOM WAS ON EDGE AFTER THE POLICEMEN LEFT. He called Jan immediately.

"Head right on over, Tom," she said.

Greg answered his knock. "Enter. I see you had some visitors."

"Yes the law was here. I need a drink real bad."

Greg pointed to the couch in the living room. "Have a seat, Tom. What can I bring you?"

"How about a scotch?"

"On the rocks?"

"Yes, that will be fine."

After Tom was seated, Jan entered the room. "Well, hello—you're really into it today, aren't you?"

"I guess I am. Just my luck to walk into another murder."

"I feel just terrible about Dalia. And Cliff—I hear he's taking it real bad. He has the flu, you know. That's why he wasn't at the store."

Tom felt embarrassed for not thinking about Cliff earlier. Cliff's name had hardly been mentioned and not at all by the detective.

"Oh boy, that must have been quite a shock. I feel for the guy," responded Tom.

Greg returned from the kitchen and handed Tom a scotch. Taking a generous sip, Tom appreciated the good feeling as it was going down.

Jan said, "Carl is in a frenzy down there. He doesn't laugh any more—eyes most everyone with suspicion. This has got to end pretty soon."

"It may be over soon. The police are about to pick up Marcil Huggins," responded Tom.

"What's this all about, Tom? What?" asked Jan, excitedly.

"Well, when I found the pool of blood in Jensen's back room, I saw someone leave via the back door. I'm not positive, but it may have been Marcil. There's not much doubt that Detective Anderson is questioning him right now."

Greg interrupted. "Bingo. We have a winner."

"It's not funny, Greg," scoffed Jan. "Besides, there are a lot of other guys on the list."

"Yeah, like who? Me, Tom?" asked Greg.

"It's no joke, Greg. Phil Bartron is about as suspicious a guy as I have ever seen. Then how about Vito and Gordon Beard," retorted Jan. "I hear Susan has quit SkyWeb."

Tom responded, "That shocks me. What's the deal?"

"I heard the company is going broke."

Jan's statement put a damper on Tom's thought regarding his upcoming visit to SkyWeb the next day. "That doesn't sound very good. What's she going to do?" Tom feebly asked.

"I hear she's out job hunting already," added Jan.

"Or man hunting," sneered Greg.

"Oh, Greg, you have a dirty mind," retorted Jan.

"Well, maybe, but this Jack and Candice split may have something to do with Susan," said Greg, raising his right arm and pointing a finger at Jan.

"Well, folks, thanks for the drink. I have to get going," said Tom.

Tom returned to his apartment, lay down on the couch and reflected on the events of the day. He dozed for a few minutes, experiencing a weird dream. *He was down in the storage room and there were several people standing by the door, blocking his exit. They were Marcil Huggins, Vito Manchino, Detective Anderson, Susan, and Phil Bartron.* He woke up in a cold sweat and was relieved to see the Minneapolis skyline through the window.

At close to 7:00 p.m., he took the elevator down to the lobby and walked to the outdoor parking lot where his car was parked. The .32-automatic was in his jacket pocket. He placed it in the glove compartment and drove to O'Leary's.

The hostess nodded to his request for a table that had access to the television. She led him to one of the high tables next to the bar.

He was pleased to see a baseball game in progress. The Twins were playing the White Sox.

Thoughts of his dream resurfaced when he saw Phil Bartron sitting on the other side of the bar. Those small, beady eyes were directed at two young ladies sitting on stools close to Tom's table. The pointed goatee was hanging about an inch off the surface of the bar.

After a waitress came, Tom ordered a Bud and a sweet-and-sour salad.

"Very good, sir," she said, and hurried off.

Tom refocused on the baseball game, watching the Twins score four runs in the second inning. A base clearing double was the big hit.

When Tom's beer came, he saw Phil Bartron get up from his stool and head for Tom's side of the bar. For a moment, Tom was concerned that Bartron was going to join him, but his fears were allayed when Phil Bartron sat down next to the two ladies.

After finishing his dinner, Tom looked over at Bartron. The lady next to Phil appeared angry—she was jawing at Phil intensely, forcing him to slip off the stool and head out the door.

Phil Bartron had been gone for only about five minutes when another player from Tom's dream replaced him. The sport-coat man, Vito Manchino, took a seat at his usual stool on the other side of the bar. Within moments, a large plume of smoke billowed over the top of his head. Vito appeared extremely fidgety and his eyes roamed around the room. Tom wondered if any of his other dream characters were going to show up.

He didn't have to wait long. Gordon Beard came in and took a seat next to Vito. Even though Gordon hadn't been in his dream, Susan had.

According to Jan, Susan had left SkyWeb. Tom assumed the two-million-dollar loss that SkyWeb showed on their books had something to do with Susan leaving.

After thinking about his most recent accounting work with SkyWeb, Tom was relieved to know his own bill was paid in full.

The conversation Gordon was having with Vito appeared to be anything but friendly. The Twins' four-run lead was down to one, and they were changing pitchers. Gordon got up from his stool and placed a finger in Vito's face. Not being close enough to hear what Gordon was saying, Tom could only guess that money was likely involved in the dispute—perhaps drugs? *I'll probably never know and don't really care*, Tom thought, signing his credit card slip.

Tom placed the credit card back in his billfold. His departure was delayed by the sound of breaking glass, followed by a loud thump.

Tom looked toward the far end where Vito Manchino and Gordon Beard had been talking. Vito was missing from the stool. Standing and looking down at the floor was Gordon Beard. Glancing around the bar, Tom noticed all the patrons watching. It was apparent that

Gordon had something to do with Vito not being on the stool. Everyone watched as Vito Manchino got up from the floor, partially leaned against the stool and pointed a finger at Gordon Beard.

Using both hands, Gordon pushed Vito in the chest and Vito went down again. The bartender was on the phone. Uh-oh, we may have some police here—and soon, Tom thought. Gordon turned, said something to the bartender and headed for the door.

Slowly, Vito got up from the floor and reseated himself on the stool, gently rubbing his chin. Drawing the eyes of everyone in the room, Manchino lit a cigarette and used both hands to pat down his hair.

Two police officers came through the door a couple of minutes later. They advanced to the bar and talked to the bartender, who pointed toward Vito. The officers proceeded to the end of the bar and began to interview Manchino. Tom got up from his chair and left the bar and grill.

After arriving at the Towers and parking in the lower-level garage, Tom removed the automatic from his glove compartment and dropped it in his jacket pocket. After exiting the car, he saw a man approaching from the opposite aisle. Seeing a goatee hanging down from a narrow face, Tom was quite certain the man was Phil Bartron.

Whoever it was, he didn't look up and proceeded quickly through the door leading to the elevators. By the time Tom got there, James the barber was waiting.

Holding the door open, he said, "Good evening, Mr. Hastings."

"Greetings, Jim. Was that you in the garage just now?"

"No, I came over from the shop. I heard it was you that discovered the body at Jensen's."

Wow, news travels fast, Tom thought. "Well, sort of. I happened to arrive there at the wrong time."

"Dalia was such a sweetheart. I wish it had been someone else that was killed," said James.

Tom pressed the number 20 button and was surprised to see that James had pressed 17. During their previous elevator encounters, he'd usually gotten on at seven.

46

Tom CHANGED INTO NIGHTCLOTHES AND CALLED JULIE.

"Good evening, Tom. How are things at the Towers?"

"The Towers is fine, but there's been another victim."

"Your kidding! Who?"

"Dalia Jensen...she's been murdered."

"Oh my gosh—not another one. Guess I didn't know her. You worked for her, didn't you? You must feel awful."

"Yes, and I was the lucky person who discovered the body."

There was a momentary silence at the other end of the phone before Julie responded, "What! You found the body?"

"Yeah, I had a lunch appointment with Dalia and showed up at Jensen's Shirts at noon. She was in the back room lying under a pile of fabric. I actually didn't see the body, just a pool of blood, and called the police."

"Tom, I've known you for only three years and you seem to walk into some pretty tough situations—more than anyone else in a lifetime."

"Where can I hide?" Tom responded.

"Tell you what—I'll take you out to dinner tomorrow evening. I'll drive over about six. How's that?" Julie asked.

"Yes, that's the type of news I like hearing."

"Okay, see you tomorrow at six, and remember to be careful where you go and what you do."

Tom sighed. "Good night."

Sleep was difficult that evening. Visions of pools of blood and a shadow moving across the room kept reoccurring in Tom's mind. The more he thought about the shadow, the more he visualized the body shape of Marcil Huggins.

After awaking the next morning, Tom was groggy from lack of sleep. He was glad the appointment at SkyWeb was not until after lunch.

Close to 10:00 that morning, Tom went down the elevator to get his mail. The lobby was busy with people—among them, three uniformed police officers and Detective Anderson. Marcil Huggins, who was facing the outside door, turned and looked straight into Tom's eyes.

Tom saw deep sadness in those eyes and somehow felt guilty for Marcil's predicament. There were doubts in Tom's mind about Marcil's guilt. Looking down at Marcil's wrists, Tom could see handcuffs tying them together.

Carl was standing in his office door watching the activity. Joining him, standing next to the doorway was Jan. Tom entered the lobby and proceeded to the mailbox wall where he fished out his mail. Looking up, he saw the policemen leaving and Marcil being seated in the back of their car.

Jan, gripping a Styrofoam cup of coffee in her hand, sat down on the couch.

Tom joined her. "What's going on, Jan?"

"They are taking Marcil in for questioning, that's all."

"Why the cuffs?"

"That's exactly what I was thinking. Marcil must have said something or perhaps resisted in some way...maybe it's routine for the cops in this area."

Carl was still standing by the door. "Maybe it's all over. Huggins killed all four."

Jan said, "Tom, that shadow you saw at Jensen's yesterday was Marcil. He admitted that, also claiming that Dalia was already dead when he got there."

Tom looked at Jan and was amazed at her knowledge. *How'd she know that?* He thought.

Jan added, "The police were real interested in why he covered her partially clothed body with fabric."

"If he did that, why not call the police right away?" asked Tom.

"Well, he heard you come in and got scared. His natural instinct was to hide. Maybe he thought you were the killer."

"Perhaps. It was quite dark back there. Well, I need to get home."

Jan remained in the lobby, and Tom could see her talking to Carl as the elevator door closed.

Later that morning, shortly after 11:00, Tom headed down to the garage. His plan was to have lunch downtown prior to visiting SkyWeb. Friday traffic downtown was more frantic than usual— Minneapolis was a city of cars and trucks without adequate transit routes.

He found an inexpensive parking lot near the building that housed SkyWeb. While circling the block, he noticed a sidewalk restaurant less than a block away. It was a quaint, dusty-looking place, but the service and food turned out to be above average.

Shortly before 1:00, he left the restaurant and proceeded to the SkyWeb building on foot. Gordon Beard's black Mercedes was not in the parking lot. After getting off on the third floor, he was shocked to see a special lock on the door accessing the SkyWeb suite. There was a notice pasted to the door: *Closed until further notice by order of the Sheriff's Department.*

Tom stood there and looked at the sign for about a minute before returning to the elevators. When he exited on the main floor, Trisha was standing in the main lobby, waiting for him.

"I'm sorry, Tom. The Sheriff closed us down just this morning. I tried calling you, but you didn't answer."

"Where can we talk, Trisha?" Tom asked.

"There's a coffee shop around the corner."

They walked in silence to the small shop and took a table by the window.

"So what happened, Trisha?" Tom asked.

"I just knew when Susan left, things were not going to turn out well. I began receiving phone calls from creditors, and they were getting real mean. Gordon was not taking any calls, leaving me holding the bag. It was a relief when the sheriff people came and locked the place up."

"So, what did Gordon tell you?"

"He said the money was gone and I would have to look for another job. I felt bad about your appointment today."

"All is not lost, Trisha. You've learned a lot. It will be useful when you apply for another job."

Trisha began to cry. Tom reached his hand across the table and placed it on Trisha's arm. "I'm sorry this has happened. You're going to be just fine. I wish there was some way I could help."

Trisha regained her composure, wiped a tear from her check and worked her words through jerky sniffles.

"There *is* something. Could I use you for a reference?"

"You certainly can." Tom reached into his pocket and drew out a business card. "Take this Trisha—my address and phone number."

"Oh, thanks, Tom. You taught me so much. I'll always remember you and will never forget what you've done for me."

After leaving the coffee shop, Tom and Trisha walked back to the SkyWeb parking lot. She gave him a big hug before driving off.

While walking back to his car, Tom was thinking about the pushing incident at O'Leary's of the previous evening. Gordon Beard had been seriously upset about something—serious enough to push Vito Manchino off his stool and then push him down a second time. Tom wondered if Vito had filed a complaint with the police officers. *Doubtful*, he thought. Vito probably wants to stay as far away from the police as he can.

47

JULIE WAS COMING. Tom spent the rest of Friday afternoon cleaning his apartment. At five minutes before 6:00, the phone rang. He insisted Julie wait until he got there.

After a long hug at the rear door of the Towers, Julie looked up sadly. "Tom, I'm so sorry about Dalia."

"Thanks. Let's go up."

Julie sat down on the couch, Tom brought back two glasses of wine from the kitchen and said, "The police took Marcil Huggins away—for questioning, I heard. He was wearing handcuffs—there may be more than questions.

"According to Jan, Marcil claimed that he found Dalia's body before I arrived on the scene. After covering the body with a pile of fabric, he heard me come in. Panicking, he hid behind the machines and sneaked out while I was standing looking at the pool of blood.

"I saw Marcil right after returning to the Towers. His tilted cap, messy clothes and strange demeanor prompted me to tell the detective."

"Do you think he did it?" asked Julie.

"No, I don't think so—could be wrong, but gut feelings tell me he's not a murderer."

"What do Jan and Greg think?"

"I really don't know, not having talked to them since Marcil was taken away. Besides all that, I have two other problems. Not only have I lost Dalia—she was a client—I am also losing SkyWeb. The sheriff put a lock on their door—apparently, it's a money problem. I was totally surprised when showing up there for work after lunch today. For my benefit, the office lady hung around and waited, to let me know what's going on."

"And who is this office lady?"

"Her name is Trisha—hey, Julie, business. Strictly business."

"Oh, I know, Tom. Just kidding."

"There's a nice, quiet restaurant a couple of miles down the street. We can get away from all of this. Let's go," insisted Tom.

When they pulled into the parking lot of the restaurant, Julie said, "Frankie's—what a unique name."

"Yup, it sure is. I've heard great things about Frankie's. Let's give it a try."

On entering, they got seated right away. The hostess and waitresses were attired in long dresses and the bartender wore a black tie and white shirt. Seated two tables away were Aaron and Kit Alhaya.

"Do you remember Aaron and Kit from Jan's party?" Tom asked Julie.

"Oh, certainly—what a nice couple."

"They're sitting two tables behind you. I haven't seen them around, even though I'm up and down that elevator a thousand times."

"Good for them. They're too nice to be involved in all the rough stuff going on at the Towers."

At that moment, Kit looked up and caught Tom's glance. She smiled, raised her arm slightly and waggled her fingers in recognition. Tom returned her gesture by raising his glass.

Julie was frowning at Tom. "Would you like to do a in-line-skating session tomorrow morning?"

"Yes. I brought my skates. They're in the trunk. Who did you wave at—Aaron or Kit?"

"Great. Let's plan on breakfast at Molly's after we finish. Ah...it was Kit."

The service and food at Frankie's were at least as good as he had expected. Tom and Julie were having coffee, when Aaron and Kit stopped by their table.

"How are you?" asked Julie, smiling.

"Nice to see you two again," said Aaron. "Nice place, good food."

"So, how are things with you and the university?" Tom asked.

"I love teaching," he responded.

Kit said, "Isn't it awful about the murders? I hear you discovered the latest body, Tom."

"Yeah, I did. Hopefully, never again."

"It must have been a terrible experience," Kim said.

Aaron piped in, "Let's hope it's over with. I heard the police took someone away in handcuffs."

"Yeah, they took Marcil Huggins in for questioning. According to the latest, he hasn't been charged yet," Tom stated.

"Well, let's go, Kit, and let these people finish their dinner."

"Thanks for stopping by. See you two again," said Tom.

"Good-bye," added Julie.

After the Alhayas left, both Tom and Julie turned down a dessert offer from the waitress. He paid the bill and they headed out to the parking lot. Tom grabbed Julie's hand and led her to his car.

"My, what a nice couple," she said.

"I'm sure glad they aren't involved in any of the bad stuff going on at the Towers," Tom responded, holding the car door open for Julie.

The next morning, after having coffee and reading the newspaper, they headed for the elevators, skate backpacks slung over their shoulders. The door opened on the twelfth floor and Vito Manchino came aboard.

He looked at Julie. "Well, you can relax now, Julie. The real murderer has been caught. I knew it was that scumbag of a Marcil all along. Your lover, Tom, and I are off the hook."

Tom was looking down and saw Julie's fists clench.

Vito coughed and added, "I think the cops owe me an apology after the way I was treated a few weeks ago."

"I'm not all that convinced that Marcil Huggins is the right one," Tom responded.

"Oh, he did it alright. He was always hanging around, watching all the chicks," said Vito, sneering.

The elevator stopped at the lobby, the door opened and Julie and Tom got off. Manchino remained, apparently heading down to the garage.

"The nerve of that guy," said Julie. "He's probably still a prime suspect himself. I wouldn't trust that guy anytime, anyplace. I had to control myself from belting him one."

"Yeah, I saw those fists of yours."

"Would you like some more coffee, Julie?" Tom asked, filling a Styrofoam cup from the large silver pot on the little stand by Carl's door.

"No, thanks, I've had enough," she replied.

They walked into the outdoor parking lot, down the steps and over to the bench that marked the beginning of the bike trail.

After donning their skates and gracefully moving onto the trail, Tom asked, "I wonder what ever happened to Richard."

"Tom, everyone I talk to from the office building has concluded that he ran off with another woman."

"Well, I'm not so sure, Julie. His wife, Maria, moved in with her parents in Madison, you know."

"What a jerk he turned out to be," said Julie firmly. "Every time his name gets brought up at work, it's with disgust. No one seems to miss him, except for possibly a couple of goggle-eyed girl pups."

About two miles up the trail, they came to a bench and sat down for a rest.

"Look up in that tree—looks like a hawk," said Julie, excitedly.

Tom looked up at a hawk perched high above. That moment reminded him of the nature walks at his country place. Julie and he had walked often. He missed his previous home, especially the nature trails and the tennis court. At times, he mourned their loss. Perhaps some day he would return. The five-year option, buy-back clause included in his selling contract was comforting to him. Thoughts of returning to the country energized feelings in him. I'll keep this my secret for now, he thought.

"Well, Julie, should we continue?"

They reversed direction and headed back toward the Towers. The trail was new and smooth and they moved along at a graceful, comfortable pace, enjoying the pleasant day and the nature along the trail. When the bench at the end of the trail came into view, Tom could see it was occupied. He visualized Marcil sitting in a jail cell.

As they got closer to the bench, Tom slowed down and turned to Julie. "You're not going to believe this, but that's Marcil Huggins sitting on that bench."

48

GROSS FEELINGS OF DISCOMFORT GNAWED AT TOM when they stopped at the bench to remove their skates.

"Hello, Marcil," Tom said.

"Well, if it isn't the informer," Marcil responded.

"Oh, come on now, Marcil. Was I supposed to lie to the police? I just told them what I saw. By the way, why didn't you call the police when you found Dalia, as you claimed?"

"I was going to, but when you showed up, I got scared and hid."

"Did you think I was the killer?" Tom sharply asked Marcil.

"How was I to know if you weren't?" he responded.

"Well, I'm not the killer, and not you nor anyone else is going to bully me into not talking to the police. Come on, Julie. Let's go home." Any previous sympathy Tom had had for Marcil Huggins vanished.

Julie and Tom met Jan and Greg later that day for cocktail hour. Their main discussion centered on Marcil Huggins and how quickly the police had released him. Greg admitted he hadn't been surprised. Jan thought the police were making a mistake. Julie agreed with Jan. Tom didn't express an opinion, in spite of his disgust for Marcil's attitude.

Julie remained until mid-afternoon on Sunday. Tom escorted her down to the parking lot and watched the little red convertible disappear around the corner as she left the Towers.

On Monday morning, close to 10:00, the phone rang. The caller was Cliff Jensen. "Tom, I need some help with the books. Could you help me out?"

"Cliff, I feel real bad about what happened. Are you alright?"

"Well, not really, but I have a potential buyer for the business and need to understand what I am selling. You could help me."

"Okay, Cliff. I'll come over this afternoon if you'll be in."

"You may think this is a little quick—Dalia dying so recently— but this buyer is persistent."

"Cliff, you do what you have to do, okay?" responded Tom.

"Yes, I'll be here all afternoon. The place is locked, so call me just before you come. I'll watch for you."

"Okay, Cliff. I expect to be there about one-thirty."

Cliff hung up and Tom wondered what that had been all about.

Tom got one more phone call that morning. Shortly before noon, Gordon Beard was on the phone.

"Tom, I don't understand the SkyWeb books. I'm closing out the company and need some help. Are you interested?"

"Okay, how about tomorrow?"

"Sure, what time?"

"Midmorning. How about ten?"

"Sure, see your then. The door will be locked, so just knock."

"I'll help you all I can."

"Thanks. See you tomorrow."

After hanging up, Tom sat and thought about the two calls. He wasn't too concerned about going to Jensen's, but the trip to SkyWeb disturbed him. In any case, he decided to take along his gun.

Shortly before the noon hour, Tom headed down the elevator. He brought along Jensen's phone number, planning to call Cliff from Molly's. On his way down to the lower-level garage, he got off at the lobby to fetch his mail.

Carl was standing in front of the couch, where Jan and Greg were seated. Tom paused on his way to the mailboxes.

"Good morning, Tom," said Carl.

"Yes, it is a good morning. What's the big talk about this morning? Hi, Jan. Hi, Greg."

Jan looked up at Tom. "Tom, Richard has been found. A couple out canoeing on the lake late yesterday evening found the body, floating."

Tom took a deep breath and whispered, "Oh my gosh. It's happened."

He thought of Maria. Sweet, little Maria must be hurting now. "I really feel for Maria. She has gone through so much," Tom said sadly.

"At least it's over with," responded Greg.

"Which lake?" Tom asked.

"The one you see from your window," Greg replied.

"Geez, Greg, I hope the police have their man; otherwise, we'll be living under constant pressure. I wonder how many other tenants are carrying guns, other than me."

"You're carrying a gun? I sure didn't know that."

"Well, not all the time, but anytime I go down to the lower level, including the garage, or outdoors."

"Maybe we should all stick together whenever we are in or near the building," said Jan.

"Oh by the way," she added. "We were on national television again last night. Well, *we* weren't, but the Towers was. They had the Minneapolis chief of police on. He said the FBI has entered the case."

"Geez, that part sounds good—the FBI. Let's hope it will be over soon. See you guys later. I have to go," Tom said, and with a troubled mind, headed for the mailboxes.

49

"GREETINGS, MR. TOM. HOW ARE YOU TODAY?" said a bright, smiling Molly when Tom entered her restaurant.

"Not so great. I just found out that one of my neighbors was found dead, floating in a lake."

"No...oh no. Was it that Richard guy?"

"Yes, Molly, it was. I need a quiet corner."

"Follow me," said Molly as her long dress swished through an aisle leading to a table away from anyone else.

She lay down a menu and asked, 'How's this?"

"Just fine. Thanks, Molly."

Tom was attempting to read the newspaper, but his mind was on Richard and what the body had looked like after being in the lake for a few weeks. Nothing on the menu looked appetizing to him as he thought of Richard's demise and the large pool of blood in the production room. He shuddered and took a long sip of coffee, attempting to remove the dreadful images. Tom ordered a grilled cheese sandwich and a glass of orange juice.

At 12:45, Tom paid his bill and left the restaurant. After getting back to his car, he called Jensen's on his cell phone. Cliff answered and Tom announced his arrival would take place in about two minutes.

"Fine. I'll wait for you by the door," responded Cliff.

Tom received a firm handshake after Cliff opened the front door.

"Come on in, and please have a seat at the computer. I'll pull up a chair," said Cliff anxiously.

Tom laid down his briefcase on the desk and positioned himself in front of the computer. The monitor was on, displaying all the icon selections in the left margin.

"How can I help you, Cliff?" Tom asked.

Cliff raised a large sheet of paper to his eyes. "I have a list. First, I need a report showing all the customer balances. Next, a report showing all the outstanding bills. A balance sheet report, which needs to show the value of the equipment. Also, I need an inventory printout of all the items, plus a total value of all the materials on hand. I have a buyer for this place, and they need to have this stuff as soon as possible."

"Cliff, would you leave that paper on the desk, and I'll get right to work? Hopefully, before leaving today all the reports that you need will be printed—if not today, then tomorrow at the latest."

"Tom, I need to leave for awhile—should be back in a couple of hours. If you have to leave for any reason, just make sure the door is locked behind you. Here's an extra key if you need to get back in."

"Okay, Cliff, see you later," answered Tom as he felt into a compartment in his briefcase to make sure the gun was there.

After Cliff left, Tom got busy with the accounting program, tracking down the customers and their outstanding balances. He noticed Joan Collison's name on the list. Her balance was zero. Uh-oh, he thought. There was someone else I know.

Juanita Valdez had an outstanding balance of fourteen hundred dollars. Tom double-clicked their listing and brought up their ledger. It didn't show a payment for the last six months. He printed their ledger and any others with a balance over five hundred dollars. Finally, he printed the entire customer list, including any customer with an existing balance.

His watch showed just after 3:00, and the door opened. As expected, Cliff appeared.

"Hi, Cliff. This is going well. The accounts payable, accounts receivable and the balance sheet are all updated and printed." Tom stapled them together and placed them on the counter.

Cliff walked over and shuffled through the documents. "Nice job. Tom—this is just what I need," he said, smacking on a wad of gum.

"I'm working on the inventory right now, and within the hour should have all the recent purchases entered. After that, I'll save the file to disk and work on it at home. The reports need adjusting and fine-tuning, and this will take some time. I hope to have that ready and all printed by late tomorrow—say, about five."

"Oh, that'll be just great, Tom. I can't thank you enough. Please have your bill ready when you come over tomorrow."

"I will," Tom replied, and returned to his work.

Within forty-five minutes, the last invoice had been entered and Tom made a backup copy onto two separate floppy disks.

Cliff was in the back room. Tom peaked in, saying, "I'm leaving now. See you tomorrow."

Cliff was working on one of the large embroidery machines. He said, "I need to get all these shirts done. Looks like I'll be here for awhile."

Tom entered the production room and quietly said, "Cliff, I feel your loss. Would you like me to stay around a little longer?"

Cliff stopped the machine and turned toward him. "Tom, life has to go on and I cannot spend the rest of it back here either. I need to start over again."

"Cliff, do you have any notion what happened last Thursday?"

"No, I was home. I didn't feel too good and decided not to go to work. I talked to Dalia about ten that morning, and everything was fine."

"Sorry I asked, Cliff. I imagine you have answered that question so many times."

"Yes, the police went over this, over and over again. I need to get out of this place and put it behind me. I need to forget."

"I feel for you, Cliff. Best of luck to you," Tom added, packing the backup diskettes into his briefcase. He left the building.

50

RICHARD AND DALIA'S MURDERS HAD OVERWHELMED Tom's mind as he was stopped his car in the outdoor parking lot. He was relieved on entering the Towers because the lobby was empty. Mental fatigue was beginning to take its toll.

Looking forward to a beer and a nap, he pressed number 20 in the elevator. When getting out on the twentieth floor, he noticed Jan and Greg's door was open. After stopping and staring for a moment, he continued down the corridor and turned the corner. Jan was standing next to his door.

She turned as he approached. "Oh, so there you are. I was about to leave you a note."

"Hi, Jan. What's on your mind?"

"I was wondering if you wanted to talk about what happened to Richard."

"Ah, yes I would, but first I need to unwind—a shower, perhaps a little nap, and then later I will come over."

"Sure, Tom, just come on over whenever you're ready."

Tom wasn't in the mood to discuss other problems. Rather, he needed to work on Cliff Jensen's request. The sight of a cluster of cold beers in the refrigerator generated peaceful thoughts. The top of one flicked off with a snap, and he kicked off his shoes before sitting on the couch. The beer was half gone when he fell asleep.

Two hours passed before Tom cleaned up and headed over to Jan and Greg's apartment. He knocked and Greg answered the door.

"Come on in, Tom. Have a seat in the living room. Can I get you a drink?"

"Sure. How about a glass of wine?"

"You drink chardonnay, don't you?"

"Yup, I sure do."

Tom sat on the couch in the living room.

Jan entered moments later. "Hello, again. Did you have a nice nap?"

"Sure did. So, what's the latest on Richard?"

Jan's chin tilted upward and she narrowed her eyes. "Detective Anderson came to see Carl early this morning. He brought the news about the body being found. According to Carl, it—the body was a mess. One might expect that after being in the water all that time."

"I guess the biggest question is whether it was an accident—or was he murdered like the others?" Tom questioned.

Greg entered the room and set a tall glass of white wine down on the small table for Tom.

"Thanks, Greg. That should hit the spot," said Tom as he took a long swig of the wine, enjoying the feeling as it hit the bottom of his stomach.

Jan shook her head. "The detective didn't know for sure how he died. He said it will take a week or two—autopsy, and all."

"Do you remember when I took you guys down to check out his car? The keys were in the ignition and his briefcase was on the floor. Richard was gone.

"A few minutes earlier, I saw him, apparently asleep."

"Or was he dead then?" offered Greg, just before he raised a glass to his lips.

"We'll probably never know," Tom replied.

"Oh, I think the cops will figure it out—modern science, you know," said a firm-toned Jan.

"Meanwhile, we still have a killer on the loose," warned Greg. "I get the willies every time I go down to that parking lot."

"Yeah, it's pretty cryptic down there, especially at night," mused Jan.

"I left my car in the outside lot this evening, and it's going to stay there tonight," Tom remarked. "Well, I better get back. I need to get some work done for Cliff Jensen by tomorrow."

"What are you doing for Cliff?" asked Jan.

"Bookwork. He's selling the store."

"Oh, that's too bad—I'll miss Dalia in that shop," added Jan.

Tom stood up. "Don't get up. I'll leave my empty glass in the kitchen. Thanks."

Tom returned to his apartment, got out his laptop and placed it on the dining room table. After copying the inventory program from the Jensen diskette, he worked on the program for about three hours. After the reports were completed, he shut down the computer and headed for bed.

Before going to sleep, he thought about the midmorning appointment with Gordon at SkyWeb. Tom wasn't looking forward to the visit.

51

FEELINGS OF APPREHENSION DOMINATED TOM HASTINGS while he sipped on the morning's first cup of coffee. He had agreed to meet with Gordon Beard because of a natural responsibility. Regardless of his feelings toward the failing status of SkyWeb, Tom felt obliged to demonstrate the results of his work and bring the job to a conclusion.

He headed down at just before 9:30. Jan and Greg were down in the lobby talking to Carl when he got off the elevator. Tom didn't have time to visit, but simply waved while continuing out to the parking lot.

The early-morning traffic had dissipated, and he arrived at the SkyWeb parking lot ten minutes early. After getting out of the car, Tom paused and looked for a black Mercedes—it wasn't there. He entered the building and took the elevator to the third floor. Surprisingly, the door to SkyWeb was open.

After entering, Tom was challenged by an armed deputy sheriff.

"Hello, I'm Deputy Sinkler. Are you Tom Hastings?"

"Yes, I am. Would you like to see an ID?" Tom asked.

"Yes, I would," replied the deputy.

Tom reached in his jacket for his billfold, slipped out his driver's license and handed it to the officer. After glancing at the license, the deputy returned it to Tom.

"I'm confused. What's going on? I was supposed to meet Gordon Beard here this morning."

"He won't be coming. I'm here as a result of a court decision. The company, SkyWeb, is under some sort of legal receivership, and its assets have become property of the court. I am here to enforce the judge's decision. According to this paper, the judge has asked you to produce a series of reports from the SkyWeb accounting file. It's up to you, of course."

The deputy handed Tom Hastings a sheet of paper. "This should explain," he added.

The letter addressed to Tom Hastings was headed with a county court title. The contents asked for the following reports: A list of creditors and amounts owed, a list of customers and the amounts due, and a list of assets and liabilities. The last paragraph requested the reports be submitted to the court within thirty days. The signature at the bottom of the paper belonged to the judge.

"I'll get going on this right now, deputy, but this is going to take some time," responded a frustrated Tom Hastings.

"For right now, the judge has asked if you would volunteer to check the integrity of the computer and the accounting program. After that, I am instructed, with your help, to disassemble the computer and printer, and deliver them to the court. In the near future, they are going to provide an office where they will ask you to generate the reports. You can start tomorrow, if you agree."

The computer booted without any problem and after Tom double-clicked the accounting software icon, the program loaded. Tom scanned the chart of accounts and everything appeared to be in order—so were the customer list and the vender list.

"It looks fine," he told the deputy. "I think there's enough paper in the printer to print the vendor list, customer list and the chart of accounts right now. I can do the rest tomorrow."

"Whoa, just one second. I think the judge's intentions are to have all that work done under supervision of the court. Let's shut the thing down, and I'll do the delivery."

The deputy handed Tom two documents and said, "You will need these to proceed."

The first one had instructions on how to access a specific room at the courthouse. The second document was a voucher form for expenses and fees. A parking permit was clipped to the second document.

"Well, okay. We'd better do it the judge's way."

Tom shut down the computer and disassembled the monitor and

printer. During the process of preparing the computer and accessories for moving, Tom accidentally pushed a pen over the side of the desk next to the wall. When reaching down to retrieve the pen, his fingers came in contact with a crumpled piece of paper. Along with the pen, he brought up a gum wrapper. After placing the pen back on the desk, he held up the gum wrapper momentarily and noted it was a common brand—Trident. As the deputy focused on the equipment to be moved, Tom dropped the wrapper in his pocket—the detective would be interested.

"The computer should be safe to transport on your car seat," Tom told the deputy, and assisted him in moving the equipment.

"Thanks for your cooperation, Mr. Hastings. Just follow the instructions on the sheet, and you should have no problem finding the right room when you come."

After the deputy left, Tom walked two blocks to the Chinese restaurant where he had lunched with Susan and Trisha. While following the hostess to a table, Tom recognized Jack Billings at the next table.

52

SMILING, JACK BILLINGS SAID, "Hello, Mr. Hastings. What brings you to this part of town?"

"I'm here on business, tying up some loose ends," Tom replied, and sat down on a chair at his own table.

"If you're alone, why don't you join me?" asked Jack.

Even though Tom preferred to lunch alone, he replied, "Sure, I'd be happy to."

Tom lifted the table setting and napkin off his table and moved.

After Tom sat down, Jack asked, "What do you think of the Towers and all the murders?"

"It's grossly uncomfortable and makes me think about moving back to the country," Tom answered with a frown and watched as a waitress filled his coffee cup.

After the waitress took their orders, Jack nodded and said slowly, "I'm out of town so much that what goes on at the Towers doesn't affect me much. Besides, I'm going to be leaving the Towers when my lease is up at the end of the year. Candice and I have split, as you probably already know."

Jack's announcements didn't surprise Tom as he lifted the coffee cup to his lips. After a couple of sips, he replied, "No, Jack, I didn't know about you and Candice."

"Yeah, Candice got involved with that funky barber—but then, I was going to split off, anyhow. It was just a matter of time."

"Well, I'm sorry it didn't work out. Those things happen. Where are you moving to?" Tom asked.

"Back to Texas. It will be more central for my work. I'm in import-export, you know?"

"Yes, I was aware that you were in that type of business—South America, is it not?"

"That's right. I do business in six Latin countries. Exporting has been on the decline due to the increase in value of the dollar and the devaluation of some of the South American currency," Jack said, subdued as he took a sip from a glass of dark wine. "It makes my job much tougher."

"Jack, have you ever heard of SkyWeb?"

"No, I haven't. What do they do?" asked Jack, looking down at the table.

"They used to create and maintain websites for businesses. Its owner is a guy by the name of Gordon Beard. The company is going under—currently going through bankruptcy."

"Oh, yeah, I've heard of Gordon Beard. His name came up somewhere—can't be sure."

The color of Jack's face turned a deep crimson. When the bill came, Jack insisted on buying Tom's lunch. While they were waiting for the credit card settlement, a package of gum appeared in Jack's left hand.

"Care for some?" he asked.

"No, thank you," Tom replied as Jack unwrapped a stick, stuck it in his mouth and discarded the wrapping on his plate.

The waiter arrived with the ticket folder. Jack penned in a number and his signature. The gum wrapper was lying upside down, and Tom couldn't read the brand. He thanked Jack for the lunch, and they left the restaurant, parting ways on the sidewalk.

Tom hurriedly reentered the restaurant, rushing back to the table. To his disappointment, it was cleared—the gum wrapper was gone.

After returning to the Towers, Tom parked in the outdoor lot and went up the elevator, seeing no one. He booted up his computer and brought up the SkyWeb accounting file, an accurate duplicate of the original. He felt that confidentiality was not at issue. The judge wanted those reports.

Tom printed a set of tests of the reports that the court had requested. Placing the reports in a folder, he tucked it into his briefcase, which was going to accompany him to the courthouse the next day.

Tom loaded the Jensen's Shirts inventory program and spent the balance of the afternoon perfecting the reports that Cliff had requested.

Shortly after 5:00, his preparation was complete. He dialed the Jensen's Shirts number, but no one answered.

Just before 7:00, he left the apartment and headed down the elevator. His right hand was fingering the gun in his jacket pocket. Jan was down in the lobby conversing with a strange woman. Tom greeted the ladies and walked out into the parking lot.

After driving his car to the strip mall, he parked in front of Jensen's Shirts. Retrieving his briefcase from the back seat, he approached the front door, noticing a light coming through a window from the reception area.

Tom turned the knob and was surprised to find the door unlocked. He opened the door slightly and called out Cliff's name. After waiting a few seconds and receiving no answer, Tom entered the room and saw Cliff sitting in chair behind the customer counter. His head was down and he wasn't moving.

Before approaching the counter, Tom unsnapped the holster strap that secured his automatic. Again, he called out Cliff's name, much louder this time. To his relief, Cliff's head jerked up and his eyes opened.

"Oh, hi, Tom. I must have fallen asleep."

"Are you okay, Cliff?" Tom asked.

"Yeah, just havin' a snooze."

"Cliff, I have the reports that you requested," Tom said, plunking his briefcase down on the counter. Releasing the two snaps, he pulled out the Jensen folder.

"They're all in here, Cliff. I'll leave them on the counter for you. You can call me later if you have any questions."

"Oh, sure, Tom. Hey, thanks a lot. What do I owe you?"

"The invoice hasn't been prepared. I'll send you a bill."

"Yeah, don't worry, Tom. You'll get paid."

"I'm not worried. Give me a call if you or your accountant have any questions. I'll lock the door on my way out."

Tom, briefcase in hand, headed for the door. While reaching for the knob, he heard Cliff say in a firm, subdued voice, "Tom, I think I know who did it."

Stopping in his tracks, he turned and stared at Cliff. He frowned and exclaimed, "What?"

Cliff did not answer. He looked up at Tom and nodded his head. "I think I know, Tom."

"Who, Cliff—who?" Tom asked.

"That meatball of a Vito Manchino," Cliff firmly replied.

"Have you told the police?" Tom responded.

"No, not yet, but I will tomorrow."

Cliff's theory was based mostly on hunch, Tom thought, and didn't take it too seriously. The recent experiences at Jensen's were on Tom's mind as he drove to O'Leary's and parked in their lot.

Discovering Dalia's body had been traumatic enough. Cliff being asleep in the chair had given Tom a scare—another body, and at the same place, would have been too much. He needed a drink. After placing the holster and gun in the glove compartment, he entered the bar and grill.

Instead of his usual beer, Tom ordered a brandy on the rocks. From his stool at the closed end of the bar, he observed that the bar and grill was only about half occupied with four people at the bar beside himself. Tom ordered an appetizer and patiently waited for a baseball game to start on television. When the food arrived, he ordered a second brandy. Taking a long gulp, he felt relieved as it went down.

His feelings of relief were short-lived. Phil Bartron soon propped himself up on a stool next to two ladies sitting on the right side of the bar. The goatee appeared longer than usual. It swept the top of the bar surface while Phil's eyes worked the room.

When Phil's beer arrived, he toasted in Tom's direction. Tom ignored him and continued to look up at the television. Out of the corner of his eye, Tom could see the distasteful look on Phil's face. He wasn't in the mood to socialize with Phil Bartron that evening. Tom's mind was focusing on his upcoming visit to the courthouse tomorrow morning and on the plight of Cliff Jensen.

Tom signed the credit card slip and was preparing to leave. Feeling a gentle pat on his shoulder, he feared the worst. Turning, he faced the tip of a goatee.

"Mr. Hastings, you can really see what's going on from here, can't you?"

"Yes. Why is that important to you?"

"Excuse me, I'm only trying to be friendly."

"I have to go," Tom sharply replied, brushing against Phil's shoulder as he got off the stool.

Phil pushed back for a moment and took Tom's stool after watching him leave.

Tom removed the holster and gun from his glove compartment after parking in the lower-level garage. Placing them in his jacket pocket, he proceeded toward the door leading to the elevators.

There was a note tucked under his door—it was from Jan. Note in hand, he unlocked the door, entered and set the paper down on the kitchen counter. After bolting the door, he read the note—an invitation from Jan and Greg to Julie and him for a lobster dinner on Friday.

53

ARRIVING AT THE COURTHOUSE ON WEDNESDAY MORNING, Tom Hastings followed the instructions he'd received from the deputy. Walking up a flight of steps to the second floor, he found the room number. Tom reviewed his instructions and entered. Two people were in the room, one of them a female deputy, the other a man dressed in a suit.

The deputy spoke first. "You must be Tom Hastings. I'm Deputy Claire, and this is Val Peterson from County Court."

"Yes, I'm Tom Hastings," Tom responded, looking around the room and spotting the SkyWeb computer.

"Mr. Hastings, you can go right to work," said the man in the suit.

Tom promptly walked to the table, sat down on the chair and pressed the On Switch on both the computer and the printer. After they booted, he loaded the accounting program and brought up the vendor list report. Because of the dress rehearsal in his apartment, Tom had an easy time displaying and printing the requested reports.

While the printer was producing the results, the man in the suit said something to the deputy and left the room. The deputy remained in her chair, watching the street and not paying Tom much attention. After the final report had printed, Tom removed a stapler from his briefcase and organized the sheets. The clicking sounds drew the deputy's attention. She got up from her chair and approached the table.

"How's it coming?" she asked.

"I'm done, Deputy Claire. Here they are—I hope that's all they need."

The deputy lifted the stack of papers and said, "Would you initial and date each report?"

Tom did as requested and watched while the deputy placed the reports in a large envelope.

"Would you fill out the fee voucher form?" the deputy asked.

"Sure," Tom said and proceeded to jot down his hours and hourly fee. He signed the sheet, and the deputy placed it into the same envelope with the reports.

After placing the envelope under his arm, the deputy said, "Thanks a lot, Mr. Hastings. Your job is done. Please shut off the computer and I'll see you out."

Tom closed down the operating system and shut off the printer and the computer. Clicking his briefcase shut, Tom headed for the door. While leaving down the corridor, he noticed the deputy lock the door and walk in the opposite direction. Tom exited the courthouse into the parking lot, feeling a sense of accomplishment and that he'd fulfilled a need. It had been a chance to temporarily escape the trauma going on at the Towers.

Driving back, he was glad the Jensen and SkyWeb reports were finished—producing them had not been a comfortable experience. Yearning for a beer, cigar and a run with the in-line-skates, Tom visualized speeding up the trail on his skates, flying in the wind. He could make that happen today.

After parking in the Towers outdoor lot, he anxiously headed for the door, briefcase in hand. Glancing back at his car, he noticed it was parked at an uncomfortable angle. Stopping, Tom returned to his parking spot and realigned his car between the yellow lines. He headed back to the Towers. As he was placing his key in the Towers door, he remembered the briefcase. Returning to his car for a second time, he found his briefcase safely sitting on the parking lot surface— a close call.

Jan and Greg were seated on the lobby couch, sipping coffee. Carl was standing over them, waving his right arm, his forefinger pointing upward. Hearing someone enter, Carl brought his arm down.

He said, "Well, Tom, we were just talking about you."

Greg piped in, "Yeah, and it was all bad."

Jan gave Greg's shoulder a push. "Oh, come on now, Greg. You know we were discussing the defective dryer on the twentieth."

"Better the dryer than me," Tom laughed in response. "Well, it's time for me to get on with the day. The bike trail awaits me."

"Oh, Tom, by the way, did you get my note?" asked Jan.

"Oh yes, you mean about the lobster dinner on Friday?"

"Yes, it included Julie, too—you know that?"

"Lobster! Did you win the lottery, or what?" Tom asked.

Greg returned Jan's push on the shoulder and pointed to Carl. "We would invite you, too, but we have only four of the crawling monsters."

The thought of wrestling with the shell was not too appealing to Tom, but eating fresh lobster...

"I'll call Julie tonight. In the meanwhile, consider it a date."

The trip up the elevator couldn't be fast enough, Tom thought as he watched the numbers change. Getting off on the twentieth floor, he unlocked his apartment door and anxiously changed clothes. He was trying to ignore the beeping answering machine while fetching his skates backpack from the closet. Just before leaving, he pressed the button on the answering machine.

"Stay away from O'Leary's. Better heed my warning," a hoarse-sounding, whispering voice said.

Tom Hastings set the backpack down on the floor and sat down on the chair by the phone. Geez, I didn't need that, he thought. The joyous anticipation of in-line-skating was destroyed. *Do I call Detective Anderson?* Tom got up from the chair and walked to the window overlooking the bike trail. Whoever called is not going to ruin my day—I'm going skating.

He opened a compartment zipper in his backpack and placed the .32-automatic inside, zipped it shut and headed for the door. Hurrying to the elevators, he was angry and determined.

No one was down in the lobby and Tom proceeded out the back door, through the parking lot and out into the street. While approaching the first bench, he felt a sense of relief that Marcil Huggins wasn't there. Hopefully, Marcil would eventually forget about the tattletale incident, he thought, *unless he's guilty of the murders.*

Tom latched on his skates, stood up to put on the backpack and noticed a paper item on the ground. There it was—another gum wrapper lying in the grass next to the bench. He almost fell down attempting to retrieve the wrapper, a Trident. Holding the wrapper between the tips of two fingers, he gently dropped it into his shirt pocket. *Probably a waste of time*, he thought.

The feeling of flying through the air, listening to the swish-swish of the skates, was fulfilling. Tom watched two birds fly across the trail. They don't have murders, Tom thought, some type of sparrow, likely. Julie was his expert on birds. Lobsters kill, he thought, their claws are weapons. Tom thought about calling Julie, hoping she could come to the lobster dinner the next night at Jan and Greg's.

"Lobster?" Julie exclaimed when Tom called shortly before 6:00.

"Yup, that's what Jan said. How does that appeal to you?"

"I love lobster. What time should I come?"

"Soon as you can."

"I'm thinking about getting off early tomorrow afternoon. I could be there by five. How does that sound?"

"Perfect."

"Julie, I had a crank call earlier today. Someone—sounded like a man—warned me about spending time at O'Leary's."

"What's this? A crank call?"

"Geez, Julie, Someone is playing games with me. I'm torn between doing nothing, or calling the detective."

"Why wouldn't you call the detective?"

"Well, by now they're probably real sick of all the tidbit calls from this place."

The phone conversation ended after some small talk, and Tom's evening was open to settling down with a book or a TV movie. Hanging up the phone, he thought about the crank message on the answering machine. Tom was still wavering about whether or not to call the detective. Resisting the urge to play the message again, he chose not to, and pressed the On button of the television remote.

Sleep was difficult that night because of the crank phone call, among other things.

At last morning came, and Tom busied himself cleaning up the apartment for Julie's visit. After working on domestics most of the day, by 5:00, he was ready. Julie's call came one minute after he sat down with a beer.

Greg answered Tom's knock a half an hour later. Julie got a hug from Greg, who gave Tom a pat on the shoulder as he escorted his guests into the entryway. Jan made her appearance and directed them into the kitchen, where four ugly lobsters were attempting to crawl out of the sink. Julie shrieked mildly and turned away from the scene.

Greg led his guests into the living room, where Tom was attracted to a stack of appetizers neatly arranged on a white platter. Julie and Tom sat next to each other on the couch, picking at the goodies while awaiting Greg's return with a bottle and glasses.

When Greg returned, he stumbled as he made his way around the coffee table. Julie saved the evening by catching the bottle as it plunged toward the floor.

By the time Jan called them for dinner, the wine bottle was empty. They were ready to deal with the hard surfaced, lifeless bodies of the clawed creatures of the sea. As they shared wine from a second bottle, Tom wrestled with the shells and broke the handle of the shell tool.

"Easy, Tom—its only dinner," remarked a bright-faced Greg chuckling.

"Here, use mine. I'm done," said Jan.

While Tom continued his efforts to break the shell, a second loud crack occurred—another broken handle.

"Anyone got a hammer?" Tom asked.

54

PLEASANT THOUGHTS OF THE LOBSTER DINNER occupied Tom and Julie's thoughts while they sipped coffee and read the *Star Tribune* the next morning.

Tom interrupted the silence when he said, "Julie, I want you to listen to that crank phone call."

She looked up from the paper. "Okay."

Tom pressed the Replay button.

Julie listened to the message, set the newspaper down on her lap and exclaimed, "Tom Hastings, this could be serious! You should call the detective at once."

"Julie, I'm not the type that jumps every time some nut makes a crank call. If it happened more than once, well, then maybe."

"Yeah, but this is different, considering the murders. I think it's your public duty to notify the police," said Julie.

"Okay, I'll consider it," responded Tom.

"Well, I've got to get going. As you know, I'm meeting Mary for dinner and the symphony concert later this evening."

Tom spent his evening at O'Leary's, where his wish for a cigar and beer became reality.

———

FERRO'S STOMACH ACHED. Knowing he couldn't handle it much longer, he left the apartment and headed down the elevator, getting off at the garage. Sitting in his car in partial darkness seemed to relieve some of his symptoms. Taking a couple of deep breaths, he was tempted to leave the garage and return to the apartment.

Two cars came in from outside. Both had a man and woman in the front seat. After they parked, the four people arrived at the Towers door at the same time. Ferro observed their smiles and gestures of happiness. Feelings of envy preyed on his mind. He wished he were like them, not afflicted with those horrible needs.

Another car entered. Slowly, it drove to the far end and parked. The senior gentleman had a difficult time walking, especially as he was carrying two packages of groceries. Ferro pitied the man's attempt to unlock the hallway door while holding the bags. *Why doesn't he set them down on the bench?* He thought. When one of the bags dropped to the floor, Ferro felt the urge to help.

The next vehicle to enter the garage was a medium-sized SUV. The driver was a woman. She drove fast, parking only five places down from where Ferro was slumped behind the steering wheel. He waited and watched while the trunk flipped open and the lady stooped and rummaged. *She doesn't turn me on,* he thought and decided to pass.

A few minutes later, Ferro heard the garage door chain clatter—at last, another vehicle entered. A slick black sedan drove down the aisle to the far end, and as Ferro had hoped, circled to an empty slot in his row, only four spaces down. He was ready, grabbing the saturated white towel from the empty seat. Leaving his car, Ferro quietly stepped toward his target.

"Oh, you scared me," shrieked Jan with surprise.

"Sorry I frightened you," responded Ferro.

When Jan turned toward the exit, he reached around her and placed the towel over her mouth. She struggled for a few moments until her body went limp. Ferro pressed the release on the mechanism that was attached to his left wrist, but the blade didn't emerge—it was stuck.

———

"LOOK AT THIS, ROD, THE RESEMBLANCE. It's too close to ignore."

"Aha! You're right. That guy—he's got pretty good alibis, doesn't he?"

"Yeah, he does, but there are some holes—I learned of some yesterday. I'll tell you about them on the way. His gum chewing fits the wrappers. Rod, I want you to get right on this—we'll need a search permit, soon as possible."

Rod removed a large envelope from his jacket pocket. He waved it in front of Detective Anderson and said, "Look what I have here."

Bill Anderson raised his right fist, his thumb pointing upward. The front teeth in his lower jaw went up and outward, overlapping the uppers. He said, "Let's go get'em."

———

TOM WAS IN A GOOD MOOD because his recent business encounters were successful and they were finished. Thoughts of the succulent lobster dinner of the night before also contributed to his mood. As he made the outdoors turn leading to the lower-level garage, he noticed two police officers returning to their car parked at the delivery entrance.

The lower-level garage was inactive when he drove up the aisle leading to his parking spot. Opening the glove compartment, he realized that he had forgotten to take his gun. Oh well, he thought, I'll be quick. Besides, the two officers were just here.

After exiting the car, he clicked the lock button on his key chain twice, hearing the expected short beep that signaled the successful locking of the car doors. Pausing for a moment, he inhaled through his nose and detected an odor not very familiar. It was definitely not the type he'd experienced at Jensen's.

Tom began the walk toward the corridor door, when he heard a shriek. Stopping to listen, he suspected the sound came from somewhere in the garage. Taking slow steps, feeling tension building in his body, he resisted the temptation to race to the door.

A thumping sound sent his heart racing. It appeared to be coming from the last row of parked vehicles. Stopping, he strained his ears to hear more. A few steps farther and he would be safely through the door leading to the elevators.

Gut feeling and curiosity overcame his desire to get out of the garage. Quietly and cautiously, he worked his way between the vehicles toward the back wall. After reaching the last row, Tom peaked around a pickup truck. Several places down, to his left, sitting on the garage floor were the bodies of two people. His feelings of fear turned to anger when he saw the long hair of a woman nestled against a man's chest. The man was in a sitting position, one of his arms circled around her chest. His other hand was holding a white cloth that was covering her face. Her motionless legs were stretched out on the floor.

A reflection of light coming from the man's arm that circled the woman's chest caught Tom's eye. Something metal? He thought. Tom's mind was racing with ideas of actions to take—the gun was up in his closet—the cell phone was in the car. *The lady may already be dead*, he thought. Another shriek eliminated that possibility. Thus far, the assailant was not aware of his presence.

Reversing his direction, Tom quickly and quietly returned to his car. Pressing the Open button on his key chain, he heard the click of his front car doors unlocking. After opening the driver's door, Tom knelt down on the front seat and fumbled for his cell phone. It dropped to the floor of the passenger seat, adding to his frustration. Sitting down in the driver's seat, he reached, probed and clumsily retrieved the phone.

The display was blank. After pushing the On-Off button a half a dozen times, the display light came on. Tom dialed 911. To his relief, there was a ring on the other end, and he heard a voice answer.

Tom said as quietly as possible, "I need help right now—the police. A man has a weapon and a woman is down. I'm in the lower-level garage of the Towers, at thirty-eight hundred Fordyce. Send someone, and hurry."

Tom heard no reply and anxiously asked, "Are you there?"

His repeated inquiries were in vain. Noticing that the display was blank, he flung the phone down on the seat. Damn battery must be dead—of all times, he thought. Frustration led to near panic.

He thought of racing to the lobby office and getting help. Only a minute ago, the lady had been still alive. Each second of delay could be fatal.

Before sliding out of the front seat, Tom clicked the Trunk button on his key chain. Hurrying around to the back of the car, he remembered the baseball bat.

Grabbing it, Tom crouched and hurriedly retraced his original steps between the vehicles, to the far row. The man was still holding the lady down. Tom's adrenaline flowed and a strong wave of courage emerged.

Shouting, he said, "Hey, what's going on down there?"

The man's dark head turned—it was Carlos. Desperately, Carlos raised his right fist and punched the mechanism, finally succeeding in releasing the stuck blade. Bringing it up to the woman's neck, he snarled, "Back off, mister, or she dies. *Entiende!*"

Tom's mind was racing with possible strategies. If I rush him, she may die, and I might die, too. If I don't, the lady will die for sure. Racing back to the office to get help would save me—that would not only be cowardly, but she would die for sure.

Carlos stood up, allowing the woman's upper body to flop to the floor. Her face turned toward Tom as it landed with a dull thud. It was Jan. Geez, he had to do something—there was no turning back now.

Tom took two cautious steps forward, his two hands holding the bat out front. "Let the lady go," Tom's crackling voice sputtered.

"Stay back, or I'll kill her—*quedarse fuera!*" Carlos exclaimed.

"It's no use, Carlos Valdez. Your game is up. The police are on their way. Killing again will gain nothing."

"Oh, so it's you, Mister Tom Hastings, the baseball man," Carlos sneered, advancing in Tom's direction.

By bending his shaky knees and crouching, Tom felt an improvement in his stability. Sliding the fingers of his right hand upward, he steadied the bat—he was sure that combat was imminent.

His memory flashed back to three years ago, when an intruder had attacked him, with only a tennis racquet for defense. His assailant's stumble on the small carpet had saved him that day.

The sharp, shiny blade extended from Carlos's left wrist. Tom held his breath. Gasping to regain missing oxygen, he swung the bat back into strike position. The sound of a moan drew his attention. Jan was beginning to stir, attempting to rise by pushing down on the floor with the palm of her hand. Seeing that Jan was alive uplifted Tom's courage.

Remaining focused on the sneering Carlos, Tom noticed movement in the well-lit area leading to the elevator doors. Perhaps his mind was playing tricks—was it Carl he glimpsed? There wasn't time to speculate. Advancing two more steps, Tom looked straight into the glaring eyes of a gleaming, excited face.

The terrifying blade extension of Carlos's left hand glittered under the overhead light. His left arm was extended forward, his right arm retracted behind his body.

Tom's extensive experience as a tennis player had taught him to focus on an opponent's racquet. Carlos's left arm and knife appeared to be the only threat. Jan emitted a louder groan and her body began twisting and contorting. She was regaining consciousness. The blade—Tom continued to stare at it. He could run—no, he couldn't leave Jan.

Glancing back at Carlos's eyes, Tom detected a hint of fear. The exhilarating feeling that Tom had experienced as a young athlete firing fastballs at home plate surged through his body. The look he noticed in Carlos's eyes resembled the fear in the eyes of a batter coming up to bat after getting hit the last time up.

Tom advanced one long step. Carlos's knees bent slightly and his left arm jerked upward. Tom was ready and took another step forward until the two men were almost touching. The blade looked smaller as it got closer. Tom jabbed the bat forward and Carlos backed off a step. Tom's confidence elevated a notch. More boldly, he pulled the bat back and faked a swing. Carlos backed up another step.

Suddenly, Carlos's face contorted and his head tipped downward. Tom saw an arm wrapping around his legs—Jan was fighting back. Taking advantage of the moment, Tom leaped forward and with all his strength swung at Carlos's head. Carlos ducked, and the bat glanced off of his chin. It drove him backwards, and he stumbled over Jan's body. Carlos recovered and was up before Tom could swing again.

Carlos put his right arm under Jan's neck and pulled her up to a sitting position. He pressed the blade against her neck. She shrieked, and blood began to drip onto the glittering metal.

"Let her go!" Tom cried.

"You come one more step and I will kill her. I mean it! *Es verdad*," snarled Carlos.

Tom spotted movement next to the hood of a car three spaces away. *Talk—need to keep Carlos talking.* Help is coming.

"Come on, Carlos, you'll never get away with it. Why harm the lady?"

The shadow was getting closer to Carlos.

"Give it up. What would Juanita say?" Tom pleaded.

Carlos was on his right knee, the blade still pressed against Jan's neck. Tom backed off a step. Carlos's left hand appeared to relax a bit. A narrow sliver of space showed between the metal and Jan's neck. Tom backed up another step. Carlos stood up.

They heard a new voice say, "Don't move or I'll shoot."

The shadow behind Carlos–it·was Carl, looking menacing as hell. He was holding a stick in both hands and it was pointed at Carlos.

Carlos turned, scoffed and said, "Not with that stick, you're not. Back!"

Tom leaped forward again and his swinging bat.struck Carlos in the back of the neck. Carlos recovered, turned and lunged at him with the blade. Tom dodged and watched in amazement as Carl leaped on Carlos's back. Wrapping his arms around Carlos, Carl groaned when the blade cut into his waist. Carlos jerked from side to side and successfully shook Carl off.

Waving his left arm, Carlos refocused on Tom. The bat was pulled back, ready for another swing. Carl was down, sitting against a bumper, holding a hand over the wound in his side.

Jan took a deep breath and grabbed Carlos around the legs again. Carlos wavered and attempted to step out of Jan's grasp, when the loud popping sound of a bat reverberated through the garage. Tom had swung the bat with all his might, hitting Carlos in the skull, dropping him to the floor.

Tom knelt by Jan and held her head. "How are you doing, kid?" he asked.

Jan began to sob.

Tom held her close. "It's all over, Jan...you're going to be alright."

Carl stood up, gasping for air. "Carl, are you okay?" Tom asked.

"Could be better," he replied meekly.

"Could you call for help, Carl? I'll stay with Jan."

Carl held a hand against his wound and loped toward the door. Tom looked at Carlos, who was on the floor, unconscious, his left arm and the blade extended.

"Jan, can you sit up?"

"I'll try," she whispered.

Tom helped her into a sitting position, walked over to Carlos and raised the bat over his head.

"Oh, don't, Tom. Please don't."

Tom looked back at her. "I'd like to put him away for good, but this will help."

He raised the bat handle in the air and brought down the thick part directly on the metal mechanism. Sound of wood striking metal reverberated through the garage–the bat went up again. Tom struck again, sending metal pieces flying and clattering across the concrete floor.

The next five minutes seemed like an eternity to Tom and Jan.

Jan shouted hoarsely, "They're here, Tom. Can you hear the sound?" The garage door had opened. "It's a siren."

55

TOM WAS SITTING ON THE COUCH, next to Julie, at Greg and Jan's apartment a week later. Jan had just returned from the hospital, where she'd been held for treatment for shallow knife wounds in her neck, and for observation. Greg was at the door answering a knock.

Detective Anderson and Carl entered the room. "Sorry to intrude. I just want to check and see if everyone was okay," said the detective.

"I'm just fine," said Jan, softly, "thanks to Carl and that man sitting over there."

"Have a seat, Carl. How's the healing going?" asked Greg.

"Oh, no thanks—just a quick in and out. The healing is fine—there's no infection. The detective asked to come up to see you guys. He says he's go something to say."

"I'm happy to inform you people that Carlos Valdez has admitted to all five murders. He's going to be put away for a long time," reported the detective smiling.

Carl asked, "What about those other guys?"

"I have good news about them also. Phil Bartron, Vito Manchino, Gordon Beard and Jack Billings have all been arrested for drug trafficking. You won't be seeing any of them around either."

"What about the crank call?" asked Tom.

"The man with the goatee, Bartron," responded the detective.

Tom gave Julie a hug, smiled and said, "Thanks for coming to see us, Detective Anderson. We appreciate the good news."

Jan stood and put her thumbs up, tears flooding her eyes. "Peace at the Towers, at last."

EPILOGUE

SNOW WAS FALLING IN MINNEAPOLIS, The final week in February had arrived at last and Tom Hastings was packing. He had a condo rented in Florida for the month of March.

His building manager, Carl, helped him load the last of his things on that early sunny morning. Are you picking up Julie?" Carl asked.

"No, I have to go it alone...at least for now. She's going to take a couple of weeks off starting next Saturday. If you think all those suitcases belong to me, you're wrong. Half of them belong to Julie. She's flying down."

"It's sure going to be quiet around here with you gone. We haven't had a murder for over six months," said Carl.

"Well, if you have a murder while I'm gone, don't bother letting me know," said Tom laughing. "At least until I get back."

"Have a good trip, Tom, and enjoy the sun."

"I sure will. Thanks, Carl."

THE HASTINGS BOOKS SERIES

BLUE DARKNESS - *First in a Series of Hastings Books*
Released February 2003
This tale of warm relationships and chilling murders takes place in the lake country of central Minnesota. Normal activities in the small town of New Dresen are disrupted when local resident, ex-CIA agent Maynard Cushing, is murdered. His killer, Robert Ranforth also an ex-CIA agent, had been living anonymously in the community for several years. Earlier in his career, Cushing was instrumental during the investigation and subsequent arrest of Ranforth by the FBI for espionage. Ranforth vanished before the trial began. Tom Hastings, a neighbor and friend of the victim, becomes a threat to the anonymous ex-agent. Stalked and attacked at his country home, he employs tools and people, including neighbors, a deputy sheriff and Allan Burnside of the FBI, to mount a defense and help solve crimes.
Written by Ernest Francis Schanilec of Vergas, Minnesota. (276 pgs.)
ISBN: 1-931916-21-7 $16.95 each in a 6x9" paperback.

THE TOWERS - *Second in a Series of Hastings Books* - *Released April 2003*

DANGER ON THE KEYS - *Third in a Series of Hastings Books* - *Soon To Be Released*

PURGATORY CURVE - *Fourth in a Series of Hastings Books* - *Soon to be Released*

❏ Check here to order additional copies of *THE TOWERS*
❏ Check here to order additional copies of *BLUE DARKNESS*
$16.95 EACH
(plus $3.95 shipping & handling for first book,
add $2.00 for each additional book ordered.
Shipping and Handling costs for larger quantites available upon request.

Please send me _____ THE TOWERS _____ BLUE DARKNESS
additional books at $16.95 + shipping & handling

Bill my: ❏ VISA ❏ MasterCard   Expires _____

Card # _____

Signature _____

Daytime Phone Number _____

For credit card orders call 1-888-568-6329
TO ORDER ON-LINE VISIT: www.jmcompanies.com
OR SEND THIS ORDER FORM TO:
McCleery & Sons Publishing• PO Box 248 • Gwinner, ND 58040-0248
I am enclosing $_____   ❏ Check ❏ Money Order
Payable in US funds. No cash accepted.
SHIP TO:
Name_____

Mailing Address _____

City _____

State/Zip _____

Orders by check allow longer delivery time. Money order and credit card orders will be shipped within 48 hours. This offer is subject to change without notice.

NEW RELEASES

Blue Darkness *(First in a Series of Hastings Books)*
This tale of warm relationships and chilling murders takes place in the lake country of central Minnesota. Normal activities in the small town of New Dresen are disrupted when local resident, ex-CIA agent Maynard Cushing, is murdered. His killer, Robert Ranforth also an ex-CIA agent, had been living anonymously in the community for several years. Earlier in his career, Cushing was instrumental during the investigation and subsequent arrest of Ranforth by the FBI for espionage. Ranforth vanished before the trial began. Tom Hastings, a neighbor and friend of the victim, becomes a threat to the anonymous ex-agent. Stalked and attached at his country home, he employs tools and people, including neighbors, a deputy sheriff and Allan Burnside of the FBI, to mount a defense and help solve crimes. Written by Ernest Francis Schanilec (author of The Towers). (276 pgs.)
$16.95 each in a 6x9" paperback.

War Child - *Growing Up in Adolf Hitler's Germany*
Annelee Woodstrom was twenty years old when she immigrated to America in 1947. These kind people in America wanted to hear about Adolf Hitler, the man who was despised everywhere in the world. During her adolescene, constant propaganda and strictly enforced censorship influenced her thinking. As a young adult, the bombings and all the consequential suffering caused by World War II affected Annelee deeply. How could Annelee tell them that as a child, during 1935, she wanted nothing more than to be a member of Adolf Hitler's Jung Maidens' organization? Written by Annelee Woodstrom (252 pgs.)
$16.95 each in a 6x9" paperback.

Damsel in a Dress
Escape into a world of reflection and after thought with this second printing of Larson's first poetry book. It is her intention to connect people with feelings and touch the souls of people who have experienced similiar times. Lynne emphasizes the belief that everything happens for a reason. After all, with every event in life come lessons...we grow from hardships. It gives us character and it made her who she is. Written by Lynne D. Richard Larson (author of Eat, Drink & Remarry) (86 pgs.)
$12.95 each in a 5x8" paperback.

The SOE on Enemy Soil - *Churchill's Elite Force*
British Prime Minister Winston Churchill's plan for liberating Europe from the Nazis during the darkest days of the Second World War was ambitious: provide a few men and women, most of them barely out of their teens, with training in subversion and hand-to-hand combat, load them down with the latest in sophisticated explosives, drop them by parachute into the occupied countries, then sit back and wait for them to "Set Europe Ablaze." No story has been told with more honesty and humor than Sergeant Fallick tells his tale of service. The training, the fear, the tragic failures, the clandestine romances, and the soldiers' high jinks are all here, warmly told from the point of view of "one bloke" who experienced it all and lived to tell about it. Written by R.A. Fallick. (282 pgs.)
$16.95 each in a 6x9" paperback.

Grandmother Alice
Memoirs from the Home Front Before Civil War into 1930's
Alice Crain Hawkins could be called the 'Grandma Moses of Literature'. Her stories, published for the first time, were written while an invalid during the last years of her life. These journal entries from the late 1920's and early 30's gives us a fresh, novel and unique understanding of the lives of those who lived in the upper part of South Carolina during the state's growing years. Alice and her ancestors experiences are filled with understanding - they are provacative and profound. Written by Reese Hawkins (178 pgs.) $16.95 each in a 6x9" paperback.

I Took The Easy Way Out
Life Lessons on Hidden Handicaps
Twenty-five years ago, Tom Day was managing a growing business - holding his own on the golf course and tennis court. He was living in the fast lane. For the past 25 years, Tom has spent his days in a wheelchair with a spinal cord injury. Attendants serve his every need. What happened to Tom? We get an honest account of the choices Tom made in his life. It's a courageous story of reckoning, redemption and peace. Written by Thomas J. Day. (200 pgs.) $19.95 each in a 6x9" paperback.

Tales & Memories of Western North Dakota
Prairie Tales & True Stories of 20th Century Rural Life
This manuscript has been inspired with Steve's antidotes, bits of wisdom and jokes (sometimes ethnic, to reflect the melting pot that was and is North Dakota; and from most unknown sources). A story about how to live life with humor, courage and grace along with personal hardships, tragedies and triumphs. Written by Steve Taylor. (174 pgs.) $14.95 each in a 6x9" paperback.

9/11 and Meditation - *America's Handbook*
All Americans have been deeply affected by the terrorist events of and following 9-11-01 in our country. David Thorson submits that meditation is a potentially powerful intervention to ameliorate the frightening effects of such divisive and devastating acts of terror. This book features a lifetime of harrowing life events amidst intense pychological and social polarization, calamity and chaos; overcome in part by practicing the age-old art of meditation. Written by David Thorson. (110 pgs.) $9.95 each in a 4-1/8 x 7-1/4" paperback.

Eat, Drink & Remarry
The poetry in this book is taken from different experiences in Lynne's life and from different geographical and different emotional places.
Every poem is an inspiration from someone or a direct event from their life...or from hers. Every victory and every mistake - young or old. They slowly shape and mold you into the unique person you are. Celebrate them as rough times that you were strong enough to endure. By sharing them with others, there will always be one person who will learn from them. Written by Lynne D. Richard Larson (86 pgs.) $12.95 each in a 5x8" paperback.

Phil Lempert's HEALTHY, WEALTHY, & WISE
The Shoppers Guide for Today's Supermarket
This is the must-have tool for getting the most for your money in
every aisle. With this valuable advice you will never see (or shop)
the supermarket the same way again. You will learn how to: save
at least $1,000 a year on your groceries, guarantee satisfaction on
every shopping trip, get the most out of coupons or rebates, avoid
marketing gimmicks, create the ultimate shopping list, read and
understand the new food labels, choose the best supermarkets for
you and your family. Written by Phil Lempert. (198 pgs.)
$9.95 each in a 6x9" paperback.

Miracles of COURAGE
The Larry W. Marsh Story
This story is for anyone looking for simple formulas for over-
coming insurmountable obstacles. At age 18, Larry lost both
legs in a traffic accident and learned to walk again on un-
tested prothesis. No obstacle was too big for him - putting
himself through college - to teaching a group of children
that frustrated the whole educational system - to developing
a nationally recognized educational program to help these
children succeed. Written by Linda Marsh. (134 pgs.)
$12.95 each in a 6x9" paperback.

The Garlic Cure
Learn about natural breakthroughs to outwit: Allergies, Arthri-
tis, Cancer, Candida Albicans, Colds, Flu and Sore Throat, En-
vironmental and Body Toxins, Fatigue, High Cholesterol, High
Blood Pressure and Homocysteine and Sinus Headaches. The
most comprehensive, factual and brightly written health book
on garlic of all times. INCLUDES: 139 GOURMET GARLIC
RECIPES! Written by James F. Scheer, Lynn Allison and Charlie
Fox. (240 pgs.)
$14.95 each in a 6x9" paperback.

For Your Love
Janelle, a spoiled socialite, has beauty and breeding to attract any
mate she desires. She falls for Jared, an accomplished man who
has had many lovers, but no real love. Their hesitant romance
follows Jared and Janelle across the ocean to exciting and wild
locations. Join in a romance and adventure set in the mid-1800's
in America's grand and proud Southland.
Written by Gunta Stegura. (358 pgs.)
$16.95 each in a 6x9" paperback.

From Graystone to Tombstone
*Memories of My Father Engolf
Snortland 1908-1976*
This haunting memoir will keep
you riveted with true accounts of
a brutal penitentiary to a man-
hunt in the unlikely little town of
Tolna, North Dakota. At the same
time the reader will emerge from
the book with a towering respect
for the author, a man who endured pain, grief and needless
guilt -- but who learned the art of
forgiving and writes in the spirit
of hope. Written by Roger
Snortland. (178 pgs.)
$16.95 each in a 6x9" paperback.

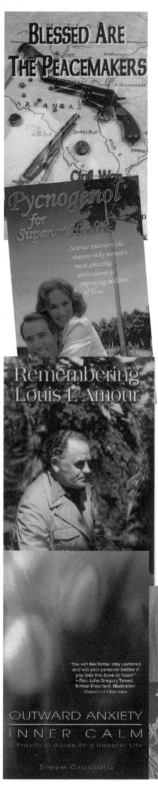

Blessed Are The Peacemakers *Civil War in the Ozarks*

A rousing tale that traces the heroic Rit Gatlin from his enlistment in the Confederate Army in Little Rock to his tragic loss of a leg in a Kentucky battle, to his return in the Ozarks. He becomes engaged in guerilla warfare with raiders who follow no flag but their own. Rit finds himself involved with a Cherokee warrior, slaves and romance in a land ravaged by war. Written by Joe W. Smith (444 pgs.)
$19.95 each in a 6 x 9 paperback

Pycnogenol®

Pycnogenol® for Superior Health presents exciting new evidence about nature's most powerful antioxidant. Pycnogenol® improves your total health, reduces risk of many diseases, safeguards your arteries, veins and entire circulation system. It protects your skin - giving it a healthier, smoother younger glow. Pycnogenol® also boosts your immune system. Read about it's many other beneficial effects. Written by Richard A. Passwater, Ph.D. (122 pgs.)
$5.95 each in a 4-1/8 x 6-7/8" paperback.

Remembering Louis L'Amour

Reese Hawkins was a close friend of Louis L'Amour, one of the fastest selling writers of all time. Now Hawkins shares this friendship with L'Amour's legion of fans. Sit with Reese in L'Amour's study where characters were born and stories came to life. Travel with Louis and Reese in the 16 photo pages in this memoir. Learn about L'Amour's lifelong quest for knowledge and his philosophy of life. Written by Reese Hawkins and his daughter Meredith Hawkins Wallin. (178 pgs.)
$16.95 each in a 5-1/2x8" paperback.

Outward Anxiety - Inner Calm

Steve Crociata is known to many as the Optician to the Stars. He was diagnosed with a baffling form of cancer. The author has processed experiences in ways which uniquely benefit today's readers. We learn valuable lessons on how to cope with distress, how to marvel at God, and how to win at the game of life. Written by Steve Crociata (334 pgs.)
$19.95 each in a 6 x 9 paperback

Seasons With Our Lord

Original seasonal and special event poems written from the heart. Feel the mood with the tranquil color photos facing each poem. A great coffee table book or gift idea. Written by Cheryl Lebahn Hegvik. (68 pgs.) $24.95 each in a 11x8-1/2 paperback.

Bonanza Belle

In 1908, Carrie Amundson left her home to become employed on a bonanza farm. Carrie married and moved to town. One tragedy after the other befell her and altered her life considerably and she found herself back on the farm where her family lived the toiled during the Great Depression. Carrie was witness to many life-changing events happenings. She changed from a carefree girl to a woman of great depth and stamina.
Written by Elaine Ulness Swenson. (344 pgs.)
$15.95 each in a 6x8-1/4" paperback.

Home Front

Read the continuing story of Carrie Amundson, whose life in North Dakota began in *Bonanza Belle*. This is the story of her family, faced with the challenges, sacrifices and hardships of World War II. Everything changed after the Pearl Harbor attack, and ordinary folk all across America, on the home front, pitched in to help in the war effort. Even years after the war's end, the effects of it are still evident in many of the men and women who were called to serve their country. Written by Elaine Ulness Swenson. (304 pgs.)
$15.95 each in a 6x8-1/4" paperback.

First The Dream

This story spans ninety years of Anna's life - from Norway to America - to finding love and losing love. She and her family experience two world wars, flu epidemics, the Great Depression, droughts and other quirks of Mother Nature and the Vietnam War. A secret that Anna has kept is fully revealed at the end of her life.
Written by Elaine Ulness Swenson. (326 pgs.)
$15.95 each in a 6x8-1/4" paperback

Pay Dirt

An absorbing story reveals how a man with the courage to follow his dream found both gold and unexpected adventure and adversity in Interior Alaska, while learning that human nature can be the most unpredictable of all.
Written by Otis Hahn & Alice Vollmar. (168 pgs.)
$15.95 each in a 6x9" paperback.

Spirits of Canyon Creek
Sequel to "Pay Dirt"

Hahn has a rich stash of true stories about his gold mining experiences. This is a continued successful collaboration of battles on floodwaters, facing bears and the discovery of gold in the Yukon.
Written by Otis Hahn & Alice Vollmar. (138 pgs.)
$15.95 each in a 6x9" paperback.

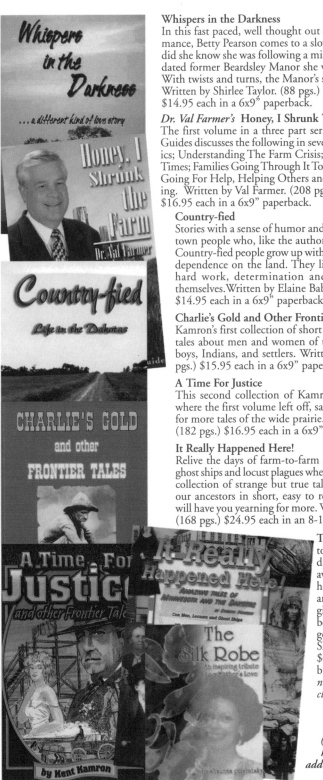

Whispers in the Darkness

In this fast paced, well thought out mystery with a twist of romance, Betty Pearson comes to a slow paced, small town. Little did she know she was following a missing link - what the dilapidated former Beardsley Manor she was drawn to, held for her. With twists and turns, the Manor's secrets are unraveled. Written by Shirlee Taylor. (88 pgs.)
$14.95 each in a 6x9" paperback.

Dr. Val Farmer's Honey, I Shrunk The Farm

The first volume in a three part series of Rural Stress Survival Guides discusses the following in seven chapters: Farm Economics; Understanding The Farm Crisis; How To Cope With Hard Times; Families Going Through It Together; Dealing With Debt; Going For Help, Helping Others and Transitions Out of Farming. Written by Val Farmer. (208 pgs.)
$16.95 each in a 6x9" paperback.

Country-fied

Stories with a sense of humor and love for country and small town people who, like the author, grew up country-fied . . . Country-fied people grow up with a unique awareness of their dependence on the land. They live their lives with dignity, hard work, determination and the ability to laugh at themselves. Written by Elaine Babcock. (184 pgs.)
$14.95 each in a 6x9" paperback.

Charlie's Gold and Other Frontier Tales

Kamron's first collection of short stories gives you adventure tales about men and women of the west, made up of cowboys, Indians, and settlers. Written by Kent Kamron. (174 pgs.) $15.95 each in a 6x9" paperback.

A Time For Justice

This second collection of Kamron's short stories takes off where the first volume left off, satisfying the reader's hunger for more tales of the wide prairie. Written by Kent Kamron. (182 pgs.) $16.95 each in a 6x9" paperback.

It Really Happened Here!

Relive the days of farm-to-farm salesmen and hucksters, of ghost ships and locust plagues when you read Ethelyn Pearson's collection of strange but true tales. It captures the spirit of our ancestors in short, easy to read, colorful accounts that will have you yearning for more. Written by Ethelyn Pearson. (168 pgs.) $24.95 each in an 8-1/2x11" paperback.

The Silk Robe - Dedicated to Shari Lynn Hunt, a wonderful woman who passed away from cancer. Mom lived her life with unfailing faith, an open loving heart and a giving spirit. She is remembered for her compassion and gentle strength. Written by Shaunna Privratsky.
$6.95 each in a 4-1/4x5-1/2" booklet. *Complimentary notecard and envelope included.*

(Add $3.95 shipping & handling for first book, add $2.00 for each additional book ordered.)